Praise for Dalton Fury's Delta Force series

"Packed with speed, surprise, and overwhelming violence of action . . . Want to know what Spec Ops really look like? Read Dalton Fury. Simply put—nobody does it better."

—Brad Thor, #1 *New York Times* bestselling author

"Crackles with gut-wrenching action and authenticity."
—*Publishers Weekly* (starred review)

"Fury is retired Delta Force, giving the action a rapid-fire, realistic air . . . Racer is locked and loaded for a series of adventures." —*Kirkus Reviews*

"Step aside, Jack Ryan—Kolt Raynor is the true hero of the new millennium . . . I kept having to remind myself this was fiction."

—James Rollins, *New York Times* bestselling author

"Dalton Fury and I came up in the Unit together, flip-flopping troops and missions from Afghanistan to Iraq. What makes his writing unique is not just the tactical accuracy . . . but his unique understanding of the geopolitical events that propel the plot[s]. He is the real deal. If you want to know what it's like on the front lines of the shadow war, pick up his book[s]."

—Brad Taylor, *New York Times* bestselling author
of *One Rough Man* and *All Necessary Force*

"An important, must-read book about real warriors. A story that so positively reflects what on the ground decision making, professional acceptance of risk and maximizing interagency cooperation can do. Dalton Fury shows us with amazing detail and insight what highly trained and motivated special operators can accomplish successfully in combat out of all proportion to their numbers."

—Cofer Black, former chief of the
Central Intelligence Agency's Counter Terrorist Center

"The most compelling and comprehensive account of the Battle of Tora Bora that I have read, heard, or seen in any format."

—COL(R) John T. Carney, author of
No Room For Error and President/ CEO
of the Special Operations Warrior Foundation

ONE KILLER FORCE

A DELTA FORCE NOVEL

DALTON FURY

St. Martin's Paperbacks

This is a work of fiction. All of the characters, organizations, and events portrayed in this novel are either products of the author's imagination or are used fictitiously.

ONE KILLER FORCE

Copyright © 2015 by Dalton Fury.

For information address St. Martin's Press, 175 Fifth Avenue, New York, NY 10010.

ISBN: 978-1-250-09198-7

Printed in the United States of America

Our books may be purchased in bulk for promotional, educational, or business use. Please contact your local bookseller or the Macmillan Corporate and Premium Sales Department at 1-800-221-7945, ext. 5442, or by e-mail at MacmillanSpecialMarkets@macmillan.com.

St. Martin's Press hardcover edition / October 2015
St. Martin's Paperbacks edition / August 2016

St. Martin's Paperbacks are published by St. Martin's Press, 175 Fifth Avenue, New York, NY 10010.

10 9 8 7 6 5 4 3 2 1

To the unsung rock stars of the 160th Special Operations Aviation Regiment, whose customer service is legendary inside the purple community. On short notice in pitch dark, at bat-out-of-hell speed and cornfield level, you can bank that the Night Stalkers are on time, on target, plus or minus thirty seconds.

PREFACE

Behind the wheel of Bessie, Scotty saw the billowing smoke and gassed it, curb-bouncing our Toyota in reverse over your garden-variety street trash prevalent in war-torn Baghdad. Next to him, wide-eyed with mouth probably open, I stared in silence at the target building as it exploded, jetting hot shards of steel, concrete chunks, and blast waves toward four unarmored Hummers only yards away.

We were hunting Zarqawi chemical weapons or their precursor material— jackpot on the materials; the blast we could have done without.

Scotty and I unassed Bessie, dashed into the smoke, and found what we hoped we wouldn't. A female soldier staggered into Scotty's arms, cammies blown out at the seams and burned over most of her body. Scotty did what he could.

I continued through the smoke, coming face-to-face with a tall soldier staggering zombielike and unrecognizable toward me. His Kevlar tilted back like a Little Leaguer's ball cap, face crushed, torched, mumbling incoherently. The soldier collapsed into my arms. I dragged his heavy body from the smoke, away from the burning vehicles, and laid him on the asphalt street. I patted out the burning clothes with my flight glove–covered hands, and unclipped and cleared his M16A4 rifle.

My Tier One mates, Tora Bora warriors like Stormin', Shrek, Blinkie, and a dozen-plus others, had moved on to service a follow-on target, leaving Scotty and me as the Task Force 626 liaison. The best medics in the world, only minutes earlier, had been on target. Now, pulling in the distinct smell of burning flesh, I tore into my personal first-aid pouch attached to my vest. The wounded soldier was breathing but expiring rapidly. He needed a lot of attention, but an open airway was priority one.

"Hang in there, man," I said, while slipping the Kevlar off his head, covering my gloves in crimson blood. "You're gonna be all right, buddy." I'm not sure I believed it myself, but I hoped he did.

I pulled the flexible nasal tube from my pouch, lubed it with a dribble from my CamelBak, wiped the blood and dirt from his nose, and tried to insert it into his left nostril. It passed fine for an inch or so before it deadended. No luck. I touched gently on his maxilla bone just under his nose. It was compromised.

The soldier's eyes were shut. I shook him gently to gauge a reflex or determine if he was conscious. I was losing him.

"Stay with me, Sergeant!"

I yanked the nasal tube out and went to the hollow, hard-plastic J-tube. Tilting his jaw back, I spotted his tongue and seated the tube, slowly pushing until it passed the soft palate, where I tried to turn it 180 degrees to direct the tube down into his throat. Again, something was blocking it from moving further.

Shit!

"MEDIC!"

I looked up, shocked to see a big red-and-white ambulance only a few feet behind me. Two Iraqi national EMTs, in white-over-white uniforms, stood with timid and nervous looks, holding an extended stretcher between them. I looked around, consciously hoping to see a Tier One medic appear out of nowhere.

The soldier was expiring, I couldn't help. Behind me, back toward the target building, the large crowd of irate Iraqis was growing and closing around us on three sides. Collapsed but still-hot power lines were sparking off the street like giant horse whips. A dozen Iraqis had jumped on top of the four burning and derelict Hummer hulks, chanting an unintelligible rant, taunting those of us who were left.

"Scotty, let's get him in the ambulance. He needs a doctor."

As the door closed to the ambulance, two shots rang out from close by. I looked toward the Hummers to see an Iraqi dressed in a brown T-shirt and U.S. desert khaki fatigue pants. He was being passed down from the top of one of the turrets, person to person in a human chain.

I looked at the platoon sergeant nearby.

"Are you up on head count?"

He hesitated. "I don't think so."

The wounded Iraqi dressed like a U.S. soldier, screaming from a wound or maybe from fear of losing his head, was being carried through the crowd to another ambulance near the intersection.

Scotty and I looked at each other, silently knowing we were both thinking the same thing. Had the locals pulled the unit's terp from the burning Hummers? Was the platoon sergeant still looking for him?

I felt a tap on my shoulder. "We're back."

It was the bearded Blinkie, an assault team leader.

The cavalry had returned and I could tell he knew what Scotty and I were thinking. I looked quickly for the platoon sergeant but he had vanished.

"Let's go!"

We took off at a dead sprint into the swarming crowd of Iraqis. I yanked my M4 suppressor from my muzzle and rocked the safety off, firing five rapid rounds into the clear blue sky to clear the way. We reached the ambulance before it departed, and stopped the driver. In the back, we opened the rear doors to find the wounded man on a stretcher with an ambulance tech leaning over him.

I jumped into the back of the ambulance, climbing over the bloody man, as Scotty and Blinkie secured the area and kept the ambulance stopped. I grabbed the man's arm and asked if he spoke English. He frantically shook his head, letting me know he was both scared shitless and not who we thought he might be. I searched both cargo pockets, pulling out some papers with Arabic writing and a pair of black leather work gloves before offering my hand to give him one more chance to let us save him. He wasn't taking.

As we did in the streets of Baghdad or the mountains of Afghanistan, fictional operator Kolt "Racer" Raynor must make split-second decisions based on his tactical acuity, tacit knowledge, and operational experiences. Shit can turn in the blink of an eye and guys can go one of two ways: either vapor lock and wait for a mate to bring you back, or turn the switch and auto-revert to your training. Just like Scotty did.

In *One Killer Force,* Racer is served up combat and chaos wholesale, forced to audible from plan A, which rarely survives the first gunshot.

Luckily for Kolt Raynor, even though many think his decision-making cycle is sketchy at times, he gets shit done. To what standard is typically debated in the hotwash and the hallways. For me, on that hot summer day in Baghdad, I should have been better. And if not for Scotty and the timely return of the Tora Bora warriors, there's no telling what would have materialized.

In the real world of spec ops, there are no individuals. It's a cross-functional team of teams with complimentary skill sets that lead to mission accomplished. From snipers to imagery analysts to helicopter door gunners to personnel clerks, if it's not a well-oiled and synchronized cast of thousands, it is darn close. In the fictional spec ops world, fortunately for me, things are no different.

To write *One Killer Force,* I needed more help than normal. Obviously, without the extraordinary support and blind confidence from my longtime editor at St. Martin's Press, Marc Resnick, and super-agent Scott Miller of Trident Media Group, Delta operator Kolt "Racer" Raynor would have remained in deep-cover status forever.

With the Delta Force thriller series at book four, I'm humbled and entirely grateful to still have Marc and Scott providing world-class top cover. I'm equally blessed to have Chris Evans back, an extremely talented writer in his own right, to tighten my shot group as my pen ran into the margins and to correct those peculiar things about writing comprehension that I admittedly gave less priority to than Coach's trick third-and-long plays or animated hand and arm signals from the third-base coach's box a few decades ago.

Besides Marc, Scott, and Chris, I'm deeply thankful to former mates and other unnamed experts that willingly provided unique and insider-knowledge-only details about special equipment, and historical perspective on real-world ops we experienced together years ago. Battling the enemy or crafting a book, no doubt about it, it's a team sport. For Kolt Raynor it's a sport that, if not for the continued support of my wife and daughters, would have him on waivers in a second. I owe all these Racer fans a deep debt of gratitude.

ONE

A small, dark shadow flitted across the waves under a waning quarter moon. Casting the shadow was a MH-6M Mission Enhanced "Little Bird" helicopter of the 1/160th Special Operations Aviation Regiment, its outer skin a dull matte black that absorbed both light and radar. Riding on the starboard pod of the bird, Delta Force Major Kolt "Racer" Raynor leaned into the headwind and wished like hell he'd never seen an episode of Shark Week.

Kolt accepted that putting his life in danger was just part of the job. Hell, it was one of the main reasons he loved being a special operator. Still, there were times when it felt like he was pushing his luck, and skimming across the cold, dark ocean was definitely one of those times.

Tonight particularly sucked for a number of reasons, which Kolt had way too much time to ponder as the Little Bird tempted fate over the ugly-looking waves way too close to the bottom of its skids. Scuzzball Iranian terrorist Marzban Tehrani and a group of jihad wannabes had hijacked the *Queen Mary 2* in the middle of its cross-Atlantic cruise. As bad as that was, the intel update made it a whole lot worse. It was believed, though unconfirmed, that Tehrani had managed to get ahold of one, and possibly two, North Korean–made miniature nuclear warheads, the legendary suitcase nuke that had been a constant fear of Western governments for decades. There was credence to this, as Marzban was known to have ties to the North Korean regime through the illicit trade of nuclear technology between North Korea and Iran.

Whatever Marzban and his compatriots had in mind, assuming it wasn't simply a massive suicide bombing, they weren't talking to the FBI's hostage negotiators. No, they were either oddly shy or operationally savvy. So far, they were only communicating through the cell phone belonging to an elderly woman from Buffalo who was on the cruise as a gift from her children. The NSA had quickly provided all the information they could find on Mildred Angelica Swanson, age seventy-three, born in Harrisburg, Pennsylvania, graduate of Vassar College, widow of one Jonathan Merle Swanson, mother of two adult children, and frequent visitor to Trump Casino in Atlantic City as well as several of the Native American–run casinos in upstate New York. Their information on Tehrani wasn't nearly as detailed.

Kolt rolled his shoulders an inch or so higher inside his rubber dry suit to close up the opening near his neck. The suit was far from a custom fit. Unlike the suits worn by the SEAL team he was flying along with, his suit was a SEAL Team Six supply-room handout, and whoever had cut out the neck area must have been endowed like Hulk Hogan. Now, the piercing winds coming off the choppy ocean water seemed to be collecting right under his Adam's apple.

Motherfucking SEALs!

Through his headset, Raynor heard the OPSKED, the code word for the helicopter assault force, or HAF for short, as they reached the point of no return. "All stations, all stations, I send Gettysburg. I say again, Gettysburg."

Kolt tilted his head forward, moving his eyes higher in their sockets to get a glimpse of the target vessel. With Gettysburg called, he figured he might be able to pick up a faint silhouette as soon as they cleared the horizon. No dice. Three MH-47 Dark Horse heavy-lift helos, the meat of the HAF, were flying staggered trail right and roughly a hundred meters in the lead, preventing Kolt from gaining eyes on the target.

Kolt knew the SEALs would be roughly thirty seconds in front of the 47s, cutting a deliberate path through the ship's rough wake. The boat assault force, or BAF, cross-loaded on four low-profile gunmetal gray Mark V Special Operations Crafts, was perfectly positioned, steering for the target ship's fantail with nobody on board the wiser.

He turned to look at the SEAL seated behind him, leaning backward, hiding from the headwind as much as possible. The SEAL was tucked in nice and tight, taking advantage of the few inches he was able to gain inside the open cabin, allowing Kolt to block every bit of headwind. The SEAL's kit was definitely custom, perfectly waterproof and buoyant.

Son of a bitch!

Kolt turned back around, moving his eyes past the fast rope hooked to the overhead, the rest coiled and lying in the cabin just a foot away, then back forward past the pilots in the bubble-glass cockpit, before leaning slightly aft to look through the opened cabin and focusing on his troop sergeant major, Slapshot. Ice-cold sea water whipped up by the pounding 47 blades, mixed with a sea squall rain, seeped into his lower neck area, running down between his pecs and settling in his belly button. Kolt wondered if Slapshot was having the same problem.

Slapshot, like Kolt, had been given the shit spot, too, just on the other side of the Little Bird. A second recruiting-poster-perfect-dressed SEAL, along with a very unfriendly-looking Belgian Malinois, were hooked in behind Slapshot.

Kolt made eye contact with the alert K9, Roscoe, a fully kitted out bomb dog. Roscoe's black, marblelike eyes reflected the waning quarter moon like a pocket mirror. Kolt shivered and looked away.

Kolt reached up with his gloved nonfiring hand to adjust his inflatable horse collar. The tactical life preserver was must-have kit when flying a bird's-eye view of the ocean, but it had already rubbed his neck raw. Embedded with hydrostatic inflator technology, the vest would automatically inflate within seconds when submerged in four or more inches of water. In an overwater emergency, with HIT, keeping your head above water was a certainty, but breathing was something altogether different.

Giving up on finding much comfort with the life vest, Kolt checked the positioning of his helicopter emergency egress device. A compact and lightweight mini-scuba bottle, the HEED III was snap-linked into his assault vest's nonfiring shoulder strap. Kolt gripped it lightly, slightly repositioning the mouthpiece toward his own mouth. Taking a quick glance down at the waves, he mentally rehearsed saving his own life. Unlike the horse collar, the HEED bottle had no auto-activate technology inside. The only way it would work was if you were conscious and had your shit together.

The bird rose and dipped before settling back into level flight. Kolt's stomach caught up a few seconds later. He knew the pilot gripping the collective inside the bubble cockpit of Twister Two-One, Chief Warrant Officer Three Stew Weeks, was one of America's best, the gold standard of helicopter pilots for sure. All the same, flying nap-of-the-earth at 152 knots, only a hundred feet above the frigid sea swell of the North Atlantic, at night, bordered between careless and reckless.

As the Killer Egg, as the Little Birds were also nick-named, dipped dangerously close to the waves before climbing, Kolt wished he'd been more aggressive in scoring a spot on one of the 47s. Being in one of those big-ass birds was like riding in an M1 Abrams com-pared to this little toy.

Kolt began to regret pushing to get clearance for op-erations from the doctors. Only a few months before, he'd been a human guinea pig as they dosed him with experimental antibiotics along with a hematopoietic stemcell transplantation at Raleigh Duke Medical Cen-ter. Kolt had tried to follow all the medical jargon and finally gave up, hoping that whatever they were doing would save him from the radiation he'd received at the Yellow Creek Nuclear Power Plant.

Hawk. She was there for him through every proce-dure, every fever-racked reaction to the drugs, every—

"All stations, I send Sumter, Sumter."

Shit. Turn the switch, Kolt.

Kolt shook his head, releasing the spell. He looked ahead, over the choppy Atlantic Ocean.

There, just visible above the ocean's flat horizon, were the soft yellow lights of the seventy-six-thousand-ton *Queen Mary 2*. Kolt looked down and saw they were already flying over her wake. The helo banked and lined up directly aft of the ship and their target, the Grill Terrace, a five-star restaurant.

Navy intelligence analysts had focused on the Prin-cess Grill during the mission planning. It was here, with a large heated whirlpool behind them, that the terror-ists would likely set up to snipe approaching rescue boats or helicopters attempting to sneak up behind the luxury cruise liner.

Kolt mentally ran through his checklist, already preparing for the post-mission joint hotwash.

BAF planning and approach, check. HAF planning and approach, check.

The restaurant's lights were still on, slightly illuminating the massive ship's wake. To Kolt, it made the dark water look that much colder. It was surprising that the lights were on, as they would serve to backlight any terrorists on the stern, but all the better for the assault team. It was a mistake to assume your enemy would always do the smart thing. You had to be ready to adapt, especially when your foe was acting stupid. Kolt knew all too well that rational action could be predicted, but stupid had a mind of its own.

Motion in the water drew Kolt's gaze down, and he spotted the boat assault force splitting to run up on either side of the *Queen Mary*'s stern. At just eighty-three feet long, the assault boats were like minnows in the shadow of the mammoth cruise liner.

Kolt couldn't make out the SEALs on board, but he knew several would be in overwatch, scopes and thermals up, eyes peeled for any terrorists brave enough to shove an AK-47 barrel over the ship's bulwark. The rest of the SEALs would be stacked behind the pole men, the two SEALs required to raise the pole while a third worried about scoring a positive first-attempt stick of the grappling hooks. Attached to the hooks would be lightweight aluminum caving ladders, which would allow the four boatloads of SEALs to silently climb aboard the hijacked cruise liner within seconds.

Everything was moving fast, giving Kolt little time to process his first mission since Yellow Creek. With aircraft now a difficult option for terrorists to hijack, they'd gone looking for other modes of transportation with far less security. It was no wonder they'd settled on a cruise liner. They were big, slow, filled with innocent people, and sure to capture the blinding lights of the media across the world. And adding to the nightmare, the *Queen Mary* was on a westbound crossing, coming from Southampton and heading toward New York City. Kolt knew that just as there were standing orders to shoot down hijacked aircraft should they pose a threat to any ground targets, the navy was prepared to sink any ship for the same reason.

Kolt scrunched his shoulders up around his ears and urged the Little Bird on. Waiting grated on his nerves. He didn't handle the middle ground very well. He wanted things to get going for another reason too. The JSOC commander, Lieutenant General Seth Allen, had done the quite remarkable by deploying both special mission alert squadrons for this mission, one from SEAL Team Six, the other nod going to Delta's Osage Squadron. While Delta didn't work in the water nearly as often as the SEALs, they could still get wet without needing water wings.

Delta and the SEALs together. It could work brilliantly, or be a brilliant disaster.

A spray of saltwater snapped Kolt back to the here and now. Scanning the restaurant area again, he detected no sign of the terrorists. Kolt shifted his focus just below to deck ten, where steady but faint lights from the outboard staterooms, the exorbitantly priced Windsor and Buckingham suites, could be seen from behind partially closed drop curtains.

He knew the assaulters would be entering those suites within a few minutes and he worried about what or who might be waiting in ambush. Delta would be clearing the high decks from thirteen down to seven, while the SEALs would be going deeper to the low decks. Marzban and his dirty bombs were expected to be down below, so the SEALs would get the hot mission while Delta drew the short straw of supporting them. Ever since the

Osama raid the SEALs had taken insufferable to a whole new level.

CW3 Stew Weeks closed Twister Two-One to a hundred yards immediately aft of the *Queen Mary*. He slowed the bird to sixty knots to give the lead 47s time to deploy their ninety-foot fast ropes from the tail ramps and front right doors. The lead double-bladed 47 maneuvered over the Sun Deck, rotated counterclockwise ninety degrees, and dropped all three ropes simultaneously. In trail, the second 47 flared nose up over the aft end of deck twelve, mirrored the lead's rotation, and dropped three ropes on top of the shuffleboard area.

Weeks held Twister Two-One offset until the Delta assaulters were off the fast ropes and the 47s cleared to the east out of the *Queen*'s deck lighting. The helicopter slid and darted as the pilot kept it in the dark, engaging in an air loiter roughly seventy yards off stern and slightly aft of starboard. Almost immediately the windchill temperature lowered, allowing Kolt to relax his face and focus on the ropers sliding down the nylon ropes at one per second.

Kolt quickly wiped the water beads off his eye pro lenses just as the last ropers from both 47s cleared his field of view. Seconds later, six dark nylon ropes dropped freely to the decks, cueing Kolt to listen for their signal to proceed to their insert point.

"Ropes away, ropes away."

So far so good; good op.

Immediately, Kolt felt his Little Bird's nose drop a foot or so, picking up forward air speed. Twister Two-One was following the 47s' approach route while remaining just off starboard so that they flew directly over the SEALs' two Mark Vs that were now bobbing midship.

Kolt uncrossed his ankles and looked down between his Multicam Salomon assault boots. Clearing the ship's wake, the lead Mark V peeled off, separating them from the hijacked vessel before picking up a bearing for the twenty-seven-mile run back to the mother ship, the afloat forward staging base conventionally known as the USS *Ponce*. Kolt knew the SEALs would have already negotiated the ladders as skillfully as triple-canopy jungle monkeys and would be moving toward the main stairwells to descend to the lower decks.

Lead boat crew, good hook, good board.

Kolt leaned forward slightly, testing the tension on his monkey strap, and spotted the second Mark V still positioned next to the ship. He knew the driver was holding the boat as close as he could, essentially attaching his Mark V like a blood-sucking leech to the ship's hull at the waterline to provide the SEALs a stable base to climb.

First hook attempt must have failed.

"You seasick yet, boss?" Slapshot asked over their dedicated frequency.

Kolt leaned back to look through the cabin and toward Slapshot. He flipped him the bird for a couple of seconds and then keyed his mike. "In case you missed my last, that was a big fuck you."

"Roger, I'm stopping by the Regatta Bar as soon as we get on board," Slapshot said.

"Might be crowded. Frogmen already boarded," Kolt said as he reached behind him to control his monkey strap snap link, found the opening lever, and gave it a slight nudge to ensure it would open quickly.

"That will be my first hotwash comment then," Slapshot said.

Twister Two-One accelerated toward the bridge, the highest point on the *Queen*'s bow, and the quickest point of entry for Roscoe to bite into a terrorist's hairless ankle or bony forearm.

Chief Weeks slowed and banked slightly left, slipped

cyclic slightly to lateral shift another few feet forward to center his customers over the fast rope point, then flared and settled to hover six or seven feet above the bridge.

"Ropes, ropes, ropes," Weeks transmitted.

Pleased with the spot, Kolt turned to see the SEAL push the coiled heavy nylon rope off the pod, allowing the twenty-five-footer to drop to the bridge wing. Kolt thumbed his snap link, releasing his tether to the Little Bird, and reached for the rope to follow the SEAL down. Standard stuff for seasoned operators like Kolt. Even though nobody kept tabs on an operator's fast rope inserts, say, like the number of HALO free falls or his long obstacle course time, for Kolt this one had to be somewhere around a thousand or two.

But this insert just didn't feel right. Kolt sensed the MH-6M was sliding left, not keeping pace with the *Queen Mary*'s forward speed.

With both gloved hands gorilla-gripping the nylon rope, Kolt hesitated. He looked down. His instincts were spot-on. His landing point wasn't fouled, just gone, and he was staring at the small whitecaps on the right tip of the bow illuminated by the distant moon.

Shit!

Kolt wasn't sure if the SEAL had successfully dropped or if he had slipped off the end of the rope and fallen into the sea. But he did know a drifting Little Bird over a moving ship was fairly common. Weeks would make the fine adjustments and get them back over the correct insert point. No drama. Kolt held what he had.

"Twister's Lame Duck, Lame Duck!" Weeks calmly transmitted.

Kolt froze. *What the hell?*

Without further warning the MH-6M jerked nose down, wobbled out of balance, and went into an uncontrollable right-hand yaw.

Blade strike? Antenna? High-tension wire?

Now that wasn't common. Kolt figured Weeks lost drive in the tail rotor from either a blade strike–induced break in the drive train or a Murphy-like mechanical failure. Either way, or anything different altogether, any barracks mechanic could tell you it was absolutely fucked-up shit.

Kolt thought to reach for his snap link, debating whether or not to hook back in. Or, just slide down the rope and safely into the water. Put distance between him and the problem, let the HIT save his ass, pop a pin flare, and get picked up later. Before he could decide, Kolt heard a hard metallic snap and yanked his neck to investigate. The tail rotor had snapped off the main cabin and was falling toward the ocean.

Kolt knew now the safest place to be was inside with the pilots, as far away from the six spinning blades on the main rotor as possible. Second to that, the open cabin just behind the pilots' seats and near the auxiliary fuel tank offered the best protection, and the best chance of surviving the impending crash impact.

Kolt also knew Chief Wecks didn't have many emergency-procedure options when the crash sequence began. He knew he would be concentrating on keeping it "wings level" as they spun downward to the drink from about fifty feet above the choppy sea.

"Fuck!"

Kolt didn't know who shouted, but it summed up his feelings nicely. Fighting the centrifugal force created by the spinning, now tailless MH-6M, Kolt struggled to push off the rope and reach for the edge of the cabin. Kolt gripped the sheet metal with his right hand, releasing his left-hand death grip from the rope, and, half launching, half pulling, he managed to get his upper torso inside. Lying on his back, his legs still hanging out the starboard side, Kolt reached out for whatever hard points he could find. As he braced for impact, his eyes rolled to the top of his goggles. Kolt blinked twice.

Slapshot?

A moment later, the MH-6M smacked into the frigid waters upside down, the rotor blades slapping the water, reducing their speed significantly. Kolt slammed into the roof area of the helo, his body armor saving him from severe blunt trauma. He took in a heavy whiff of engine oil and JP8 as ice water gushed into the door-less bubble cockpit and cabin.

Kolt knew the pilots' shoulder harness reels would lock on impact and that they would free themselves. Assuming they were conscious, their extensive training and basic mission qualification standards ensured that much. But, just as instinctively, Kolt figured he was screwed.

He remembered his pool workup and Slapshot's adolescent scare tactics about some bullshit called the gasp reflex. Something about the average schmuck can hold his breath for 103 seconds in room-temperature air, but maxes out at about 12 seconds of air when immersed in cold water. The gasp reflex was involuntary, Slapshot explained, and didn't give two shits how badass you thought you were.

The HEED!

Kolt held his breath as the MH-6M held him entombed and dragged him below the choppy water. But forgetting to close his mouth, either from the hard slam against his chicken plate or simple shock, he took in a gulp of seawater. He tried to spit it out but, already submerged, he had no choice but to close his mouth tight and fight the urge to panic.

He reached for his HEED, stoked to find it on the first try, but fumbled to turn the white rubber mouthpiece toward his face. He jammed it in his mouth, closed his lips tight around it, and purged the regulator and most of the water in his mouth. Kolt coughed, having not cleared all the salt water, and struggled to remain calm.

When submerged at night, without reference points and unable to see, Kolt knew the key to survival was actually counterintuitive. Swimming out of the crashed helo was the last thing he should do, as the arm strokes and kicks were more likely to hang his kit up on some unseen hazard. If that happened, he would suck his HEED empty trying to free himself. Once he was out of air, seawater would rush into his lungs, shallow water blackout would be rapid, and he would simply drown, sinking to the ocean floor with the wreckage. Really, Kolt certainly knew, no different from Yellow Creek.

Kolt did his best to stay calm, but with only two to five minutes of air, and a sinking helicopter, he needed to move fast. He used basic hand-over-hand and controlled pulls, working his way free of the wreckage by feel. Once he cleared the fuselage he knew his body's natural buoyancy would right him head up and point him to the surface. With the HIT horse collar, even better.

But Kolt had swallowed too much seawater and struggled to juggle air from the HEED and the water in his lungs. Feeling with his hands, he found the outer edge of the submerged cabin, and felt the weight of the wreckage pull his hands downward. He let go to prevent himself from being dragged to the ocean floor and pushed off from an unseen hard point with his right assault boot.

Unable to see, even with his goggles still in place, the front end of Kolt's Ops-Core brain bucket bumped into something blocking his escape route.

The surprise startled him, knocking the HEED from his mouth. Kolt reached out with his right hand to assess the obstacle while he ran the length of the dummy cord to secure his HEED and reinserted the mouthpiece. Again, he pressed the top of the air bottle to purge the regulator. Again, he coughed deeply, fighting the natural urge to spit out the mouthpiece.

A human!

Kolt quickly grabbed the upper body of the person in front of him. He ran his hands along the edges, determining the body was actually upside down and unconscious. Or quite possibly even dead.

Kolt wasn't exactly sure if the guy on the opposite pod was the SEAL or his troop sergeant, Slapshot. He ran his hands up to the human's waist, and felt around the open water for a monkey strap. The operator's buoyancy and horse collar activation were working against the downward-sinking movement of the MH-6M. He followed the taut line to the snap link with his left hand, thumbed it open, and felt the lanyard yank upward, signaling the operator's horse collar was pulling him to the surface.

Fuck!

Kolt felt the hard bite on his right forearm, the sharp teeth easily penetrating the polyurethane dry suit and puncturing his skin.

Roscoe!

The bomb dog didn't loosen the bite, and began to shake his head rapidly from side to side, threatening to tear Kolt's arm off at the elbow joint. Kolt thumbed the snap link gate open and unhooked it from the helo O-ring. Immediately Kolt felt the snap link pull up and out of his hand, confirming the SEAL was free and ascending to the surface.

With Roscoe still working the bite, thrashing back and forth as if he had the lungs of an alligator and wasn't thirty feet under the ocean surface, Kolt suddenly recalled a glimmer of Slapshot just before impact. He reached toward the left edge of the outer pod and moved his hand back and forth, searching for Slapshot's safety line. He would be inverted now, like the SEAL was, but still tethered close enough to the outer pod for Kolt to know for sure.

Nothing but space.

Kolt reached for Roscoe's neck with his left hand and ran his thumb up to the dog's right ear. He pinched hard, giving Roscoe something else to think about. Feeling the bite pressure release, Kolt yanked his right forearm free and reached for Roscoe's snap link. He couldn't find it initially as he ran his hands along the outer pod, and was forced to expand his search area. Just as he touched it with his right hand, one of Roscoe's front paws slashed downward, pulling Kolt's eye protection off his face and leaving a long scratch on Kolt's right cheek. The cold salt water flooded his eyes just as a second paw slash knocked the HEED from his mouth.

Screw the dog, I need to get to the surface, or drown in this lonely ocean.

Kolt thought he had decided. Leave the dog and save himself. But his conscience grabbed him, reminding him that Roscoe wasn't just a stray mutt in the Hindu Kush. Or, maybe God's hand was working. Kolt knew that, even before 9/11, working dogs had proven to be must-have assets on target. Not everyone was a PETA extremist, but nobody could argue that their nose wasn't a combat multiplier or that they didn't take years to train. Kolt knew they had saved the lives of countless operators, either from sniffing out IEDs or taking down scumbags like the Chechen Black Widows at the Sochi Games.

Aw shit! I can't leave Roscoe.

Kolt put both hands on Roscoe's snap link and unhooked it easily. He held on to the snap link as he found his HEED again and reinserted it.

Fuck me. Empty!

Kolt pulled on the inverted outer pod above his head, and felt himself moving free of the still-descending Little

Bird. Out of breath and feeling the early effects of shallow water blackout, he knew he needed to get to the surface immediately. Sure, he knew drowning was actually peaceful, once you reached your limits. Kolt certainly knew his, but the panic before the peace was a mankind equalizer.

Kolt pulled stroke with both hands and frog-kicked, thankful for the horse collar and no longer worried about the cold water that had entered his neck area or the rash. Two more long pulls and Kolt's helmeted head popped out of the water, with Roscoe surfacing a moment later. The silence from inside the sinking helo was interrupted immediately by the rotor blades of a hovering MH-6M, most definitely Twister Two-Two.

Just as Kolt raised his hand to wave at the hovering Little Bird, a white beam of light from an operator's rifle illuminated Kolt, Roscoe, and the immediate area. Kolt noticed several objects floating nearby. Kolt wasn't surprised to see an obvious pilot seat cushion, and what looked like a pilot's map board that is usually strapped to the thigh, but the third item floating nearby was oddly out of place. He tried to focus on it, squinting into the rotor wash of the hovering Twister Two-Two and fighting the bright white light.

He rubbed the salt water out of his eyes.

A fucking doggie toy!

TWO

USS **Ponce**, *Atlantic Ocean*

Son of a bitch! Delta commander Jeremy Webber did his best to count his blessings, but found them few and far between. The joint training mission to assault a large ship at sea was a bust as far as Delta was concerned, but at least the men had all been plucked from the water alive and in relatively good shape.

Webber drew in a deep breath and did his best to compose himself as he walked with SEAL commander Hank Yost from the planning bay up to the main hangar deck of the USS *Ponce*. They knew the MH-6M Little Birds would be landing on the flight deck soon, signaling the soggy return of the rescued men. Webber gave way to his navy peer, letting him navigate the galleys and the shortcuts through a string of heavy watertight doors, before they reached the main hangar deck.

"Your boys took a hell of a dunking tonight," Yost said.

"No wetter than yours," Webber said, annoyed that he rose to the bait. It was no secret DOD was considering combining Delta and the SEALs, or even getting rid of one altogether. It was one of the reasons this joint exercise had been planned.

"So much for the training exercise," Yost said.

Is he looking for an elbow to the teeth? He and Yost had been friends for years, but right now Webber was ready to pop him one. "I'm happy everyone is okay," Webber said, exerting more control over himself.

Webber climbed the last set of aluminum stairs from the second deck and lowered his head as he followed Yost, stepping over the bottom of the watertight door-jamb. The hangar deck was bustling with activity as sailors and troops ducked in and out of the unit's and the 160th's open equipment containers. Maintenance crews were seen behind the roped-off area that held the spare AH-6 gunships, their wooden rocket cases, and the MH-6Ms, prepping to launch if the order came.

Hangar deck elevator number two lowered from the flight deck on the starboard side of the ship. Backlit by the moonlight bouncing off the dark blue sky, a dozen or so silhouettes stood on the elevator as it slowly came into view.

Webber saw Kolt's feet first as the elevator cleared the outer edge of the flight deck and continued to lower a half foot per second. Behind Kolt, Slapshot was visible, and nearby two SEALs, one holding a K9 in his arms, and just behind them the two Little Bird pilots. Webber marveled at Raynor's nine lives. The soldier was a lot like the USS *Ponce* in that regard. Two years ago the ship was to be decommissioned, but all that changed when U.S. Central Command realized they needed a floatable forward staging base to handle contingencies in the Middle East and off the coast of Africa. Now, instead of being so many car parts or flying the flag of some third-world ally, the USS *Ponce* was a refitted fighting machine, and had become the first ever laser weapon system.

Webber and Yost stood a few feet from Kolt as the medics went to work. They used medical scissors to cut off his horse collar and assault vest, then drew the scissors up his arms, cutting the polypropylene dry suit away from his body.

"You cut into me and I'll sic that damn dog on you," Kolt growled. "And I could have just taken the assault vest off. You didn't have to ruin it."

Webber chuckled to himself.

As Yost moved off to check on his SEALs, Webber moved in closer to Raynor. A dozen or so medics were checking the survivors' vitals. Webber noticed the blood running down Kolt's face.

One of the medics shone a small flashlight into his eyes and told him to blink, while holding pressure on the gash with a piece of Kerlix. A second medic inserted an ear thermometer for a few seconds, while a third medic did a full 360 of his head and upper torso. As they worked, Webber couldn't help but notice the half dozen or so battle scars smattered over Kolt's six-pack, pecs, and right upper arm. The cold water had turned the scars bright pink, contrasting heavily with his beach-bum-like tanned upper torso.

Kolt's scars of war were no surprise to Webber, but the massive shoulder tattoo certainly was. It stretched from just above the base of his left bicep, captured the entire swole deltoid, and engulfed his entire left pec muscle, depicting Spartan warriors with their battle shields tactically aligned and raised in defense as arrows rained down on them. As Webber neared, he realized the tattoo was pretty fresh, maybe a few days to a week, still slightly swollen and burnt red. Then he noticed the phrase "Molon Labe" and smiled. The mark was as significant as the statement. Webber understood Kolt was covering the vicious scarring from the blue-on-blue bullet he took at Yellow Creek.

But, something wasn't sitting right with Webber. Something was strange about Kolt's demeanor. His eyes were distant, barely blinking naturally. He couldn't be sure, but the Delta commander had seen this before in other operators over the years. For a second, he thought Kolt Raynor was showing the classic signs of shell shock.

"New ink, I see, Major," Webber said.

No response. Webber took a few steps closer to Raynor, raised his right hand to wave it in front of Kolt's eyes.

It worked. Kolt's head shook slightly as if he had just been pulled from a deep trance. "Uh, yes, sir, sorry," Kolt said, coming around and seemingly not worried at all. "Nice night for a swim."

Webber tried not to smile. He knew Raynor, if anybody, had earned the right to ink his body any way he saw fit. As long as he didn't go full sleeve, or full auto chop shop and ink his neck and face, at this point, after over a decade at war, Webber didn't give two shits.

He also knew Kolt's recent meetings with the unit psych, Doc Johnson, had revealed potential flaws in Kolt's mental capacity to command a Delta squadron, something Webber didn't plan to share with the special mission unit board members. Something he wasn't entirely surprised about, given the trauma Raynor had suffered during the Yellow Creek debacle. But something Webber hoped like hell was a temporary condition that his top officer would soon overcome. All things considered, as long as Kolt didn't fall off the wagon, Webber figured he could manage the trauma.

"You okay, Raynor?" Webber asked, extending his hand out to shake Kolt's.

"Yes, sir, I'm all right, just a little cold at the moment," Kolt said.

"No, listen to me. Are you okay?" Webber asked, speaking low and slow.

Raynor blinked and looked around the flight deck before looking back at him. "It sucked, but I'm fine. My reflexes were fast and I kept my head. Hell, I saved that squid's mutt. I'm one hundred percent. Well, high nineties, anyway."

Webber held Raynor's gaze for several seconds. If Kolt was bullshitting him, he was brilliant. Webber nodded. "Right. Get yourself squared away, knock out a quick hotwash with Slapshot and the pilots, then get to my quarters," Webber said. "I've got a job for you."

"Something that is more important than hot chow first, sir?" Kolt asked, surprised at the urgency, considering he was almost dead less than fifteen minutes ago and still wet from his crotch to his toes.

"Afraid so, Racer," Webber said. "I'll fill you in soon enough."

"C'mon, sir," Kolt said as the medics started to pull his dry suit down past his ass and to his ankles, revealing Kolt's black Under Armour Boxerjocks. "Can't you give me a mad minute or warning order now?"

"All right, Kolt," Webber said, knowing the old Kolt had come back to earth. "We've got intel on a high-priority target in Syria. It's actionable, but only if we go now. I want you on the mission."

Raynor didn't react, which was impressive considering he'd nearly lost his life not half an hour ago. And now here he was asking Raynor to go put it on the line again. And that wasn't the worst of it.

"My team—" Raynor started to say, but Webber cut him off.

"No. You're going without them."

"Don't tell me you're putting me in command of SEALs?"

Webber shook his head. "Not SEALs . . . and not in command."

Afrin, Syria—April 2014

Delta Force operator Major Kolt "Racer" Raynor considered his lot in life and decided it was definitely . . . interesting. Only two weeks ago he'd been fighting for his life in the cold waters of the Atlantic Ocean. Now he was sitting in the back of a nondescript van deep in Syria, on the lookout for a Syrian Army officer known as the Barrel Bomb Butcher. Not satisfied with rockets, mortars, and chemical weapons, the Syrians had begun dropping fifty-five-gallon drums filled with explosives from helicopters onto civilian areas. The Butcher was a particularly zealous proponent of these massacres, and so he was now on the target list.

"You got the ass you aren't gonna kill anyone today, Racer?" Noble Squadron commander Lieutenant Colonel Rick "Gangster" Mahoney asked, his voice filled with sarcasm.

"Just a dude in the back today," Kolt said from six feet behind in the rear cabin seat closest to the back doors, "strap-hanging with no dog in the fight."

Kolt let Gangster's smart-ass comment roll off his back like a heavy rucksack dropped after a forty-mile suckfest. He didn't need to be reminded. He knew he wasn't there to do anything but watch. Hell, Colonel Webber had warned him back at Bragg, several times actually, not to start any shit.

Yes, maybe Kolt could take some mental notes, but, as every operator knows, on target trouble can find you, whether you like it or not.

"SITREP, over," Gangster said from the front seat of the panel van as he released his push-to-talk.

"This is Jackal Two, no change."

Jackal Two, one of the sniper teams perched inside the vacant third floor of a half-finished block of flats, had scoped out the target at exactly 247 yards. The hide was good enough to easily range the old adobe-brick-and-plaster house's huge front door, painted with odd-looking multicolored geometric patterns, and the small courtyard. Even a massive crystal chandelier, a favorite Syrian decoration even in the poorer villages, could be scoped from two and a half football fields away.

"Rog. Thirty mikes till sunrise. If the Butcher loved his mother as much as the agency said he did, he's there," Gangster said.

Speaking into a handheld mike connected to a coiled black cord that ran to the SATCOM radio positioned just behind the black curtain, Gangster was calm and collected. And why shouldn't he be?

Gangster was a shit-hot Delta Force squadron commander, on the very short list to someday command all of Delta Force. In fact, the word on the street was that he was being specifically groomed for it. Kolt knew the type for sure. The kind of guy always picked first when choosing sides during a neighborhood pickup game, or the guy that scored the hottest cheerleaders in high school.

Like everyone else, Gangster had his skeletons. But nobody expected him to be perfect all the time. To most guys in the building, his flaws were manageable and easily massaged. But to Kolt Raynor, his peer Delta officer for many years, a risk-averse reputation was a deal breaker. Kolt didn't care if the guy had won two of the last three Unit annual triathlons.

Behind the wheel and up front with Gangster sat a dirty-blond operator named Trip Griffin, one of the few guys in the Unit whose first name was so unique that it became his de facto code name. Kolt sensed Trip's pucker factor fully pegged as he kept a keen eye on the dense bed of gray and tan adobe single- and two-story homes about a block or so away and about two hundred feet lower. The black curtain separated the front seats of the panel van from the two guys in the back, but more importantly it hid the red and green radio lights from being seen by curious locals outside.

"Let's go to one hundred percent from here on out, over," Gangster transmitted over his push-to-talk.

"Rog. Jackal's up."

"All assault elements, you roger my last?" Gangster asked, checking on the three assault teams loitering in their rolling LCCs, or last covered and concealed positions.

"This is Echo One, up!"

"Golf One, we're up."

"Fox is good."

"This is Noble Zero-One, roger all, out!" Gangster said, sounding pleased his teams were set, alert, and ready to turn the target.

Bumpered on a pseudo-discreet piece of high ground, overlooking the ancient municipality of Jindires, the lemon-looking Peugeot panel van wasn't necessarily out of place. Even though it had a finicky ignition, like an old John Deere, nobody could argue that it wasn't *local*-looking enough. Syria's northern neighbor, Turkey, only thirteen miles away, had hundreds of thousands of them. If well-paid CIA assets were good at anything, acquiring suitable assault vehicles for high-risk, high-yield, low-visibility ops topped the list.

Tilted slightly on the shoulder of a one-lane muddy road and adjacent to one of the village's four local cemeteries, the van was located more out of necessity than choice. Not a perfect spot for Gangster's command and control element, but it did provide excellent radio line of sight with his assault teams, just over a mile away. They had driven the hills in a light rain for over an hour, pushing their luck darting in and out of the village, checking possibles identified during the planning phase, before bumpering up. For the second day in a row the spot would have to do. As long as the tires could tame the mud-slicked road, they were good.

"Guys, hate to break it to you, but I need to lock out a SEAL team," Kolt Raynor said from the back of the van.

"You gotta be kidding, Racer," Gangster said in disgust, ripping the curtain open to look in the back. "A shit? Now?"

Kolt didn't appreciate the attitude one bit, but he understood the death stare he was currently getting from Gangster, now turned around in his seat. Gangster had an op to run. The Unit, particularly Gangster's squadron, had been on the Barrel Bomb Butcher's trail for some time now, with a couple of near misses and several agency-provided nuggets that took them down dead ends. The dead ends, although not resulting in the loss of any mates, were becoming a running joke within the halls of the Joint Special Operations Command. To the point that the Delta commander, Colonel Jeremy Webber, had to convince COMJSOC to not push the Butcher kill/capture op to SEAL Team Six. All this led to the sketchy decision to stake the Butcher's mother's house two mornings in a row.

Sure, the CIA had reported that the Butcher's mother was terminally ill. And their assets in the Aleppo Governorate likely had good intel that her days were numbered. Actionable enough for the National Command Authority to cut an oh-dark-thirty deployment order and push a troop from the alert squadron to a CIA safe house in the Turkish border town of Kilis. Whether the intel was legit or not was still to be seen.

"Man, I'm sorry, but those Turkish meatballs have me jacked up," Kolt said, ashamed at his predicament and feeling like a jackass, especially knowing the pressure Gangster was obviously feeling to score the Butcher.

"Can't you hold it? We're thirty minutes from show-time," Gangster said. "I'm not losing the Butcher like the Mossad lost Marzban."

"Afraid not, partner," Kolt said, realizing that Gangster was more amped up than he thought.

Bringing up Marzban Tehrani—the former leader of the Iranian dissident group the Mujahedin-e-Khalq, or MEK, and now the current bane of the Israeli prime minister's existence, was about as random as you can get. Besides, Kolt figured, they couldn't talk much smack, as they hadn't positively identified the Butcher yet.

"I'll pop out the back doors and find a tree. Be back in a flash," Kolt said.

"Unbelievable!" Gangster said. "All right, make it quick, heat tab's almost up."

Kolt unslung his suppressed Flat Dark Earth–colored HK416C ultra-compact rifle and laid it on the van's carpeted floor. He tapped his Caspian .45 cal single stack placed against his appendix on the right and under his wife-beater tank and local-enough turtleneck wool sweater before reaching into a small zippered bag.

"JoJo, cover the radio lights for a second, will ya?" Kolt said to Gangster's squadron communicator.

"Yeah, good idea."

"Three knocks on the window and it's me, cool?"

"Roger," JoJo said. "You got shit paper?"

"Right here, partner, saw it coming," Kolt said as he held up a fresh roll of foreign-made two-ply tissue paper like a panning forty-niner discovering a piece of gold.

"Hurry up, Racer!" Gangster chimed in from the front.

Yeah, asshole! I didn't ask for this gig anyway.

Kolt was right, actually. Right-seat riding with Gangster was Colonel Webber's big idea, and Kolt, hell, even

Gangster wasn't all that fired up about the arrangement. Kolt and Gangster knew Unit standard operating procedures required it, though. Any guy on the bubble for special mission unit, or SMU, selection for squadron command strap-hung with current commanders during an operation. No big deal to Kolt. Definitely not necessary either, as he'd been around long enough to know how to synchronize multiple troops on target and in combat.

Kolt pulled the inch-thick blast curtain away from the back double doors and reached for the handle. He peeked out the back window for a few seconds, making sure he wasn't going to bump into any early-morning strollers or punctual market workers, and eased the door open. Kolt stepped out into a thick fog bank, felt the light rain hit his dark brown hair and short cropped beard, and felt his leather boots sink a full inch into the chocolate-colored mud.

Shit! Footprints!

Kolt stepped to the left to gain the tall grass, toward the two-foot-high cemetery wall made of aged and stacked gray and light brown quarry rocks. If the defaced and broken tombstones were any indication, some vandalized with spray-painted phrases in Arabic, they had to have been laid in at least two hundred years ago.

With his tracks better concealed, Kolt moved twenty feet or so to clear the corner of the rock wall and spotted a patch of thin trees just off the military crest of the hill. He moved down and in behind the second tree in line and, using the heel of his left boot, scraped the pine needles away before carving out a small slit trench. He turned his back to the tree, dropped his cheap designer jeans, careful to keep his mini-blaster from falling from its holster, and squatted.

Not a moment too soon either.

Kolt looked out to the south as he prepped the first folds of shit paper, happy to find a few of the trees not harvested by locals for timber or firewood. He remembered what the intel analyst had said about not even thinking about finding a forest to hide in. Supposedly, in ancient times, Syria was richly forested, until forest fires and basic human needs depleted the vast majority of European black pines and kermes oaks.

Not yet finished with his business, Kolt turned his attention to the southeast, toward the hotly contested city of Aleppo, some forty-eight klicks away. Dawn had yet to appear, and the heavy ground fog that seemed to cling to their little hilltop limited his visibility to a few hundred yards max. He knew it wouldn't be long before the Syrian rebels and government forces would trade fire and jockey for terrain. Today, like every day for the last few months, Aleppo residents with ties to the city for generations would become refugees and flee the bombings, or simply relocate in search of much-needed food, clean water, and safe shelter.

Just as uncertain, Kolt wondered if he was close enough, once the fog lifted, to spot Russian-supplied Mi-8 and Mi-17 helicopters dropping barrel bombs on the slower, or more stubborn, innocent civilians.

Kolt brought his focus closer, down the hill, following the dirt road to the old wood-and-concrete bridge the agency assets had assured them was impassable. He couldn't see the bridge itself, but did see half of two large logs lying across the road, near where he figured the bridge was.

Must be the locals' way of saying "bridge closed."

Kolt began to fold another few layers of shit paper together, careful to keep it dry. He froze.

He heard what sounded like a truck approaching off to his left and slowly turned to look. He spotted the dim headlights through the fog, barely illuminating their path of travel. Metal objects could be heard bouncing around in the back of the truck bed.

Kolt finished his business, wincing as the two-ply sandpaper rubbed his cheeks, and slowly stood to a crouch to pull his drawers up. He moved behind the tree and followed the headlights as the truck came to a stop on the far side of the cemetery.

What the hell? Not good!

Kolt could barely make out two, maybe three voices. He didn't recognize the language as Arabic, figuring maybe Kurmanji, a Kurdish dialect spoken by Syrian Kurds mentioned in the target folder. It didn't really matter; Kolt wasn't in town to mingle with the locals. The Syrian mystery men obviously weren't worried about waking them either as they laughed about something while removing some equipment from the bed.

Kolt worried that they would see Gangster's van across the cemetery, now more thankful for the ground fog than ever. Then, three men, two middle-aged and one younger, maybe twenty or twenty-five, stepped over the rock wall. Two wore colorful wool hats to ward off the cold, one with the hood of his black leather jacket up, front zipper at the neckline and the top dropping over his eyes.

Shovels! Folding chairs? Shit!

Kolt reached down and grabbed a few handfuls of pine needles, shaking his greasy bangs out of his eyes before dropping the needles over the slit trench. He crouched down and moved toward the rock wall. Worried he would be spotted, he went into a high crawl, slithering through the dew-covered grass while hand-railing the rock wall to his right. He could still hear the voices, now more hushed, but the unfolding and squeaking of metal chairs and shovels piercing piles of dirt was telling.

Now at the van, completely soaked through at the thighs and elbows, Kolt slowly moved to a knee. He tapped lightly on the back door three times as he stole a peek back toward the three workers. Kolt paused for a second, giving JoJo time to cover the radio, then slowly opened the door and moved the ballistic blanket out of the way. Holding his forefinger extended vertically in front of his lips, Kolt crawled inside.

"Shhhhhh."

Kolt reached for his rifle, quickly reslung it, touched the selector lever with his thumb to ensure the weapon was still safe, and checked the red dot in his EOTech holographic weapon sight. "We got company."

"No shit?" JoJo said. "They make you?"

"Negative," Kolt said, moving forward in the van, just past JoJo, to open the curtain separating them from Gangster. "Hey man, three males and a truck. Far side of the cemetery. Shovels and folding chairs."

Kolt took in a whiff of a recognizable odor, an odd cross between Frasier fir Christmas tree and raspberry vinegar. He had smelled it before, many times back inside the Spine at the Unit, and knew it to be the signature body wash used by Gangster.

Gangster raised his hand in the air, showing Kolt his palm and giving him another death stare out of the corner of his eye.

"Assault One, stand by!" Gangster said, obviously irritated, before turning around in his high-back seat to address Kolt. "You had to get out and compromise us."

"Negative," Kolt said, now a little irritated. "They didn't see—"

Gangster quickly cut him off. "How can you be certain?"

"Look, man, they are a work crew, not troops, probably not armed," Kolt said, hoping to calm Gangster down a little.

"Bullshit!" Gangster said. "You should have never left the van."

"Hey, asshole, any of you guys spot the vehicle?" Kolt said, trying to control his volume. "If I didn't go out there, we wouldn't have any idea. They are setting up a funeral right now, you hear them?"

"No, I don't hear shit!" Gangster said.

"Exactly!" Kolt said. "Trust me."

Gangster turned his head from Kolt and moved his right hand to his earbud, reaching for his hand mike with his left.

"Boss, we've got movement," Jackal One said from their sniper hide 130 yards from the red side of the target house. "Forty-something male, stepped out the front door, on the porch now . . . just kicked a bony dog."

"Positive ID on our man?" Gangster asked.

"Not sure. This guy looks the part but no facial hair, over," Jackal One said.

"Bald guy?" Gangster asked.

"Can't tell, black over blue jeans, wearing a tan skullcap and pulling hard on a lung dart."

Kolt listened intently to the transmissions between Gangster and his sniper team on target.

Kolt knew the Butcher wasn't necessarily bald, but he did shave his head. He also was hardened from years of war, with tough features, wide, oversized jade green eyes, and sported a thick salt-and-pepper beard that covered most of his face. Yes, Kolt was pretty sure from what he just heard that the man the snipers were currently observing could very well be a dirtbag, maybe a body guard, or even a cousin, but not the Barrel Bomb Butcher himself.

Not our man.

Gangster broke his silence. "We have positive ID on the house, it's most likely the Butcher."

Kolt shook his head in amazement. *Most likely? Where did Gangster get that from?*

Kolt shouldn't have been surprised. He knew Gangster led like he read it in a field manual: rigid, afraid to audible off the elaborate charts and tables he was force-fed at

West Point or in one of his formal military schools. Gangster was encyclopedic with doctrinal terms and phrases, big-picture mission planning and decision-making process stuff. Shit Kolt avoided like a fat girl the morning after.

To Lieutenant Colonel Rick Mahoney, everything had a step, a specific sequence, and he wasn't about to stray even for a second from what the book said. Indeed, things like intuition and gut instinct, things that Kolt Raynor placed the most importance on, were taboo inside Gangster's brain housing group.

But even with all his vices, Kolt allowed, Gangster needed it to be the Butcher after so many dry holes.

"All elements, this is Noble Zero-One, depart LCCs, over?" Gangster transmitted with authority.

"Echo One, roger, moving."

"This is Golf One, moving."

"Fox, moving."

Kolt understood Gangster's desire to grab the Butcher, but he wasn't tracking with his thought process. It wasn't Kolt's op though; he wasn't anywhere in the chain of command on this one. No, he was there to learn the ropes of squadron command, not punk out the squadron commander. He may not have shared the warm and fuzzy with Gangster, but he knew the assault teams would figure it out. Even if it wasn't the Butcher out for a morning stretch, he likely was rolling out of bed about now.

Kolt settled back in his jump seat in the rear of the van, content to give Gangster some space and mind his own business. The Delta commander, Colonel Jeremy Webber, had counseled him—rather, warned him—not to interfere. Be a fly on the wall and nothing more.

Kolt pulled up the left sleeve of his tan wool sweater to reveal his quarterback-style armband. Two passport-size photos of the Butcher were taped to the upper right side of the grid target graph, or GTG aerial that showed what the CIA had fingered as the target house. He looked hard at both CIA-provided photos, studying the distinct features, further committing the Butcher's hard look to memory.

A ten-year-old could pick this guy out.

"Gangster, you seeing this?" Trip said from behind the steering wheel.

"What the hell is that?" Gangster said loud enough for both Kolt and JoJo to hear from behind the curtain.

"Hard telling, but I'm counting twenty, maybe thirty," Trip said. "They're coming up the road right at us."

Kolt bounced out of his seat, moved back past JoJo, and threw open the curtain again.

"Shit!" Kolt said, taking it all in and somewhat shocked by what he was seeing through the raindrop-splattered front windshield.

"We need to bug out," Gangster said as he reached for his HK416C placed muzzle down on the floorboard between his legs.

Kolt jumped in as he saw Trip reach for the ignition. "Trip, don't start the vehicle."

Surprised Gangster didn't respond to his comment to Trip, Kolt pushed his luck.

"We aren't compromised, this can be easy . . . unless we make it hard," Kolt said. "We try to leave now and we'll have problems, unless you are willing to mow over three dozen noncombatants with the van."

"That's gotta be the YPG," Gangster said, fidgeting in his seat. "We're hard compromised."

Kolt looked hard at the mob. He knew Gangster could be spot-on. The YPG, the odd acronym of the Popular Protection Units, had run Syrian president Bashar al-Assad's government forces out a few years ago and claimed the city, establishing their answer to America's red beret–wearing Guardian Angels to make sure the war didn't reach the city's edge again.

Trip quickly turned to the right, his fingers still on the keys in the ignition, just a few pounds of pressure away from turning the engine over, and looked at Kolt.

"Gangster, it's your call," Trip said, obviously wanting some guidance, unsure of who to listen to, his squadron commander or the strap-hanging Kolt.

"No, we need to go. Now!" Gangster said, shaking off the momentary vapor lock. "Back down the hill and we'll cross the creek."

"The creek?" Kolt said. "The bridge is out, man. Intel was right about that."

Gangster turned toward Kolt. "And you know this how?"

"Dude, I just confirmed it outside. There are two big-ass logs across the road anyway. Only way we are driving out of here is straight ahead."

Kolt looked through the windshield toward the crowd again. As he peered through the rainbow-shaped dirt streaks left from the worn wipers, he noticed something odd about the group. The group was all men—that he was now sure of. But it didn't appear to be a gang of thugs. They were dressed mostly in black, which wasn't odd to Kolt, but if truly the YPG, they would be armed. More telling, Kolt saw no women or children holding hands. No grown men carrying toddlers in their arms. Some distance into the middle of the moving crowd, they were carrying something on their shoulders.

The Butcher's mother?

"Gangster, hear me out, man." Kolt tried to maintain eye contact with him. "They are heading to a funeral. It fits. All males, the work crew with shovels, the folding chairs. Shit, this is probably the Butcher's family cemetery."

"Speculation, Racer—that's a definite stretch. We don't know that her funeral is today," Gangster said.

"We don't know it's not, but it's logical," Kolt replied.

Before Gangster could reply, Trip cut in, "We gotta do something, boss, crowd is fifty meters, I can practically read their lips."

Just then, over the assault net, they all heard the Phase Line Pinto call confirming the three assault teams were thirty seconds out from the Butcher's mother's house.

Kolt spotted Gangster keying his mike in his peripheral vision, but kept his eyes peeled on the crowd slogging up the muddy road. The wooden casket being shouldered, covered with red and white flowers and green garlands, was now clearly visible as they neared.

"Roger, Pinto," Gangster said.

More sure than ever now that this very well could be the Butcher's mother's funeral, Kolt broke in.

"Gangster. Look, bro, think it through," Kolt said, trying to keep calm in the face of what was turning out to be a certain shit sandwich. "Abort the assault on the house. The guy smoking out front doesn't match."

"What are you, Racer, psychic now?" Gangster was clearly fed up with Kolt's interference in his op.

"No, but that crowd out there is about to deep-six someone. If the guy out front of the target house was the Butcher, why would he be at the house and not with these guys?" Kolt said. "It's not him. You don't have PID. Abort the hit!"

"Negative, Racer, I'm not aborting the hit. It could be the Butcher out front of the house. This could be anyone's funeral," Gangster said as he keyed his mike to transmit to his assault teams approaching the target house. "All elements execute, execute, execute."

Nothing Kolt could do about it now. Either way, the Butcher or not, they would know soon enough. Kolt kept his attention on the closing crowd.

"Trip, Gangster, at least close it down and get back here behind the curtain." Kolt slid back to his seat to make room. "Make sure the doors are locked, and pull the keys."

Somewhat surprised they actually listened to him, Kolt watched Trip peel into the back, quickly followed by Gangster. JoJo put his fist up to get everyone's attention and give the hand and arm signal for *freeze*.

The procession moved closer, faint sounds of singing and chanting in Arabic seeping through the van's thin aluminum skin, tinted windows, and blast blankets. Kolt and the team were trapped.

THREE

Kolt held his breath. Of all the times he could have died and all the ways he imagined he might someday buy it, stuck in the back of a damn minivan had never entered his mind. The sound of the crowd grew louder as they reached the van and began to move around it.

A few moments later it felt to Kolt as if the crowd was bumping into both sides of the van as they made their way for the cemetery entrance. Funeral or not, Kolt knew the more switched-on men would be window-shopping the interior of the cab, probably looking for anything valuable like food or items to barter with at the Aleppo souk.

Kolt looked at Gangster, now squatting next to the radio. He could tell his nerves were pinging.

A few seconds later the crowd of men screamed in unison before breaking into what sounded most certainly like chants of Allah u Akbar, *God is Great*! Kolt looked around and thanked their training that no one had their finger on the trigger. He couldn't speak for the others, but that collective scream had startled him.

Kolt looked at Trip, then to JoJo. Both men looked

ready to explode. "*American Idol* material?" Kolt said, offering them a slight grin.

Neither man responded.

"That was close," Gangster whispered as he looked at Trip.

"Too close," Trip said.

Kolt reached for the blast blanket and slowly peeled it back an inch or two to peek out of the rear-door window.

"Shit!"

Kolt quickly let go of the blanket after seeing the blade edges of a hand just leaving the window glass and a male face turning from the van.

"Someone just tried to look in the window."

Kolt waited a few moments and tried again.

"Crowd passing the coffin over the rock wall," Kolt said as he watched the men gently but efficiently pass the wooden coffin from one group to another to clear the short wall without losing a single flower.

And then he saw someone that looked familiar.

Kolt let go of the blast blanket and quickly yanked his left sleeve up his arm. He moved his forearm closer to his eyes, fixated on the two pictures of the Butcher.

"I'll be damned!" Kolt whispered. "That's him!"

Before anyone could respond, the assault net came alive. "Noble Zero-One, target secure, over."

"Roger. Do you have jackpot, over?" Gangster asked.

"Possible, controlled pair to the face though, unrecognizable now. Three more fighting-age males, questioning them now, stand by."

"Roger. Finish it and exfil, over," Gangster said.

Finish it? What the hell does that mean? Kolt thought.

Kolt went back to the rear window. He looked again but his angle was off; he was barely able to see the backs of a few of the men halfway into the cemetery.

"Grave-side service under way," Kolt whispered.

Gangster took the ball. "Let's initiate exfil, best time is right now."

"Gangster, you don't have PID on the Butcher yet from your assault teams," Kolt said, turning away from the window to make eye contact. "I'm pretty sure I spotted him outside, let's hold for a few more."

Gangster didn't respond. He looked at JoJo and then Trip, likely trying to gauge their opinion. Kolt knew Gangster couldn't argue with his logic. He didn't have PID from the target and he damn well knew it. They all knew it. This hit was too important to the Unit to bug out before they knew for sure.

"Damn it!" Gangster said, trying to keep his voice down. "It's illogical that the Butcher is in that cemetery. What are the odds? Ridiculous!"

Kolt looked at Trip and JoJo, surprised they hadn't chimed in yet, one way or the other. Kolt didn't expect them to specifically stiff-arm their commander, but he did expect all Unit members to speak their mind to help solve the problem.

Nothing.

Gangster had had enough. He made his decision.

"All elements, this is Noble Zero-One, we're moving, acknowledge, over."

"This is Assault One, we are target clean at this time, all Eagles up, en route to linkup point."

Kolt watched Gangster slowly climb back into the front seat, allowing Trip to control the black curtain behind him.

Son of a bitch!

Kolt knew his influence on this op, if there ever was any, was shot. This wasn't his squadron. No need to push it now. He knew Webber would already be pissed once he got an earful from Gangster at the post-mission hotwash.

As Trip settled into the driver's seat, Kolt decided to

take another look out the rear window. If for nothing else, to simply cover their six as they pulled off the shoulder and gained the muddy road.

He pulled the blast curtain out of the way one last time.

Holy hell! The Butcher! No doubt.

There, with the edges of his hands against the window, his nose pressing flat on the glass, his unmistakable large gemstone eyes peering into the van, goatee and shaved head obvious, was the Barrel Bomb Butcher. The shitbag responsible for the death of thousands of innocent men, women, and children throughout Syria stood only a few feet from him. This was the man controlling the helicopter force dropping barrels filled with high explosives, oil, and shrapnel on civilians, and he was literally two feet away from the only man in Delta told by the commander not to get involved.

Fuck that!

Kolt snapped his telescopic buttstock up to his firing shoulder and with the precision of a NASCAR tire changer cleared the blast blanket with the four-inch SureFire can, thumbed the selector switch from no bang to bang, and pulled trigger slack. Without an ounce of hesitation or second thought, he indexed the EOTech's bright red dot on the Butcher's cranial vault, center mass above the bridge of the nose and between those signature eyeballs, and broke the trigger.

Dead trigger!

Dang! Did I forget to lock and load?

Kolt took immediate action, reaching up with his nonfiring hand and two-finger ripping the charging handle to the rear, and slightly turning the rifle to ten o'clock to observe a round eject. Nothing.

Holy shit! I did forget. Kolt knew immediately he'd screwed up, a total rookie mistake. He had taken his strap-hanger status for granted, failed to turn the mental switch, execute his own precombat checks like a simple brass check.

Kolt slapped the bottom of the magazine to ensure a full seat before releasing the charging handle, slamming the bolt forward and into battery, shoving the mag's top cartridge into the chamber. He looked up, back to the window, at who he was absolutely sure was the Butcher.

Outside the back of the van, the Syrian's right hand was balled into a fist. He circled the fist, wiping the raindrops off the window, and touched his nose back on the glass to peer back in.

Again, Kolt seated the buttstock, fingered the trigger and pulled slack, simultaneously looking to red-dot the bridge of the Butcher's nose.

The Butcher turned his head at the exact moment Kolt expected the trigger to break. Too late to stop the rearward pressure, in an instant, a single 5.56 mm full-metal-jacket bullet screamed down the nine-inch cold-forged-hammer barrel and through the baffled suppressor at close to 2,400 feet per second.

Kolt thought he saw blood splatter simultaneously with the rear window tempered glass shattering. Hundreds of pea-size pieces of glass fell into the back of the van and out onto the muddy ground.

"Holy shit, Racer!" JoJo said as he fumbled for his rifle.

Kolt heard Trip try to crank the van but it wouldn't turn over.

As Trip held the ignition, certainly hoping for a spark and most likely pumping the gas pedal, Kolt ripped the bomb blanket open to look out the broken window.

Son of a bitch! He's not down.

The Butcher was hit all right, definitely a head shot, as Kolt saw him holding both hands to his face. He was stumbling away from the van, bent over at the waist, the back of his weathered black jacket facing the van.

"He's not dead," Kolt said, turning around to look at Gangster as he grabbed the SureFire suppressor's cam ring to untighten it. "Toss me your bangers, I don't have enough."

"Absolutely not!"

Kolt slid the end mount suppressor off the muzzle as he turned back to the rear door.

"We can't leave a target wounded," Kolt said, digging his two nine-bangers out of his nylon pouch, "I need to put him down."

"No way, Raynor, leave him," Gangster said. "He'll likely bleed out anyway."

Kolt knew Gangster was right; the Butcher could bleed out for all he knew. He could pull out of it too, maybe with Allah's will, and especially if the bullet just grazed him or his people carried him to a clinic soon enough. But, Kolt knew the mission statement was crystal clear, they always were. You don't go halfway with a kill mission.

No, as much pain as the Butcher was currently in, he was the specific target that they were there to see about. He was a problem that the United States wanted solved, not just warned, not just wounded.

"I really don't want to do this," Kolt said. "Options?"

"I said leave him, damn it!" Gangster yelled.

Kolt dropped his rifle to his chest, letting it hang by its sling as he pushed aside the bomb blanket to open the rear door, hoping to get a clear finishing shot. Instantly, the van awoke, the engine turning over a second before Trip slammed the gas pedal to the floor. Kolt lost his balance, falling toward the shattered rear window. He was unable to stop himself—the van's forward momentum sent Kolt tumbling out of the back. The rear tires kicked mud all over him, forcing him to roll to the side, farther out into the road.

Now caked in muck, as if he had hit the Kiss of Mud

obstacle in a Tough Mudder run, Kolt struggled to both knees. He fumbled to pull the slippery pin from his first nine-banger. As he did, he looked toward the Butcher, now leaning over the rock wall with at least a dozen very concerned men at his side. Initially stunned by what they had just witnessed, a stranger tumbling from the odd-parked panel van, Kolt could see in their eyes that a chocolate-covered commando solved the riddle.

Don't have a lot of time here. Make it quick!

Kolt lobbed the first nine-banger at the crowd, just clearing the rock wall. The nine rapid detonations were deafening, forcing the funeral party to scatter like scalded apes. They quickly moved away from the Butcher, giving Kolt clear visibility of his prey. Kolt immediately yanked the safety pin from his second and last banger and sailed it farther into the cemetery, where it landed in a cluster of old tombstones. The crowd continued to flee, some faster than others, most moving away from Kolt and the Butcher.

Kolt first pushed up to one knee, took tactical control of his slippery rifle, and tried to stand. Taking the first step toward the Butcher, he pulled his left leg out of a large sludge puddle that threatened to suck his boot off his foot. Kolt brought the rifle up to a low carry and slogged forward to reach the grass.

Kolt saw the Butcher turn to face him, rolling over to his back but remaining against the wall. The bullet with his name on it had clearly struck his face—blood ran down both sides of it. It must have gone through both cheeks, probably busting several teeth.

Lucky bastard!

Kolt looked back at the crowd. Several Syrian men, yelling something in Arabic, right fists raised high in the air, were moving back into the cemetery and toward Kolt. Rifle up, both eyes open, he scanned for threats, looking at their hands. Nothing.

The nine-bangers had served their purpose. But, with his personal load spent, and with the crowd's rage now obvious, Kolt had to give himself more margin.

Sure, more than one guy in the funeral party probably needed smoking—this, Kolt was certain of. But the pissed-off guys yelling at Kolt from inside the cemetery weren't on the Unit's kill list, not yet anyway. If they were, Kolt wouldn't have dicked around with the non-lethal flash-bangs, but would have been popping frags. No, only one target today. One terrorist. One man that needed to be dumped.

Kolt lifted his muzzle toward the overcast sky, thumbed the selector to Fire, and ripped half a mag. The supersonic sound of bullets racing skyward reverberated across the fog-covered small hills and valleys, and bounced off the outer walls of half the village homes. The riot-control rounds helped, giving the crowd pause, as they knew bullets were much deadlier than the flash-bangs.

It wouldn't last, and Kolt knew it.

Kolt took a few more steps toward the Butcher, lowering his rifle in preparation for the kill. And that's when he made his second rookie mistake.

First, inside the van, he'd forgotten to rack a round when they departed the safe house, resulting in a dry gun and failure to fire. Now, instead of just stitching the guy, control-pairing him center mass of the chest, he let himself look directly into the Butcher's bloodred and green eyes. Everyone knew you didn't look a dead man walking in the eyes before you pumped him full of holes.

Invariably it causes a man to hesitate, putting himself and his mates at risk. Not only does it put you at a distinct disadvantage on target, the souls of your confirmed kills haunt you for life.

"Your mother is a whore," the Butcher said, spitting up blood.

Kolt ripped three rounds into the Butcher's chest. From point-blank range, Kolt watched him first slide down the short wall to a sitting position, then fall half over to his right, his eyes locked open, thick auburn-colored blood slowly spilling from the crook in his mouth.

Kolt stepped closer, bent over, and delivered an eye thump, flicking him in the left eye with his middle finger to ensure the Butcher's nervous system was compromised.

Confirmed kill.

Certain he was dead, Kolt immediately turned and began to beat feet down the road, in the same direction the van had gone after his not-so-acrobatic dismount.

Staying on the grassy edge, Kolt gained speed. He looked up, surprised to see JoJo and Gangster moving uphill toward him, split with one on each side. Relieved, Kolt watched Gangster stop first, taking up a kneeling position behind a tree to cover Kolt's egress. Behind JoJo, who was still moving up but now slowed to a tactical pace, the van was reversing back up the road.

Kolt watched two objects sail over his head, toward the point he left the Butcher crumpled in death. He knew that JoJo must have air-mailed them, or maybe Gangster. A second later, Kolt heard the distinct detonations, nine rapid-fire explosions each, mirroring the speed and ear pounding of a runaway machine gun.

Within a few seconds Kolt reached JoJo and Gangster.

"Last man!" Kolt said, just loud enough to be heard by his mates. He had kicked a hornets' nest, but the true nationality of the kicker didn't need to be shared with the neighborhood.

Kolt reached the stopped van first and turned to cover JoJo and Gangster. Both had collapsed their positions and were already just a few yards behind Kolt. Gangster continued to the shotgun seat while JoJo opened the rear door and jumped in. Kolt followed and closed the door behind him before quickly scooting on his muddy knees to behind the protection of the ballistic blanket.

The van jerked forward again, struggling to gain purchase on the muddy roadway. Trip worked to gain downhill speed and keep the van from slipping off the edge.

Getting his shit together, Kolt managed to slip back into his seat and lean against the skin of the van. He thumb-checked the safety of his weapon, consciously slowed his heartbeat, ripped the partial mag from the rifle, and leaned slightly forward to grab a fresh mag from the pouch on his left hip. He jammed it up into the mag well, tugged to ensure it held, eased the charging handle to the rear until he eyed brass before releasing the bolt to put the gun back in battery. With a confirmed loaded rifle, he flipped the dust cover closed before very nonchalantly keying his hand mike for the first time during the entire two days on target.

"Butcher KIA, let's make tracks."

I screwed up and Webber's gonna shit!

FOUR

This asshole seems to be enjoying this.

Delta Force commander Colonel Jeremy Webber knew he wasn't the only one who was thinking this. The eyes of his buddy and mostly friendly rival, SEAL Team Six commander Hank Yost, seated on his immediate right, told the same story.

A junior National Command Authority representative flown in from Capitol Hill on that gorgeous cloudless morning confirmed the secretary of defense's 2015 budget plan would look to reduce the military force structure to the smallest postwar number since World War II. Indeed, as the stuffed suit continued, Webber stole another look over the top edge of his bifocals, confirming he and Yost were on the same page.

Typical shitbag politician that's never broken a sweat for his country in his entire thirty-something years of life.

"In closing, gentlemen, I can't reiterate enough how serious the president is about exploring options to reduce the force. One option included a plan for either combining the Tier One special mission units into one organization, or to disband one or the other."

Webber almost swore out loud. Worst-kept fucking secret was finally confirmed. He was careful to hide his body language, not moving a muscle, keeping the two nineteen-inch flat monitors at his seat between him and the board president.

Webber knew, as did the others in the room, that defense budget cuts were standard practice after a long war. Delta and ST6 hadn't been around after Vietnam to feel the brunt of deep, across-the-board budget cuts, and both Webber and Yost knew their commands had actually grown during the post–Cold War drawdown. Now, though, they were hoping they pulled enough weight within the special operations community that they would be hands-off. A safe assumption, given that they'd carried the nation's war effort on their backs for a decade and a half by now.

The suit continued droning on. "We are seeing bipartisan support in Congress as well. Many believe that the two organizations' force structures are redundant and that they appear to be equal players with redundant, mirrorlike capabilities."

I'll bet this Harvard-mouth jack wagon doesn't even know we are the commanders of those units.

As much as the guy's speech grated on him, Webber got it. He knew that the president, or his pencil-neck geek chogy boys like Mr. Pinstripe here, had no idea about the nuances of Delta and Six. No comprehension of their capabilities, or even the details on how and what they had done since their activations many decades ago. Presidents and cabinets shift on schedule mandated by the U.S. Constitution, but Delta operators and Six frogmen stay long enough to span four or five consecutive administrations. Webber and Yost were pretty much proof of that.

Even though the president, or the liberal-leaning SECDEF for that matter, didn't see the necessity for maintaining the current numbers within both the nation's premier ground and maritime counterterrorist units, Webber was certain of one thing. *I'll be damned if they think Delta is gonna disband on my watch.*

"Gentlemen, I thank you for allowing me to interrupt your important work here. I've satisfied my requirements so I shall leave you to reconvene."

Colonel Webber leaned over to Captain Yost. In an effort to make light of the confirmation of the president's desires and ensure their camaraderie trumped whatever decision was made, Webber broke the ice.

He let go of the hard-wired mouse and reached up, pulling his wire-rims from his face. "I can give twenty of your beach boys a slot at our next tryouts."

Not missing a step and with a straight face Yost replied, "I'd return the offer but I know you don't have twenty guys that can even doggy paddle. Your boys looked like half-drowned puppies when we fished them out of the Atlantic last month."

"It was my guy that rescued the puppy," Webber said.

Yost opened his mouth to reply, then closed it.

Webber smiled at Yost before returning his attention to the desktop screen in front of him. He held the mouse softly and scrolled to the next page, halfheartedly reading the board instructions they were required to read.

The terrorist that had been the target of the *Queen Mary 2* exercise was the topic. "What do you make of the agency's claim that Marzban Tehrani and his scientist buddies are holed up in eastern Ukraine?" Yost said.

"My analysts haven't bought into the Russian–North Korean connection just yet, but who knows?" Webber said.

"I'm with you," Yost said. "Catching that guy alive is going to be tough."

Webber looked past his screen and noticed the visitor being shown the door by the desk officer from the

special management division. He closed the door behind
him, appeared to lock it, and turned to speak to the
assembled board members.

"Gentlemen, we are now ready to review the nominees for our Tier One special mission units. Naturally,
due to the sensitive nature of these nominees, our cyber
security protocol requires these particular files remain in hard format, so you will not see them on your
screens."

Webber turned his attention to his own Unit personnel noncommissioned officer, the sergeant in charge of
the human resources troop, stunning as a toy soldier in
his dress uniform. Webber watched as Master Sergeant
Brewer, right on cue from the desk officer, began passing out the classified nomination packets he had hand-
carried from Fort Bragg.

"Thanks, Sergeant Brewer," Webber said as he took
the three files and set them in front of him. As the sergeant moved around the oval-shaped table passing them
out one by one to the seated gentlemen, some in their
respective services' dress uniform and some in coat and
tie, Webber thumbed through to locate the file he was
concerned about the most. Finding it third in the stack,
Webber opened the bottom of the file just a few inches.
He wasn't expecting to see a Department of the Army
photo, and was a bit shocked when he found one; a current one at that.

"As a reminder, gentlemen," the desk officer said,
pausing to ensure he had everyone's attention again, "we
will potentially be discussing top-secret special-access
program information with reference to these nominees,
so please ensure all two-way communication devices are
powered off." Webber watched the desk officer catch up
to Sergeant Brewer with a cardboard box, placing a
handheld magnifier in front of each board member.

Webber reached for the provided three-by-five index

card and laid it perpendicular over the four-by-six color photo. He slid it up an eighth of an inch at a time, revealing specific areas that standard promotion boards home in on to determine the littlest of flaws. There was a proper length for the jacket sleeves, a perfect alignment of both corners of the service jacket, and a sure-bet method to determine if a nominee was trying to hide a rubber tire underneath the jacket. If you had gotten soft, sucking it in or smoke screening it behind a hundred medals didn't make a difference.

Before leaving the midsection, Webber counted the overseas service bars, gold hash marks sewn to the candidate's right sleeve, one for every six months in combat. Seeing the edges of the small patches just slightly signaled a skilled and meticulous Unit personnel shop.

Brewer's folks are all over it, as usual.

Webber followed his right index finger center line up the midsection, stopping at the nominee's right breast pocket. Webber drilled down to ensure the combat service identification badge was correctly centered. The red arrowhead with upward-pointed black dagger worn by all army special operations command forces combat veterans was free of smudges and fingerprints.

Webber shifted his focus to the upper chest area, pausing at the fruit salad of ribbons on the left breast. He studied the photo, keying on the medal ribbons pinned to the dark blue service coat. Reaching for the magnifier, he brought the photo closer into view.

What the hell?

Webber focused on the two rows of ribbons pinned to the dress uniform. If you were in Delta you had accumulated at least five rows of ribbons. Webber also knew, like every other board member in attendance that day, that all authorized medals and awards should be present in photos submitted to promotion and command select boards.

The two Distinguished Service Crosses by themselves were enough to draw any professional military man's attention. But, after counting the Purple Hearts, Silver Stars, Bronze Stars, and the half-dozen bronze and silver oak leaf clusters, along with the two bronze "V" devices denoting valor on the battlefield, Webber came up for air. He wasn't surprised at all that he could connect the gold hash marks' timelines to pretty much every one of those valor awards. And, unfortunately, he knew he could connect a few of the names engraved in the black granite-and-marble Memorial Wall inside the Unit garden back at the compound.

"That son of a bitch!" Webber said just a little too loud, drawing several of the attendees' attention momentarily.

Moments later Webber felt Yost's pointed stare, his peripheral vision picking up Yost's head turned to him. Being too lazy to display all your medals and awards was one thing. Even Webber recognized that the bottom two rows of ribbons were bullshit anyway, more about Napoleon Bonaparte's famous statement about conquering the world if he only had enough ribbon than the wearer actually earning anything. Webber of course knew that the top two rows told the story of the man, of his combat actions, of what he did when the chips were down and the elastic moment wore off. Sure, the two rows of medals were irritating enough, and definitely out of protocol, but the disheveled and nonmilitary haircut, a thick lock threatening to cover his left eye, and the salt-and-pepper goatee were enough for Webber to execute a controlled detonation.

Fucking Major Raynor, doing his own thing as usual.
Webber looked up to lock eyes with Master Sergeant Brewer, his sapphire blue coat and Persian blue Army Service Uniform pants contrasting nicely with the charcoal gray sound barriers secured to the wall of the win-

dowless and secure basement conference room. Brewer was already returning the glance, but unaware that one of his Unit nominee packets had caused a stir. Webber made note of Brewer's own attire, proud but not surprised of how his mirror-polished black leather jump boots were like beacons. Webber marveled at how the custom fit of his white collared dress shirt and black tie was only obvious to a trained eye. The sergeant's fresh and mandatory military-style haircut met the expected standards. Webber nodded from behind the desktop screen at the poster-boy sergeant, motioning him to come over.

Webber remained locked on Brewer as he slipped and side-stepped around a half-dozen other board members. The JSOC commander, Lieutenant General Seth Allen, was there, seated next to the SOCOM commander of all services' special ops soldiers, sailors, and marines, who was up from Tampa, Florida. Three more general officers detailed by the army chief of staff, all with some special ops experience in their careers, had seats at the table.

The real players were the few former SEAL Team Six commanders and two former Delta commanders, whose opinions on nominee strength would be weighed heaviest. Basically, any former SMU commander who was healthy enough to make the trip and had a dog in the fight was welcome. The dog being one of their former shit-hot subordinate officers, and now the guy who he wants to see get the nod for a squadron command or take the Unit.

The immaculately dressed Sergeant Brewer leaned down to his commander to listen to the concern.

"What the hell is this?" Webber whispered as he pointed to the ribbons and goatee.

The sergeant stared at the photo for a second before his face reddened. To Webber, the surprise on Brewer's face was genuine.

"Sir, uh, umm, I'm not sure how Major Raynor was able to take that picture without a haircut or all his ribbons present," Brewer said. "That wasn't taken in the Unit photo lab."

"I'm not sure either, Sergeant," Webber whispered back as he pointed to the upper left corner of the photo. "Looks like this photo was taken last Saturday morning."

"Yes, sir, it won't happen again, sir," Brewer said.

"Let's knock out the army officers first," marine three-star general Chuck Swacklion, the promo board president, barked to break the room silence.

Webber saw relief come over Brewer's face and watched him move back the way he came, within a few seconds posted back at the wall near the front door.

"First up, gentlemen, Major promotable Zachary Shents," Swacklion said.

Webber put Kolt Raynor's file down, picked up Major Shents's file, and thumbed it open. He pulled the DA photo first, and just like with Raynor's photo, he moved from bottom to top like a skilled diamond trader with a gold jeweler's loupe. Again, along with the other board members, he studied the haircut, the overall facial expression, and the overall physical fitness of the candidate.

Webber and the others had an important job to do. They had to ask themselves, does this cock-strong type A look like a potential senior officer? Is he still in shape? Sloppy? Confident posture, square jaw, eyes still rational?

The board members would be zooming in on the uniform's fit, then the spacing of the accoutrements, and comparing the number of awards to what was in the nominee's Officer Record Brief. The carefully typewritten ORBs were stamped Top Secret and practically captured an officer's entire career on a single page.

Lieutenant General Swacklion spoke up, somewhat as a joke but certainly to share a point. "Gentlemen, I think it goes without saying that any man that can't get his own dress uniform squared away according to the army's strict rules and regulations concerning the wear and appearance of the military uniform has no business assessing at an SMU board for a squadron command billet."

Webber saw nods around the table, other heads bobbing from behind the computer screens.

Webber looked at Shents's photo again. He knew him to have been a sound troop commander years ago. Nothing like Kolt Raynor for sure, but definitely solid. Webber was of two minds when it came to the dog-and-pony show and the emphasis placed on how an officer looked. Whether a nominee's infantry crossed rifles or Special Forces crossed arrows were crooked on his lapel, or if faint thumbprints could be seen on buttons or shined brass, was pedantry taken to a whole new level. On the other hand, attention to detail mattered. But even then, he could forgive an eccentricity or two if the officer demonstrated one thing above all else.

Can this guy lead action heroes or not?

"Looks to be a top-notch candidate for a squadron," Ambassador Bill Mason, the former Joint Special Operations commander, said, not entirely unexpectedly.

That didn't take long, Webber thought.

Motionless in his high-back leather swivel chair, Webber didn't bother to acknowledge Mason's comment, playing it off as if he was in another room or at a different board meeting.

If asked, Webber would be lying if he said he wasn't a little uncomfortable at the lickies and chewies table before the meeting kicked off. No way he could have avoided talking to the former JSOC commander. But he knew he wasn't the only one that wasn't too keen on Bill Mason's leadership style, or a little queasy about small-talking with the former navy three-star.

More pressing this morning, and working against Webber's desires, was that at least a dozen men in the room knew of retired and now ambassador Mason's personal dislike for one Delta Force Major Kolt "Racer" Raynor.

"Webber?" General Swacklion said. "Any reason to go on? Major Shents looks like a six-plus rating to me."

Webber was cautious with his response, knowing Swacklion and Admiral Mason were pretty tight. Webber continued to read Shents's previous units of assignment and his awards and decorations listed in the accompanying ORB. More for show than concern, as he knew his man's file cold.

Webber remembered Shents's potential years back, but the major had gotten soft over the years, lost some of his mojo taking cush assignments, and, some would say, dodging combat. Sure, Shents was a good man, he just wasn't a good choice for what he was being assessed for now.

A six-plus? I was thinking a low three rating, barely qualified.

"He is, sir, top notch for sure," Webber said, stalling for time. But Webber knew he was there to only fill one squadron command slot, with two other nominees, including the long shot, Raynor. Webber knew exactly who he wanted selected, although he was unable to outwardly show it for fear of showing signs of favoritism.

Unfortunately, for two of the three Delta officers being assessed today at the special mission unit command board, their time in Delta was over. The board was known around the community as "death row select," because not being picked here put your true name back on the army or navy open rolls, out there again for all to see, and condemned a special ops man to a conventional unit battalion command, an instructor slot in one of the many schoolhouses, or even an assignment pushing papers inside the halls of the Pentagon.

Webber looked over at Hank Yost and lowered his glasses to the edge of his nose. Yost picked up on the gesture.

"Mr. President, Major Shents is certainly qualified," the SEAL commander said, "but I recommend we review the other two candidates before we put it to a vote."

Admiral Bill Mason was quick to pipe in. "Qualified, Hank? I'd say top-three graduate at West Point, honor graduate at Command and General Staff College at Leavenworth, makes him the front runner."

"Yes, sir, nothing against Major She—"

Still reading from the file and without even a courtesy look toward the Navy SEAL, Mason interrupted, "School of Advanced Military Studies grad and Best Monograph saber awardee for his paper on 'The Equity and Efficiency of Conventional Military Units in a Shifting Global Framework.' And two years on the joint staff."

Webber bit his tongue. Jousting with Mason now wouldn't be doing any favors for his man Raynor. Webber knew this board was unique from the rest of the military. Besides the fact that background checks of each nominee had already been completed, unlike on other boards, open discussion and personal firsthand knowledge were encouraged and authorized for consideration during voting.

"Sir, I think we all recognize Major Shents's outstanding service record and accomplishments in CONUS over the past what, three, four years that we have been at war," Yost said, trying to hide the obvious sarcasm.

Webber pushed his glasses back to the top of his nose and went back to the file. He was careful not to seem too interested in the verbal tilt between Mason and Yost.

"Gentlemen, I agree, we are here to give all the nominees due review before we vote," General Swacklion said, subtly reminding everyone he was the president of the board.

Webber noticed Swacklion opening up a second folder and pulling out what he was certain was one of the other nominees' official photo and ORB. He aligned them on the table and leaned forward with the issued magnifier.

"Major Raynor have a hard time figuring out the rest of his ribbons, Webber?" General Swacklion asked without showing any signs of sarcasm.

Not knowing exactly how to respond, Webber went all in. "I recall a bit of a wardrobe malfunction at our organization not long ago, sir."

That didn't sound right.

"Impressive number of valor awards," General Swacklion said, shaking his head and obviously not hiding the fact that he was impressed. "Very Audie Murphy–like indeed."

"Gentlemen, we can't base these critical decisions off of any perceived, or otherwise, combat actions," Mason barked as he stood up for all to see. "This process is too important to the nation."

"We got that, Bill, relax, please take your seat," General Swacklion said, holding his hand up to Mason from across the mahogany table.

"Am I counting those oak leaf clusters correctly, Colonel Webber?" Swacklion said, lowering his face closer to the magnifier. "I count seven Purple Hearts."

"I believe it's actually eight, sir," Webber replied.

Webber took a quick sip of lukewarm coffee before reaching for Raynor's unmarked manila folder. He started to place Raynor's photo and ORB back inside.

"God damn it!" Admiral Mason said. "With all due respect, Mr. President, this file is indicative of the crass

nature of this officer. I can attest to Major Raynor's re-
petitive and consistent bouts of insubordination over the
past four to five years alone."

"I see, Bill," General Swacklion said calmly. "You
have history with Major Raynor you'd like to share?"

"Raynor is hardly someone we should be seriously
considering to lead a Delta sabre squadron, particularly
in light of the White House's proposed merger initiative," Mason said.

Webber quickly looked at Admiral Mason with a
faint look of disgust. Even in retirement, Mason's hair
was picture perfect, slicked back and thick, not a brown
hair out of place topping the fade of gray around the
ears. A diet of apple fritters and full-sugar Coca-Colas
like Mason had lifted from the snack table before taking his seat most likely accounted for the ten, maybe fifteen pounds the former JSOC commander had put on
since Webber last saw him.

I wish that goofy bow tie would choke him out.

Webber looked up over his glasses at Lieutenant General Swacklion. "Sir, Admiral Mason is right. Major
Raynor is a little eccentric. I'm not going to sit here and
tell this board that he hasn't been on my carpet a time or
two. But, I have thoroughly counseled Raynor and can
assure everyone here that he won't step out of line again."

Deep down, Webber knew Kolt Raynor was a rock-
head at times, pushed it more often than not. He also
knew guys like Raynor were what made the world safe
and whose combat exploits got guys like Mason stars
on their collars.

"Colonel Webber, I have to admit this file does seem
oddly peculiar to me. Can you explain why this board
is being withheld information that we need to make a
full and thorough assessment?" Swacklion asked, practically ignoring Webber's weak comments about Raynor
learning his lesson.

"Information, sir?" Webber asked as he looked up from the file. "Not sure I am following you there, sir."

Webber hurried to locate the written ORB hidden inside Raynor's folder.

"Well, Colonel, specifically, for starters, the excessive redactions on Raynor's written ORB here. The blacked-out stuff is a little extreme, no?" Swacklion asked.

"Uh, yes sir, we may have been a little overzealous with the security classification," Webber said. "But, as I mentioned, this is part of his uniqueness. I'm just not prepared to go any further than that in the present company."

"Is this the guy that took the lethal dose of radiation a while ago?" General Swacklion asked as he quickly thumbed through the remaining papers in Raynor's file, appearing to look for more information. "Down in Mississippi?"

"Sir, given the attendees today, I request we caucus off line. I'll have to ring the attorney general's office for authorization as well," Webber said, trying not to come off as a jerk or seem as if he was sidestepping the board president's question.

Marine General Swacklion locked on Webber for a long, uncomfortable few seconds. Webber maintained eye contact with the leatherneck general, careful not to blink or appear intimidated. No matter how many stars that bulldog marine had on his collar, Webber knew he wasn't going to spill highly classified information in mixed company.

The board president broke first, turning his fresh side-walled marine cut away from Webber and focusing on the only active Navy SEAL in the room.

"Captain Yost, you and this Raynor fella are the same year group; looks like he fell way off the pace for promotion."

Webber sensed the marine was trying to acquire an ally in his naval half brother. The marine general was right, Raynor and Yost were peer officers years ago, but Yost stayed on the fast track and moved up quickly through Six's ranks, while Kolt partnered with Jack Daniel's, rode the black Chinook a time or two, stiff-armed all formal schooling, and moved laterally in the ranks to stay operational as long as possible.

"Sir, Raynor and I tooled around the thick forests in Bosnia together back when we were hunting war criminals. We made a couple of in extremis penetrations across the Drina river to grab a couple of sealed Hague indictees and brought them back to Eagle Base near Tuzla. If he was a stronger swimmer I'd bring him to the beach. If there is one person I can vouch for today as much as any of my frogmen, it's Kolt Raynor."

Webber watched Yost place the photo and papers back into the folder and lay it on the edge of the table.

"We appreciate your insight, Captain Yost," General Swacklion said. "It's refreshing to hear that your SEALs and Colonel Webber's men can work together, particularly given the administration's desires for one killing force."

"No problem, sir," Yost said.

Webber shivered. *One killing force?*

The Delta colonel gritted his teeth, knowing he needed to remain calm. General Swacklion was talking out of the side of his neck, that much Webber knew. Swacklion had no idea of the complexity of the two organizations and how trying to mix them had been tried many times before, with disastrous results. Even Yost knew that the two units were the yin and yang of the counterterrorist world, equally skilled and committed, just with fire and gasoline DNA.

"In fact, that speaks well to the president's initiative to get you two aligned," Swacklion said, pointing with two fingers extended to both Webber and Yost. "I understand you had a mostly successful exercise recently."

Webber nodded. Yost gave the typical navy sir sand-wich, "Sir, yes, sir!"

"By the way, Captain Yost, great job at Sochi," Swacklion said.

Holy hell, a shout-out to Six!

"And, I almost forgot, that hijacked 767 last year over India," Swacklion added, "super work by you guys."

Webber felt his forehead turning red hot. First, Swacklion's comments about combining Delta and Six to support POTUS; now congratulating Hank in front of the entire board. Sure, Yost's SEALs had pulled off two open-air hits on moving buses during the Olympics in Russia, stopping seven Chechen female suicide bomb-ers, Black Widows, before they reached the Olympic village. But, holy hell, the SEALs had nothing to do with the hijacked American Airlines flight in India. That was all Kolt Raynor and Delta.

I'll be damned!

Webber wasn't necessarily jealous; he was a team player, and proud the SEALs saved lives, for sure. He was also pleased that the president's administration, in an effort to appease Russian president Vladimir Putin, hadn't let leaked information go viral. But, since Mr. Pinstripe's announcement a few minutes earlier, Webber realized that every attaboy pulled in by Six was going to be an ass wound to Delta's staying power, and for Web-ber, more than anyone, the kind of thing that he knew would keep him awake at night.

"Please pass on this board's congratulations to your sailors," Swacklion said.

"I will, sir," Yost said. "Thank you."

Webber sensed Yost was a little uncomfortable with the personal attention, particularly in mixed company and given the president's initiative.

"Gentlemen, my apologies for letting us get side-tracked, let's get back to the matter at hand," Swack-lion said.

I guess taking the Barrel Bomb Butcher off the target list doesn't rate? Well fuck this. Webber was going to go down swinging for Raynor!

"Actually, sir, about that hijacked plane in India . . ."

FIVE

"Would you show the dogs your neck?"

"I would hope for the firing squad." Kang Pang Su, the Korean Workers' Party's sixty-seven-year-old deputy secretary of science and education said, remaining laser-focused on the center of the caged pen. "His feet are slipping."

"As your son, Dae-Jung, did?" Pak Yong Chol said, remaining statue-still as well.

Kang's narrow shoulders slumped at the mention of his boy, his heavy hands dropping an inch lower, closer to the wet concrete balcony. It had only been a few months, but the horror of losing his granddaughter, then his last son, threatened to buckle him at the midsection. He bent slightly at the knees, ensuring blood flowed to his lower extremities, and fought back a wicked sense of nausea.

"He might have saved himself this day," Pak Yong Chol said. "Better to take care of matters while inside the concentration camps."

"Too late!" Kang said, relieved his old friend had left his son alone. "Could you take your own life?"

"The Juche religion forbids it," Pak said, referring to

Kimilsungism and that there is no god but Kim Il Sung, the country's eternal president. "But, if I was a traitor to the Motherland, I certainly would, with honor."

Kang squinted slightly in the misty rain, hoping the demons would depart, leave his conscious thought at least long enough for him to get through one night without the nightmares. Yes, Kang Pang Su still had his head, full of slicked-back black hair, maybe pushing the government's five-centimeter limit. Barely a touch of gray near the ears, nor any sign of male-pattern baldness. He wondered what it must be like. What it would be like to lose his head. How horrible it would be to be discovered as a longtime stooge of the American imperialist bastards' Central Intelligence Agency.

Surrounded by the Dear Leader's crack security troops, whose dark shifty eyes, from under their olive drab hockey-puck-shaped, flat-brimmed dress hats, were famous for slewing to suspect behavior or signs of potential collaboration with the guilty, Kang and Pak stood motionless side by side. Their demeanor was nothing new to Kim Il Sung Square, where party officials, especially at a public execution, made it a point to be Mr. Incognito.

No, not new at all, because Kang knew that one slip in his body language, even an innocent one, could have him snatched up out of the crowd by the secret police and dragged to the dungeons in no time. It had happened before, to others, over the past few years. On overcast and colorless days, at least in the last three years or so, it seemed to happen quite often. And, Kang knew, more than once a simple nod from the vigilant man next to him was all it took to start a countryman on the road to the concentration camps.

No, Kang didn't dare flinch. He fought the urge to shift his eyes down toward his rubber galoshes, protecting his hard-won leather shoes from the puddled water and light mist, afraid his mirror reflection would scream out, revealing his true feelings. Or, even worse, his reflection might wink in sequence at Pak Yong Chol, sending some centuries-old code to the most cut-throat senior party leader in North Korea, something that would tighten the screws on Kang, force him to explain. If anyone could pull the plug on Kang's three-decade life as a mole within the Democratic People's Republic of Korea, the Kool-Aid-drinking potbellied Pak Yong Chol certainly could.

"Those days are behind us, Kang," Pak said. "You know the defenders of our homeland must account for every bullet."

"The dogs are always hungrier than the people," Kang said, carefully monitoring the rise and fall of his chest underneath his white collared shirt, gunmetal gray necktie, and flat black suit made of Vinalon, a stiff and shiny synthetic material unique to North Korea. His arms remained locked and arrow straight down his sides, his digits thick as cigars curled naturally but tense against the seam edge of his dark dress slacks.

"I wonder how long the people will allow these dogs to live before they are steamed and mixed with rice and seaweed?" Pak whispered.

"With their bellies fattened, maybe a day or so," Kang replied.

Kang was smart to conceal his smile from his friend. Not so much as even a glance in Pak's direction. His eyes remained locked on the center of the cage, focusing on the metal stake that had been sledgehammered three feet into the hard dirt before the rain. Kang's eyes followed the length of sixteen-millimeter-gauge chain, some ten feet or so of rusted steel angling upward until it wrapped around the bony wrists of a mostly naked man, a pair of off-white boxers allowing him to retain some modicum of dignity even before certain death.

After a half day of hard, at times horizontal rain, it had let up enough to get on with the published agenda. In less than an hour, just enough time to unfurl the red-and-white DPRK flags and banners and lift them to their prominent positions overlooking Kim Il Sung Square in the center of Pyongyang, the distinguished attendees and security forces were able to take their box-seat-like positions for the show, with a direct view of the large bloodred-and-ribbon-blue banners, a large red star left-centered in a white circle on each, the national flag of communist North Korea. Even more so than the party leadership gathered just east of the Taedong River, the real audience that government officials very much wanted to view the execution of a party traitor was the hundreds of thousands of citizens that had slogged their way from the fields and factories to the square that day.

"Have you any reason for concern?" Pak said.

Me? Why me? What does Pak know?

Kang froze for a moment, feeling his wobbly knees lock to the rear, practically killing the blood supply to the fat feet he would need to run from the brutal hands of the secret police. And Kang knew he wasn't a fast runner, as the flat feet were something he could thank his parents for. Yes, Kang had watched his weight over the years, remaining fit and trim through the seasons, closer resembling the citizen workers than the portly party members, but he knew that wasn't enough. If he was singled out on suspicion, Kang knew he wouldn't get off the puddled balcony before he was corralled by some of Kim Jong Un's henchmen.

No, Kang knew he had been careful, very careful over the years. Kang would have to admit that he and Pak weren't as close as they used to be during the glory years when they shared a cabin on the president's ar-mored train, traveling the trams and railroads to all parts of China and Russia, and visiting all parts of North

Korea, but he knew he hadn't showed so much as a frown or a turned-up eye during official party meetings.

Kang Pang Su had toed the party line.

But what about the trips to Sonch'on, his boyhood home? Had he pushed it over the last two months, taking leave ostensibly to tend to his parents' belongings and prepare the home for market sale? What about the smuggling of the small electronic parts? Three trips wouldn't arouse that much suspicion, but what about the naturally curious locals? Had the workers or peasants seen something out of the ordinary? Had they heard the machine talking from the living room? Had they noticed the new wires running from just under the tiled roofline to the power pole nearby? The antenna?

No, Kang had been as careful at home as he had been at work in Pyongyang. And even though he accepted no money, never had, as that would have been impossible to hide from the authorities, he was definitely no rank amateur.

Three decades now, and the secret still held. Sure, it had been almost twenty years since Kang shared a state secret with the CIA. It had been on the tail end of the Cold War, in fact, when he relayed secret information that caught Chinese scientists in a lie about American use of biological warfare during the Korean War. Big news at the time, but not much to speak about since, and Kang hoped nobody ever would.

The relationship was clear. The mystery CIA man, the man with the dark skin tone, maybe of Middle Eastern descent, or possibly Latin American, promised they wouldn't push Kang. No, Kang would only communicate if and when his heart took him there. The CIA never considered Kang Pang Su their international asset of the year for a treasure trove of national secrets, because, frankly, Kang hadn't provided squat.

Kang was certain he didn't need to run today, but he did need to answer Pak's question.

"My loyalties have always been to our republic's eternal president, Kim Il Sung," Kang said.

"And to his grandson?" Pak asked. "Kim Jong Un?"

The knots in Kang's stomach bounced about as he watched General Ri Myong Suk's skid-row-looking body, barely an ounce of body fat visible, wrists shackled together behind him, pull with all his strength. Ri had turned from the savage sounds of the dozen or so spastic starving dogs licking their chops in the metal cages only forty feet away, seemingly as if by facing away when the rabid jaws and razor-sharp nails arrived, his pain would be less. Or, maybe Ri had already been stripped of all sense of reality and believed he might even survive.

Fingered by Pak over a year ago and purged from his position as the minister of security for the Korean Workers' Party months ago, General Ri had to know there was no escaping. There would be no stay of execution. No reconsidering by President Kim Jong Un for ole Uncle Ri, as chubby little Kim used to refer to him when the general bounced him on his knee, having the good favor of Un's father, President Kim Jong Il.

Once the cage attendants pulled the rope to raise the three metal gates, the recently purged senior party leader, who also had close ties to Jang Song Thaek, would brace himself at the end of the chain. With his age-spotted back to the attacking dogs, he'd really only have one choice and that was to stick his neck out, offering it to the animals in the hopes of a quick death.

General Ri was not unlike the others caught up in the sweeping purge of party officials tied to Jang and the Kim Jong Il era. All of them had been part of the DPRK political culture, and had been removed to allow Kim Jong Un to consolidate his authority over military affairs. Like all the other party members, Kang and Pak were happy not to have made the list.

But, as party leaders like Kang and Pak knew very well, Pyongyang purges are sometimes a matter of flushing the suspect from cover and concealment out into the open ground. And now, Kang wondered if Pak was doing that very thing, spooking him into exposing his extraordinary distaste for the young, flamboyant current party leader, Kim Jong Un. The recent decisions by the short, fat, thirty-two-year-old on the final weaponization of miniaturized nuclear warheads and on the party's secret plans to finally exact their revenge on the puppet-master United States and reunite the people of Korea had not sat well with Kang.

Just as Kang had rehearsed his reply to Pak, deciding to throw out a bald-faced lie, music blared without warning. The lyrics to "No Motherland Without You," the signature song of the late Kim Jong Il, the man that handed down the key to the hermit kingdom in 2011 upon his death to his son, Kim Jong Un, bled with static from the large speakers surrounding the city square. The peasants and workers, packed in chest to back, tight like fat library books sitting on the white-painted curbs, began to chant from behind the line of tall trees with white-painted trunks. Trees marked by the government, forbidding harvesting for much-needed firewood.

"DEATH TO THE TRAITOR AND COLLABORATOR DOG!"

"DEATH TO THE TRAITOR AND COLLABORATOR DOG!"

Kang couldn't hear the pulleys rotate, drowned by the music and shouting, as the metal cage doors rose less than a foot off the ground. The pack of rabid dogs jockeyed for position, lowering their slanted heads to stoop under the gate's bottom, and pushed their shoulders through the opening. They dug their front paws into the mud, clawing and scratching in an effort to pull the rest of their scrawny bodies from the cages, eyes locked on the prize.

Kang could feel the energy on the balcony. He had been there many times before, and with each execution, more vile and horrific than the previous, he had always been amazed by the mental impact this type of killing had on the human psyche. He knew bullets were expensive, but the sight of a ravaged dog tearing a man limb from limb, a man who used to stand on the same balcony as Kang and Pak now stood, a party leader, a man who could crush every peasant in the crowd at the flick of a finger, was utterly priceless propaganda. People talked.

As the first few gangly dogs cleared the cages, somebody killed the music, cueing the chanting crowd to put a lid on it, as if some giant hand had held up an index finger vertically in front of two lips, or run its hand menacingly across its throat.

General Ri turned his head to see the first three dogs, one brown and spotted white, two darker but pure, taking the forty feet at a greyhound racing gallop. Ri's eyes widened; Kang figured twice as wide as if he'd been facing a firing squad with no hood.

Kang turned back to the pack of canines closing in, now seven or eight free of the cage, kicking mud out from under their paws as they pulled and pushed through the slippery surface. Their eyes beamed death.

Two of the dogs, the two darker ones, met each other's pace, and from six feet away, just a few feet past the metal stake, launched themselves into the air like flying monkeys. One bounced off Ri's right shoulder as the general flinched to defend himself and fell to the mud, landing on his side. The other dog clinched a mouthful of Ri's left triceps, practically tearing it off with one bite, scratching its four paws on Ri's naked back to secure purchase. The dog shook his head violently left to right, tearing a large piece of Ri's arm away from the bone, as the second dog, now back in action, sank his teeth into Ri's narrow side just under the rib cage.

Kang tried not to listen to Ri's screams, eerie horrific sounds of imminent death and shock that Kang was sure could be heard across the Taedong River easily into southeastern China and as far southeast as the Korean Demilitarized Zone and the border with South Korea. But Kang knew breaking his disinterested, statuelike demeanor to cover his ears would likely condemn him to a similar fate. Pak had not flinched; neither would Kang.

With all dozen dogs now fighting for flesh, feeding their insatiable appetite, the last few faint screams of General Ri, traitor to the Motherland, were all but muffled by the slurping and chomping of large pieces of bone and flesh. Part of a bloodied arm being worked over by a few there, a hand fought over nearby, two dogs playing tug-of-war with a lower leg near the metal stake, the blood mixing with the muddy surface and changing the color to a dark brunette.

Pak spoke first, breaking Kang's trancelike stare at what was left of his former colleague, General Ri. "The honorable thing to do would have been for the conspirator to show the dogs his neck," he said, "not hide it."

"A cleaner kill, yes," Kang said as the balcony party members began to stir, with the spectacle complete. "Less suffering."

"I will not rest until I expose all the traitors," Pak said. "It is my duty."

Kang's stomach tightened and his chest bounced. Nervous and threatened, he looked at his wristwatch as if he had somewhere to be. The small picture of dictator Kim Il Sung's face on the dial reminded him of what he knew he needed to do.

"I must do my duty as well," Kang said.

Kolt Raynor lifted the dark green .50-caliber ammo can a few inches off the tile floor, felt the weight to gauge how much ammo he had left, then placed it back on the floor. He opened the can's hinged top, confirming that the contents matched the can's yellow paint pen mark denoting 5.56 mm rounds by seeing close to a thousand loose and brilliantly shined brass-and-copper-jacketed bullets dumped inside, and refastened the top.

Next, Kolt turned to his HK416, opening the battery compartment on his EOTech day optics and his new ATPIAL/LA-5 High Power Advanced Target Pointer Illuminator Aiming Laser, and swapped the batteries for fresh ones. He pulled his PSQ-36 Fusion Goggle System, the latest in combined night vision and thermal imaging, from his Ops-Core helmet and replaced those batteries as well, ensuring he was all set for his solo night fire on range 19C.

Kolt locked his team room's vault, threw on his Multicam fatigue top, and headed for the squadron bar. He opened the large refrigerator, pushed the various foreign and domestic beer bottles out of the way to get to the partially frozen entrees in the back, grabbed a Red Bull from the door rack, and moved to the microwave.

Three minutes later, Kolt wolfed down the turkey and broccoli in a half-dozen swallows, slammed the last bit of energy drink, and made tracks for the Spine, headed to the Unit cafeteria. He was late for the Unit Informal, as usual, and since it wasn't quite dark enough for his liking, he knew Webber would frown on him not making an appearance.

Kolt entered the cafeteria, took a few hard stares from some of the boys for his tardiness, and spotted Slapshot and Digger near the keg. Heading their way, he shook hands with a couple of former operators, old-timers in town for the annual get-together, and nodded to several others, knowing he'd get over to them to say hello soon.

It was standing-room only, jam-packed with type-A males either in civvies or fatigues, both current and former operators and support personnel. Near the back windows, Kolt spotted the big hair-salon do of Webber's old lady, who, after catching Kolt's eye, waved him down like she was flagging a cab in Times Square.

Kolt cringed. *Damn!*

Typically, the occasion was reserved for Unit members, not necessarily their better halves, but as everyone learned years ago when Webber took command, his wife not only liked to buck the system, crash the party, and throw her husband's rank around, she liked to spike the punch and hug the keg.

"We were wondering if you would ever grace us with your presence, Kolt," Mrs. Webber slurred, grabbing Kolt's left arm as she tried to balance herself in her heels.

"Yes, ma'am," Kolt said, catching an invisible headwind of barrel-aged cocktail before helping her from making a scene on the floor.

"I'm expecting you again at this year's Unit picnic," she said. "The kids always love the pool and you are my best lifeguard."

"Uh, yes, ma'am," Kolt said, catching her from stumbling a second time and immediately wondering how he could pawn that duty off to some other schmuck this year.

From behind, Kolt heard Colonel Webber. "Lilian, dear, can you excuse us? I need to speak to Major Raynor for just a moment."

Mrs. Webber grabbed the colonel's arm and spoke rhetorically. "Lighten up, Jeremy, it's close of business already," practically falling into him, before peeling off and turning to the nearest group of mingling operators.

Webber smiled and looked at Kolt, shrugging his shoulders as if to say *Women!*

Kolt couldn't tell if Webber's brush contact was the prelude to crushing news or happy, happy, happy. Going in the Atlantic last month during the training exercise hadn't been Delta's fault. Taking over the mission from Gangster in Syria and killing the Butcher was another matter. Yes, a wanted war criminal was dead, but would the higher-ups reward him for that or punish him for yet one more "irregular action"?

"The SMU board results are in," Webber said.

Kolt nodded. *Here it comes.*

"Congrats, you're taking a sabre squadron."

Kolt was ready to say fine, to hell with them anyway, so hearing he'd been selected caught him off guard.

"Say again, sir? A sabre squadron?"

"No one is more surprised than me, except perhaps Mason, but you got it."

Kolt could only imagine how much Admiral Mason was surprised. *Asshole is probably having a coronary right now.* Kolt smiled.

"I'm guessing you had more than a little to do with that," Kolt said. He knew his track record was far from standard, but that's what you got when you jumped in the shit as often as he did.

Webber shrugged. "Your DA photo bullshit was a little much, but I just helped the board see past some of your rough edges."

Kolt nodded. "No easy feat, I'm sure. Thank you, sir."

Webber's smile vanished. "Your squadron just deployed to Ukraine."

Kolt blinked. He knew they'd deployed, but he didn't know why.

"The agency has a bead on Marzban Tehrani," Webber said. "Intel sounds legit, both Iranian scientists are with him as well, they say."

Kolt shook his head. Iranian scientists in the Ukraine with a terrorist like Tehrani could only be bad fucking news.

"Wait a second, my squadron?" Kolt said. "The alert squadron? Noble Squadron? That's Gangster's command."

Webber looked Kolt dead in the eye and paused. "Was Gangster's squadron," Webber said. "You are the new Noble Zero-One."

"He lost his command? Shit, sir, was that because of Syria?" Kolt said. Relieving troop commanders during wartime was one thing, but replacing a squadron commander was entirely uncommon.

"Wasn't your call, so don't sweat it," Webber said.

"Look, things got fucked up, but we accomplished the mission in the end," Kolt said.

Webber hesitated before speaking again. When he did, his voice was lower. "Kolt, bad news doesn't get better with time. Most of the building knows by now, but Noble's entire chain of command has been relieved for cause."

Kolt whistled quietly. "What the hell is going on?"

"Syria. The Butcher hit. The four men that day, they were innocent. Agency intel was incorrect. But they weren't the first."

Kolt nodded. "I wondered why squat was said at their hotwash about the hit on the house."

"The target house was not correct. The CIA asset's info was faulty, and no weapons were found," Webber said.

Kolt shook his head, rubbed his hand across the top of his head.

A peal of laughter followed by a roar made them both turn. Lilian Webber was regaling several operators standing around her with a story that clearly tickled their funny bones.

Webber rolled his eyes. "As I was saying, the target house was wrong. This is why, despite your charming lack of orthodoxy, you get the command." Webber's voice was growing in volume again. "Your instincts were bang-on on that mission. The culture of Noble Squadron has deteriorated in the past few years. It has to change."

"So what am I up against, coming in behind Gangster?" Kolt asked. Suddenly, getting command of a sabre squadron didn't sound so appealing.

"Kolt, it's bad; I'm not putting you in command without full knowledge of the scope of the problem. The entire squadron was privy to the sketchy killings, lifting gold and cash off targets, random vandalism," Webber said. "Gangster was giving out cash awards for the most kills on each rotation to the box."

Any sympathy Kolt had had for Gangster evaporated. "Bloody pirates," Kolt said, shaking his head. "How? How could they have slipped through the assessment and selection process? That's supposed to weed those guys out."

"I don't have the answer for you, Kolt. I wish I did, but I don't," Webber said. "But I do know we have been at war a long time. Not an excuse, just fact."

Kolt took a deep breath. "I'm not sure I am the right guy, sir."

"I understand the hesitation, Kolt, that's natural," Webber said. "I've given this a lot of thought. Bottom line is we need you to fix the problem. You've been down range more than most guys. If anyone can relate to the ugliness of war, it's you."

"I know Noble has lost more operators than any other squadron, but this is something entirely different," Kolt said. "It's not about turning targets, it's about integrity and a lack of respect for basic humanity."

"Look, Kolt, I can't force you to take the command, but I did go to bat for you at the SMU board, as did Captain Yost," Webber said. "There are things brewing, besides Ukraine, something in North Korea, and others that can't be shared just yet. Suffice it to say that not only does Noble need you to take the squadron, but the entire Unit does as well. It's isolated in Noble, it's not prevalent in the Unit."

"That asshat, Yost?" Kolt said as he smiled ear to ear, almost ignoring Webber's last gloomy comment.

"He referred to you in a similar way as well," Webber said. "But you impressed him in Bosnia way back when, and he never forgot."

That surprised Kolt. He had a tendency to think everyone took a dim view of his actions. Maybe they were able to see beyond that. It made him realize his own impressions of people were too often immediate and set in stone.

"If you see him before I do, sir, please pass along my thanks."

"Can do. Now, I need to hear it from you. Will you accept command?"

Kolt was about to say yes when a thought occurred. "Sir, who is my squadron sergeant major going to be? I want Slapshot."

Webber looked hard at Kolt. "You can have Slapshot, and I need you to take Hawk, too. If she gets through Whistle-stop and the board she'll need a commander that will give her a good and fair test."

That surprised Kolt. He hadn't seen Hawk in months and wasn't exactly sure where the two of them were at.

"Sir?"

"You've operated with her the most, and the pilot program deserves an honest and thorough assessment," Webber said.

Kolt tried and failed to come up with a good counter, mainly because there wasn't one. Kolt knew Cindy "Hawk" Bird was solid, proven, and as brave as any male operator. He knew Webber's pilot program to knight a female as an operator had many critics, not just inside the building with the old-timers, but even inside JSOC. And Webber had stuck out his neck for Kolt at the SMU board. That couldn't have been easy.

Kolt nodded. "Throw in Digger, sir? I need a master breacher and he has the language skills."

"Deal," Webber said.

Kolt's smile was ear to ear.

"Sir, it is my honor to accept command."

Webber smiled back. "You're damn right it is."

He held out his hand and Kolt took it. For better or worse, he'd just gotten what he wanted.

SIX

Carlos Menedez II closed his eyes and worked his jaw until his ears popped. After an interminable twenty-four-hour flight with a four-hour layover at LAX, his Virgin Australia International flight, 6862 from ATL, was finally making its descent into Brisbane, Australia. Leaning forward in his seat, Carlos opened his eyes and strained to get a visual on Pine Gap, the National Security Agency's prime Southern Hemisphere intelligence collection center, from the air.

As director of Tungsten's Department for Special Services, the blackest of black U.S. counterterrorist organizations, Carlos knew the facility, though he hadn't had a reason to visit since the Cold War, some thirty years earlier. That he had reason now was both troubling and intriguing. You didn't request the presence of a busy Tungsten director for trivial things. Few in the intelligence business even knew of Tungsten's existence, for that matter.

Carlos nodded when he caught a glimpse of the giant golf-ball-looking objects that cut through the middle of the Pine Gap compound. Requiring unobstructed line of sight to orbiting satellites, the massive golf balls were impossible to hide. These were no weather radar units, no matter what the official statement said. These were state-of-the-art omnidirectional radome antennas that helped the National Security Agency pull metadata from the secret global surveillance networks ECHELON and PRISM.

If of suspicious mind—and after the Snowden affair, that was a given among large swathes of the public—it would be hard to miss the strategically located but shady defense spy facility that conspiracy theorists blogged about. They swore it was jointly run by the CIA, NSA, and National Reconnaissance Office, the NRO, and in that sense they weren't entirely wrong.

Carlos sat back and closed his eyes. Twenty-four hours in an aluminum tube to travel around the world in the age of Skype and FaceTime. This had better be worth it.

Two hours later, Carlos walked toward an empty chair in a small conference room inside Pine Gap with no clearer idea of why he was there.

"The place has changed," Carlos said.

"Yeah, we have to fight for funding every year," Stephan Canary said. "NSA wolfs down funding like it's candy; we get the crumbs left over."

"I meant not much of a secret these days," Carlos said. "Google is all over it."

"We can thank Snowden's big mouth for that." Carlos chuckled at the Snowden comment before taking a seat in the maroon-colored leather chair, taking a sip of his coffee as he slid closer to the table. He placed his cell on the tinted blue glass table next to the facility-provided blank notepad and pen. The pen engraved with JOINT DEFENSE FACILITY PINE GAP was another sign that keeping Pine Gap a secret was long out of the barn.

Canary took a seat across the table, nonchalantly

reached up to yank a cable from the sleek black video teleconference speaker, and tapped a few buttons on the ivory-colored portable keyboard.

"Can I get you to power off your phone, sir?" Canary asked politely, not hiding his reverence for a man that many in community considered a pioneer in covert communications.

Carlos obliged, tapped the screen a few times, and turned it toward Canary to show a dead screen. The sign on the wall out in the hallway was hard to miss.

"Twenty-first-century bugs," Carlos said as he placed it back on the table. "I'm surprised you guys even let them inside Pine Gap."

"We didn't use to," Canary said. "One of those convenience things. It's a pet peeve of our director these days."

Carlos nodded. He understood. He stared at the flat screen on the wall and watched as Canary skillfully drilled down through a half-dozen code-named file folders. The screen was oddly placed, high on the wall and not centered, almost as if some annoying interior decorator had insisted the screen hide the only wall electrical outlet. The angle from Carlos's chair, coupled with the wicked glare on the screen from the flat ceiling lights, obscured at least half of what he could make out clearly.

Canary settled the arrow cursor on a folder obviously titled with a computer-generated code name. Carlos thought he read "Satin Ash" before Canary double-clicked, but he couldn't be sure.

"How long you been here?" Carlos asked.

"Third tour, twelve years total now," Canary said.

"You haven't picked up the Crocodile Dundee accent."

"I'm lucky if I get out of the basement twice a day."

"Just the two of us?" Carlos said. "No offense, young

man, but I dropped everything for a twenty-one-hour nonstop in coach. Figured I'd at least be seeing the vice, or maybe the director of ops."

"My apologies, sir," Canary said, "the director and ops officer are in Washington, D.C. Vice Director Fontaine planned to be here this morning, but with the latest developments, he said he might not make it."

"Fontaine? Derrick Fontaine?" Carlos said, raising his eyebrows. "Big fat guy? Dirty blond hair?"

"Um, you are on Vice Director Fontaine's itinerary immediately after lunch, though."

Carlos saw Canary look quickly at the door, obviously concerned someone might barge in at the wrong time, then look back as he held his bladed hand near his mouth. "He was body-weight challenged but just had Lap-Band surgery. No longer dirty blond either," Canary said just above a whisper. "His major comb-over is shiny gray now."

That ass clown Derrick Fontaine. Can't believe he is even allowed in a place like this, much less running the place.

Carlos wanted to ask Canary a little more about Fontaine. Maybe ask if he was still as much of a self-serving jack wagon as he remembered him to be. See if he had lightened up a little over the years or if he was still as rigid as a nun in a whorehouse.

"Got it!" Carlos said. "Fontaine and I go way back."

"Yes, sir!" Canary said before turning toward the flat screen and drawing Carlos with him. "Does this gentleman look familiar?"

Carlos locked on the screen. A fussy black-and-white of a twenty-something Asian man filled the center. His hairline pushed down his forehead, full thick black hair combed up several inches and off his forehead, cropped just above the ears. The man's eyes were narrow, ice dark, and slightly menacing, topping a proud, square jaw. His mouth was frozen slightly open, as if caught mid-thought when the camera snapped, maybe questioning his decision to become a traitor. Two oversized front teeth were obvious. The top three buttons of his too-big white collared shirt looked unfastened, letting the collar hang open, the upper neck rim of a ribbed, probably soiled, tank top undershirt just showing.

Everything about the man told Carlos that he was either a caricature artist's wet dream or some asset that had been recently compromised and likely smoked. He looked vaguely familiar, but Carlos couldn't place him.

"Is he supposed to?" Carlos asked without taking his eyes off the screen.

"I believe you took the picture, sir," Canary said, showing a little unease, "using a covert matchbox camera in the fall of 1985. Same one the OSS used during World War II, right?"

Carlos's head jerked forward. He rubbed his dark gray slicked-back hair from his forehead back to the locks just touching the collar of his pearl-colored, pressed dress shirt. His eyes narrowed, bunched tight, as he squinted hard to get a better look. He stood, took a few steps around the first two chairs to get closer to the screen, and pulled out his custom wire-rimmed eyeglasses from his denim blazer pocket. He quickly seated them on his ears and the bridge of his nose, and studied the screen from only a few feet away, as if he had seen a ghost.

"Kang Pang Su," Carlos said before he removed his glasses and returned to his seat. "No doubt now. Code name Seamstress."

"Yes, sir," Canary said. "We have good reason to believe he is still active."

"Swiss model thirty-five millimeter," Carlos said as he looked back at Canary, "concealed inside of a small leather tobacco pouch. You advanced the film roll with a small spring-wound mechanism."

"Amazing," Canary said. "Old school!"

"Back then I didn't think the damn thing would work."

"We're thinking the back and side shots didn't develop," Canary said. "The records were kind of vague."

"Hell, it's been close to thirty years, but I seem to recall being told that," Carlos said as he heard a loud knock at the door behind Canary.

Canary tapped some keystrokes to whiten the screen, stood, and opened the door. In an instant, every bit of Derrick Fontaine's body filled the doorway. Carlos noticed the man hesitate, balancing two donuts on a yellow napkin on his iPad and holding what looked like a jumbo Diet Pepsi bottle in his other hand. Kolt sensed Fontaine almost angling his body to get past the doorjamb, watched Canary close and lock the door behind him, then turn and pull the closest leather chair back several feet to allow Fontaine to sit down.

"You didn't start without me?" Fontaine barked, setting his iPad and soda on the table.

"No, sir," Canary lied, "just getting started."

"Good!"

"Mr. Menendez, I'd like to introduce you to our vice director, Dr. Derrick Fontaine."

"Have we met?" Fontaine said as he reached for a glazed donut and brought it to his mouth. He took a healthy bite, transferring obvious flakes of glaze onto his droopy cheeks.

"I can't recall," Carlos lied. "Certainly possible."

Yeah, I remember you, motherfucker. And unless you are senile, or have dementia, I know damn well you remember me.

"You're way overdressed for this place," Fontaine said.

"The last time I was here everyone was in suits and ties."

Canary keystroked to bring up the picture of Kang Pang Su again.

"I'm sure you know this man," Fontaine said as he wiped his mouth with the back side of his hairy, Popeye-size forearm.

"Been a while," Carlos said. "I do."

"You recruited him, we know."

"His father's death made him a rare breed as the child of a martyr of the Fatherland Liberation War," Carlos said. "The family even got a certificate."

"We also know you provided him covert communications," Fontaine said.

"You didn't bring me all the way over here to confirm what you already know from my operational folder, did you?" Carlos said.

"What system did you provide?" Fontaine asked as he nodded to Canary to hit the next slide. "The HAL DS-3100?"

Carlos looked at the screen. He noticed the "June 1985" at the bottom of a brochure from HAL Communications out of Urbana, Illinois, advertising four different systems.

"The top left one is what you gave Seamstress. Someone found with one of those dinosaurs ought to be arrested," Fontaine said, obviously jabbing the older Menendez. "I can't believe we got anything done back then with that Tinkertoy junk."

"They'd do a lot more to Seamstress than that if they busted him with one," Carlos said.

"Indeed," Canary said.

"But that's not the one he has."

"It's not?" Canary asked.

"Nope. Bottom right," Carlos said, "the HAL CWR6850 Telereader."

"Impossible!" Fontaine said before choking down another swallow and crumbling the napkin with his donut holders. "I spent seventeen years with the agency, working communications abroad. No way you got your hands on a 6850 back then."

"And why's that?" Carlos asked.

"Because those were tightly controlled. Nothing to the USSR, China, or North Korea."

"The DS-3100 was the size of a 1970s television and needed an external ST-6000 modem; the 6850 was an all-in-one unit more suited for our needs," Carlos said.

"I know that, but how did you come by one?"

"Japanese manufacturing, HAL was the U.S. distributor. Hard to find but I stumbled on one at the Friedrichshafen Ham fest."

"Bullshit! They wouldn't sell a radio teletypewriter to an American even in Germany," Fontaine said. "Not overseas during the height of the Cold War."

"They did once to a Ham enthusiast with a heavy Hungarian accent and a good tan," Carlos said. "Folks loved Eastern bloc countries back then."

"Whatever system he has, we are pretty much convinced he is a nut job," Fontaine said, obviously tired of matching commo knowledge with the slick-dressed Carlos.

"Can you fill me in?" Carlos said.

"Seamstress has transmitted two messages over the past few months," Fontaine said, "something about nukes. We're not even sure the guy on the other end is the real Kang Pang Su."

"Did you authenticate him?"

"No way to do that," Canary said.

"You guys should have reached out to me months ago," Carlos said. "Send him a message requesting the code word. If he is the real deal, he will know it."

"What's to say he wasn't compromised?"

"The only thing written in English was the cover name for the real authentication word. He wrote the word 'smoke.' I watched him scribble it in block letters."

"After thirty years, how do you know he hasn't forgotten the real code word and just used 'smoke'?" Fontaine asked.

"Only a fake would send the word 'smoke.'"

"Why's that?" Fontaine asked.

"Because I had Kang hold my camera decoy."

"The tobacco pouch?" Canary asked.

"Yep, he rolled the leather with his fat fingers," Carlos said. "I remember clearly his larger-than-life hands, definitely out of symmetry with his smaller frame."

"Damn," Canary said with a wide smile. "Fascinating stuff."

"Well, what is it? What is the correct authentication, then?" Fontaine asked. He fidgeted in his chair. "Tobacco? Leather?"

"Cigar," Carlos said.

"Cigar?" Fontaine said.

"That's it!" Canary said. "Both transmissions we've received on the teletype have included the word S-E-E-G-H-A-R."

"I'll be damned," Fontaine said. "It's him."

"Kang was attending university at the time, but his English was shit. He could pronounce 'cigar,' though," Carlos said as he lifted his coffee cup. "A bit of a Mongol accent, but we enjoyed the stogies just the same."

"If the guy on the other end of the RTTY transmitted 'cigar,' then I'm absolutely confident it is Kang Pang Su," Carlos said before sipping his coffee. "I recall he went to ground early, maybe sent one or two things. Figured he'd be dead by now."

"How'd he get the code name?" Fontaine asked.

"Standard stuff back then. Culturally relevant, at least

thirty years ago. Today it might be Nail Salon Artist," Carlos said.

Canary smiled at the comment; Fontaine reached for donut number two.

"Seamstress going to assassinate Kim Jong Un, or what?" Carlos asked.

So far, Carlos had been providing all the answers. He was expected back in Atlanta ASAP, back to running his embeds within the NCA's ultra-top-secret Tungsten program. But he wasn't rushing to squeeze his designer clothes back into coach seating. For sure, killing another day's worth of life with the twenty-one-hour return flight was unavoidable, but he'd take some answers with him.

"Absolutely not!" Fontaine said.

"Share nuke secrets? Defect? Make JSOC's kill list?" Carlos said, simply outlining the logical possibilities.

"You're warm, sir," Canary said.

Fontaine slammed his soda bottle down the moment Carlos mentioned JSOC, swallowed heavily, and barely allowed his colleague to get his last syllable out before jumping in.

"That's enough!" Fontaine held the palm of his right hand up in front of Canary's face. "Mr. Menendez might have the appropriate security clearance, but he hasn't been read on to the SAP and doesn't have a need to know."

"Pardon me, sir," Carlos said without hiding the sarcasm, "that's bullshit. I dropped everything to fly here; you can tell me what is so urgent. You owe me that."

Carlos felt the heat of Fontaine's pointed look but didn't dare budge. After a few uncomfortable seconds, Fontaine turned to look at Canary, whose face was pink from embarrassment. Carlos couldn't be sure exactly what was up, or what America's plans might be for Kang Pang Su, but he did know one thing for sure. You didn't need to be an intelligence genius to know that Kang

Pang Su had finally tired of being one of Kim Jong Un's improved citizens.

"Okay, but just the basics," Fontaine said. "Marzban Tehrani. Kang Pang Su says Tehrani is linked to North Korea."

"Tehrani?" Carlos said. "Linked to the nukes?" Carlos already knew all about Iranian Marzban Tehrani. For over a year, Tungsten had been tracking the CIA cable traffic that placed Tehrani in Pyongyang several times. In fact, he had initially considered embedding Kolt Raynor for the mission, if the National Command Authority had green-lighted them. But, since Kolt's flare-up at Yellow Creek power plant and his subsequent return to Delta, he was considering other options. No, Fontaine didn't need to say another word. Carlos could put the pieces together now.

"I said the basics, Mr. Menendez. You understand."

SEVEN

Whistle-stop, final phase

This college punk touches my thigh one more time, I'm taking him out.

It had been a relatively simple and peaceful train trip returning from Pyongyang, North Korea, that Saturday morning. Hawk and the other tourists had boarded the domestic train before the sun was up to return to Sinuiju, the open port city on the western edge of North Korea. Sinuiju was the last stop before crossing the Yalu River, which also served as the international border.

Hawk and her fellow tourists had offloaded the train before being herded into a large train station that Hawk couldn't help notice was relatively devoid of locals, but full of the same straight-faced and uber-suspicious uniformed types she had come to expect after her seven-day tour inside the hermit kingdom.

Consistent with every other dreary place Hawk and the other tourists had visited in North Korea, the station was adorned with chintzy chandeliers hanging from the ceiling and crooked gilded mosaics of the Great Leader Kim Il Sung stuck on three of the four boring white walls. Closer to the marble floor, other brass placards and dioramas pimped the history of Sinuiju's commercial growth. First with logging lumber down the Yalu, then advancing to the chemical industry after the hydroelectric Sup'ung Dam was built farther up the river.

Hawk's attention had been drawn to one placard in particular, and she had been relieved when her tense reaction hadn't alerted the minders to finger her for further scrutiny. The display was a large overhead photo, taken from a plane for sure, of the city after it sustained heavy damage, including to the dam, from U.S. Air Force strategic bombing during the Korean War.

Customs officials had asked the usual questions, reminded them about the punishment for smuggling out Korean artifacts or contraband, and warned of passing information about North Korean citizens to outsiders. Just as they had done when they entered a week ago, the officials had the Korean conductors and tourists open all their packages before finally returning their passports and their mobile phones, sealed in yellow envelopes marked with the owner's passport number.

Having to operate without her tech gadgets hadn't been an issue for Hawk. The country study she'd read before deploying was clear about that. North Korean officials would definitely confiscate all electronics, forcing her to commit her tasks to memory. The silver lining, she knew, was that she had less to keep track of and therefore less that might get her in trouble. Sure, she wasn't there on a simple culmination exercise, as every other Whistle-stop had been for hundreds of wannabe operators before her. In Hawk's case, she was thrown to the wolves after the CIA had come up empty on their longtime deep asset, Kang Pang Su. Nobody in Langley seemed to have a clue about Su, much less be able to distinguish him from the Korean owner of the dry cleaner's on Dolly Madison Boulevard. No, Hawk wasn't asked to assassinate anyone in North Korea, rather work her God-given magic, and her operator skills and instincts, to grab a bead on the asset himself—enough, it was hoped, to sit down with an FBI sketch artist, to give the agency a starting point.

But, hope wasn't an operational method, and on this particular mission, Hawk was an abject failure.

Hawk repressed the urge to curse. Sure, she'd had no luck with locating the asset, but she had learned some interesting things during her weeklong visit. Nothing anyone would really consider a state secret, but at least she wasn't leaving empty-handed.

There was the drunk at the government-monitored hotel who had a problem with insam-ju, a Korean vodka infused with ginseng roots. Making a meager income shining tourists' shoes by day, the rickety old man spent twice that each night at the bar. Hawk was still slightly ashamed for taking advantage of a drunk and horny guy, as eliciting sensitive information from him had been truly elementary. With her iPad back, she'd type up the stuff about the stealth netting supposedly protecting Kim Jong Un's armored train from remote IEDs and secure message it to Bragg, but that could wait. She'd get to it, maybe in the morning; no need to share the bad news too early with Webber and the intel shop back at Bragg. No, it could wait, she decided, and figured she'd seek out one of the flat-screen TVs, maybe the one in the recreation car, where tourists could relax a little and have a drink or two.

Nonchalantly opening her passport to ensure it hadn't been mixed up with someone else's, she noticed some kind of registration stamp and another odd stamp, ostensibly the magic mark allowing them to leave the isolated country via Sinuiju.

Hawk held up her left hand and turned her diamond wedding band toward the twenty-something with the hard-on. "You've had too much. I've told you a dozen times, I'm happily married."

Hawk knew the Pyongyang-to-Moscow trip would take 211 hours, but feel like a million if she stayed cooped up inside her sleeper, or *kupe,* a four-bed-compartment car. Sure, she was amped up in a good way, knowing that as soon as she returned to Bragg she'd be sitting down for her Commander's Board, the final gate in her quest for knighting as an operator. But, even with her Droid back, and her iPad 4, she knew she needed to let her hair down after the stressful, and equally unsuccessful, visit inside North Korea.

Yes, vagabonder Carrie Tomlinson—at least that's how she was known to anyone asking—had been stoked to finally cross the Yalu and enter China. It was the longest direct train connection in the world, some 10,272 kilometers in all, and she figured no harm, no foul if she spent the first couple of thousand partying like Paris Hilton before her liquid breakfast settled.

In fact, at the moment, Hawk had to admit she was buzzed enough that focusing on her front sight if she was busting plates back at the Unit might be a little challenging. Even so, Hawk, rather Carrie for this op, was comfortably kicking the shit out of these spring break college kids from West Virginia University in some adolescent drinking game.

It was well known for being one of the biggest party schools in the United States, something Jerud (or was it Jason; one of the six undergrads from Mr. Beckle's International Studies and Enrichment Club) must have shared a dozen times by now. Cindy Bird knew working an alias was everything, and if she had learned anything over the last few years within Delta, it was that cover is truth, truth is cover.

But Hawk couldn't deny the kid was pretty Brad Pitt hot.

"C'mon, Carrie, chill out, girl," Jerud said. "A ring don't plug no hole."

Hawk couldn't believe the arrogance of this kid. She had been out of college for a good six or seven years now and she was pretty darn certain no other male had ever hit on her with the free spirit of a wild animal in, well, the wild. Hell, even her Green Beret boyfriend, the cock-strong and cocky Troy toy, was never this aggressive.

No, Hawk knew, assuming she could keep it together, this kid wasn't adding a notch to his trophy stock on this spring break. Maybe he would with one of the two university bimbos who were totally shit-faced across the table, the one two-fisting locally made Taedonggang beer bottles all night, or the one trying to make whistle noises by blowing over the mouth of an empty. Just not with Hawk.

"Look, pal, you're cute, I'll give you that much," Hawk said as she lifted the kid's left hand off her right thigh. "What was all that you said earlier about having an obligation and responsibility to conduct research? Something about your mission of gathering and analyzing data to inform the discussion and understanding of various issues affecting the lives of others around the world?"

"You've got a good memory," Jerud said, slurring words. "But what's your problem? Live a little, it's just social sex."

"You're doable," Hawk said. "Not my type, though."

"C'mon, no way you're married and in North Korea getting liquored up by yourself."

"We're not in North Korea anymore, but maybe it's just a lifelong desire to travel the world's oddest places," Hawk said. "And apparently meet the world's biggest assholes."

"Whatever," Jerud said as he leaned toward Hawk, his left arm circling around her before coming to rest on her shoulder blades.

Hawk looked at Jerud, sending a silent but deadly

warning with her eyes. Jerud obviously wasn't worried, or he couldn't effectively gauge the coiled snake, taunted by an intruder, through his beer goggles.

Jerud leaned into Hawk, his eyes turning savage and his lips now bunched. Hawk froze, turned her face away from his beer breath, and stuck in an elbow just below the floating rib.

"Enough already!" Hawk said.

"Relax, baby," Jerud said, "you might like it."

Jerud reached up with his right hand and squeezed Hawk's right breast.

Son of a bitch! That's it!

Hawk raised her right arm high and circled it over Jerud's left arm, coming down with enough force to break his touch and trap his left hand under her right armpit.

"Now you're talking," Jerud slurred. "You like it rough, huh?"

Instantly, Hawk let go of the half-empty bottle of Tae-donggang beer she was nursing in her left hand and made a half fist, leaving two fingers sticking out. She looked Jerud in the eye.

"Yes, I guess you could say that, college boy."

Hawk spread the two fingers and jammed one in each of Jerud's eyes. Jerud's head bounced back and he let out a raging cry. Still controlling the left arm, Hawk slipped out of her chair and in one smooth motion delivered a face-palm with her left hand, just below his freckled nose, then pulled his left arm forward and to the right.

Defenseless, Jerud fell out of his chair and doormat-ted to the car's white-tiled floor, flat on his back. Hawk stood, catching the other partiers out of the corner of her eye, now standing as well. They were screaming some-thing, likely wanting to see what the chaos was about, but Hawk ignored them, focusing instead on the correct attack angle.

Controlling the left arm from the right side of his supine torso, Hawk stepped over Jerud's chest with her left foot and simultaneously jumped into the air. She fell back on her ass and brought the arm with her, locking her left leg over his chest and her right leg over his face. Not entirely textbook, given the alcohol, but the arm lock was good enough to hear Jerud squeal.

Hawk turned Jerud's thumb upward toward the *ob-shchiy* passenger car's white ceiling, centered by a gaudy brass chandelier, and aligned the elbow joint as she gave slight pressure.

"Now, Jerud, you have a choice," Hawk said as the other college kids were fumbling with their cell phones, probably to capture the scene on Instagram. "You can go back to the frat house with a broken arm, or you can go back to your sleeper for the rest of the night. Your choice."

"Let go!" Jerud screamed. "Get this girl off me!"

"Nope, Jerud, that isn't one of your choices," Hawk said as she applied more pressure to the elbow joint. She didn't want to break the kid's arm; in fact, even though Jerud and his friends didn't know it, Hawk was just bluffing. She knew he was just another hard-up spoiled frat boy used to getting his way, not a hardened terrorist intent on jihad.

Jerud screamed again.

"Choose, Jerud," Hawk said, just before hearing one of the bimbos screaming.

"Get off of him," she said. "Oh my God!"

"Which one, Jerud?" Hawk asked again.

"Okay, okay, I'm sorry," Jerud said as his face tightened in obvious pain. "I'll leave your ass alone, let's just get back to the game."

"Broken arm or sleeper car?" Hawk said.

"Okay, shit, fucking shit, man, I'll go to my sleeper," Jerud resigned himself to say.

"You're familiar with the honor system, right, Jerud?" Hawk said. "You leave your sleeper before the sun comes up and you've sobered, and I'll break both your bony-ass legs, got me?"

"Okay, okay, honor system," Jerud said. "I got it."

Hawk rotated Jerud's arm to allow it to bend at the elbow, gave up wrist control, and somersaulted backwards. Just in case the asshole had any thoughts of immediate retaliation, she put some distance between them.

If this wasn't Whistle-stop, assholes, I'd—

Before Hawk could finish the thought, two Korean customs officials corralled her, bookending her on both arms, and practically lifted her off the ground while dragging her toward the end of the car.

She turned back toward the table and the college bimbos who were huddling around Jerud now, babying him like a first-grader just hit with a wild pitch. Hawk saw Jerud look up, still half bent over and holding his left elbow with his right.

"That bitch is crazy!"

EIGHT

"My damn leg has been asleep for two hours now," Slapshot said.

"Be glad you have two legs," Digger replied.

"It's like listening to Ralph and Norton," Kolt said, wondering how the hell he scored the spot on the rear cabin floor between his two mates. "I'm tired of being all pretzeled up myself. My pistol light is killing me."

"What squadron are they in?" Digger asked.

"Ralph and Norton? The Honeymooners," Kolt said.

"What, they gay?"

Kolt rolled his eyes. "One of these days . . ."

It had been just under five hours since the three newest members of Noble Squadron had landed in Kiev and off-loaded at the end of a discreet and fogged-in runway. Dressed in roughs, T-shirts over jeans, they shouldered their packs and hoofed it into the shadows before turning to watch the contract Embraer ERJ 135 extended range, painted in civilian colors, execute a three-point 180, power the twin Rolls-Royce engines, and tear down the runway to depart in the opposite direction on a moonless night.

Within a minute, a midsize cargo truck, sporting four

bald tires and sounding like it had seen better days, had appeared from an unseen road. Its headlights were off as it pulled onto the asphalt apron, and seconds after Digger offered two flashes of a red-lens flashlight, the driver flashed his headlights twice, completing the signal that it was safe to load.

"Fucking reeks in here, man," Slapshot said. "Smells like death."

"Indeed, brother," Kolt said, trying to brace in anticipation of the next pothole. "We're probably inside a field ambulance."

"Shit!" Digger said. "The floor is sticky on this side."

"Any reason we don't have more support here?" Slapshot asked.

Kolt sighed. It was the age-old lament of every soldier everywhere. "We were supposed to, but Dmitry's boys are turning a target tonight."

"It couldn't have waited?"

"No. They got something actionable on Marzban Tehrani. A courier he uses is supposed to be somewhere near Donetsk, three hundred klicks east of the safe house."

"Lovely," Slapshot said.

A knock on the front cab's rear window ended their bullshitting in the rear. More than a knock really; more like a warning.

"There is an auto in the road ahead," Olga said. Her companion, Dmitry, continued driving.

Kolt and the others had heard rumors that Ukraine's antiterrorist unit, officially named "Alfa," had women in their secret ranks, but linking up with one face-to-face was still a surprise. Kolt quickly got over it. He knew the opposite sex definitely had its advantages, staving off scrutiny in certain circles. The SBU, the odd acronym of the Security Service of Ukraine, had only established Alfa in 1994, their activation a result of presidential decree. Delta turned seventeen that same year.

What the hell is taking our graybeards so long to see the value of female operators?

Kolt looked to his right and left, taking in the black smudges of his mates' heads. He was confident that they didn't consider Olga inferior simply because she was dickless. Sure, Olga was hard on the eyes, but her sunken cheeks, dark and cold eyes, and proud chin under razor-thin lips represented a fighting spirit. Kolt himself had done a double-take when he noticed her dark hair bunched up inside a pleated denim hat with a small bill, something similar to what a train conductor from the Wild West might wear, which made her all the more hardened. She had a look that told others she had seen the elephant.

Not feeling the truck stop, or seem to slow its pace, Kolt turned to the window.

"I thought there were no checkpoints on the back roads?"

Kolt fingered his mini SureFire on, holding the red beam of light an inch from his folded acetated map, trying to determine exactly where they were. He knew they had passed the town of Poltavs'ka an hour or so earlier, the spot where Dmitry had said they would have to sacrifice the luxury of fast-moving asphalt roads for the security of the back roads. After that, he could only swag it.

"No checkpoint. Just headlights," Dmitry said from behind the wheel.

"What about the curfew?" Kolt asked.

"Ahhh, some don't bother," Dmitry said.

"Shouldn't we turn around?" Kolt asked, uneasy that their Alfa escorts didn't seem too concerned.

A few seconds went by and still no answer. Kolt resisted the immediate urge to ask again. He felt Slapshot and Digger roll from their asses to their knees. Kolt could tell they were going for their bags, likely to fumble in the dark with mating their concealed HK416 uppers to their lowers.

"Hang tight," Kolt whispered, as the truck slowed and eventually stopped in the middle of the dirt road. "Pistols as primary. Maybe we're turning around."

"I fucking hope so," Digger said, "we're kind of flapping in here."

"I agree," Kolt said, as he yanked the large smelly tarp off the three of them, releasing the trapped odor and allowing them to take in some fresh air.

"Fuck, we have company!" Slapshot said as he peeked out from underneath the truck's canvas top, letting a small beam of light penetrate the dark cabin, finding Slapshot's red beard.

"How close?" Kolt asked as they heard the obvious sound of the driver's side door open.

"We are on the X, boss," Slapshot said.

Just then, from inside the cab, Dmitry shouted in his native language. Outside, in front of the truck, angry voices countered. It was heated, definitely not a friendly encounter, at least not yet. The two voices jousted, stepping on each other as the words and the decibel levels increased.

"How many?" Kolt asked.

"Don't see any," Slapshot said. "Just bright headlights."

"What are they saying, Digger?" Kolt asked, knowing Digger was Russian trained in Fifth Special Forces Group before assessing for the Unit.

"Hard to understand, man," Digger said. "Something about credentials and neighborhood. Dmitry is telling them to get out of the way."

Kolt scooted on his knees to the opposite side of Slapshot. He peeled the tarp back a half inch or so, enough to see in front of the truck. The opposing truck's high beams met Dmitry's, highlighting the thick ground fog. Kolt strained to pick up movement, hoping to assess the intent of those shouting.

With their truck still idling, the driver's door slammed shut.

"Dmitry got out," Slapshot whispered. "He's pushing it."

Don't be a dumbass, Dmitry, get back in the truck.

Kolt picked up Dmitry's lanky body as he stepped in front of their right headlight. He barked like he owned the place, throwing both arms in the air repeatedly, his baggy T-shirt slipping down to his shoulders each time, exposing his bony upper arms. Dmitry gave another command, shooing with his hands like he was clearing a herd of cattle from an open gate.

A second later, a figure stepped into the light and buttstroked Dmitry with the stock of an assault rifle, dropping him to the ground.

"Shit! Dmitry's down," Kolt said. "I've got three, you?" Kolt took inventory of his voice, hoping the truck's running engine was loud enough to muffle his words.

"Only see one from my angle," Slapshot said. "Uniform and AKMS on this one, folding stock."

"Russians," Kolt said.

Kolt watched as one of the Russian soldiers slung his rifle. Slapshot was correct; no question they were sporting AKMS 7.62s. The Russian reached down to Dmitry, and Kolt figured he was likely turning him over to his chest, securing his hands behind him, and frisking him for identification or valuables. The other two Russians came into Kolt's view, shouldered their rifles, aimed up at the windshield, and began yelling commands at Olga.

"They want her to get out," Digger said as he peeked

through the front cab's back window just enough to see Olga's head and shoulder blades. "She's slipping to the driver's seat."

"This ain't good," Slapshot said from across the truck bed.

The distinct sound of AKMS fire broke the eerie silence. Kolt noticed Digger duck out of instinct, probably thinking the rounds were directed at the windshield. Bullets impacted the thin metal of the truck's front end, and louder thuds of heavy rounds shook it as they hit the engine block.

The Russians yelled again.

Kolt noticed smoke billowing from underneath the hood. A second later, the truck spurted, shook slightly, and died.

"Olga kill the engine?" Kolt asked, hoping it wasn't the 7.62 rounds.

"Negative," Digger said.

"Secure route my ass," Kolt whispered to himself.

Slap's right, this ain't good.

"She's getting out," Digger said. Kolt heard the sound of the driver's side door opening again.

Olga stepped down from the truck and moved in front of it. One of the Russians grabbed her by the arm and threw her to the ground.

"She got balls," Slapshot said, "but she just took a nosedive."

Kolt tensed. He realized he was breathing fast, and centered himself. They needed to do something, and quick. He knew as soon as they were done searching them, they'd be tearing into the front cab for contraband. After that, the truck bed for sure. There was no hiding, not in the back of the truck, not with just the tarps they'd hid under during the long drive so far.

"We gotta do something here," Slapshot said, still peeking out the opposite side of the truck bed from Kolt.

"You make out any other trucks behind that one, Slap?" Kolt asked as he processed the data points he had available.

"Hard to tell," Slapshot said. "My guess is no, or they'd have joined the party."

Kolt couldn't argue with Slapshot's reasoning, but he wasn't convinced. As Kolt thought it over he saw one of the troops stand straight up, remove his own hat, and put Olga's conductor hat on sideways. The Russians laughed. One appeared to kick at one of the two on the ground.

They had the correct crypto loaded in their MBITR radios. Kolt could dig it out of his bag fairly easily. Maybe call the boys at the safe house near the town of Krasnoarmiisk and request some help. *Fuck.* Kolt remembered they were going after Tehrani's courier and were unavailable.

Just as Kolt thought it would be a good idea to make the Mayday call anyway, he realized he had no idea how far they were from Krasnoarmiisk. The radio's maximum line-of-sight range was limited. The signal would never reach them. He'd need to throw up a satellite antenna to make the connection, a piece of equipment none of them had deployed from Bragg with.

Damn, no good options here!

"Boss?" Digger asked, obviously wanting some guidance on where they stood. "Long guns?"

Kolt weighed their options and knew they had only one.

"Yup. Time to get into a gunfight."

Sonchon, North Korea

The sexagenarian Kang Pang Su bent over at the waist, coughing and hacking so that his entire body shook.

Still struggling to breathe normally after his bike

ride, he rolled the bicycle up the short stone-covered pathway and held it steady as he opened the front door to the traditional tile-roofed rural home with his left hand. Kang pushed it fully open, glanced one more time down the wide road lined with large plane and acacia trees with their government applied white rings.

Kang looked hard, but quick, hoping not to spot any of the Public Standards Police who dropped by to check the condition of the Workers' Party–distributed pictures of the Great Leader, or one of the teenagers wearing an armband denoting them as part of the Maintenance of Social Order Brigade wanting to spot check to see if he was wearing his government badge. He knew either of the two must be following him.

Kang had grown tired of being watched. He'd decided a long time ago that a powerful nation shouldn't be proud of a national pastime of spying on their neighbors.

Kang kicked off his vinyl loafers and rolled the bicycle's bald tires through the doorway. He closed the door quietly, leaned the rusted light blue bike against the concrete wall, ensuring it wouldn't fall, and headed for the kitchen sink to quench his thirst.

Kang lifted the aged small white cooking pot, the same one his wife had boiled cabbage and seaweed in for decades, and swirled the cloudy water around. He inspected it for signs of insects, then put the pot's hard, worn edge to his lips. He tilted it high as he leaned back, not stopping until he had downed about a quart. After thirteen miles on the wobbly single-speed bicycle, of which at least four or five miles were simply precautionary, intended as a simple but prudent countersurveillance measure, Kang was ready to lather cream in his crotch before collapsing onto the flat stone-slab floor to rest his bones and lock his eyes shut.

But those decisions had been made long ago. There

would be no rest, at least not until he sent the most important message of his life.

Kang had lived in North Korea his entire life and never cared much about what happened around the world. He shunned the South Korean propaganda that told of the wonders of capitalism, the freedom of expression, and the limitless opportunity. If not for the treatment of his wife so many years ago, Kang Pang Su would have spent his life in comfort and privilege like the ever-curious Pak Yong Chol and all the other party leaders fortunate to carry one of the family names somehow associated with the late Kim Il Sung.

No, when Kang's wife passed, the mourning, hatred, and feeling of betrayal percolated to the point that Kang couldn't control them. He hated the regime and what it had done to him, what it had taken away. At some level he knew his anger drove him to seek out the contact he'd made with the CIA all those years ago, but it was still his choice.

He'd resisted reaching out to the CIA while he was in university despite their entreaties. It wasn't so much about principle as it was the desire to protect his wife and children. Things began to change during the famine of the 1990s, when the collapse of the Soviet Union halted all supply of oil, technology, and foodstuffs the hermit kingdom had relied on for survival. But what ultimately turned Kang Pang Su was something he bore eyewitness to, given his high position within the Central Committee. When President Kim Jong Il decided to route revenues into his personal account, even the "Military First" policy, which prioritized the Korean People's Army, the upper-class people, were robbed of national resources.

Both of Kang's boys served proudly in the army, but only one, Dae-Jung, survived on the scant four hundred grams of food a day. Chung-ho, the youngest, perished after developing beriberi, which led to nervous system compromise and, within thirty-six hours, total heart failure.

Kang would have gladly helped the Americans then, but their humanitarian aid, along with that from China, replaced the Soviet losses and Kang once again pushed down any thoughts of treason. It wasn't that Kang liked Kim Jong Il's potbellied boy, Kim Jung Un; far from it. He found the new leader's nuclear aspirations to be very troubling, as they only served to further isolate the country when the good people needed so much humanitarian aid. But Kang knew his place.

And then Dae-Jung did the unthinkable. Rumors swirled about the country, telling of the extreme measures people were going to in order to stave off the continuing famine. Tears came to Kang's eyes as he thought of his granddaughter, and the madness that drove his son to kill her for food.

Kang took another swig, finishing the pot, and set it back in the sunken sink. Ignoring his fatigue, he wiped his mouth with the sleeve of his tan jacket, then dried his eyes. He shuffled down the narrow hallway to the lower room. It had been months since he'd felt the warmth of the floor, heated by channeling warm air and smoke through a system of under-the-floor flues from an exterior fireplace. But Kang hadn't needed heat under the floor for the past few months as much as he needed the hiding space.

Kang slipped up to the edge of the window, careful not to knock over the gallon-size paint cans, kick the dried paintbrush pans, or get tangled up in the drop cloths. He was careful not to show himself through the window to anyone who might be looking his way.

He reached down to feel his right knee, softly squeezing the puffy tissue. The fluid had already swollen to softball size. Kang shifted his focus from left to right, then back to the left. He looked for any sign of the high-level party committee cadres dispatched to each provincial city and district in order to flush out questionably loyal party members, or one of the propaganda trucks that barked out North Korean successes through screechy roof-mounted speakers.

Kang knew government cadre were going house to house, searching for party membership cards or Great Leader portraits stashed away in cupboards, their owners' loyalty having shifted to the faces of foreign men on U.S. greenbacks. Although they were driven by different motivations, Kang knew that, like him, they were party members in name, but not in deed.

With no time to waste, Kang stood upright and pressed on to the familiar lower end of the room, the *araemmok,* the room for honored guests and the seniors of the household. In North Korean winters, a night of heat could feel like winning the lottery, which is why the room his parents and grandparents slept in as far back as Kang could remember was closest to the outside fireplace.

Favoring his sore knee, Kang shuffled toward the upper end, the spot where he and his brothers and sisters, those with a lower social status, slept. The *ummok* was close to the front door and farthest from the heat source. Both rooms were floored with the same century-old large pieces of flat stone, tightly covered with several square-yard-size pieces of lacquered paper. The light golden-brown paper had aged nicely. Besides meeting his mother's decorative eye, the paper shielded the rooms from gas and smoke, and was easy to come by at the market in Sonchon.

Kang had to hurry. He was expected back in Pyongyang for a fourth and final meeting to confirm the nuclear arms agenda with the joint Swedish/South Korean delegation. But the last train out of Sonchon Station for

Pyongyang would push off in less than an hour, and with at least fifty minutes of hard pedaling, even without worrying about a tail, he would practically be boarding as it started down the track.

It would be the fourth meeting in the past three weeks, as they prepared for the very rare assembly of high-level delegates at Panmunjom, on the 38th parallel. Nothing they shared at the meeting would resemble the truth in any form or fashion. Nevertheless, he needed to get back for the meeting as much as to preserve his actions in Sonchon, which meant he had no time to actually do any cleaning in the yard, or fix the things still needing fixing, all an elaborate charade to ensure the local appetite for nosiness was sufficiently suppressed.

Kang delicately knelt down, sliding a dingy pillow under his knees as he kneeled on the stone floor and reached for the corner of the golden-brown lacquer paper. He peeled it up and away from the square slab, smooth cut roughly three feet by two feet, and reached for the metal fire poker leaning against the wall. Kang slipped the narrow end into the thin space separating the square stones and leaned his body into it, lifting the stone enough to angle it up and out of its century-old position. Kang laid the poker down and with both hands pulled at the edges of the stone to slide it out of the way before bending into the prone.

Kang reached into the heat space underneath the ondol flooring and secured the aged teletypewriter, pulling it up and out, careful not to dislodge the power cable secured to the back side with small pieces of chicken wire and burlap straps. Kang wiped his fingers across the small window screen of the HAL CWR-6850 electronic terminal to clear the dust, and fingered a few cobwebs off the keyboard.

Before the computer mass storage era, an age still unseen in North Korea, most radioteletype stations, known simply as RTTY, stored text on paper tape, using paper tape punchers and readers. With Kang's engineering and science degree from Kim Il Sung University he was a quick study, easily following his CIA handler's operating instructions. He knew all he had to do was type the message on the RTTY keyboard, authenticate it with the code word he had remembered for thirty years, and let it punch the code onto the tape. The tape could then be transmitted electrically across the waves at a steady, high rate.

If there ever was a paper tape message that he needed to get out of isolated North Korea, this was the one. Without the RTTY message, the only people on earth that could safely extract him from North Korea would have no idea of his plans to defect while at the meeting in Panmunjom. More importantly, the same people that needed his time-sensitive intelligence more than anyone, the Americans, were the only ones that could use the information to stop World War III.

Kang flicked the red plastic toggle switch up to power on the teletypewriter, the white switch up to send, and impatiently waited, tapping his fingers on his thighs while the normal twenty-second warmup sequence ticked off. He selected manual mode and then initiated the magnetic tape test, studied the screen, waiting patiently for the fuzzy bright green digits to change from WAIT to OUTPUT. Only then could he begin typing the message that would either save him or kill him.

NINE

Options raced through Kolt's mental Rolodex and he quickly dismissed each one. With both of their Alfa operative guides now facedown in the dirt and surrounded by Russian Spetsnaz, the only course left was kinetic. The Russians had to go.

Kolt let the edge of the tarp fall back in place, closing the peephole he was using to keep tabs on the chaos unfolding outside. He scooted on his knees back to the center of the truck bed, closer to Digger and Slapshot. Now that he was no longer under the cloak of the heavy tarp, his night vision had come around enough to make out his mates' faces, the headlights still penetrating the sliver of space at Slapshot's perch.

"This is fucking nuts," Slapshot said.

Kolt didn't disagree with his squadron sergeant major, not at all. No doubt things were spiraling out of control quickly. But that was the easy answer; they needed options. Kolt sized it up in warp speed, rapidly searched for left and right limits, ran the contingency through context, and settled on an idea. A crazy idea.

"Digger, can you be the retarded cousin?"

"Don't even go there, boss," Digger said, shaking his head from side to side.

"Look, man, hear me out," Kolt said. "You speak the lingo enough to play the part. Strip down to your underwear and remove your leg. Hop out there, full-on stupid, and draw their attention. Slapshot and I will circle around and take them from behind."

"I thought landing on a moving 747 in India was crazy," Digger said, "but this is fucking insane."

"Which is why it might work," Slapshot said, surprising Kolt that his new squadron sergeant major was immediately supportive. Slapshot's blessing told Kolt one of two things: either he was desperate and had no better ideas, or he thought the unconventional idea might have some legs. Well, one anyway.

"What? Are we back in fucking selection?" Digger whispered, still resisting.

"C'mon, Digger, if you have a better idea you need to share it now," Slapshot said.

"Hop out there?" Digger said, amped up at the suggestion. "On one leg?"

"Digger, look," Kolt said, "even those assholes won't shoot a naked one-legged wacko."

"How the hell do you know?"

"They haven't shot the other two yet," Kolt said. "We only need a little time to get behind them. If the three of us break cover and start shooting, we'll be grouped together and too vulnerable."

"Son of a bitch," Digger said as he pulled his T-shirt and sweatshirt over his head, half tossing them to Slapshot. Kolt watched him slide on his knees to the tailgate of the truck, his V-shaped triathlon-like upper body obvious even in the dark. Digger slipped over the gate like he was negotiating the high bar on the obstacle course, controlling his weight as he dropped to the dirt road. Kolt scooted toward him, as did Slapshot.

Digger handed his Glock, pistol grip first, up to Slapshot. He unbuckled his belt and dropped his cargo jeans, before balancing against the tailgate. Digger struggled to pull his boots through his baggy pant legs, one at a time, and left his drawers on the dirt road. Kolt looked at Digger, proud that he was willing to risk his ass, and realizing Digger wasn't wearing any creature comforts. Digger bent over, unlocked his prosthetic lower leg, and handed it up to Slapshot.

"Don't be too long," Digger said as he held on to the tailgate and hopped to the truck's back left corner.

"Give us one minute if you can," Kolt said, "and make it loud so we can hear you."

Without speaking to Slapshot, Kolt slid over the tailgate, careful not to tear off the bandage on his right forearm, and went to a knee. He lifted his shirt a few inches, checked to ensure his pistol light hadn't activated, and drew his concealed M1911A1 from his appendix holster. His head now even with Digger's white ass, he was struck with the idea that maybe they had better options. Feeling Slapshot drop behind him, Kolt shook off the worrywarts and turned around.

Kolt led as they backtracked down the road about ten meters, keeping the truck in between them and the laughing Russians, careful not to be white-lighted by the dueling headlights. They crouched as they left the side of the road and went down a grass embankment, both hands on their sidearms, Slapshot running a Gen 4 Glock 23 like Digger, Kolt running a .45 caliber single-action. Ready to slot the first hostile they bumped into, they turned to head back toward the dueling trucks.

Realizing they were below the road, they moved with tactical purpose, picking up a slow gait on the soft terrain. Keying off the truck lights and the top of the Russian truck, reminiscent of a crime scene, Kolt and Slapshot stepped over a dozen fallen and limbless trees. The strong aroma of burnt wood filled his nostrils, giving him the impression they were moving through a recently burned-out area. Now just past the Russian truck, they crawled out of the ditch on two knees and one hand. Making the road's edge, they paused to look right into the darkness, searching for any other trucks or troops previously unseen.

"Clear right," Slapshot whispered.

"Moving."

Kolt took point as they ninja-upped in behind the Russian truck. Fat bald tires, cheap steel, Eastern European military all the way. Kolt motioned for Slapshot to take a peek in the bed, letting him know he would cover him. Slapshot holstered his pistol, pulled up on the tailgate, testing his body weight as he ascended, until he was looking in the back from a good pull-up position.

"Crates," Slapshot whispered as he dropped back to a knee and pulled his pistol.

Kolt pied around the back right corner of the Russian truck to assess the situation. The edge of Dmitry's truck's headlights illuminated just outside Kolt's position, leaving him concealed for the time being.

Kolt turned around. "We don't want to go loud here, Slap. Let's see if we can take these guys and squeeze them for intel."

"I don't know, boss," Slapshot said. "Odds aren't in our favor."

"I know, but—"

Just then, AKMS fire erupted from in front of the truck. Kolt and Slapshot moved closer to the group, spotted one of the Russians firing single shots at Digger's single foot. Kolt watched his mate hop around in his birthday suit while spouting off what sounded like every

Russian cuss word he knew. The bullets kicked dust in the air as Digger covered his face with one hand, his groin with the other.

Digger was playing the part better than expected. The other Russians broke out in laughter, the one wearing Olga's cap hopping around on one foot too, a bottle of liquor in his hand, mimicking Digger and making fun of his handicap.

Kolt and Slapshot eased closer to the front end of the truck, just far enough to see where Dmitry and Olga were, trying to size up the situation before they sprang.

Dmitry was facedown, motionless and quiet. His hands were tied behind his back. Kolt shifted to Olga. One of the Russians was sitting on her back, holding her down as she struggled to get up. Without her hat, Olga's long brown hair had fallen in front of her face. Her pants had already been yanked down around her ankles, her underwear down to her knees. Kolt wasn't going to let this go any further. Rape was a trigger line.

The hopping Russian handed the bottle to his partner before unbuckling his utility belt and dropping it to the dirt. He said something in Russian, something obviously evil and dark, as he unbuttoned his pants, letting them free drop to the ground only a foot behind Olga. The Russian waddled forward as if he were a convict in chains on death row, staring hard at her backside.

Olga yelled out, but not in fear. It was pure hatred.

Kolt turned his head half back to Slapshot, trying to keep one eye on the three Russian troops fully illuminated by the facing truck's headlights.

"I'm left, you got right," Kolt whispered. "On three."

"Rog."

"How do you say 'hands up' in Russian?" Kolt asked.

"I'd try something crazy like 'Drop your weapons!' " Slapshot said.

"That'll work," Kolt said, ignoring his mate's sarcasm.

A single rifle shot rang out from close by.

"Shit! Moving!"

Kolt raised to a crouch and advanced forward, leaving the security of darkness. He extended his 1911 at full elbow lock and sighted the gold bead front sight post on a Russian eye orbit. He knew Slapshot would be mirroring him, his weapon up, looking to eliminate the threat in his sector.

The Russian that had been sitting on top of Olga was now on his feet, standing victorious over Dmitry, his AKMS in both hands, pointed at the Alfa man's supine body. The Russian struggled to yank his thirty-round magazine out of his rifle, then reached under the rifle and pulled the charging handle to the rear.

Weapon jam!

The Russian must have felt the presence of unwanted company as he turned his head half around to the right. In an instant, he alerted on the unknown danger, high-stepped over Dmitry's body, dropped his rifle and magazine to the dirt, and kicked it into high gear.

"Putin's a pussy!" Kolt yelled, following the threat as he cleared the front right corner of Dimitry's broke-dick truck.

Kolt left the danger of the headlights and tracked the Russian into the dark. The Russian was in a dead sprint, yelling like a baby, having lost the killer persona he played so well when things were going his way.

Kolt wasn't about to chase him all night. There were two other shitbags still back there and he didn't want to miss out.

Kolt braked, spread his boots shoulder width apart for balance, and pushed the gun to full extension. He thumbed the ambi switch of his SureFire X300 Ultra to momentary-on with his support hand, capturing the fleeing Russian from his hatless head down to his asshole inside a white beam of five hundred lumens. Kolt leaned into it, driving the front sight to center mass of the Russian's shoulder blades, and broke the trigger twice, putting a controlled pair of .45 caliber ball into the man's narrow back.

Kolt let off the light, then back on, picking up the crumpled man's body lying on the edge of the dirt road.

Kolt turned back to his mates, wondering what had happened. He hadn't heard any shots from Slapshot. In a few steps, he was close to the right fender of their truck.

"Eagle, Eagle!" Kolt said, letting them know he was a friendly.

Kolt squinted as he stepped in front of the dueling headlights, his left boot inadvertently finding a slick puddle, causing him to lose his balance.

Dmitry's blood.

Catching himself before he tumbled, his pistol at the low ready, Kolt went down to both knees, landing on Dmitry's skinny legs.

"I thought we weren't going loud?" Slapshot asked. "Intel value, wasn't it?"

Kolt tried to make sense of the scene. Digger, still naked, was on his back. He had one of the Russians in what looked like a solid rear naked choke, obviously holding pressure on his larynx as the Russian flapped his hands wildly, desperate for oxygen. Digger's left leg was wrapped around the Russian's waist, just over his half-limp penis and hairy, white thighs. His right stub leg, pointing skyward, provided leverage as he locked in the choke.

Close by, Slapshot's target was facedown and lights out. Slapshot had just finished flex-tying the man's wrists behind his back and was moving down to the Russian's ankles.

"He dead?" Kolt asked, hoping he wasn't the only one

that had used lethal force. After all, the whole capture idea was his.

"I pistol-whipped him."

Kolt shook his head, half in disbelief, half in amazement, before breaking the spell and moving to help Digger. Slapshot threw Kolt two flex ties, which Kolt used to fasten the other sleeping Russian's ankles. Digger rolled out of the way, letting Kolt turn the guy over and secure his wrists.

"Get dressed, brother," Kolt said. "That was legend right there."

"Bite me, Racer," Digger said, unable to hide his relief that the ruse actually worked. "You owe me big-time."

"Indeed," Kolt said as he watched Digger hop out of the headlight's footprint and back to the tailgate.

Kolt turned to Olga, happy to see her alive. She had pulled her pants up and was leaning over Dmitry, her hand under his neck, checking for a pulse, not wanting to give up on her fellow operative just yet.

"These are Starinov's babies," Olga said.

"Who?" Kolt asked.

"Colonel Starinov. He is the grandfather of Russian special forces."

"Spetsnaz?" Kolt asked. "For sure?"

Olga collected herself and stood up. She noticed her cap on the ground and knelt like a woman to retrieve it, bending at the knees and not the waist. With one hand she whipped her hair into a bun and slipped the blue-and-white conductor's hat back on her head, taking a long second to position it just right.

Kolt watched her every move, impressed by her demeanor and composure with Dmitry's blood-puddled body so close. Kolt assumed the two Alfa operatives were tight, at least as compatriots, maybe more.

"We gotta get going, boss," Slapshot said. "We taking these two with us?"

Kolt let the question sink in for a moment, until his thoughts were interrupted by Olga walking toward him.

She kneeled next to the Russian soldier Digger had napped out and reached toward his head, grabbing a piece of two-inch-wide orange-and-black ribbon attached to the soldier's left shoulder epaulet. She rubbed the knot between her fingers to untie it.

"The Order of St. George," she said, holding the ten-inch-or-so-long ribbon in the air. "Russia's nationalist pride. All Spetsnaz wear one when the Kremlin declares war."

Olga handed the ribbon to Kolt. He studied it for a few seconds before sharing with Slapshot.

"If you wear one of these the locals know you're Russian special forces?" Slapshot asked.

"Yes," Olga said, not taking her dark eyes off of the defenseless Russian sprawled at her side. "Even the traitors, Ukrainians who are pro-Russian separatists, are afraid of them."

Kolt stood, holstered his blaster, and started toward Dmitry's body. "No debate. We're taking everyone. Even the dead."

Kolt grabbed Dmitry by the left arm and rolled him over on his back.

"NO!" Slapshot yelled.

Kolt turned, surprised by his mate's disregard for noise discipline, but intrigued by what he was yelling about. It was too late.

Two-handing a knife, Olga lifted it out of the back of the neck of the Russian she had pulled the St. George's ribbon from. She spoke in Russian, saying something poetic for sure, certainly laced with vengeance and horror for Dmitry's death.

Slapshot jumped in to grab her.

"Slap!" Kolt said. "At ease!"

Slapshot froze, looked hard at Kolt, then, understanding, stepped back.

Olga turned to lock eyes with Kolt, but only for a moment before turning back around. She raised the knife with both hands high in the air, like a wounded woman possessed, and slammed the bloody blade down like she was swinging a sledgehammer at the pivotboard of a traveling carnival.

Olga retracted the knife from the neck, repeated her deep-seated verbal hatred, and struck again.

And again, and again.

TEN

Kang Pang Su powered up the teletypewriter, knowing his life as he knew it was coming to an end. It should have been more shocking, he thought, but everyone had their breaking point. His had come slowly over the decades until he simply couldn't take any more.

A message blinked onto the screen—DISPLAY ERROR/ POWER. Kang sat back. Now that he'd made up his mind, would he be thwarted by a technical malfunction? Forcing himself to remain calm, Kang reached behind the teletypewriter, feeling for the 1985 operator's manual taped to the back. He yanked it off, and turned to the back section.

Yes, turn the RTTY off and retest the initiation sequence.

Kang reached for the red toggle switch to power down the device, but before he did, he noticed an odd message display.

ERROR 143.

Kang quickly thumbed to the back of the manual and ran his right index finger down the two-page list of error codes until he found the number 143. Out to the right the noun nomenclature read SYMBOLIC INPUT POWER—UNCONDITIONAL ABORT.

Oh my!

Again, Kang froze in confusion, unsure what to do. He instinctively looked back toward the window, then through the kitchen to the door in the distance as he thought it over. He looked up at the old wall clock, positioned just below the Workers' Party–distributed portraits of the Great Leader, Kim Jong Il, and the Dear Leader, Kim Il Sung. He had to get moving, had to get the message off.

Power! That's it. It must be.

Kang reached for the RTTY, rotating it 180 degrees to see the rear connections. He touched both terminals, feeling for slack in the connections. Nothing.

Kang pushed himself to his feet and moved back to the window, pausing to quickly look outside at the makeshift antenna, ensuring the radial poles buried just below the dirt hadn't been disturbed. It was the same garden spot where his mother buried the kimchi bowls in the winter so they would stay cold but not frozen.

Things looked in order.

Kang followed the thirty-foot antenna made from metal fence pieces and barbed wire from the ground to its apex, finding nothing odd or disturbed. Satisfied, he returned to the front door, opened it, and stepped outside, gingerly slipping back into his loafers. Forgetting to close the door, Kang stepped off the low porch and walked around the drab wall of the aged and gray house, hugging the side and trying to conceal his movements using the sporadic bushes off to the side.

Kang reached the power pole just six or seven feet from the wall, and followed the white power cable from the hole under the tiled roof across the open space and down the pole until it reached the breaker box. Kang looked closely; nothing out of order to the naked eye. He looked around the immediate area, searching for a stick to protect him from the hot line. Finding one that might do, an old soiled garden hoe, he delicately touched the ends of the wire, immediately realizing one of the wires was obviously loose.

No time to fix this!

Kang again found the end of the power cable, gently jamming the wooden side of the garden tool up and into the old wooden box, attempting to connect the cables enough to provide enough power to operate the RTTY. He let go of the stick cautiously, ensuring it held, before returning to the RTTY and the open space in the ondol flooring.

Back kneeling on the dingy pillow, Kang wheeled the brown metal RTTY back around to face the screen and keyboard. Waiting for him was the message he had prayed for.

OUTPUT1

Attacking the olive drab keys with eight fat fingers, Kang banged out the required character string *RYRYRYRY* needed to test five-level teleprinters. Known as Baudot, this stressful test sequence for electromechanical teleprinters forces the switching between the two characters. Repeated over and over, it outputs a carrier wave that regularly and rapidly shifts back and forth in frequency, allowing for testing of signal polarity.

The test took only a few seconds and Kang found the keys again to craft his message, not forgetting to properly front it with BOM, *beginning of message*, generating green 5-bit characters every time he pressed a key.

BOM. MTNG 38th NEXT—

Kang stopped typing at the sound of the knock at the door. Someone must have seen him outside, either before he hid the bicycle inside, or maybe when he checked the power cable connection. Kang knew he didn't have time to put the RTTY away and make the last train out before the electricity shut off. No, it would take too long to even politely dismiss any of his neighbors bringing fresh radish and turnip kimchi to simply mask their nosiness. And if his visitors were government men, or a few of the four million Worker-Peasant Red Guard paramilitaries, he would need much more time to properly sterilize the ondol flooring and return it to its natural state.

Ignore it, keep typing, send the message. It's your last chance!

Kang continued hacking, finishing the message, his nerves forcing him to backspace twice to correct, just as a second and distinctly louder and longer knock was heard at the door.

MTNG 38th NEXT WED. SOS. SEEGHAR. EOM.

Kang hit Enter twice, initiating the Send sequence.

Damn it! The noise!

Kang had forgotten about the noise the RTTY makes as it begins to transmit, and reached for the tubular silver volume slide. He slid it down, from level five to zero.

A third knock.

Kang yanked the pillow from under his knees and placed it over the face of the RTTY. Chancing a power failure again, he lifted the teleprinter up and gently placed it back into its hiding place. Looking one last time at the front door, he shoved the flat stone back into place and refastened the golden lacquer paper.

"Yes, I'm coming, please wait."

Kolt, struggling to keep his forefinger following the correct road on his map, didn't realize they had arrived at the safe house until Olga brought the truck to a shuddering halt. They'd commandeered the vehicle the three Spetsnaz troops had been using, an Ural-315 general utility truck, to replace their destroyed truck. Kolt motioned for Olga to kill the lights.

"Keep the engine running," he said, grabbing his .45 from its position between his legs and bringing it up to just below the dash. "We have no idea who's here."

Kolt was pissed, but mostly at himself. He'd told Olga not to drive straight up to the house, but to stop a quarter mile out. Obviously, he should have told her again. He studied the aged two-story brick building and burnt-out vehicles in the surrounding area. The war had clearly run over this place. He counted three holes in the wall facing him, most likely from RPGs. The front corner of the structure was completely gone, leaving a ten-foot-wide gap clogged with rubble and wood beams hanging down from the second floor. Every window he could see was shattered. The place looked abandoned, which was good. If his team were inside, they were practicing excellent light discipline.

It was still dark, which normally worked to Kolt's advantage, but after their run-in with Spetsnaz he found himself wanting more than the artificial kind provided by SureFire.

"I check," Olga said, apparently reading his mind.

Kolt grabbed her arm before she could step out of the cab of the truck. "Stand by, I'll join you." He turned and saw Slapshot staring at him through the rear window. Kolt slid the glass panels back. "I fucked up. We're too close."

"You want us to take a look?" Slapshot asked.

"Just cover us from either side of the truck. We'll go to the door. If it goes south, don't be strangers," he said.

"We'll try to discriminate, but," Slapshot said, lightening the mood a bit.

A knock on Kolt's window startled him and he swung his auto pistol up and to the right. Trip Griffin was staring back at him, his smile evaporating as he stared at the business end of the 1911.

Kolt quickly lowered his pistol and reengaged the thumb safety.

"Welcome to Ukraine," Trip said.

ELEVEN

Kolt stood inside the living room of the war-torn safe house and tried to make sense of what he was seeing. Three bodies were laid out on a filthy blue and gray carpet in the center of the room. Placed abreast of each other, the bodies were dress right dress, maybe an inch between them. They were two Delta snipers and a 24th Special Tactics Squadron combat controller. Each one was wrapped tight with the red, white, and blue of a full-size American flag and then inside an olive green plastic Skedco litter, the kind infantry troops use to drag their casualties.

Kolt took a few steps closer to the bodies and took a knee. It was the last thing he expected to see upon arriving at the safe house. He didn't know the details, at least not enough to determine what, if anything, could have been done differently. On occasion, they'd lose an Eagle on a hit, usually by some freak accident, a lucky rabbit round, or something unseen and uncontrollable. Kolt knew losing a mate left the survivors feeling one of two ways. Either they'd be stuffing more frags in their assault vests and topping off mags, or they'd dump their kit in a pile and mentally shut down for a while. Losing one guy on a hit was tragic enough, but three guys in one hit was entirely uncommon.

"It was a fool's plan in the first place," Trip Griffin said, breaking the silence. "We should have waited for better intel."

"What happened?" Slapshot asked.

"Jackal's op car hit a land mine during the exfil."

Kolt gritted his teeth. It was a tough break to lose their sniper team.

"What about Marzban's courier?" Kolt asked, immediately regretting the comment. Kolt didn't intend to be insensitive to the casualties, and felt a pang of guilt in his throat. If his men fingered him as a commander more concerned about the mission than the men, his first operation with his new squadron would only get more difficult.

"Slotted him. But that ain't the half of it. Marzban was there, too," Trip said.

Kolt looked at Trip. "Intel only had the courier."

"Yeah, well, they got part of it right. He had extra muscle with him. When we realized it was him, he was already making a run for it. I'm sure I tagged him; Dealer shot, too. He probably has two bullets in him."

"Dealer?"

"One of the SEALs," Trip said. "They had the cordon."

Kolt paused for a second. He knew who Dealer was, but was surprised to hear his name. Kolt knew Colonel Webber had never said anything about the SEALs tagging along on this mission.

"Any word on him?" Kolt asked, hoping something positive had come from three KIAs on a failed mission.

Trip shook his head. "Last we saw of him he was holding his belly. He jumped in a dark-colored sedan and bolted."

"The Iranian scientists?" Kolt asked. "Any sign of them?"

"None," Trip said. "They weren't there."

"Marzban's got a girlfriend," Kolt said. Again, he caught himself, hoping his tone wasn't too snippy.

"No," Trip said, "bitch was probably behind the wheel."

Kolt took his eyes from Trip's dirty face and disheveled hair and looked down at the three corpses lying on the floor behind him.

"Who are they?" Kolt asked, a knot forming in his stomach.

"Philly and Max," Trip said, "and our new combat controller, Carson. His first time out with us."

Mother Fuckers!

Even the impetuous Kolt Raynor knew it wasn't worth Marzban, not dead or alive. But he knew he wouldn't turn off the mission because of casualties. The Ukraine in 2014 was not Somalia in 1993, where after too many special operators were lost, weak-kneed politicians pulled the plug, aborting the original mission before it could be realized.

A different time, a different place.

Marzban Tehrani wasn't simply stealing from a United Nations food distribution center to cement his power base. He was the pivot point for North Korea's miniature nuclear warhead program, responsible for smuggling nuclear scientists from his home in Iran, across Europe into Russia, and on to Pyongyang.

"Same route you took in?" Kolt asked. He stood back up, wanting to refocus.

"Yeah, the other routes were blocked. Separatists had the place locked down."

"Dumb luck on the infil?"

"Pressure-plated mine. We missed it going in."

"Damn. Why did you guys launch if the intel was weak?" Kolt asked, careful not to sound as if he was second-guessing their decision to execute, especially since he hadn't been there to help.

"Hell, sir," Trip said, "I don't really know. I guess because it was written that way on the sync matrix."

"Sync matrix?" Kolt asked, surprised at Trip's comment. "Even if the intel wasn't actionable or vetted?"

"Yeah, seems like we always do it that way," Trip said, "at least when Lieutenant Colonel Mahoney was our commander."

"Sync matrices don't think, don't process, and don't audible," Kolt said, looking Trip dead in the eye.

Trip didn't respond, just turned slightly and looked down at the three bodies on the floor. Kolt wasn't sure if the comment even registered with Trip or if he was too shell-shocked to comprehend it.

Kolt bit his tongue, felt the pointed stares from Slapshot and Digger, and took a deep breath. He looked at them both, read their minds, and let it go for now.

"Where'd you guys score those digs?" Trip asked, as if he finally broke out of his trance and noticed the oddball uniforms Kolt, Slapshot, and Digger were wearing. He pointed with both thumbs at his own chest. "We thought this was the Ukrainian uniform?"

"No. Russian," Slapshot said. "Spetsnaz, in fact."

"We scored them on a pit stop en route from Kiev," Kolt said.

"They smell like shit." Trip waved his hand in front of his nose. "Are those bloodstains?"

"Not ours," Kolt said.

Kolt studied Trip's outfit, impressed that his men had dug into the commando toolbox, opting to don deceptive Ukrainian uniforms to protect their cover for action. Kolt noticed the blue-and-yellow Ukrainian flag sewn to the right shoulder of the puke yellow-green camouflage smock.

"Drop your kit," Kolt said. "We'll watch over them. Get something to eat."

"I lost my appetite."

Trip walked through the closest doorway and out of sight. Kolt realized then he hadn't even had a chance to address his entire squadron. Hadn't huddled them up and given them the obligatory *I'm honored to be your new squadron commander* speech, or told them how valuable they were. He always knew, if he ever got a squadron, he'd make it a point to let his boys know how important each and every one of them was to obtaining the national security objectives of the United States of America. Not that they would need the reminding, or would even expect the kudos; to Kolt it just felt right.

Major promotable Kolt "Racer" Raynor had only been the new Noble Zero-One for less than forty-eight hours. Not long enough to move his kit from his team room in Mike Squadron across the hall to Noble Squadron's bay. Not long enough for the rigger shop to cut and sew him some new callsign patches. Not long enough for that damn dog Roscoe's bite to heal. Not even long enough to let them know that Slapshot, Digger, and maybe even Hawk were part of the package. But there had been time for three Eagles to be killed in action on his watch.

From behind, Kolt heard someone address him more formally than he was used to.

"Major Raynor, sir. You need to look at this."

Kolt turned, seeing it was one of the Unit's intel analysts, Sergeant John Simminski. Even though Kolt couldn't remember how to spell his last name, he recognized the man easily enough. Sporting wire-rimmed glasses, the scruff of what could be the attempt at a hipster beard, and a potbelly definitely set him apart from the operators. Still, Sergeant Simminski wasn't there for his shooting skills.

"Show me," Kolt said, noticing Olga was on his tail. Both of the Alfa operative's hands were chest high, holding the leather sling tight, as if the AKMS she had claimed at the truck standoff and now carried on her back was throwing her natural balance off. Her left hand also clutched her conductor's hat, the dried blood on her hands and around the edges of her fingernails serving as a stern warning that she shouldn't be tested.

Olga's shoulder-length hair had fallen naturally to the sides with a center part, as greasy and matted as John's. Five, maybe six days of facial growth put ten years on him. Kolt figured John hadn't had a shower in a week, something not uncommon for Unit intel analysts, who put in more time at the office than anyone.

Kolt looked at the palms of his hands and wiped the dried blood on his thighs. He took the paper from the analyst and started reading, but John injected the information anyway.

"Marzban is at the hospital in Donetsk," John said, also handing Kolt an eight-by-ten color printed map with the thin black horizontal and vertical lines of a standard grid target reference already superimposed over the satellite photo.

"Big-ass hospital," Kolt said, studying the photo for possible high ground spots for his snipers and infil routes for his assaulters.

"Donetsk Regional Trauma Hospital," John said. "Believed to be still under control of the locals."

"What's the source?" Kolt asked.

"SIGINT," John said, offering the acronym for signal's intelligence. "Cell phone chatter has been smoking hot."

"Who's doing the monitoring?" Kolt said. "Not an airborne platform."

"My compatriots," Olga said. "Our intelligence group is very skilled in this."

Kolt listened but continued reading. "John, let's push ISR over the hospital," he said, "develop the vehicle activity pattern."

"Can't, boss," John said. "All of Incirlik's Predators are committed to Iraq and Syria. The Kurds have more power than I do, it appears."

Kolt thought about it and nodded knowingly, seeing in John's eyes his genuine frustration with the lack of airborne intelligence assets. With the recent territorial gains of the Islamic State in Iraq and the Levant, everyone in JSOC was expecting POTUS to issue a deployment order to send Tier One assets back to Iraq. The ISIL had recently steamrolled through Iraq from the west, cutting off heads from Fallujah to Ramadi, and held mass executions from Mosul to Baiji to Tikrit, which meant the United States was about to butt in again.

Kolt read on.

"Looks like we have Marzban, his girl, and the two eggheads in one spot, boss," John said, showing he was becoming a little impatient with the time Kolt was taking to finish the note.

"We have current PID photos of all four?" Kolt asked.

"Already printed, sir."

Kolt turned to Slapshot. "Whatya think, Slap?"

"I think we don't know shit about this target, don't know shit about what or who is there, don't know shit about what room they are in," Slapshot said. "Should I go on?"

"You're right," Kolt said. "We just can't go in there full-up green machine. Too many breach points, target too big, and even though he probably is wounded, we don't know how ambulatory he is. And it's a hospital," Kolt added, almost as an afterthought.

"Can't let him squirt again," John said. "If he does, he probably won't stop until he is across the border in Russia."

"What's the drive time from here to the hospital?" Slapshot asked, his tone revealing his clear lack of enthusiasm for some harebrained, half-baked course of action.

"Hour at least," John said, "forty-five miles."

"Forty minutes," Olga said. "I know a way."

Kolt looked at Slapshot then slewed quickly to John. "Okay, I need a no-shit assessment here from both of you."

"Yes, sir," John said.

No response from Slapshot.

"Our working assumption is Marzban is wounded. This message says the four of them are together, not necessarily in the same room, but likely nearby. A waiting room or something."

"Just spill it, boss," Slapshot said.

"Can we afford to wait till the next cycle of darkness?"

"My best assessment, sir, is there are no guarantees," John said. "We don't know how bad he is. For all we know he could be stitched up and walking out with a prescription for Motrin."

"My people will know when he leaves," Olga said.

Kolt looked at Olga, impressed that she was participating in the hasty mission analysis.

Kolt looked at Slapshot, hoping to get his take next. Silence.

"Sir, if the trigger is a call from Alfa, he won't be heading toward us," John said. "Probably looking to make Volgograd."

"I agree," Kolt said. "We're irrelevant this far away."

"Racer, it's daylight, man. Marzban knows he is being hunted. He won't risk a move until nightfall," Slapshot said, reaching for the overhead photo of the hospital Kolt was holding.

Kolt watched Slapshot look it over, stoked that he was

at least engaging. He knew Slapshot's opinion was better
than most. Sure, Kolt knew, it was simple gut instinct
and operator intuition, nothing that could be proven, but
Slapshot was rarely wrong.

"We need a squadron-plus for this," Slapshot said,
passing the photo back to Kolt. "Even with the SEALs,
it will take hours to clear that thing."

"Okay, we all need to get out of these filthy uniforms
and clean the blood off before we get sick," Kolt said.
"Let's huddle up with the boys for a minute and I'll
issue some planning guidance."

Digger and Slapshot turned to head through the same
door that Trip had used, entering the large open area.

Kolt handed the photo and message back to John and
looked at Olga. "You need to clean up, too."

Before Olga could answer, Kolt heard Slapshot
barking from the other room. "Noble! Get everyone in
here."

Kolt led John and Olga through the door and into the
middle of a crowded room. It was tight, all of his operators upright on the concrete floor, a few standing on
some crates in the two opposite corners. Kit bags lay
about in small groupings, each team having found a
place of their own.

Kolt looked around, measuring each man's mettle,
wondering if he could pick out the guys that weren't
fans. He knew many of them, but definitely not all. To
an outside observer, they would look like just one more
group of militia and Ukrainian troops, but looks could
be deceiving. While many of his men carried AK-47s
and the smaller-caliber AK-74s, others had stuck to their
own weapons, the tried-and-true HK416, based on the
older AR-15 rifle.

"Slapshot and I don't give a shit what you have done
in the past," Kolt said, scanning the room for raised eyebrows or unbelieving smirks, and setting the standard

early that he considered the new squadron sergeant major, Slapshot, his peer in everything.

"We all have demons. We all have to answer to a higher authority one day," Kolt said, pausing for effect. "Right now, tonight, we will turn another target, without Max, Philly, and Carson. If you are in here you have a clean slate as far as we are concerned."

Kolt looked at Slapshot. "Slap?"

"Roger, a new day."

"Men, it's behind us. Make sure it's behind you," Kolt said, knowing he didn't need to dwell on it anymore. He knew the boys would understand the implication. They'd understand that their new squadron commander was treating them like adults, being careful not to sound too threatening or condescending.

Kolt turned around to see if anyone behind him had anything to say. He spotted Navy SEAL Tim Kleinsmith, and immediately rewound his every word, concerned he'd screwed up and shared Unit business with their sister Tier One unit.

"Good to have you guys here, Dealer," Kolt said, approaching the SEAL and shaking his hand. "How many do you have?"

"A dozen plus me," Dealer said. "Nice duds."

Kolt offered a quick smile and turned back around. They all looked tired, some still in the Ukrainian uniforms, some having stripped down to tees, others now topless. He was pleased to see he still held everyone's attention. Either they were all standing around with breacher brain, not caring what the new squadron commander had to say, or they were willing to give him some rope.

"We're turning the hospital in Donetsk after dark. Let's stay with the Ukrainian uniforms you have on. We have a few hours to knock out a solid assault plan. Get some re—"

From behind, a booming voice interrupted Kolt. It was John, the intel analyst, with Olga in tow again.

"Sir, Marzban is moving!" John said. "Can I talk to you offline?"

"Just put it out, John," Kolt said, turning to the squadron. "Listen up!"

John didn't waste any time. "Alfa is monitoring the local police radio frequency. Marzban, both big brains, and his squeeze are leaving the hospital."

Kolt turned around. "We have good intel that they are at the hospital in Donetsk. You guys must have hit him on the assault."

"The intel vetted?" a voice from the crowd asked.

Kolt turned to Olga, then back to his men. "This is Olga. She's with Alfa. She got us here. Her mates are monitoring Marzban's comms."

"We must go," Olga said, loud enough for the entire room to hear her.

"It's frickin' daylight, lady," Trip said, deep in the crowd.

Kolt knew it was time. If they hesitated now, Marzban would soon be free and clear into Russia. They had no hot pursuit authority to venture into Russian territory and really no external assets or combat multipliers to speak of. They'd have to be vigilant not to get overextended, knowing the Russians had been massing troops on their side of the border for weeks now, but they had to act.

"All right, disregard my last. We don't have time to debate this. We are going," Kolt said. "Get it on and load up."

"That's crazy, boss," Trip said. "This isn't Syria. There's pro-Russian separatists all over the area."

"They know what we're driving," another voice said. "We're sitting ducks in the daytime."

Kolt knew they were right. It was suicide, at least going with the same assault plan they'd used early that morning. They had the cover of darkness on their side then, and launching now, without the advantage of their night vision goggles, leveled the playing field. But, Kolt thought back to the days when they hunted Abu Musab al-Zarqawi and al Qaeda in Iraq, to the several hundred missions they conducted in the heat of the day. Saying the sunlight was a disadvantage was fine; saying they couldn't figure it out to increase their odds was blasphemy. Kolt turned to John.

"We have the cell phone sniffer?"

"No, sir," John said, slipping his hands in his jeans pockets, obviously embarrassed.

Without the ability to locate and track Marzban's cell phone, and geolocate it down to ten meters inside the hospital, they had no ability to focus an assault plan on even a specific wing of the hospital, much less the exact floor or room.

"Boss," Slapshot said, "we have the Russian truck. These three uniforms, too."

Kolt looked at Slapshot, barely able to contain his excitement that the squadron sergeant major was providing options. Using a different vehicle, one the Ukrainian separatists wouldn't spike on as it approached, made perfect sense. It would likely get them close to the hospital without any drama. Once they were on the ground, the Spetsnaz uniforms, soiled and bloodstained or not, would provide enough cover for action to enter the hospital, possibly get to Marzban.

"Dealer, I need you guys to take one of the hospital wings. We'll take the other two," Kolt said.

"Yes, sir," Dealer said, not offering any open resistance to what Kolt knew most thought was a wacky plan.

Kolt addressed his men. "Plan B is Digger, Slap, and I will stay in these uniforms. These are Spetsnaz. This orange-and-black ribbon is their recognized friend or foe unit symbol. We'll enter the hospital with Olga. She can run verbal interference for us, help us figure out where

Marzban's room is. Once we know, we'll direct every-one else to the crisis point and free-flow it from there."

"What's plan A?" Trip asked.

"If we get better intel on the drive, we'll develop one," Kolt said.

"What's the big hurry?" someone asked. "We have been chasing this clown for a long time. Why don't we let it play out for a while, see what develops?"

Kolt appreciated the challenge, immediately recog-nizing he needed to use kid gloves here.

"Look, no guarantee the intel will get any better than this. Hasty security at the hospital won't expect anything like us. We'll look like Spetsnaz. The separatists think they are heroes of the Motherland."

Kolt looked around the room. Maybe they were gun-shy after the revealing of the money-for-kills scheme? Maybe just torn about their lost mates?

"What the hell, sir," another voice said. "What about a concept of operation here? How about a sync matrix?"

"No time for that," Kolt said, looking at the operator across the room. He couldn't place his name at the mo-ment, but he knew he had been around awhile.

"How are we going to sync our assets?"

Kolt was losing his patience, realizing it was much more difficult to get a squadron to throw caution to the wind than it was his Mike assault troop.

"What assets?" Kolt asked. "We're about it, don't you think?"

"We'll never get approval that fast."

"At ease!" Slapshot barked. "Damn it! You just got ap-proval. Your squadron commander just ordered the hit. You either kit up and load, or drop kit and let me know what line unit you want to go to when we get home."

TWELVE

Squadron commander Kolt Raynor leaned against the door, his right elbow chicken-winged outside the window of the Russian truck. He muttered something about giving Olga a little more room in the center jump seat between him and Slapshot, but the real reason was the stench.

Kolt kept sticking his head out into the wind stream, filling his nostrils with fresh air to kill the aromas emanating from his and Slapshot's bloodstained Spetsnaz uniforms, and Olga's body odor.

"We're getting close," Olga said. "A few more turns. About five minutes."

Kolt turned toward Olga, leaned over until his face was inches from hers, and grabbed a quick study of the satellite imagery showing on the Toughbook laptop sitting on Olga's lap. He tapped the Down arrow, zooming in two levels to focus on the last few miles to the hospital.

Kolt reached up to key his hand mike. He noticed his hand shaking and paused. He looked at Olga, certain she noticed too, as her eyes were locked on Kolt's.

"All elements, this is Noble Zero-One. Five minutes."

Kolt heard six reply transmissions in sequence, one

from each of the other vehicles tactically spread out to lower their signature and, just in case, to ensure an IED wouldn't take out more than one vehicle.

"Noble Zero-One, this is Satan Seven-One," Navy SEAL Dealer said. "Any plan A yet?"

Kolt looked at Olga, knowing she hadn't received an update since they left the farmhouse. If she had, she would have shared it.

"Negative."

"Turn left at the next intersection," Olga said, speaking to Slapshot behind the wheel.

Kolt wished he could provide an update to his men. He'd hoped he would have been able to issue some better guidance on the assault plan, but had nothing so far.

Kolt leaned back toward Olga, realizing he was holding his breath, and exhaled heavily.

"All elements, we are looking for the black side," Kolt said. "Digger, Olga, and I will enter the back door and look for Marzban. Dealer has the white side. Golf One take the red side, Fox One has green."

Kolt let his teams acknowledge his last order before transmitting again.

"Hold in the vehicles until we can identify the correct wing."

"That it?" Slapshot asked, pointing to the roofline of the four-story hospital through a series of trees in full bloom, fronting thirty- to forty-foot Italian poplars.

"Yes," Olga said. "Turn right up ahead, past the Jaguar billboard."

Kolt rubbed his AKMS, mentally rehearsing the steps to clear a malfunction and how to drop a magazine. He'd prefer his trusted HK416, but the cover demanded the Russian rifle.

"Thirty seconds."

Kolt took in the industrial city's high-rise apartment

buildings, most easily twenty stories high. Looking back at street level, he was surprised by the colorful buildings. Even more jarring were the modern billboards advertising high-end foreign automobiles or pints of expensive vodka, mounted above abandoned sandbagged positions with coiled razor wire stretched about. The scene reminded him of one of those zombie movies. Empty bright green and yellow mini-buses sat idle, hiding a few of the shops that lined both sides of the street. The scene told any visitor that on normal days, when people weren't in the middle of a nationalist struggle, these streets were popular with the residents of Donetsk.

"Nothing like Sarajevo," Kolt said. "Hard to believe there is a war going on here."

"It's crowded, boss," Slapshot said, as he pulled the truck into the hospital's back parking lot.

Kolt looked around, rolled his window up quickly, and tried to look like he belonged there. He didn't need to count the bodies, intuitively knowing they were looking at three, maybe four dozen separatists standing around in the parking lot in small groups.

"Probably smart for the locals to stay home today after all," Kolt said.

Dressed in a mix of civilian clothes with random camouflage, some pulled hard on cigarettes, expertly sending mini smoke signals into the atmosphere. Behind them, their weapons were stacked muzzle up, five to six to a group. Some AK-47s were leaning up against the redbrick building under the first-floor windows. Several of the fighters had turned to eyeball the Russian truck as soon as it had pulled into the parking lot.

"Looks like the boys will stand out around here," Slapshot said. "We should be good."

Slapshot hugged the curb and slowed to a stop.

"The door!" Olga said.

Kolt spotted the movement too, confirming at least two thugs just inside the front entrance.

"Stay cool," Kolt said. "Remember, we are supposed to be here. Act the part."

"Yes," Olga said. "I'm okay."

Kolt stepped down from the passenger seat and slung his rifle as if he were on a mission from Putin himself. He helped Olga down from the cab, immediately wondering if overt politeness was smart, and handed her her rifle. Kolt turned and spit on the ground, hoping that would counter any perceived weakness on his part.

Kolt keyed his mike. "Foxtrot at this time."

"Lead the way," Kolt said without looking at Olga, realizing he truly was making it up as they went.

Kolt heard Digger drop from the back of the truck, the racket telling him his master breacher wasn't as worried about noise as he had been back at the truck headlight standoff with the three Spetsnaz troops. No, Kolt knew Digger knew the deal. Live the cover, until living might be fleeting.

The three of them headed for the front door.

"No gunshots," Kolt said, "until we have to."

Close on Olga's heels, Kolt and Digger followed her through the wooden-framed right-side glass door and stepped into the hospital foyer. Instantly, Kolt picked up the telltale aromas of antiseptic and lemon-scented floor cleaner and immediately assessed the purchase his boots had on the slippery tiled floor. Memories of his long stay in the hospital after Yellow Creek began to surface, but he quickly pushed them down.

A large, middle-aged man shaped like a half-full lister bag, in high-water polyester pants and woodland-pattern camouflage of greens, browns, and blacks, strode up to Olga and slammed his palm into her chest. Olga didn't hesitate, grabbing the thug's hand and wrist. She tried to free his hand from her chest, exchanging desperate words in her native tongue.

Kolt looked at Digger just as his peripheral vision caught a second thug moving from behind a check-in counter. Digger's eyes grew wide, telling Kolt that what he was hearing translated into major problems.

Kolt nodded, silently signaling to Digger that he had execute authority.

Digger lifted his rifle and delivered a savage muzzle tap to the shiny forehead of one of the separatists, dropping him like a rag doll in camo to the vinyl-squared floor.

Kolt pulled his blade from his belt sheath with his right hand, circled like a cat, and grabbed a handful of the pear-shaped man's left shoulder. He spun him counterclockwise, until they were chest to chest, maintaining his grip control. Kolt took in the man's cigarette breath and noticed his right hand had moved from Olga's chest to her throat.

Kolt shoved the knife into the man's upper stomach at a forty-five-degree angle. He felt the knifepoint pierce the empty space in the traitor's lungs, watched his eyes squint shut and his mouth curl in shock. Kolt jammed the knife upward, until the hilt slammed into the man's lower rib, feeling the slight but soft resistance of the right ventricle as the cold steel punctured the heart.

Kolt looked at Olga, still holding on to the thug's right wrist, and watched her calmly let him drop to the tile floor.

"Drag them behind the counter," Kolt said.

"I don't need protection," Olga said as Kolt and Digger began dragging the two bodies across the floor. "These are my countrymen."

What the hell?

Coming from behind the counter, Kolt wanted to ignore

the comment, figuring he didn't need an argument at the moment, but he couldn't. Hearing Olga's obvious sympathy for the separatists startled him, forcing him to realize that maybe they didn't share the same enemy on her native soil. And worse, to wonder if she was now a liability.

"Anti-Ukrainian government fighters," Kolt said. "They'd treat you no different than the Russian troops."

"Some of their concerns are legitimate," Olga said. "Some might even be blood."

"We don't have time to debate this," Kolt said. "You should have told me. I can't promise we won't have to kill others. You can go back to the truck, but we really need your help."

"This isn't America's war," Olga said.

"Not looking to make it ours. We're here for one thing only—Marzban and the Iranian scientists."

"These aren't Russian soldiers," Olga said, "they are different."

Kolt looked at Digger, who was pulling long security deeper into the hospital.

"Shhhhhh," Olga said, "the stairs."

Kolt hadn't heard anything. He looked toward the back of the building, at first not seeing any stairs, as they were hidden. He could see the double back doors, each with a square-foot glass window, head high, that certainly provided a view into the back parking lot where the idle separatists were.

"What stair—"

Kolt stopped mid-question and froze, subconsciously raising his right hand as if to hold Digger from moving closer. He saw Olga's concern as two camouflage-laden separatists appeared from the back right corner, short-jumped onto the floor, then busted the crash bars on both back doors, continuing outside and allowing the spring-loaded doors to shut behind them.

"Upper floor!" Kolt said.

"Three floors, boss, which one?" Digger asked.

"Second floor!" Kolt said, figuring it was as good a place to start as any, and it gave them options.

"Olga?" Kolt said, offering a hand, motioning her to lead the way.

On Olga's ass for the move to the stairs near the back doors, Kolt updated the rest of the squadron. "We're moving to second floor, red side. Three rooms with curtains closed."

"Roger. We have eyes on the windows now," Golf One said. Kolt knew Golf team was postured in the parking lot on the north side of the target, and was pleased they were overwatching the same room windows.

Kolt took the bottom steps two at a time, heading for the first landing, and heard his radio squawk.

"You on to something?" Slapshot asked over the assault net.

"Nothing yet. Working a hunch."

"Don't get overextended, boss," Slapshot said. "Plenty of help out here."

"Roger," Kolt said. "If we confirm target location we'll need to flood all sides minus the black side. Parking lot party out there."

"Standing by," Slapshot said.

Kolt heard Russian voices and looked up the stairs, both Olga and Digger now in the lead, and saw two separatists quickly turn the corner. The first thug, his AK slung over his right shoulder, bumped into Olga accidentally, a few steps below the upper landing.

Olga fell back into the white guardrail, bounced off, but before she fell Digger bear-hugged her. The lead separatist stopped for a second, appeared to apologize, then continued down the stairs and past Kolt.

Both separatists descended to the bottom of the stairs

and the sound of people crashing out of the back doors could be heard again.

Kolt looked at Olga, who had dropped to her rear end, sitting on the stairs. Her eyes were distant, her hands on the top of her head holding her blue denim conductor's hat tight to her tied-up hair.

"Thank you," Olga said.

"Later," Kolt said, moving up and grabbing her under the left armpit. "We gotta move."

"They said they were about to leave," Digger said. "I couldn't get the rest of it."

Olga nodded, agreeing with Digger's understanding of what the two men had said before they had startled them at the top of the stairs.

"Follow me." Kolt took two steps to clear the stairwell and gain the tiled second floor.

The hallway was empty, save for a lone gurney halfway down. Kolt found the first open doorway on the left and took it, rifle raised to high ready, clearing his corner before collapsing to his secondary sector of fire by sweeping his rifle back across the room until he met Digger, now posted up in the opposite corner.

"This is Golf One. Two trucks just departed to the east. Full of troops."

Kolt eyed the internal door on the far corner, assumed it was a bathroom, and moved to it. He reached for the doorknob, slowly turned it to ensure it was unlocked, nodded to Digger, and pulled it open. Digger picked up as number-one man and flowed past Kolt, who followed, clearing in the opposite direction.

"Open door," Kolt said just loud enough for Digger to hear, "hallway."

Just then a group of men, cammie over civvies, blew by the doorway heading for the stairs Kolt's team had just come from. Two stretchers passed, a litter bearer on each side, hauling two patients still dressed in civilian clothes and half covered by white bedsheets.

Kolt turned to Olga. "Those men on the stretchers, locals?" Kolt asked.

"I can't be sure," Olga said.

"Digger, take the door."

Kolt moved to the window, pried open the gray curtain, and peeked out. He waited for a few seconds, scanning the deck where the ambulances were parked and the separatists had been lounging around, pulling on lung darts.

"They're armed up," Kolt said. "Maybe a dozen left."

"Gotta be him, boss," Digger said.

Movement on the back stairs outside caught Kolt's eye. The stretcher bearers were carrying two men, which he was now certain of. Their skin color was definitely darker than the Ukrainians', they both had jet-black hair, and one was wearing wire-rimmed glasses.

"I agree," Kolt said, quickly referencing his GTG before reaching for his hand mike.

"This is Noble Zero-One, target PID black side." Kolt watched the group move toward the open back doors of one of the blue-and-white ambulances. They stopped, slowly slid both litters into the back, and closed the door.

"All elements, three ambulances," Kolt said. "Marzban is inside middle ambulance. Lock them down with total isolation. Weapons tight."

The acknowledgments coming over the radio from his men bumper-upped in the vehicles outside barely registered as Kolt turned back to Digger.

"Moving directly to the three rooms," Kolt said. "No time to clear all of them."

"Rog."

Kolt led the way into the hallway, moving in a careful

hurry, not an uncontrolled sprint where he might throw a shot. With both eyes open, Kolt looked just over the Soviet-made rifle's iron sights at three closed hospital room doors. He felt Digger on his right rear, covering the right side of the hallway as they pushed.

"Center door," Kolt said, pausing for Digger to pass him to check the lock.

Digger slowly turned the knob, shook his head left to right, signaling no breach, and rotated his back to the door. Kolt kept his rifle trained on the door, but quickly looked left and right at the other two doors, ensuring they wouldn't be caught flatfooted.

Digger lined up his titanium lower leg, raised it horizontal to the white tile floor, and delivered a powerful mule kick just below and to the left of the doorknob. The door flew open with a sharp crack. Digger hopped out of the way, wincing as he did so. Kolt could check to see if he was injured later. He charged past him and into the room.

THIRTEEN

Kolt cleared the right corner quickly, pushing his focus beyond a wooden chair and small desk. Then, in the mirror on the wall, he saw a figure's reflection from the opposite side of the room. Kolt spun, set his trigger finger, and pulled a pound before his mind arrested his actions.

"Get down!" Kolt said, feeling Digger roll in the room and catching Olga in his peripheral as she stopped in the fatal funnel of the doorway.

Two people stood locked together a few feet away; only a bloodstained hospital bed stood between them. The first was a skinny man, dressed in a white button-down shirt over dark, wrinkled slacks and soiled shoes, a look of genuine fear in his eyes, his body language signaling he had accepted his fate. Holding him from behind was a larger woman.

Assuming she was Marzban's old lady, Kolt was impressed with the Iranian terrorist's taste, but only from the neck up. She was fairly attractive, dirty-blond hair just hitting her neckline, but that's where it ended.

Kolt immediately knew her look was all business, having seen the same in many others who had made a stand against a Delta operator. Her hips were super-size in the area most heavyset women despise, both sides bookending the narrow man she held with a strong arm over his bony chest. Her other hand, wearing a thin black glove, held the muzzle end of what looked like an antique Makarov 9mm to the frightened man's forehead.

Olga spoke first but her words were met with a vicious retort as the woman only tightened her hold on the man, shook the Makarov, and inched closer to the drawn curtains, keeping the bed between her and the strangers.

"Boss," Digger said, not loud enough to interrupt Olga's verbal interrogation. "Look familiar?"

With his rifle still at the high ready, aimed at the tethered man and woman, Kolt took his eyes off the target for a moment, turned his left forearm slightly, and looked down at the GTG. He knew he didn't have a passport photo of Marzban's girlfriend taped to the satellite photo of the hospital, but he had mug shots of Marzban and the Iranian scientists.

"Olga?" Kolt asked.

"She is not from here!"

Kolt raised his Soviet AKMS rifle an inch or so, placing the front iron sights on the Iranian's pointy Adam's apple, and fired one round. The copper bullet tore into the man's neck, locking his eyes open, likely severing his larynx and vertebrae, before blowing a massive exit wound out the back. The bullet, having lost some energy but still deadly at less than twelve feet, entered the woman's right clavicle, forcing her to release her hold.

The scientist collapsed in a heap, his body weight dragging the woman to the floor with him. The Makarov, still connected to her black-gloved trigger finger, flopped harmlessly to the floor.

Kolt stepped around the hospital bed, intent on safing the Makarov, and failed to notice the open bathroom door. Another man, holding a surgical scalpel, lunged toward Kolt. The razor-sharp blade found Kolt's right forearm, piercing his Spetsnaz sleeve and the bandage over Roscoe's underwater bite, and penetrating deep into the bone.

Kolt stumbled, tried to turn his rifle to the threat, and tripped over Olga and the scientist. As he fell, a radio transmission from Slapshot boomed through his earbud. The assailant jumped on Kolt's side, and frantically beat him over the head with a barrage of flailing but effective hammer fists.

Kolt reached up and circled his arms around the man's upper body, bringing him close before rolling him over to his back and taking the mount. Kolt held the man's right arm down against the floor, his elbow at a perfect ninety degrees from his body. With his right hand, Kolt pinned the man's right wrist, then slipped his left hand under the man's right triceps, fishing it forward until Kolt found his own wrist. Kolt locked it in and rotated his hips forward, applying a form-perfect jujitsu paintbrush. Applying upward pressure, Kolt torqued the man's elbow and bent it in a way God never intended.

Kolt held the lock as the man screamed, trying to squirm out of the hold. A second later, Kolt felt and heard the man's shoulder dislocate and the radius bone in his forearm snap. Kolt released the grip, began to push away, and saw Digger's muzzle placed on the screaming man's head.

"NO!" Olga yelled.

"Hold up, Digger," Kolt said, slowly pushing the rifle muzzle away.

Kolt stood, looked down at the damage, and adjusted his sling to realign his rifle. Next to the scalpel-wielding man, the skinny scientist was clearly dead, maroon blood already pooling underneath him. Marzban's girlfriend was on her thick back but still alive, her softball-shaped breasts rising and falling rapidly. Kolt noticed her hazel eyes locked on the ceiling, her dark eyelids flapping like Morse code, fighting her body's natural descent into shock.

Another transmission from Slapshot captured Kolt's attention, this time sounding concerned. "Gunshots; you good up there?"

"Roger, hold tight," Kolt said. "One scientist KIA, girlfriend critical. What do you have out there? Any sign of Marzban?"

Kolt stepped toward Digger as he waited for Slapshot's sitrep. He raised his right forearm, eyed the silver scalpel sticking out three or four inches, and motioned to Digger to yank it out.

"Serious?" Digger asked.

"Do it!" Kolt said, grabbing a handful of the bedsheet, balling up one corner, and placing it in his mouth. He laid his arm on the small desk and took a knee, looking away from the wound.

Digger stepped forward, gripped the scalpel fully, and held the arm down with his other hand. Kolt noticed Olga had moved to the man with the broken arm, kneeling next to him as if she was offering comfort.

"Son of a bitch!" Kolt yelled, his voice muffled by the bedsheet.

Kolt stood, took the instrument from Digger, and walked to Olga. He bent over, placed the blood-covered blade in front of the Ukrainian man's open eyes, and looked at Olga.

"You do it," Kolt said, "or I will."

"No. He is innocent."

"Ask him where Marzban is."

"He doesn't know," Olga said, her eyes pleading with Kolt to leave the man be.

"Ask."

Olga looked at Kolt as if she was about to make a decision on who the real enemy was, Kolt or the Ukrainian national with the broken arm.

"Last time," Kolt said. "Ask him."

Olga stood, took the scalpel from Kolt, and quickly turned back to the man lying on his back. She delivered the toe of her boot to the man's ribs as if she were taking a World Cup penalty shot. She slammed her right knee down onto the man's chest, waved the blade in front of his eyes, and machine-gunned two dozen harsh words.

The man shook his head, panted heavily, visibly challenged to get out a verbal reply.

"He ain't talking, boss," Digger said.

Olga placed the scalpel on his neck, letting him feel the seriousness, and then reached over to the dead scientist lying in his own blood. She slammed the scalpel down into the man's chest, looked back at her problem as if she wanted to confirm he noticed, and pulled it up and out. She spoke again, from what Kolt could tell, obviously losing patience with the man's resistance.

"Do it," Kolt said,

The man shook his head violently side to side a few times, before finally speaking.

"He said ambulance, boss," Digger said, understanding at least one of the Russian words.

Kolt reached down, grabbing Olga under the arm again, and lifted her to her feet.

"Let's go!"

"What about them?" Digger asked.

Kolt looked at Olga, then back at Digger. He knew the girl would bleed out, figuring she wouldn't get much medical attention now, not any that could save her. As for the other guy, he held a different status than the scientist. Killing the scientist and the girlfriend was the mission. Killing the scalpel-wielding Ukrainian was illegal as shit. If Kolt wanted the man dead he should have choked him out versus sticking him with the paintbrush.

Kolt also knew killing the Ukrainian in cold blood would certainly turn Olga against them. Yes, Kolt knew, if he valued Olga's indigenous skills, it just might be worth letting the man live, to preserve that.

"Leave them," Kolt said. "We're heading for the ambulances."

Olga and Digger led the way, Kolt a few feet behind. They blew by the dozen rooms on either side of the hallway and passed the empty gurney without seeing any sign of other humans. Kolt watched Digger corner-clear the stairwell, then hit the stairs.

Now at the back door on the ground floor, Kolt stopped to peek out the door's window, hoping to get a visual on the situation. He strained his neck to look both left, then right, hoping to see his operators posted nearby. Nothing.

"Damn," Digger said, looking out the other window. "Can you believe that?"

Kolt turned his head, moving his focus toward the ambulances, all three still parked side by side. A row of knee-high bushes partially blocked his view, but the vehicles hadn't moved an inch from where he saw the two stretchers loaded earlier.

Kolt keyed his hand mike. "Whatya got, Slapshot?"

"Count fifteen on the deck," Slapshot said, "all face-down."

"Dead?" Kolt asked, confused by Slapshot's last.

"Behind the bushes, boss," Digger said.

Kolt looked closer, focusing between the main shafts of the bushes, and realized there were bodies lying in the parking lot.

"I didn't hear anything," Kolt said, "did you?"

Kolt knew his men were running with suppressors, and that from inside on the second floor they wouldn't hear anything. But, earlier, he was sure he had seen at least a dozen separatists from the second-floor window. He hadn't counted them at the time, but that many bad guys usually drew a basic load of fragmentary grenades.

"Mexican stand-off at the moment," Slapshot said from somewhere outside. "What's your status?"

Kolt keyed his push-to-talk. "We're up. At the blackside double doors."

"Nothing's moving out here," Slapshot said.

Kolt thought it over, somewhat relieved that his men hadn't smoked the Ukrainians outside. They were just in the way, not the mission, and being a nuisance didn't come close to the threshold for declaring them a hostile threat. Not when they were lying on the ground. But Kolt knew they didn't need any prisoners besides Marzban Tehrani.

"All elements, this is Noble Zero-One. We're about to execute a call-out. Olga is leading out the back door."

Kolt heard Slapshot acknowledge first, then heard Dealer break into the net.

"Be advised, the white side is unsecure. Watch your own six."

Immediately, Kolt and Digger turned around and looked back toward the front doors and the counter where they had stashed the two separatists upon entering the foyer. Hearing Dealer's warning, a situation they both knew was prompted by Kolt's total isolation call on the ambulances out back, pegged Kolt's spider senses, making him realize they had been careless with their security.

"Listen to me, Olga. We need you to walk out there and tell them we are here to take custody of the two men in the ambulance. Understand?"

"Digger, Russian lingo from here on out," Kolt said.

"Rog," Digger said.

"On what authority?" Olga asked, questioning Kolt's order.

"Motherfucking Stalin's authority!" Digger said.

Kolt turned to Digger and gave him the chill-out look before looking back at Olga.

"Look, we don't want any more bloodshed here," Kolt said, hoping to reason with her. "Whoever's authority you think will work will do. Maybe Vladimir Putin."

"They don't resist Kiev because of Putin," Olga said. "They think he is the devil."

"Pick someone," Kolt said. "Make it up for all I care. The others could return any moment now."

"Sergei Kadyrov," Olga said.

"Fine!" Digger said. "Let's go."

"He is known as the Chechen caretaker," Olga said. "All in Ukraine fear him."

"Perfect!" Kolt said. "We are right behind you. Keep them scared shitless, and Digger and I will go for the ambulance."

Olga took a deep breath, reached up with her dirty hands and straightened her hat, then pushed a few fallen locks back up under the brim with her straight fingers.

"Moving!" Kolt transmitted.

Digger broke the door, letting Olga lead the way, and he followed her outside. Kolt made one last check of their six o'clock, Dealer's warning still fresh in his mind.

Satisfied they were clear, Kolt caught up and passed Olga, barely letting her begin the ruse. Knowing their target was finally within grasp, he resisted the urge to run to the back of the ambulance, and the desire to raise his rifle tactically. He knew they were vulnerable, but for the plan to work, to accomplish the mission and limit the bloodshed of anti-Ukrainian government forces, he needed to trust the Spetsnaz uniforms and Olga's acting skills.

Not knowing what waited for them inside the back

of the ambulance, Kolt stepped to the side of the door, grabbed the handle, and looked back at Digger. Kolt yanked it open, stepping out of the line of fire, and waited for his master breacher to engage or not.

"Clear!"

"Cover me," Kolt said as he rotated the AKMS to his back and jumped into the cabin of the ambulance.

Kolt slid on his knees, closing the distance with the two men still lying on stretchers. He slipped in between them and studied both of their faces for a few seconds. The one on the right was easily recognizable. Even with his eyes closed Kolt was sure, without having to refer to the mug shots again. It was the second scientist.

Kolt placed two fingers on the scientist's neck and held them there for a few seconds, hoping to find a pulse. The skin beneath Kolt's fingertips was cold and clammy, and there was no pulse. Kolt delivered a quick eye thump to test for responsiveness. Nothing.

Fuck.

Kolt turned to the second stretcher, the one he hoped held their primary target. He looked at him closely, could see he was still alive, but couldn't be positive it was Marzban. Kolt yanked the white bedsheet off the man's upper torso, pulling it back to reveal his chest and stomach, and looked for the gut wound that Trip had reported back at the safe house. The man's dark brown shirt was soiled, making it hard to tell.

Kolt grabbed the bottom of the shirt with one hand and pressed down with a balled fist into the man's belly. The man jerked, spitting up blood that ran down the left side of his face.

Kolt reached for his hand mike. "I need a medic, Kevlar vest, and helmet, ASAP."

Within a few seconds Kolt heard his men outside the ambulance behind him. He turned, saw them flex-tying the prone Ukrainians, and yelled to Olga.

She looked at Kolt, and responded to his wave for help. He leaned over to help her climb in the ambulance.

"I need you to positively identify this guy. The other one is dead."

Olga scooted closer, looked hard at the dark-skinned man, who was returning the stare under labored breathing.

"Yes," Olga said. "It is him."

"Him, who?" Kolt asked, needing to hear her identify the man.

"It is Marzban."

"Are you positive?" Kolt asked, turning away from Olga and looking back at the man on the stretcher.

Before Olga could answer, three rapid-fire shots rang out. The distinct sound told Kolt they were from a pistol, and he ducked out of habit, scrambling to lower his silhouette. He turned, looking over Olga's body, as she was down too. Outside, he picked up the larger-than-life image of Marzban's girlfriend, the thick-hipped woman they'd left barely breathing in her own blood back in the hospital room.

Kolt saw the barrel end of the Makarov, the pistol still up in front of her face with the slide locked to the rear, just an inch below her dark eyes. She was a mess, but seemingly oblivious that she had run the pistol dry, still acquiring a sight picture.

Kolt immediately second-guessed his decision to leave her to die in peace. He'd followed the law of land warfare and their combat rules of engagement to the letter by not executing her, and now it had come back to bite him in the ass. Before he could reflect more on his decision, the side of her head exploded, blowing brain matter and the distinct dark mist of blood into the air.

Two of Kolt's men quickly closed on the threat, one

of them pumping two more 5.56 mm suppressed rounds into her chest at close range.

Kolt looked around the interior of the ambulance, surveying the immediate area, unsure of where the three bullets had impacted.

"Olga!"

Kolt grabbed her by the shoulders and turned her over, her train conductor's hat falling off her head, her brown hair dropping past her shoulders.

"Shit!"

Kolt held the back of her head, immediately feeling the warmth of blood as it seeped through his fingers. He laid her head down gently, knowing there was nothing to be done. In that moment, the fact that she was a woman didn't even register. Olga had been a fierce warrior, and that's what he would remember.

Kolt turned to Marzban, noticed more blood coming from the side of his mouth. His eyes were closed. Kolt shook him several times.

Don't die, you son of a bitch. Olga's death and those of the operators before her weren't going to be in vain.

Kolt heard a familiar voice. It was one of his medics. "Whatya got, boss?"

"Don't know."

Kolt ripped the bedsheet completely off Marzban, throwing it to the side of the ambulance, out of his way. There, plain as day, fresh blood was covering Marzban's groin and upper left leg and Kolt realized that either of the Makarov's bullets could have had his name on them. Kolt found the tear in the trousers and ripped it open to expose the wound.

"He's hit!"

Kolt jumped on Marzban and tilted his head back to open his airway. Blood gushed from his now-open mouth. Kolt didn't bother to check for a pulse, going immediately to rescue breathing, squeezing his nose with two fingers and connecting his lips to Marzban's.

Two quick breaths and Kolt went to the chest, placing the heel of his right hand on the breastbone, covering it with his left hand. Kolt leaned over Marzban and pressed hard downward, depressing his sternum several inches. Kolt repeated the thrusts, counting out loud with each depression. Blood bubbled from Marzban's mouth with each thrust.

Kolt felt his medic climb into the ambulance, crawling around him to Marzban's exposed neck, and check his pulse.

Kolt hit a count of thirty, moved back to Marzban's head, and administered two more rescue breaths.

"He's gone, boss."

Kolt barely heard his medic. He had to save this miserable fuck of a terrorist. Killing Marzban was not the mission. The United States wanted Marzban captured. He was tapped as an intelligence bonanza—with a little luck, ripe for enhanced interrogation techniques—and was the only link to the North Korean miniature nuke warheads. Killing Marzban equated to mission failure.

Kolt rose up over Marzban's chest again, rapidly depressing the man's sternum deeper and deeper, hoping to jump-start the man's heart.

"Boss!" the medic said. "No pulse. He's dead."

Kolt ignored him, continuing to press.

"C'mon, damn it," Kolt said, "don't you fucking die on me."

"He's lost too much blood," the medic said.

"Damn it! Help me!" Kolt said, picking his count back up at twenty-two.

Then, before he could give another chest thrust, Kolt felt a massive bear hug squeezing both of his arms tight to his sides.

"Racer!" Slapshot said. "It's okay, man. Let him go."

Kolt's heart pounded. He couldn't break his stare from Marzban's slack, lifeless face.

"Gotta have him alive, Slap."

"Allah's hands now."

"He's too important," Kolt said. "We need this guy."

"More important than Max or Philly?" Slapshot said, letting go of Kolt. "Fuck this asshole."

That snapped Kolt out of it. He looked at his squadron sergeant major. He knew Slap was right. Marzban had valuable intel. They'd been after him a long time, and not bagging him alive meant they would be at a dead end on the mini nukes and back to the drawing board. But when it came right down to it, Kolt could live with this outcome, especially because it meant his men would, too. Kolt would rather Marzban take his martyrdom trip here while the squadron lived to hunt another day.

Fuck him. Kill 'em all and let Allah sort them out. Kolt smiled at his very politically incorrect thought.

"We ready to exfil?" Kolt asked.

"All flex-cuffed, and vehicles standing by," Slapshot said.

"Get a few proof-of-death pics of Marzban and let's roll."

FOURTEEN

Startled awake by the sound of bells ringing, Cindy "Hawk" Bird sat up in her sleeper cabin on the train. Bundled in tension and confused, she rotated on her panty-covered rear end, steadied her hands on the side of the bed to save a tumble, and placed her feet on the floor. Puzzled as to why she had only one sock on, she scanned the tiny room but found nothing amiss. She rubbed her wrecked eyes and shook her head.

Where is my sports bra?

Hawk stood, caught a trace of her own body odor, and paused to balance the nausea in her stomach. She felt K27/K28's cold passenger cabin floor beneath one foot, and wiped her neck-length auburn hair out of her eyes. The ringing seemed to be getting louder. She reached for the water bottle on the small table and slipped the nozzle under her nose to be sure it was plain water, and not full of the dog that bit her, before taking a long pull.

Hawk felt the train slowing, recapped the bottle, and dragged herself to the dingy red curtains hiding the filthy windows. She pulled one curtain aside, rubbed a balled fist on the glass, peered through the clean spot, and tried to focus on the buildings buzzing by. Yes, they were stopping, all right, and dusk was falling, barely offering an opportunity to make out the blurry signage on the drab gray and whitewashed buildings. It was enough, though, to confirm that they were now somewhere in China.

Where the hell are we? How long have I been asleep?

A series of buildings and the glimpse of a river jarred a memory. This had to be Harbin, a city of seven million inhabitants straddling the Songhua River. Her cramming of Asian geography didn't let her down. Once a small rural settlement, its name literally meaning "a place for drying fishing nets," Harbin embraced the major technological advances in the twentieth century and had been launched from backwater to one of the largest cities in Northeast China.

Feeling every bit like a rotting crab net, Hawk looked at her watch, fumbled with some basic math, and realized she had slept for the last eight hours. That meant she'd slept through their previous scheduled stop at Shenyang, the railway hub of Northeast China.

Hawk turned too quickly from the window to head back to the bed. The room spun and she held her hands out to her sides like a child pretending to fly. She tried to shake the cobwebs, get the blood flowing, and stimulate her short-term memory about what led her to be unfit for duty.

That bastard Jerud! The bimbos taking pictures! The arm lock!

Hawk sat back down, rat-fucked the covers to find her other sock, and felt something hard on her butt cheek. She reached down, touched her iPad, and rescued it from her unpredictable state.

Hawk opened the tablet and began cycling through her mental Rolodex, sensing her memory wasn't going to be entirely cooperative. Vaguely remembering bits and pieces, she knew she wasn't going to get the whole story.

Hawk mashed the power button and stared at the iPad screen as it came to life. She sort of remembered bowing up to eye candy Jerud, was pretty sure she remembered being dragged back to her room by uniformed customs officials, and thought she remembered banging out the sitrep over the secure e-mail link to Fort Bragg before getting horizontal. But, she was pretty darn certain, unless it was part of an alcohol-induced nightmare, that her antics on the hard floor of the restaurant car had been captured. Her photo had probably been snapped more than once, which scared the attitude and hangover right out of her.

She knew that if the college bimbos had already posted images of her slippery arm lock all over Instagram and Twitter, maybe even uploaded a short video to YouTube, Delta Force commander Colonel Webber might have seen it by now. The Unit intel analysts that troll the Web twenty-four/seven while operators, or in Hawk's case, wannabe operators, were overseas under alias, didn't miss shit. And if Webber had seen it, he'd do more than just shit, for sure; he'd detonate. Moreover, this would likely doom the pilot program and kill her chances at the Commander's Board. Webber would have no choice, no matter what he felt personally; the voice of the naysaying graybeards would certainly rule the decision.

Truth be told, Hawk couldn't deny that she was the one that had brought up the big idea of playing a friendly drinking game. It had been a long, whirlwind Whistlestop so far, beginning back in Raleigh, North Carolina, with CONUS stops in Atlanta, Houston, Denver, and Los Angeles, where her skill sets were tested with a boatload of dead drops, personal meetings, covert comms, and brush passes. Over the past two weeks, planes, trains, and automobiles had taken her from the States, through South Africa, Istanbul, Croatia, and Moscow, before her last stop in North Korea. So far, she had knocked it out of the park.

But she also knew letting her hair down around the tourist bar after finishing her final mission in North Korea might have killed her chances at gaining operational status.

Fuck!

As Hawk swiped and tapped, drilling down to the secure e-mail link, she tried not to stare at the desktop picture. A picture only a few weeks old, Photoshopped by the cover shop to help cement her status as a young high school teacher interested in European and Far East culture, with a personal penchant for foreign languages. Hawk had been proud of the cover photo and pleased to use it, but now, after her exceptionally poor judgment, she was ashamed at the sight of her standing proud among a group of unknown teenagers at work in her own classroom.

What have I done?

Hawk knew she was Delta Force's experimental flower child to answer the president's top-secret tasking of exploring the pros and cons of opening up operational positions to females within the special operations community. Webber and her father, former Delta squadron commander Michael Leland Bird, had been close mates before he was killed in action in Baghdad. She knew very well that Colonel Webber had gone to bat for her numerous times over her two years in the Unit, and she cringed at the idea of letting both of them down. Granted, Hawk hadn't created one-tenth the problems for Webber as Major Kolt Raynor had over the years, but give her time.

Aw shit!

Hawk felt her stomach tighten as she opened the Send folder, subconsciously holding her breath, hoping like hell to confirm she had indeed pushed the sitrep to Bragg before she'd passed out.

Thank God!

It was there all right, and she slumped forward, quickly opening her sent message. Hawk quickly read the report, noticed a few typos, a grammar issue or two, but was satisfied that she had pecked slowly enough to get the key information out. It was all there, most importantly the unique discovery of details pertaining to Kim Jong Un's private armored trains and the claims of stealth netting the shoeshine man had bragged about.

Hawk read it a second time, slower, and closed it out. She noticed her Inbox folder highlighted, telling her she had an unread message.

That's odd.

She wasn't expecting a message from anyone. Even though the link was secure, part of Whistle-stop was the ability to remember your taskings and itinerary before you left Bragg to begin the solo journey. Whistle-stop was a final culmination of sorts, the last test before attending the Commander's Board, where her fate as an operational member within the command would be decided, one way or the other.

Hawk tapped the Inbox folder and saw the top unopened message. She didn't recognize the sender, but figured it was just some innocuous coverspeak. It had to be from Bragg, that much she was certain of. She paused, seeing the subject line blank, but only for a few seconds before she tapped it open. She swiped the touch screen with two fingers, enlarging the message, and was surprised again to see the body of the message empty. She swiped her fingers again, this time closing her fingers to reduce the screen, simply to ensure she hadn't missed anything. She searched, befuddled as she found nothing, but noticed a file attached.

Hawk opened the attachment, studied it for a few seconds. It was obviously an itinerary of some type for her—she saw "Carrie Tomlinson" in bold letters in the upper left corner. She was expecting another five days or so on the K27/K28 before catching a plane out of Moscow and heading back to Bragg.

Maybe I'm finished. Is Whistle-stop over? Is this my itinerary to fly home?

She read it quickly, running her right forefinger from left to right, ensuring she didn't skip a line, given her present state of mind.

She read it once, stopped, then said it out loud, unsure of what she was actually reading.

"Depart Harbin International at zero eight thirty, layovers in Beijing and Amsterdam, arrive Stockholm at twenty thirty."

What the hell is in Sweden?

Pine Gap, Australia

"Mr. Menendez, we have a secure connection confirmed from our end," Stephan Canary said, leaning toward the video teleconference microphone resting in the center of the conference table. "How do you have us?"

"This is Menendez, I have you secure voice on this end. No video yet."

"We'll look into that," Canary said, waving to the audio technician to troubleshoot appropriately to allow Carlos Menendez II to view the attendees inside the Pine Gap soundproof conference room from his secure location at Tungsten headquarters in Atlanta, Georgia. "Give us a few minutes to work on it, please. Our director is still stateside but Vice Director Fontaine is in here with—"

"Nonsense!" Vice Director Fontaine barked. "We can see you fine, Mr. Menendez, we don't have time to wait around."

Canary looked at Fontaine, and then up at Menendez on the screen high on the wall. Canary, the forty-two-year-old career analyst, aware he was wearing a perpetually greasy and shiny forehead, and knowing his early gray hair was longer than anyone cared to look at around the office, grew increasingly tense. He knew the time difference between Australia and Atlanta meant that Carlos Menendez had been most certainly woken up in the wee hours of the morning and asked to come in to take this top-secret secure call that Fontaine forced him to arrange. And now, as Canary watched Mr. Menendez's reaction to Vice Director Fontaine's annoying and crass comment, he was happy that his embarrassment couldn't be seen just yet by the man they believed held the answers they were looking for.

"By all means," Carlos said, obviously signaling he would play well with others and maintain his professionalism. "I'm a morning person anyway."

"Well I'm not," Fontaine said. "Where exactly are you in Atlanta?"

"A secure facility," Menendez said. "It's fine, I'm alone."

"You wear a tux when you sleep?" Fontaine asked, as Menendez's patterned bow tie and coat gave the on-screen impression that Carlos Menendez had just come in from the Governor's Ball.

"It's off the rack," Menendez said. "Was just about to drop it off at the Goodwill trailer."

"We need you to get back over here immediately," Fontaine said.

Canary held back a smile, knowing Menendez wasn't

a pushover, and recalling very well that Menendez and Fontaine didn't hit it off the other day. The texture of Seamstress's former CIA case officer's bow tie was certainly in harmony with the texture of the suit fabric. He knew his boss, Fontaine, liked to throw jabs and then duck and cover, getting his rocks off by ignoring his off-balance opponent's response and getting to it, but Canary thought Fontaine might have met his match.

"I have you secure video now," Menendez said as he looked away from the screen for a moment.

"When can we expect you?" Fontaine said. "Tonight? Tomorrow at the latest."

"Impossible," Menendez said in an even tone.

"Impossible?" Fontaine asked, as if he was insulted by the negative response.

"That's what I said."

"This has the highest priority within the administration's senior cabinet."

"Wonderful," Menendez said. "I wish you luck and I guess that ends this VTC."

"Now wait one damn minute here," Fontaine barked. He stood up and walked away from the microphone and toward the screen as if Menendez was standing in front of him. "I demand you clear your schedule and return to Pine Gap."

Canary sat up straight, almost as if he didn't want to be seen by Menendez onscreen for fear of being roped in as part of Fontaine's ass-hattery. Canary was surprised that Fontaine didn't push Menendez on his exact location. That was something. Canary had no idea where Menendez was sitting either, other than the city he was in, but was hopeful that Fontaine wouldn't waste any more time trying to dig it out of Menendez.

"Sir, it sounds as if Mr. Menendez is preoccupied," Canary said, playing it as if he hadn't picked up on the tension in the room. "Maybe we can satisfy our concerns with Mr. Menendez over this VTC. It's too important."

Fontaine ignored Canary's positive slant, his refrigerator-size body remaining locked on the screen as if he was a big schoolyard bully trying to intimidate a smaller kid.

Canary heard Menendez break the ice. "I'm willing to answer your questions. I did drag myself in here on no notice this morning."

Canary looked at Fontaine, who turned to wobble back to his chair. Fontaine huffed like a tired elephant, wiped his nose on the back of his yellow-striped right shirt sleeve, and checked his watch on his left wrist before collapsing back into the soft leather. Canary looked back to the VTC screen, noticing Menendez's dress. A wave of embarrassment rose in Canary as he realized how just about every one of the eight hundred employees around the office these days seemed to stretch the dress code, especially Vice Director Fontaine.

"I'm listening," Menendez said, remaining gentlemanly still as if the screen had frozen.

Canary looked at Fontaine and nodded, silently admitting defeat and letting him know to proceed.

"Mr. Menendez, have you ever known of Kang Pang Su having family ties to the Japanese?"

"None, at least not thirty years ago," Menendez said without hesitation. "Do you guys know different?"

"Well, lately, the Japanese have been holding secret talks with North Korea and China against U.S. wishes. We believe—"

"We'll have to limit what we share with you, Mr. Menendez," Fontaine interrupted. "You understand."

"Yes, sir," Canary said, addressing his boss. "My mistake."

Fontaine didn't reply, just turned his head back to

Menendez, which Canary took as the okay to continue, although cautiously.

"Seamstress must have checked in again," Menendez said.

"Why would you assume that?" Fontaine said.

"The fact that the moon is still up?" Menendez said, not hiding the sarcasm.

Canary jumped in, hesitant to provide too much, but also showing he'd had about enough of Fontaine's micromanaging the video-teleconference. Hell, Canary felt himself allying with Menendez for no other reason than knowing Fontaine had gotten more sleep last night than he and Menendez likely had, combined. He couldn't go full-up insubordinate, not if he wanted to keep his job, and he certainly did. But, he could be a little more creative, as long as he understood when too much was too much.

"Do you believe Kang Pang Su is capable of treason?" Canary asked before catching the pointed stare of Fontaine.

"Every asset has the potential, which is what makes them attractive to a case officer," Menendez said. "Some take longer than others, but simply signing on speaks to a recruited asset's potential and innate desire for change."

"I see," Canary said. "How about weapons of mass destruction? Say, miniature nuclear warheads placed on long-range ballistic missiles? Seamstress capable?"

"North Korea has long believed that having a nuke makes them a player in world affairs, not susceptible to the wastebasket of history," Menendez said, his situational understanding impressing Canary.

Fontaine jumped in. "Is that a yes?"

"Saddam Hussein was ousted because he didn't have nuke capability, regardless of what the world likes to espouse, a lesson the North Koreans learned quickly," Menendez said.

Canary knew Menendez hadn't exactly answered the question, but decided to take an implied *yes* and move on.

"So we are going after Seamstress, I assume," Menendez said.

"The one thing the president took from his top-secret transition of power briefing from the outgoing president was the disappointment of allowing North Korea to obtain the nuclear bomb years ago," Fontaine said, now showing some impressive insight, seemingly giving way to Menendez's assistance as he dodged the question.

"There have been some developments," Canary said.

"Like Marzban Tehrani being taken off the deck?" Menendez said.

Canary and Fontaine locked eyes, both a little startled to hear Tehrani's name.

"We received a third teletypewriter message from Seamstress. Just after you left for your flight the other day," Canary said. "He is visiting Panmunjom with some colleagues to restart nuclear talks. A Swedish delegation will attend, along with the South Koreans, of course."

"Not the ideal place to execute an asset extraction," Menendez said, "but compared to downtown Pyongyang, it's perfect."

"Are you serious?" Fontaine asked.

"No, of course not. That would be suicide."

"Well, we don't have a lot of time to slow-burn contingencies for Satin Ash," Canary said. "Seamstress's last RTTY message puts the date of the conference in just a few days."

"Then I'm sure the Joint Special Operations Command has been alerted," Menendez said. "A high-risk mission like that requires their specific skill sets."

Canary looked at Fontaine, letting him know he was

satisfied with what they had learned from Menendez, and that he was ready to end the VTC.

"Are you familiar with the LIPS program Mr. Canary here is chairing, Mr. Menendez?" Fontaine asked.

"Something to do with all the Skoal cans on his desk?"

Canary broke a smile, impressed Menendez had remembered the half-dozen empty dip cans on his desk.

"Negative," Fontaine said, "LIPS stands for 'locate information pulled by Edward Snowden,' a POTUS-directed crisis management team."

"Oh, I thought it was a play off the small signs hanging just past the main entrance out there," Menendez said. "The ones that say *loose lips sink ships*."

"Consider yourself read on," Fontaine said. "We don't need another Snowden on this one."

Canary watched Menendez stand up, revealing his shiny gold belt buckle and designer trousers, as if he was reaching for something. A moment later the screen went black.

I guess the meeting is over.

FIFTEEN

Standing at the head of the drab thirty-man classroom, Major promotable Kolt Raynor remained poker-faced in his rugged range shorts and tan T-shirt as he looked into the eyes of each of the thirteen operator candidates. Slightly spread out, each sat behind a gray table, outfitted in an unmarked Crye Multicam assault uniform, his new Unit access badge hanging from his neck. These men were more than just fresh meat.

Kolt surveyed the group a little more as Jason, the cadre member in the back, drilled down into the correct folder inside the Unit secure local area network to pull up the aircraft training slides and video. Most of the students had the early stages of relaxed grooming standards already going on, and were probably pushing it a bit based on their candidate status. These thirteen candidates had been the chosen ones, the ones still standing after the long walk and the Commander's Board at the most recent Delta tryouts. Of the 132 that had started assessment and selection at an undisclosed location in the northeast, they were the only ones to have gotten by the intrusive psych interviews, kept the unpublished physical and mental pace over the thirty days in the mountains, and not gotten hit with a DUI while celebrating their new permanent change of station orders to report to Delta Force.

Kolt's efforts today were common practice in the Unit. Guys with certain experiences during combat ops were often asked to speak to the Operator Training Course candidates to invoke a sense of realism and share lessons learned. Unlike in Kolt's OTC class, too many years ago to count now, every member of this class had seen the elephant already, half with valor awards on their official records, several with Purple Hearts.

Kolt slipped his bandaged forearm into his right cargo pocket, yanking out a half-full bag of Red Man. He opened the pouch, shoved two fingers in to tear away a wad of the moist leaf tobacco, and worked it into his right cheek.

He knew his standing there was odd, what with him still nursing battle wounds from the op in the Ukraine. Kolt knew that wasn't lost on any of the alert candidates, as he caught most eyes surveying his bandage. Kolt also knew that the operator candidates had already heard about the three operators from Kolt's squadron that bought it. Word travels fast inside the Spine.

"We might as well get started," Kolt said, his voice barely audible as he tried to seat the tobacco and wipe his fingers on his range shorts. "I'm Kolt Raynor, or known around here by most just as Racer. Don't ask me how I got the code name and I won't ask about yours."

The class was deathly silent, but Kolt noticed a few of them breaking smiles and looking down at the desk as if they were breaking the class rules, worried about the cadre, or something. Kolt stepped over to look down into the trash can, pulling out an empty water bottle, removing the cap, and wiping the nozzle on his shirt.

"You can call me Racer, Kolt, or boss, if you get across the hall into my squadron," Kolt said, fanning back and forth to ensure he had eye contact with the entire class. "We're informal around here, nobody goes by, or answers to, 'sir.' "

Kolt took a long spit into the bottle. "I'll tell you guys one thing: you all look like you wouldn't know what to do with a piece of pussy if they served it up with a Sledgehammer Stout at Huske's Hardware House."

That loosened them a bit. The entire class broke out in laughter, trading looks with each other as if what Kolt was saying was already true about several of them.

"Go ahead and run it, Jason," Kolt said, "someone kill the lights."

Up on the large white screen at the front of the classroom, in simple black bold letters, appeared the long-winded words CLOSE QUARTERS BATTLE (CQB) DURING TUBULAR ASSAULTS—PLANES, TRAINS, AND AUTOMOBILES.

"I'm pretty sure all of you can read, so I'll just let it roll," Kolt said.

As the title screen faded out, several still pics of actual assaults made by Delta over the years popped up. Several trains, a few buses, and a half-dozen planes, all with captions of the mission name and location.

"That bus was stopped with a couple of volley shots with a SIMON device," Kolt said rhetorically. "Some of you might know it as the GREM, the grenade rifle munition, or some shit."

Kolt noticed a couple of smiles as he deposited another stream of tobacco juice into the clear plastic bottle.

The last few pictures showed the roof hatch breach from on top of the American Airlines 767 that allowed Kolt and a few mates to retake the plane while airborne over central India a year or so earlier.

"That breach was done with the harpoon; first time it was used real world, actually," Kolt said. "You guys will get some good training on both of those during your advanced breaching training."

Kolt looked into the crowd, keying on the wide eyes of all thirteen reflecting in the projector light. He took another long spit into the bottle, and as if on cue, the room erupted to the sound of heavy metal rock.

"In honor of the late, great Jeff Hanneman, if you don't like Slayer, you probably suck at CQB," Kolt said loud enough for the entire class to hear him.

Flashes of Delta Operators doing CQB on tubular targets in training, intermixed with real helmet cam footage from actual targets down range in Iraq and Syria, rolled by as the music blared. There was more action on this screen than in ten Hollywood blockbusters combined.

Kolt let the video play out, another thirty seconds or so, until the thundering sound of "War Ensemble" faded. "Lights, please," he said.

"Gentlemen, how many of you think you know how to do CQB?" Kolt asked, scanning the room. About half the candidates raised their hands tentatively as they looked around, hoping they weren't the only one sticking their neck out.

"That's a damn shame, isn't it, Jason?" Kolt said as he looked to the back of the room. "Guess you've got a lot of bad habits to break, then."

Again, a few smiles and abbreviated laughs, the students not exactly sure what to make of the forty-something and obviously seasoned operator.

"Men, I know the Unit command sergeant major told you the three things that will end your time in Delta," Kolt said. "Someone help me out."

"Women, booze, and money," much of the class spouted out almost in unison.

"Good," Kolt said, "but after over a decade at war, we like to add 'CQB with two left feet' to the list."

No response from the crowd.

"Now, on target, especially in a confined-space tubular assault where there is no cover, multiple, simultaneous breaches are critical to overwhelm the enemy thought process."

Just then a familiar female voice came over the building's intercom. Kolt recognized Joyce, Colonel Webber's secretary. "Major Raynor, call four-zero-zero-five please. Major Raynor, four-zero-zero-five."

Kolt recognized Webber's office extension and noticed cadre member Jason stand up and begin walking to the front of the class.

"I'll take it from here, Racer; thanks for coming in to talk to these guys," Jason said.

"No problem. Happy to help." Kolt shook Jason's hand, mentally gauging his grip strength against the stocky sergeant's, and tapped him on his right shoulder. Kolt looked at the candidates one last time as he walked down the side of the room toward the back door.

"Make your own luck, men," Kolt said. "Hope to see you all down range in a few months."

Stockholm, Sweden

Staff Sergeant Cindy "Hawk" Bird had grown tired yesterday of waiting by the hotel phone for a call from her in-country CIA contact who she knew was only about a quarter mile away on the second floor of the U.S. embassy. After checking in early yesterday afternoon, Hawk couldn't resist taking a quick walk around the area to clear the jet lag, or, truth be told, to clear her mind after a whirlwind Whistle-stop and having been rerouted at the last minute away from the Commander's Board she had so anticipated.

It had been a beautiful day with carefree locals walking their dogs, clear plastic doggie bag and leash handle in one hand, cell in the other. She had walked only a block from the hotel parking lot, careful, though, not to be too obvious when she glanced back over her shoulder while passing the Norwegian embassy, to check if her tails were still on the job. She then continued west down Dag Hammarskjolds vag another six hundred feet along the noticeably clean sidewalk, and stopped. She had paused there, playing it cool and trying to blend in. She had peered through the gray-painted embassy fencing and razor-topped chain-link fence, willing her x-ray vision to pierce the tinted windows of the U.S. embassy.

She wasn't able to see inside, but she just knew Myron Curtis was in there somewhere.

C'mon, Myron, you knew I was coming.

Hawk turned south, taking Laboratoricgatan Street toward the bay, passing by several walkers of various cultures and skin colors, and noticed the Turkish and South Korean embassies. She reached the edge of the bay and stopped, taking in a deep breath of fresh Swedish air. She was amazed by the sheer beauty of the sailboats, dozens and dozens moored at the nearby docks. She looked for swimmers and wondered how warm the water might be, before coming back to reality.

Hawk gained the sleepy Nobelparkan dirt trail that hugged the north bank, allowing her to complete a lazy circular route back to the Villa Kallhagen in just over thirty minutes. No calls, so she had waited, killing time in her room by flipping through the flat-screen channels, trying to find a station in English or one not showing a soccer game.

After a late breakfast at the Villa's five-star dining area, Hawk waited in her suite for contact from her host, bored, antsy, and tired of the waiting game. She checked her watch, then the desk clock on the nightstand next to the pearl-covered phone. Both were close to 1 P.M., her watch just two minutes ahead of the clock's red digital numbers.

Hawk ran her fingers through her hair, expending trapped energy just for the hell of it. She tapped both hands on the edge of the bed, hummed for a few seconds, and popped straight up. With no word from the CIA, she walked across the plush pink carpet, threw open the beige blinds, and absorbed the gorgeous Djurgårdsbrunnskanalen, the peaceful paradise-colored canal water surrounded by towering emerald pines interspersed with shady spruce trees. In the distance, maybe a half mile away, she marveled at the top half of the 110-year-old haunted-looking Nordic Museum.

Fuck it! Truth is cover, cover is truth.

The phone in the suite rang, startling Hawk and pulling her from the window. She closed fast, nibbling nervously on the end of her fake fingernails, and watched it ring a second time. Answering on the first ring was too desperate, almost as if she was expecting an awkward prom invitation from that cute boy in algebra class.

On the third ring, Hawk moved. "Hello?"

"Miss Tomlinson, my apologies for the disturbance, but you have a call from overseas. I'll patch you through."

It sounded like the same guy that checked her in, the tall one with wandering eyes, but she couldn't be sure.

"Thank you," Hawk said, wondering why the front desk would think a call from the Swedish embassy down the street would appear to be an international call. Possible, she allowed, and maybe smart for operational security issues.

Hawk heard the phone switch over, leaving her with a hollow silence.

"Can I help you?" Hawk said.

"You alone?"

"You're the last person I expected to hear from," Hawk said as she plopped onto the white bedcovers.

"Sounds like all is okay over there," Kolt said.

"The old man have you checking up on me?" Hawk asked, figuring Colonel Webber might be having second thoughts about sending someone on such a unique singleton mission, one that could go sideways on so many levels in a heartbeat.

"Well no, actually," Kolt said, "just wondering myself."

"Bullshit," Hawk said. "I'm sure you have a hundred better things to do."

"Look, Miss Tomlinson, it's important you get this one right," Kolt said. "We're running out of time."

"Time for what?" Hawk asked. "I'm not tracking."

"Just don't let the navy push you around," Kolt said. "They prefer their women heavily buzzed and in gangs."

"Uhh . . . okay," Hawk said, "that's random."

"I know you're busy. Glad all is good," Kolt said. "Remember, if you can, find a way to squeeze us in. It's political but important."

"Are you drinking again?" Hawk asked. "What the hell are you talking about?"

"Better face-to-face. Just the rumor mill turning around here. Nothing specific," Kolt said.

"Not buying it."

"Listen, I need to run but if there is a valid reason, ask for help," Kolt said. "Our survival may be at stake here."

"Holy shit, Frank!" Hawk said, reverting back to Kolt's cover name from their guy-girl urban recce team back in Cairo.

"Gotta go," Kolt said. "You'll be fine either way, and we'll see you when your vacation is over."

"Wait a sec—" Hawk said before hearing a dial tone. *What the hell was that all about?*

Hawk set the phone in its holder and stared at the lampshade. She wasn't sure what Kolt was getting at, but knew few things could prompt Kolt Raynor to risk a cold call while she was under cover. He wasn't liquored up, that she was certain of. No, the call was deliberate, and she was disappointed in herself that she wasn't able to read between the lines to solve the riddle Kolt had just leveled at her.

"I gotta get some air!" Hawk whispered to herself as she bounced up and turned for the bathroom.

Hawk threw a super-soft hotel bath towel over her shoulder, grabbed the elevator down to the lobby, passed the dining area scattered with limo drivers and tails in dark three-piece suits, eyes buried in their cell phones or rapidly swiping a touchscreen, and made for the gift shop.

Browsing quickly, she yanked a skimpy all-black two-piece from the rack and threw a twenty banknote and a five-kronor coin down, thankful she had thought ahead and dumped what she had left of North Korean won and Russian rubles just before catching her flight out of Berlin.

Kolt had told her back in Cairo to never enter a new destination looking too much like a tourist, or an arrogant American flashing greenbacks all over the city, and converting it all to Swedish krona had been a smart move. One of the simpler, but crucial lessons she was flooded with during her recent Whistle-stop planes, trains, and automobiles exercise. Dying her hair blond with the hair-coloring kit she picked up at the duty-free store in Beijing was another one.

Hawk took her change, stepped into the ladies' room, and slipped into the new suit. She hesitated before putting her clothes back on, staring at her image in the full-length mirror and a little bent at the fit. Standing in her stocking feet, she realized she hadn't been in a rocking set of heels in weeks.

Hawk pushed the inside portion of her right thigh an inch or two to see the gunshot scar, still no more faded than the day before. She looked at her right upper chest before tugging at both sides of the bikini top, trying to cover the scarring from the sucking chest wound.

Out the back glass double doors and heading toward the canal, Hawk caught herself moving too fast, in too big of a hurry, out of character, and eased back into a carefree glide. She'd had a lot on her mind before Kolt's unsolicited call. Yes, heavy head stuff, but after Kolt's out-of-left-field mind fuck, she felt like the weight of the world was on her shoulders.

I haven't even been to the Commander's Board yet!

In third gear for less than a hundred feet, Hawk gained the flat gray stone walking path, passed under the Villa Källhagen Gästbrygga, the sign telling hotel guests they were welcome to enjoy that particular dock, and crossed the shaky arched footbridge, sliding her palms along the wooden rails. She stepped off the plank bridge, onto the ten-foot-wide floating aluminum dock, and noticed the ducks weren't startled at all by her presence. Walking down the dock she noticed the five buoys, identifying the shallow zone for boaters, and the Nordic Museum's pointed peaks of Renaissance architecture, and stopped a stride short of the far edge of the 130-foot-long dock, before spreading her egg white towel on the deck.

Balancing on her belly with her feet overhanging the edge, Hawk reached behind herself to untie her top, careful to keep her breasts on the deck. She knew she was being tailed since she arrived in country—everyone was tailed that stayed at the Villa—but she'd be damned if one of those rent-a-cop perverts with a zoom lens was going to get a freebie today.

They are so Captain Obvious!

After fifteen minutes, she gingerly rolled to the left, careful to keep an even tan. Hawk looked toward the footpath that she'd enjoyed the day before, noticing an African American in mauve shorts, a wolf gray man purse hanging off his right shoulder, a matching gray tee, and a pair of beat-up tan deck shoes. Not entirely out of place for the neighborhood, given Embassy Row and that Sweden has a huge minority population of Africans and Middle Easterners, but something about this man was odd.

Hawk lowered her sunglasses to her eyes, concealing her rude but curious death stare on the guy, and keyed in on the unique hiccup in his gait, his weight supported by a wooden walking cane, and a miniature jet-black thick-haired dog on a short leash.

I'll be damned, the son of a bitch still takes his field-craft seriously.

The man certainly looked the part. His hair had grown into more of an unkempt fro look since she last saw him in the streets of Cairo. In fact, he looked a whole lot better now than he did back then, with a bad arterial bleeder, ashen-faced, and well within the golden hour. She knew the cane was courtesy of one of Kolt Raynor's impetuous command decisions, but given the choice, she figured the guy preferred the hiccup more than death.

Hawk watched him pass under the Gästbrygga sign, cross the arched footbridge, and continue down the floating dock headed straight at her.

Hawk retied her bikini top, rolled over as if she were on a jujitsu mat, and crossed her legs in front of her. She wasn't too keen on giving the guy an eyeful. A few feet from Hawk, the man stopped, leaving his dog just enough leash to flaunt his cuteness and score some love.

He eased down to his rear end, sitting with his lower legs dangling over the water.

"You know Swedish law now allows women to swim topless," he said without looking Hawk's way.

"Not getting out enough?"

"You'd think not, right?" he said. "This is the most overhyped country on the planet. Most think every girl here is a blond bombshell, but that's urban legend. The talent level competes very poorly with other countries in Eastern Europe."

"How did you find me?" Hawk asked, quick to limit the small talk.

"Surprisingly, Sweden is fat. Likely the fattest country in all of Scandinavia," he said, "though it's a close call with Denmark."

"That was my biggest concern, the competition," Hawk said. "Is that why you drag this little hairy chick magnet around with you?"

"Gustav. He's a Swedish Lapphund," he said, "the country's national dog."

Hawk smiled sarcastically and rubbed the prickly ears and wedge-shaped head, causing the excited wavy tail to rotate like a top.

"He doesn't get in the way of your cane?" Hawk asked, immediately second-guessing bringing up bad blood.

"I guess that will pass for bona fides," he said, now looking at Hawk for the first time.

"Miss Tomlinson, I'm not so sure I'm happy to see you again, given our shared experiences," he said, "but I do need to be blunt with you."

"You can call me Carrie," Hawk said, again sarcastically. "I'm listening."

"I didn't ask for you, I didn't even ask for Delta, I asked for the SEALs."

"We do have a lot in common, Myron," Hawk said. "I didn't ask for you, and I wouldn't ask for a SEAL even if the entire U.S. Marine Corps was tied up on an amphibious landing somewhere."

"Do all Delta operators have a chip on their shoulder?" Myron Curtis asked.

Hawk thought about that for a moment as she petted the dog. Sure, some of the Unit guys were a little cock strung at times, but most were average dudes—married, two and a half kids, pickup and minivan in the driveway. Type A, confident, sure, but not genuinely arrogant assholes. But that wasn't what was giving Hawk pause. No, Myron Curtis's specific word choice was the problem.

Had I not been pulled early from Whistle-stop I'd be a Delta operator by now!

"I wouldn't know, Myron," Hawk said.

"I know you aren't an operator, Carrie," Curtis said. "I was talking about the guys like that Kolt Raynor and his partner, Slapshot."

Whatever, you bastard!

"Look, Myron, can we just cool it and agree to work together to get this mission done?" Hawk realized the last thing she needed was Curtis crying to his bosses on the seventh floor at Langley over cable traffic.

Go along to get along, Cindy Bird. Kolt isn't here to underwrite the conversation.

"I guess you aren't one of those elitist Swede disco bimbos with striking blond hair after all."

Damn, he is pushing my buttons today.

"Truce, Curtis!" Hawk said. "Fill me in now or call in someone else."

"Holy shit!" Curtis pointed to the battle scars above Hawk's right breast. "Those birthmarks or did you take a round in the chest?"

Hawk reached up and gently pulled the bikini top

over slightly, trying to cover the scars without looking too obvious.

"Old news, Myron, like your leg. Can we get on with this mission, please?"

"Okay, since you dyed your hair already I assume someone has read you on," Curtis said. "Basically, one of our deep assets has passed a covert message requesting extraction."

"How sure are you the message is legit?" Hawk asked.

"No doubt. It's too unique for it to be a false flag," Curtis said, "besides, the signal has been in play for almost twenty-three years now."

"North Korea, right?" Hawk asked.

"Yes, which is why you are in Sweden. All U.S. diplomatic discussions are handled by the Swedish government."

Please don't tell me I'm going back to North Korea? I just left that shithole.

"I knew that," Hawk said.

"We're putting you in the delegation that is meeting a senior delegation from the Korean Workers' Party at Panmunjom," Curtis said, "hosted by the South Koreans right on the most heavily guarded border in the world."

What? Curtis is fucking with me.

Curtis continued as if he were passing information during a personal meeting he was having during his training back at the Farm in Williamsburg, Virginia.

"You'll wear a pair of high heels, the higher the better," Curtis said. "Wedges, stilettos, or platforms will all flatter your legs and make them appear longer. Height intimidates the North Koreans and will put you on an even playing field. Nude-colored heels worn with cropped trousers or a skirt add to the illusion, because they blend with skin tone."

Okay, now this is getting freaky! Is he referring to Yellow Creek?

"Okay, to do what?" Hawk said, deciding to play along in case someone had gotten to Curtis about her using a two-and-a-half-inch pump to kill a terrorist at the nuclear power plant over six months ago.

"To help extract the asset."

"Why?" Hawk asked. She scratched behind both of Gustav's ears.

"You'll be fully briefed tomorrow."

"C'mon, Myron, at least tell me what the big rush is."

"The asset has some information on North Korean miniature nuke warheads," Curtis said.

"Crap!" Hawk said, the seriousness of being yanked off the K27/K28 in Harbin and pushed to Stockholm with no notice finally making sense. "We'll need an assault troop or two to extract him properly, right?"

"The SEALs have that covered. We just need you to tag the asset at the meeting," Curtis said.

"With a homing device?" Hawk asked, still uncertain of Curtis's sincerity.

"A radar responsive device, or RRD for short," Curtis said. "It's a tag developed at Sandia. Like the RFID tags the store clerk removes at Belk's, but a longer-range version, one that can be located twelve miles out."

"Are you crazy? How am I going to get close enough to this asset and clip a theft-prevention beacon to him without anyone noticing?" Hawk said. "Don't they run a wand past everyone when they leave those high-level meetings?"

Damn, Cindy, what's with the negative vibes?

"We'll know more tomorrow," Curtis said, pulling out a cell phone from his shorts pocket. "This is yours, don't run the minutes up, my number will show up as four letter Zs."

Hawk took the phone, thankful that Curtis didn't detonate on her last comment. She knew better than to spout off about the mission before she had all the facts, before all the assumptions were validated. She started to think Kolt Raynor's style was wearing off on her, and he was 4,500 miles and five time zones away. And without him here to hold her hand, she knew she needed to curb the attitude.

"What other assets are in play?" Hawk asked, hoping to smooth over the poor attitude stuff. "Any quick reaction force going to be available on a carrier?"

"Probably not. Staging time and distance issues won't meet our rigid execution window."

"How about ISR?" Hawk said. "The Global Hawks based in Japan?"

"Doubtful," Curtis said. "Busy monitoring Chinese naval ops."

"My God, Myron," Hawk said, "the two G-hawks were put at Misawa Air Base to spy on North Korea's nuke sites, too. Seems kind of relevant here."

"I didn't say no, I said doubtful. We're working it."

Well, at least I'll have my nude-colored heels.

SIXTEEN

Colonel Webber's office, Delta Compound

Moving to exit the selection wing of the building, Kolt passed by the large plexiglass display as he gained the hallway. The box contained thousands of rounds of spent brass, with the small display placard claiming the amount to be the number of bullets an operator candidate fires during his initial training. On both walls, extending the length of the hallway, dozens of framed eight-by-ten black-and-white photos of every OTC class since the Unit's inception were hung in perfect alignment. Once past them, Kolt opened the heavy light blue doors and gained the Spine, spitting his tobacco into the plastic bottle as the doors shut behind him. He jumped into the nearest bathroom, swirled some water around in his mouth to make sure he got it all, and quickly washed his hands.

Entering the command group area, he made eye contact with Joyce sitting at her desk with the phone to her ear. Kolt mouthed a silent hello and gave a wave.

"Go on in, Major Raynor, Colonel Webber is waiting," she said as she cupped the phone's voice box with her right hand.

Kolt continued past her desk, but stopped at Webber's office door. He opened it slowly, peeked around the doorjamb, more out of respect than in a sneaky manner, and saw Colonel Webber on the phone, seated, with only his tan T-shirt on.

Webber had a look of deep concentration on his face, but when he looked up to see Kolt, he waved him inside. Seeing Webber point to the two leather seats near the left side of the desk, he took a seat in the closest one, immediately knowing this was more than a simple social call.

"I got it, the CG wants it minimal force and low vis and yes, I understand his hesitation with Noble," Webber said into the phone, "but you know I'm not sending Mike Squadron, they are on alert cycle. With Osage Squadron heading back to Iraq, sending a troop-plus from Noble is it."

Hearing his squadron's name pinged Kolt's radar to max power, but he played it cool in the chair, careful not to appear overly excited. Over the years, he and his men back in Mike Squadron had stood up, then stood down, more times than any of them cared to remember. So much so that they had been desensitized to the rumor mill of deploying, learning not to get too fired up about anything until the deployment order had been cut by the National Command Authority.

But, Kolt was pretty sure Webber was talking to the JSOC J3, Colonel promotable Kevin Tanner, and that was usually a sign that something was brewing on short notice. Webber quickly looked up at Kolt, catching him eavesdropping. Too late to play it off, Kolt simply stared back at him, poker-faced. Kolt figured that if the commander didn't want him to hear the conversation, he would have never waved him into his office.

"Major Raynor just walked in, give us a few minutes

to talk and I'll get back to you," Webber said, leaning toward the phone as if he was in a hurry to hang up. "Hour, tops."

Kolt watched Webber hang up the red phone, pull out a side desk drawer, and fish out what looked like a glossy eight-by-ten photo before abruptly standing.

Kolt stood and accepted the picture from Colonel Webber.

"Hawk?" Kolt asked. "Where was this taken?"

"Twitter!"

"Recent?" Kolt asked as he brought the photo closer for further analysis, realizing Webber wasn't in the mood to share the exact spot the pic was taken. "Not Whistle-stop?"

"I'm afraid so," Webber said. "In less than a hundred and forty characters we learned Hawk was tanked and psycho."

"This it?"

"Only one so far."

"Cultural studies cover, wasn't it?" Kolt asked, handing the photo back to Webber.

"What the hell does that matter?" Webber said, opening the drawer again.

"Well, sir, as long as Carrie Tomlinson wasn't pulling the chastity-like nun cover, snapping some asshole's elbow probably fit her cover for status okay."

"Let's get some dark roast," Webber said as he came from behind his desk, reached for his camouflage top hanging on the wooden coat rack, and continued out the door.

"Uh, yes, sir," Kolt said, standing quickly and trying to catch up. He had been in and out of Webber's office a hundred times, for both attaboys and ass-chewings, but never been turned around like this to head to the dining facility.

This can't be good.

"I'll be in the DFAC, Joyce," Webber said without looking at his secretary or making eye contact.

"Yes, sir," Joyce said.

Kolt followed Colonel Webber down the hall as he slipped one arm into his fatigue jacket, then the other one, pausing to button it fully before entering the double doors to the dining facility.

Kolt reached around Webber, opening the door for him, feeling a little awkward, and let the colonel lead the way inside the empty cafeteria. He followed him past the long, clean tables and perfectly dressed chairs, still a couple of hours before the lunch crowd showed, and to the coffee dispensers. They grabbed a cup each, Kolt declining Webber's offer for the artificial sweetener.

"Darker the better, sir," Kolt said.

Webber pulled out a chair and sat at one of the tables offering a view through the large windows of the manicured bushes and small shade trees. The compound's main parking lot was full of pickups and SUVs basking in the already uncomfortable sun. Kolt stepped around the opposite side and took a seat facing Webber.

"I need to quit this," Webber said.

"Sir?" Kolt said, not sure what he was talking about.

"This damn coffee, fourth cup today," Webber said, taking a delicate sip so he wouldn't burn his lips.

Feeling a little more relaxed now, Kolt decided to keep the mood light. "Chewing tobacco is a good alternative, sir."

Webber just nodded.

"JSOC seems ready to execute Satin Ash Two," Webber said.

"Satin Ash Two?" Kolt asked. "Marzban is history."

"North Korea," Webber said. "CIA is positive that one of their deep-cover assets knows what Marzban knew about the miniaturized nuke warheads."

Kolt played it off as if he wasn't up on the target folder

yet, hoping Webber would fill in some gaps from what he had read the day before, down in the SCIF, the secure compartmented access facility. Kolt had a habit of unofficially checking in with the intel analysts often, sometimes twice a day when he felt something was brewing.

"Which option, sir?"

"The Six option. They are the main effort," Webber said.

Son of a bitch!

Kolt tried to hide his disappointment, but it made sense. If option one had been chosen, it would have been his old squadron, Mike Squadron guys deploying, but hearing the phone conversation with the JSOC operations officer, it made sense now. Noble Squadron was on tap.

"Got it, sir. Damn shame, but I'm sure they'll get it done," Kolt said, immediately sensing he was unsuccessful in trying to hide his disappointment in front of Webber.

Hell, he could see Webber was disappointed. With the momentum behind disbanding the Unit, or Six gaining speed, even within JSOC channels, leaving just one killer force like POTUS was reportedly leaning toward crushed Webber as much as everyone else in the building.

"Yost's men will do fine, it's Red Squadron," Webber said. "Master Chief Kleinsmith's boat crew is the main effort."

"Good man, Kleinsmith," Kolt said, "but he just got back from the Ukraine with us."

"You remember Carlos Menendez?" Webber asked.

"Who?" Kolt said, leaning closer to the table as if he was in a crowded room. "My Carlos? Tungsten's Carlos?"

"That was him on the phone."

"No joke, sir?" Kolt said. "I figured the J3."

"Kolt, close hold, but JSOC didn't tell me about using Six for Satin Ash," Webber said. "Carlos did. As a favor, I owe him one."

"What, like the bin Laden hit?" Kolt said. "JSOCs back to playing faggot-ass hide-and-seek games again?"

Webber didn't answer.

"I thought we were past that stupid shit?" Kolt asked.

"Afraid not. In fact, it's worse, given the competitive and backstabbing environment these days."

"You didn't buy me a cup of coffee, sir, to tell me you caught up with Carlos," Kolt said, confused as to why they couldn't have had this discussion in Webber's office, and moreover, how it involved him if the SEALs had already been given the nod.

"I'm pretty sure I can get the J3 to go to bat for us with the CG," Webber said. "I'm pushing for us to have, rather your squadron to have, the QRF piece."

"Sir, you know I'm not big on turning down a mission, but why can't the SEALs handle their own quick-reaction force?" Kolt asked, both confused and becoming frustrated. "Besides, we've got the Fallen Eagle memorial service in a few days."

"Kolt, this might be it." Webber sounded a little more desperate than Kolt was comfortable with. "Word is the NCA is about to make their final recommendation to POTUS."

"Sir, c'mon, this is a kiss-your-sister mission," Kolt said. "I'll send my newest troop commander, Captain Banner, to cover down on this one. He could use the exposure with his guys."

Having just redeployed from the Ukrainian op, Kolt had barely had enough time to drag his kit across the Spine from Mike Squadron to his team room in Noble Squadron. He was hoping for some downtime after the memorial services for his guys, and knew he had three funerals still to attend. After that, he needed time to get to know his squadron a little better, meet some of the guys' wives and kids when the atmosphere wasn't so gloomy, do some planning for their upcoming squadron-building training, maybe fix the leak in the singlewide.

"That's not the issue," Webber said. He started to say more, then checked himself.

"I have no doubt about Banner," Webber said, "but your Mike troop was the last to do a train assault trip with Amtrak. You've got the most current quals. You're the best for tubular assault if it comes to that, so I need you to deploy, but I'm a little ambivalent about it."

What in the hell does he mean by ambivalent?

"Banner doesn't need me micromanaging him forward," Kolt said.

"Deploy your squadron command group, run interference for Banner."

"With all due respect, sir, that's exactly the kind of thing I hated from my squadron commanders," Kolt said. "Hell, sir, I believe you've told your squadron commanders several times over the years not to spoon-feed their subordinate troop commanders."

Kolt picked up the death stare, practically feeling Webber peering through his head and out into the courtyard. Then it hit Kolt like a spin kick to the floating rib.

"Sir, you concerned about my mental status or decision-making or something? Ambivalent?" Kolt said, trying to remain respectful but definitely playing his hand.

Webber took another exceptionally slow sip of his coffee and set the Styrofoam cup back on the table.

"Son, I'm not going to bullshit you. Doc Johnson, and frankly me, too, are concerned that the radiation may be handicapping you to a degree," Webber said, laying it out like a Shoney's breakfast buffet.

"The Unit surgeon cleared me, sir," Kolt said, trying

not to get too defensive. "I've CrossFitted my ass off the last few months, best long obstacle course times in years. I'm good."

"Look, Kolt, there is more to it than just your physical abilities," Webber said, somewhat surprising Kolt. "But now isn't the time."

"Sir, the day I can't meet the Unit standards, I'll turn in my kit," Kolt said.

"If you fuck things up on the SEALs' op I'll pull you from command," Webber said, not really showing that he wasn't entirely serious.

"I have no doubt, sir," Kolt said.

"All right, let's drop it, we don't have time for this right now," Webber said. "If I can swing it with the CG, I'll need you to get to Sweden ASAP."

Sweden? Hawk's in Stockholm.

"Hawk having issues?" Kolt asked, trying not to show how happy he was that Webber dropped the bullshit concerns or that he was worried Webber might suspect he had made an unauthorized call to Hawk on an unsecure line two days ago. "She's still good with the Swedish delegation, isn't she?"

"Yes, she made a secure call this morning," Webber said. "She has some major concerns about the tactics, techniques, and procedures the SEALs are using for the mission."

"What's her beef?"

"She hasn't been briefed yet," Webber said, "just worried about what the agency's in-country representative told her about the SEALs' tactics."

"That doesn't sound like Dealer to me. He's solid," Kolt said.

"She thinks using the radar-responsive device to tag Seamstress without a backup method is shortsighted. She learned a little about the armored trains during Whistle-stop, something about some stealth technology that she thinks will prevent the device from being tracked."

"I read her sitrep this morning. What's the J2's take?" Kolt asked, knowing the JSOC chief intelligence officer would have an opinion. "There is another option."

"The J2 doesn't discount Hawk's information on the North Korean president's train but he is green and typically noncommittal, probably afraid to interfere with Six's tactical planning," Webber said. "What's the other option?"

Kolt did a quick look around the cafeteria, just to be sure nobody had slipped in a side door unannounced.

"Quantum dots," Kolt said.

"That's what Hawk said."

"Hawk knows their capability, as does Slapshot," Kolt said. "He is fully read on to the SAP."

"I thought the Tagging, Tracking, and Locating Task Force had some issues with the liquid nanocrystals not being clearly distinguishable after impact?"

"Those were the originals. We're on mod three now. We messed around with the corrected prototype sent from Sandia last month in the boneyard, tagging vehicles. The optical-property issues were fixed and we pick them up easily under nods."

"Hawk isn't tagging a vehicle."

"We had an old-fashioned egg fight with the dots leftover. The crystals attached to the skin and clothing fine, and were easily seen through goggles."

"Look, Raynor, Hawk is your operator, or will be soon if she gets past the Commander's Board, and your old squadron is on alert cycle for the never-ending Ukrainian mess." Webber was obviously growing frustrated with the entire situation. "Noble has the mission and you are going, unless you want me to tell the CG just to leave it Six pure."

"Not a chance, sir. We'll dip pouch the quantum dots overnight to Hawk," Kolt said.

Webber sipped on his coffee, seemingly becoming a little more comfortable with the situation. Kolt was making it sound easy, but he knew Webber knew it wouldn't be. Webber would have to sell it, and quick.

The diplomatic pouch was the quickest way to get Hawk the quantum dots in time. The container came with unique legal protections in carrying official correspondence between a diplomatic mission and its home government. The lock and tamper-evident seal prevented even the most curious unauthorized third parties from peeking inside. As long as the pouch is externally marked to show its status, the old-ass Vienna Convention decision ensures it enjoys diplomatic immunity from search or seizure.

"Why doesn't Six seem to know about these dots?" Webber asked, signaling Kolt that he wasn't seriously countering the dip pouch idea.

"Not sure, sir," Kolt said. "My guess is we never told them."

"You know how important it is for Six and us to be aligned on everything," Webber said, "but in this case I might be able to leverage that."

Kolt didn't dare let on even a half smile. Webber was starting to sound like his old self after hearing the reassuring news about the quantum dots.

Webber took the last mouthful of his coffee, slid his chair out from under the table, and stood. Kolt followed him past the trash cans, where they both threw their cups in and moved to the double doors.

Kolt turned to Webber. "Can I bring Captain Banner in tomorrow morning after the staff meeting, sir?" Kolt asked. "I'd like him to get some face time with you and brief you on the concept of operations."

Webber didn't immediately answer, he just stared at the door, his hand still on the crash bar.

What's up with the old man?

"Kolt, I can't tell you how important this is," Webber said, as if his mood ring was on a pendulum. "You can't mess this one up, it's truly no fail. Failure in North Korea is likely going to be the knife in the Unit's back."

Kolt tensed at Webber's last comment, subconsciously scratching his head and adjusting his neck as a chiropractor might do. A little uncomfortable, for sure, but Kolt opted to keep it from getting too awkward. "Damn, sir, we don't even have deployment authority yet. Don't jinx me."

"I'm serious, Major," Webber said, stepping forward and busting Kolt's personal space. "The Unit, the female pilot program, our careers in army special ops, all of it is on the line here."

"Yes, sir," Kolt said, realizing the time for smart-ass comments was long gone, "I won't let you down."

"I know you won't, Kolt, you're not my biggest worry," Webber said. "It's Bird and—"

Hawk?

"Hawk's switched on, sir. You know that," Kolt said. "The Twitter pic is nothing to worry about."

"I'm worried she might be in over her head on this one," Webber said.

"Sir, I know your personal connection to Hawk with her dad and all; hell, everyone in the building knows it," Kolt said, "but I'm telling you she has it, she's all over it. The fact she questions Six is a perfect example."

"Yeah, she's got her dad's instincts, no question," Webber said, referencing Hawk's father, former Delta officer Michael Leland Bird, code named Major League Ballplayer. "MLB sure left us a blue chip."

Webber turned back toward the door as if to open it, then sighed and turned back to Kolt.

"Look, I've got it from a good source that the J-staff has provided POTUS with a recommended command structure and organization for a new composite unit."

"Really?"

"If I hear even a hint around the building about what I'm going to tell you, with God as my witness, I'll pull your badge for life," Webber said.

"Damn, sir," Kolt said, "that bad?"

"There is a high-level initiative to disband us or ST6. Part of the Defense Department's 2015 budget and post-war downsizing. Maybe combine the two of us."

Kolt knew his mouth was open and closed it. He'd heard the rumblings around the compound, which had prompted his spontaneous call to Hawk in Stockholm, but hearing it directly from the Delta commander made it horrifyingly real.

Everyone and their brother knew special ops forces had been increasing in numbers since 9/11. It was public knowledge. But, Kolt allowed, it wasn't entirely an uptick in operators, as even POTUS had finally realized the men at the tip of the spear couldn't be mass produced. No, America had enough operators. What she needed was help with the support side of the house. Trained professionals required to maintain special ops helos to get guys like Kolt on target, folks to maintain personnel records on guys like Kolt, drone operators to give guys like Kolt some real-time intel, and intel analysts to let guys like Kolt know what it all meant.

"Us or Six?" Kolt said. "That's unimaginable, sir, we have different missions, unique legacy tasks."

"Many disagree, Kolt, but that's a debate for later. You need to know that JSOC has penciled in Mahoney as one of the subordinate commanders of this composite unit option."

Kolt impressed himself that he didn't curse out loud.

"Gangster? After all that shit with his squadron in Syria?"

Webber looked up to the ceiling before replying. "You know how it works. Suspected of everything, charged with nothing. The asterisk beside his name is huge and invisible."

Kolt nodded. The army was legendary in blacklisting people, but still keeping them on.

"I got this straight from Carlos. Gangster is JSOCs senior rep forward. He'll be at the forward staging base in Inchon, South Korea. Same as you and your men."

Kolt didn't say anything. What the hell could he say?

Webber seemed to read his mind. "There's nothing I can do. Gangster still has his supporters. Hell, maybe he really does deserve a second chance. And he was All-Army swim team captain," Webber said, the sarcasm in his voice unmistakable.

Kolt thought about that. As far as he was concerned, something about Gangster over the years didn't add up. Kolt mentally threw up Gangster's full profile; everything about the guy since day one of the Operator Training Course implied that he was tailor-made for the Unit. He was the epitome of a Delta operator in every way, they all said. Sure, Kolt knew Gangster looked the part, no doubt, but as he focused on the image in his head, the obvious lit up like a giant neon sign in Manhattan. Gangster's wingspan was asymmetrical with his torso, as if a kid had yanked GI Joe's arms out of the sockets to help him fly. Olympic swimmer Michael Phelps had nothing on Rick Mahoney. More so, Kolt noticed, Gangster's eyes were bunched above the bridge of his long, thin nose, perfectly shaped for those tiny swim goggles that leaked around the edges on most folks.

Son of a bitch!

"So if they do combine Delta and Six, they plan on

making it a SEAL-heavy unit," Kolt said, working out the political machinations. "So Gangster gets his shot at redemption, what with his great butterfly stroke, while the rest of us dog-paddle."

"Looks that way."

"That sucks, sir," Kolt said.

"It does, and you'll deal with it," Webber said, taking in a breath and fixing Kolt with a stare. "This won't be Syria. You'll play nice, and whatever you do, don't start the Third World War over there."

Kolt nodded, but the thought occurred that if a new war did break out, all this shit about combining Delta and Six would vanish.

SEVENTEEN

CIA safe house, Stockholm, Sweden

Hawk couldn't say Kolt hadn't warned her. Eight minutes into the first planning session, she had already been undressed and eye-fucked a dozen times.

Talk about your stereotype hard-up testosterone junkies.

Happy she'd dressed down for the night, Hawk listened intently to the three SEALs that had flown in to coordinate the operation with the CIA and the Swedish delegation. She watched them run through their mission analysis slides (put together back at Dam Neck), read through the JSOC staff's sync matrix, and give their concept of operations.

Not bad, but not Delta planning.

For Hawk, she knew the SEALs were checking the block, covering all the bases, and simply being courteous to Myron Curtis. As the senior agency rep read on to the operation, Curtis was a critical piece of the approval chain, but given the agency guy's constant head nodding, the SEALs could have said they were putting on clown suits and pole vaulting the DMZ and he would have nodded in the affirmative.

Curtis is smitten with these guys.

The SEAL leader, Master Chief Tim Kleinsmith, continued to lay out the phases of the operation, taking them through the infil of the SEALs from Inchon Air Base in South Korea, into the Yellow Sea and then up the Yesong River a few miles north of the border.

"Once we go feet dry about right here, we'll transition into phase two," Kleinsmith, the taller of the three SEALs, said, throwing commando buzzwords out like a Gatling gun while pointing a red laser pointer at a large satellite map shining on the wall from a small one-eye projector.

Hawk was surprised by the lack of questions from Curtis, but chalked it up to part nerves, not having the experience to even question the tactical plan of the top SEAL unit in the navy, and part backstage-pass groupie.

The SEAL continued, flicking the red laser pointer on and off the wall, unable to steady the dot, as if he was hung over or showing early signs of Alzheimer's.

"We'll take these abandoned structures, about seven klicks southwest of Kaesong, by force if necessary, and lay up during the day until the next cycle of darkness."

By force? Murder innocent North Korean noncombatants?

"Charges go here, at this bridge we've named Objective Beaver," the shaky SEAL said, bouncing the red dot over half the screen, "and at this bridge further east, Objective Bear."

Myron Curtis broke in with his first comment. "We haven't solved the North Korean airspace issue yet, so you're still prepared to go in without Predator coverage, right?"

"That's our understanding, yes," Kleinsmith said.

"Once the train is trapped between the two blown bridges, how are you going to secure Seamstress?"

Hawk looked at Curtis, proud he shook off the

starstruck act and finally asked a question. And a good question at that.

"Actions on target are boat team specific," the SEAL said. "I'm not prepared to share that information."

"Oh, yes, of course," Curtis replied apologetically.

Jesus, Curtis, you a SEAL junkie or what?

"That about does it." Kleinsmith looked around the crowded living room, keying on Curtis's reaction. "If no questions, we have a plane to catch."

Hawk looked at Curtis, sitting on one of the kitchen bar stools, shaking his head as if he had no concerns.

"I appreciate the briefing, Master Chief Kleinsmith," Curtis said. "You guys have really outdone yourselves. I'll send a cable immediately to Langley, and to our station in South Korea, letting them know we are on schedule."

"That's good to hear, Myron," Kleinsmith said, the projector's light illuminating his long blond hair like a beat cop busting two locked-up teenagers in the back-seat with a high-powered flashlight. "Give us a few minutes to grab our gear and we'll be ready for a ride back to the airport."

"I'll drive you guys," Curtis said. "Would love to hear more details about the bin Laden hit you guys were talking about earlier."

Holy shit!

Hawk sat there dumbfounded by what she was seeing, wondering if someone was going to walk in and try to sell her a Navy SEAL workout video with a free T-shirt. Was this an actual mission brief for CIA approval or was this just a quick TDY trip for the SEALs to secure another month of tax-free income?

Hawk was still clueless about what the SEALs were actually going to do inside North Korea. Sure, she knew they were infiltrating subsurface, using the Yellow Sea and the Yesong River to circumvent North Korean defenses. She now knew about the animal cracker names, Beaver and Bear, and that the bridges would be blown to trap Seamstress's train. Beyond that, she had no idea what the plan was. She wondered if it was designed that way; maybe she didn't need to know the details? But what about her part in this operation? How the hell does a critical mission briefing like this, a mission that includes the first JSOC covert op into denied North Korea in the history of the command, start and end without anyone giving fuck all about Hawk's role in this?

If Kolt was here, this shit wouldn't be over, not yet!

"Gentlemen, I have a few concerns," Hawk said, interrupting the CIA–SEAL Team Six love fest.

Curtis whipped his head toward Hawk, eyes narrowed and mouth open as if he was preparing to absorb the overpressure on a heavy wall breach. The three SEALs, now with an excuse to overtly grab an eyeful of the blonde in the room, focused their attention no higher than Hawk's breasts.

"Sure, Candy, isn't it?" Kleinsmith said. "What are you, intel?"

Hawk looked at Curtis before answering, surprised to see him pick up on the odd question. Kleinsmith's question wasn't entirely surprising. She remembered Curtis had been shocked to see a woman get off the plane back in Cairo, a full team member of Kolt Raynor's AFO cell, but her hunch was he would keep quiet for the meantime.

"I'm sorry, Master Chief, I should have started with introductions. This is Carrie Tomlinson from Fort Bragg," Curtis said.

"Bragg? Delta?" Kleinsmith said, noticeably surprised and looking at Curtis. "I thought she was with you guys."

"Well, ye—" Curtis began.

"Now why would that make any of you guys nervous?" Hawk said. "ChemBio by trade, but intel works, too, if it's important."

"No offense, Carrie, ease up," Kleinsmith said. "What are your questions?"

"Yeah, sorry, jet lag and no sunscreen don't mix," Hawk said. "Not trying to pry here, but how many North Koreans do you think you'll have to go through to secure Seamstress?"

"Go through?" Kleinsmith asked, trying to hold back a smile and not appear too offended by the lady's oddball question.

"Neutralize clearer?" Hawk said, not appreciating Mr. Stud's facial expression.

"Perfect world," Kleinsmith said, "zero."

The SEAL leader's response was not only surprising to Hawk, but more than a little irritating. Not five minutes earlier this same guy deliberately mentioned taking a barn by force.

Hawk couldn't let it drop. "Isn't that a little unrealistic?" she asked. "Nobody gets shot?"

"I didn't say that," Kleinsmith said, "but we are using nonlethal munitions. They will break skin and, no shit, hurt like a bitch, but the targets live."

Damn! Okay, Cindy, major cool points lost?

"Got it. Makes sense." Hawk tried to hide her embarrassment but already knew her response wasn't fooling anyone.

Hawk tried not to notice, but she could sense the men in the room teaming up, testosterone-supplemented and stalking a keg party, ready to dog pile her in the coat room.

"Anything else?" Kleinsmith asked.

Screw it, I'm still not happy.

"Are the South Koreans read on?"

Hawk watched Kleinsmith turn to Curtis, laying his

hands out in front of him as if he were shoveling her question to the CIA.

Curtis rubbed his Afro for a second. "No, POTUS decided against it."

"Since when did the South Koreans become the ISI?" Hawk asked. "We're not actually going after bin Laden here."

Curtis raised his eyebrows at Hawk, visibly unimpressed with her know-it-all attitude. "That's not something we can affect, Carrie."

"Pictures to PID this guy?" Hawk had seen the one quartering photo from the rear in the SEALs PowerPoint. More current than the grainy black-and-white, decades-old asset photo of a much younger Kang Pang Su, but not much more helpful. Without something more current, unless Hawk was sneaking up from behind, she knew her ability to positively identify Seamstress would be iffy.

"The two pics you saw are it," Curtis said. "Anything else?"

"Since I'm tagging Seamstress, I wanted to talk about the radar-responsive tags you guys carried over."

Hawk watched one of the SEALs walk a few steps over behind the couch and pick up a small black pelican box. He opened it and pulled two small tan objects out, with what looked like the instructions.

"Yes, those things," Hawk said, gathering some confidence and wondering if anyone else in the room realized that a major piece of the operation had yet to be discussed, particularly since no intelligence, surveillance, and reconnaissance assets were available. "I'm concerned they may not work on the armored train."

"And that assessment is your opinion or—" Kleinsmith said before being cut off by one of his men.

"They've been tested, lady, they're good through four feet of reinforced concrete and double-plated titanium," the SEAL holding the tags up said with obvious sarcasm.

"Roger, but Kim Jong Un's trains are equipped with additional security features that the tag hasn't been tested against," Hawk said as she walked over to the SEAL, nearly stepping on a sleepy Gustav in the middle of the floor. She took one of the RRDs from the SEAL's hand and motioned for the red laser from Kleinsmith. "Without ISR coverage, these things will make or break us."

"Can you back up a few slides, back to the overhead of the two bridges?" Hawk asked, happy at the surprise of Gustav now rubbing against her leg to draw her attention.

Hawk didn't dare look at Curtis, knowing he would be getting a little annoyed at the Delta girl's interference after he had just told the SEALs everything was grand.

"That's it," Hawk said, steadying the red dot on the U-shaped railroad track that connected the two bridges, Beaver and Bear. "All of KJU's trains are protected by a stealth net that blocks or scrambles all wireless-frequency communication for about fifty feet on all sides of the train."

Curtis jumped in. "Where are you getting that intel from?"

"I got that from my North Korean minder in Pyongyang, who had a little too much soju," Hawk said. "Did Seamstress ever pass that info along?"

"We didn't know about it, neither does the J-staff," Kleinsmith said before Curtis could answer. "How positive are you?"

"I'm not at all positive, just worried that if my drinking buddy was correct, then this mission might already be set up to fail." Hawk looked around the room to assess her allies and see if her comments pulled their attention away from her ass.

The SEALs all stirred, looked at each other, then over to Curtis. They might not have been too thrilled with a female interfering, but they damn well knew they didn't want to tiptoe into North Korea knowing the mission could already be a bust.

"Now damn it, wait one second here," Curtis said, "how exactly do you know about this, this blanket thing?"

"Stealth net, at least that's how the guy described it," Hawk said. "I was on a train in North Korea a few days ago and the minder told me that if I was on the Great Leader's train that my cell phone wouldn't work."

"I thought you were in Istanbul and Moscow?" Curtis said with a twinge of disbelief.

"I was, Curtis, right before hitting Pyongyang," Hawk said, trying not to sound defensive.

"You that girl that's trying to be an operator in Delta?" the poster-boy SEAL with the RRD box said.

The room fell dead silent. Hawk froze. She wasn't exactly sure how to respond to that but she knew enough to either change the subject or ignore the question.

"You believe the guy?" Kleinsmith asked, saving Hawk from her discomfort. "Sounds pretty farfetched to me."

"Who knows?" Hawk said. "But he did mention that the 2004 explosion in the North Korean town of Ryŏngchon was believed to be an attempt to assassinate KJU's father, former president Kim Jong Il, and that cell phones were outlawed because of it."

"Makes sense, I guess," Kleinsmith said. "We probably need to relook this thing."

"I'm not voting for an abort," Hawk said, amazed they were finally listening. "I'm just suggesting we need a contingency method to mark Seamstress at the DMZ."

"Any suggestions?" one of the other SEALs chimed in.

"You guys familiar with quantum dots technology?" Hawk said. "We have been experimenting with them for a while now."

Hawk looked around to see all of them shaking their heads back and forth. She had their undivided attention now. She looked at Curtis, back on his bar stool and expressionless.

"Can't say we have, Carrie," Kleinsmith said, "mind giving us the one over the world on it, if it's not too secret squirrel for us?"

Ass.

"Basically, they are nanocrystals that change their optical properties based on size. The dots are made of cadmium selenide and can be hidden in clear liquids," Hawk said, trying not to sound too technical.

"So how do you detect them?" Kleinsmith asked. "Spacely's Space Sprockets?"

"Your night vision goggles," Hawk said, ignoring the childish reference to the animated sitcom *The Jetsons*.

Kleinsmith looked at his two partners and then at Curtis. "I think we're past the good idea cutoff time here. I'm not introducing something untested this late in the game."

Before Hawk could return Kleinsmith's latest backhand, Curtis stepped up.

"Sounds smart to me," Curtis said. "Better to have a backup planned and ready if this stealth net deal turns out to be correct."

"Can we get the quantum dots shipped here?" Curtis asked.

"Yes, I'm pretty sure," Hawk said, "but Curtis, let me go through my channels versus your formal cable traffic channels; a lot quicker that way."

South Korea

Under the cover of a near moonless night, an Air Force C17 Globemaster III landed and taxied to a quiet far end of a sleepy runway where it killed its four Pratt & Whitney megaton-thrust engines and waited. Seven minutes later, two tractor trailers from Korea Express, South Korea's largest total-cargo-delivery company, turned onto the taxiway and approached the massive but silent plane. The lead orange-and-white truck, with 대한 통운, *KOREX* stenciled in large black Hangul lettering, banged a controlled U-turn before backing up to the rear of the plane. As soon as the large hydraulic-operated tail ramp lowered to horizontal, two U.S. Air Force special ops loadmasters jumped the last few feet to the tarmac, moved to familiar positions, and began backing the truck up to the horizontal ramp, controlling the speed with small green and red ChemLights cupped inside the palms of their hands.

Kolt stepped off the C17. The clock was ticking. He stretched his back and looked around the tarmac. Four flat-black-packaged and fully fueled MH-6M Little Birds, their six rotor blades each pinned and side personnel pods stowed to narrow their width, were being wheeled nose-first out of the Globemaster and into the first trailer. Several operators stood watch on each side.

Chalked and strapped in place, the Birds were followed by some black rolling Pelican boxes, flexible fuel bladders resembling overstuffed black pillows known as z-bags, and the rest of the troops, about a dozen mixed of Delta assaulters and 1/160th Night Stalker pilots. Tractor One cleared out immediately, allowing the second truck, Tractor Two, to repeat the process, loading a mirror image of helicopters, equipment, and personnel.

The operation was hurried, but smooth. Time was pressing.

"We're ready to go, boss," Digger said, walking up to Kolt.

If Kolt didn't know Digger had a prosthetic he would have thought he'd twisted his knee. Digger's gait was strong and balanced, but his titanium prosthesis must be giving him some trouble.

Digger looked down at his leg then back up at Kolt. "You think I'm playing the retarded cousin again, you're nuts."

Kolt smiled. "That was inspired."

Digger snorted. "I just hope this op has a few less surprises."

I wouldn't count on it.

Inchon Air Base, South Korea

Crowded around a small Toughbook laptop with a few staff members, Lieutenant Colonel Rick "Gangster" Mahoney, the senior JSOC officer in the host nation country—for the time being—nervously watched the medium blue icon on the screen. The Raptor X satellite signal, beaming from the inside of one of the SEAL Team Six operators' ruck sacks, seemed to have frozen in place for the last hour.

Gangster noticed his reflection in the laptop screen, fixed a piece of hair out of place, and turned to the SEAL liaison officer, the LNO, to get his take.

"They're good, man," the SEAL said, picking up on Gangster's vibes and wanting to reassure him all was good.

Gangster hoped the LNO was right. Odds are, the SEALs would slow their pace as they negotiated the rice paddies and neared the final point of their movement inside North Korea. They would be careful to skirt the small fishing village of Ryeohyeon in the south and the farmers of Kyejong-gol to the north, staying out of the shit trenches and staying off the radar of any starving stray dogs that hadn't been sacrificed yet and served to a dozen Red Guards' hungry families.

"No worries, probably just getting settled into the barn," the SEAL LNO said. "They'll make a SAT shot as soon as they are secure for the night."

Gangster simply nodded, careful not to show any signs of micromanaging, and equally careful not to appear nervous or not completely in control. Gangster knew he was on the bubble, certainly aware either character flaw could deep-six his career. And with the recent behind-closed-doors information he had received about his slating for a new composite unit, he knew keeping the SEALs happy and successful on this operation would pay off in the near future.

Maybe my skills will be appreciated more in this new gig?

Gangster had a lot to lose on this operation, and a lot more to gain. It had been several months since he was reassigned from the Unit, sent a few miles across Fort Bragg to JSOC headquarters, where a revolving billet desk inside the J3 section awaited him. His reputation had taken a huge hit with the discovery that he promoted a culture of questionable ethics as a squadron commander, allowing cash awards for the most kills on combat rotations and party to his men consistently stretching the combat rules of engagement. Yes, most believed Gangster had done enough to be relieved of command, but given the environment where everything SEAL Team Six and the Unit did these days was under a microscope, General Allen and Colonel Webber had few options.

He was a player again, and would be a bigger star in the new organization. Multicam-upped and, at least at Inchon, the main motherfucker in charge, Gangster was on top of his game. He had been surprised, shocked really, about the opportunity to head up the operational portion of Satin Ash II, but he'd be damned if he would let anything or anyone screw up his comeback tour.

"Yeah, they've been spot-on with their OPSKEDS," Gangster said, looking back at the screen.

"I anticipate the final call of the evening soon, sir," the LNO said.

"Roger," Gangster said.

From a table away, Gangster heard his name called.

"Colonel Mahoney, we have Tomlinson up on secure Skype," the JCU communicator said.

A small wave of tired men shifted to their right, closing on the next fold-up table, and moved in behind the laptop screen. Gangster jolted at seeing Cindy "Hawk" Bird's face fill up the entire screen. He wondered if the others were just as surprised.

Gangster wasn't shocked because she was a female, conducting a singleton mission like no other ever handled by a male operator, but because she had managed to alter her appearance enough to make everyone in the hangar believe they were looking at Sweden's representative to the 2015 Miss Universe competition.

Gangster knew Hawk, but he'd never had the opportunity to work directly with her, and definitely not on any real world target. Hawk's bottle-blond flirty hair hanging over her turquoise blue eyes, topping a deep beachcomber tan and partly hiding a dark gray Bluetooth device in her left ear, seemed strikingly out of place given the circumstances. But, if pressed for the truth, Gangster would have to admit he was one of those old-fashioned status quo conventional-minded officers that never bought in to Webber's thesis that a female would make a good Delta operator.

Not only did Gangster not see the value, but he

thought it was stupid to have to use her cover name in front of the rest of the J-staff inside the old hangar.

"Tomlinson, good evening," Gangster said, before immediately letting everyone in earshot know that he wasn't much for small talk. "What's your status?"

"Sir, all settled in the Grand Hilton, Seoul's finest, they say," Hawk said, her voice and mouth movements off sync by a second like a bad kung-fu movie. "Swedish delegation is tucked in for the night, on schedule for a zero two hundred Zulu meeting in Panmunjom."

"Roger," Gangster said, not ready to show too much appreciation for Hawk's efforts just yet.

"I do have some tactical concerns though," Hawk said as her tantalizing eyes stared directly into the camera.

Just then, the back door opened, drawing Gangster's attention. He watched as one of the staffers, dressed in dark blue mechanic's coveralls, common to the airfield, walked quickly toward the tables.

"Sir, they're here," the staffer said, "Smokey just pulled up."

"Stand by, Tomlinson," Gangster said, speaking into the laptop microphone and leaving Hawk hanging.

Gangster turned his wrist over and looked at his G-shock.

Three-plus hours late.

Yes, Noble Squadron was several hours late, but they had kept Gangster and the JOC informed via SAT of each delaying detail, allowing the J-staff to check off each key event on the sync matrix. But with the SEALs already forced to launch to stay on schedule, the fact that Noble hadn't made it yet ate at Gangster.

Indeed, the consecutive digs from Murphy's Law were nobody's fault per se, but Gangster was in no mood for hiccups, not several hours into the infiltration phase. Gangster knew, had he still been the Noble Squadron commander, given the late start from Pope Army Airfield, delay in hitting the aerial refuel tanker—the Air Force KC-135 over the Pacific Ocean, and the three-hour-and-change drive on narrow, congested roads, he wouldn't have sweated it too much. But these were different times, with much more at stake. Gangster's former men, now Kolt Raynor's men, were fucking way behind schedule and pushing his commanding general–approved abort threshold to the limits.

Racer bullshit, I'm sure.

Conversely, things for the main effort, SEAL Team Six, were moving along without as much as a broken and distorted commo check or stubbed toe.

The SEALs successfully launched from Inchon, negotiated the Yellow Sea from thirty feet below surface, dodged the underwater mines rigged along both banks of the Yesong, and were now tactically pushing from their feet-dry point four klicks up from the river's mouth. Meanwhile, Kolt and his squadron-minus had flown into the U.S. military air base near Osan City, just north of Pyeongtaek.

Yes, Gangster knew the details of how a Smokey and the Bandit package worked, he just wasn't all that impressed.

Gangster turned back to the laptop and Hawk. She had backed up a foot or so, showing she obviously had gotten comfortable inside her own suite. Now, competing for attention with her crisp facial features, her defined cleavage, showing at the top of the thin pink-and-white underblouse and centered between muscular shoulders, held the attention of the exhausted men at the table.

Before he could get back to Hawk, the large hangar door opened behind Gangster again. He took a deep breath and made a mental note not to appear to hold a grudge. This was to be the first time he had seen Kolt

Raynor, and really anyone from Noble Squadron since he reluctantly turned in his Unit badge and last drove away from the compound gate.

Slapshot and Digger led the way into the hangar, followed by Gangster's old communicator, JoJo. All of them were wearing identical dark blue coveralls, much like several of the J-staffers.

Well isn't that a bitch?

Gangster tried to prepare for the shock of it, but it hadn't truly sunk in until he saw JoJo enter the hangar. He had been inside the panel van with him and Kolt Raynor months ago, bumpered up outside the cemetery on the outskirts of Afrin, Syria, and witness to Raynor's cold-blooded execution of the Barrel Bomb Butcher. Now, looking back, Gangster knew his instincts about letting Kolt tag along were pretty much right. Had Raynor not been there, Gangster knew he might still be riding high as Noble Zero-One, still the top runner to replace Colonel Webber one day as the commander of all of Delta Force.

JoJo spotted Gangster and made a beeline for him.

"Great to see you, sir," he said.

Gangster made light of the delay with his former men as he shook their hands. But the elephant in the room was still chomping, taking chunks of his ass. Their use of "sir" was very telling, and he hoped like hell nobody else in the hangar had really noticed. Squadron commanders, the respected ones anyway, are addressed as "boss" by their operators, with the more formal "sir" reserved only for officers not in Delta, or the ones they didn't think should be. It was a significant community slight, not intentionally insulting, but also not lost on Gangster.

"You guys, too," Gangster said, offering them a smile. *I'll be back on top, just you wait and see.* "Was beginning to think you guys landed in Japan or something."

EIGHTEEN

Right on JoJo's ass, Kolt closed the door behind him, giving the handle a slight tug to ensure it held secure. He turned and scoped out the hangar. Even though outside smelled like a fish hatchery, the setup somewhat impressed him. He noticed the black plastic tarps covering the windows, trapping the sheltered odor of the place, maybe filtering the raw-seafood aroma and keeping it from clinging to the hangar walls.

Kolt now understood why they were unable to see any artificial light escaping from the hangar as they drove up in the orange KOREX trucks. Lights on in an abandoned hangar, or any safe house for that matter, could potentially compromise the mission should a local South Korean out for a late-night stroll pay any attention.

Kolt heard Gangster before he saw him in the small crowd. "Major Raynor, we're in a hurry."

Yeah, good to see you too, Gangster.

Kolt picked up on the sarcasm quick, but ignored the dig on his rank, the "major" part, knowing Gangster was making a point that he, as a lieutenant colonel, out-ranked his replacement as Noble Squadron commander.

For years now, Gangster had gone out of his way to

trigger Kolt's rage. It was well before Kolt had been loaded on the black Chinook and disgracefully booted from the Unit after he had ignored his commander's orders. That was a decision that resulted in several dead mates and 160th special aviation operators, not to mention the capture of several others.

Kolt wondered if his work ethic was the issue; maybe it was Kolt's success, or maybe it was Kolt's luck. Probably all of the above. And if Gangster had any clue, he would know Kolt Raynor gave no fucks about rank.

Kolt walked toward the tables where a small group of men stood, several dressed in civilian clothes to conceal the U.S. military presence as much as possible. South Korea was a permissive environment if there ever was one, but they had learned long ago to respect operational security regardless of the area of operations.

Kolt locked on Gangster, backlit by one of the few major light sources inside the hangar, one of the laptop screens. He noticed Gangster, still with his Oakleys up on his thick hair, first nod, then smile and pat JoJo on the back. He did likewise with Digger.

Holy shit! Is that who I think it is?

Kolt had to blink a few times as he focused on the facial features of the light-skinned black man standing in the crowd. The four- or five-inch Afro was a little out of character, at least for the guy he thought he was looking at. But the cane, yes, the cane was a dead giveaway.

Motherfucking CIA man Myron Curtis!

"I thought we did everything in Cairo we could to make sure you lost that bum leg?" Kolt said, smiling and walking directly to Myron Curtis. "We must be going to the bench early, huh?"

"Racer, I guess we are desperate," Curtis replied, showing everyone in the hangar he was willing to give as good as he got. "I think I made a promise that I'd shove this cane up your ass if I ever saw you again."

Kolt laughed and shook Curtis's hand before stepping in for a pretty natural man hug.

"I guess you two know each other." Gangster was obviously a little annoyed that Kolt Raynor was already taking center stage. "Let's get done briefing Tomlinson before you guys go off into a corner."

"Yeah, no problem, Gangster," Kolt said, respectful of Gangster's position as the JSOC lead on the ground. "Curtis and I spent some time together in Libya and Cairo, good ops."

Curtis nodded, twisting his lips a little as if to say it wasn't all that good.

"I figured as much," Gangster said.

"General Douglas MacArthur carve his initials in the shitter around here?" Kolt asked rhetorically.

"Place left behind by the army, Second Infantry Division owned it until they downsized and repositioned brigades to support the War on Terror," Curtis said.

Kolt looked around again. The discreet hangar, just a stone's throw from the western beach and the limitless Yellow Sea, now without electricity, aging at the mercy of the forces of nature, was serving an important purpose once again.

Kolt followed Gangster and Curtis to the open laptop on the table a few feet away. The screen was frozen on Hawk's face, capturing her in a very unflattering pose, eyes half closed and tongue slightly out of the left side of her mouth. Kolt barely recognized her with the deep tan and blond hair, easily six inches longer than the last time he had seen her.

The SEAL LNO leaned in toward Kolt and whispered. "Dealer just radioed Minnesota; we're a go."

Kolt nodded, understanding that Kleinsmith and his SEALs had reached their hide site without drama. One of the JCU communicators noticed Hawk's frozen face and jumped in, fingering the mouse trackpad, and clicking on the refresh button to unfreeze the image.

Gangster took over. "Miss Tomlinson, sorry for the interruption. We're back."

"No problem, sir," Hawk said, "I thought we might have lost the connection, but I've got plenty of time."

"Major Raynor and Noble Squadron just arrived," Gangster said, obviously still unable to call them Kolt's men.

Impressed that Gangster respected Hawk's cover name, but not really surprised given the mixed company in the hangar, Kolt leaned down a little to get his face in front of the mini camera.

"Good to see you, Carrie," Kolt said. "What do you still need from us? What building is the meeting in?"

"They said the main conference building, center blue hut, straddling the military demarcation line," Hawk said.

"Okay, you good on your end?" Kolt asked. He knew the military demarcation line, or MDL, was the specific line in the sand that separated the two Koreas, buffered by two klicks on either side that comprised the demilitarized zone, or DMZ.

"Yes, Racer, she is good," Gangster said, showing a little irritation. "You're coming in a little late on this; everything is in place, except you guys."

Kolt looked at Gangster quickly, then back at Hawk. "Did the dip pouch arrive? Do you have the contingency items?"

"No, they didn't make it before we got out of Stockholm," Hawk said, showing obvious concern.

"You're fucking kidding." Kolt looked at Curtis. "Those damn things suck ass."

"What contingency items?" Gangster demanded.

"Sir, I wasn't able to brief you on this, but Curtis

knows about it," Hawk said. "We, or maybe just I, had some concerns about how I was marking Seamstress tomorrow. I'm worried the RRD tags won't be picked up by the assault force once the target is inside the armored train."

"No, Carrie, it's not just you, we have some concerns as well," Kolt said, jumping in before Gangster or Curtis could reply.

"Negative, negative, negative, it's way too late for the good idea fairy," Gangster said. "The RRD tags have been fully tested and rehearsed. The SEALs tested them while inside a C5 Galaxy and an M4 Bradley. We are good."

Kolt noticed Gangster quickly look at the SEAL LNO, who nodded a few times in agreement.

"We need another set," Kolt said, practically ignoring Gangster's last comment. "Where are you, Carrie?"

"The Grand Hilton in Seoul," Hawk said, "room—"

"Miss Tomlinson, this discussion is over," Gangster interrupted, "we are going as planned. The SEALs are in place, less than a klick west of the train track and bridges; it's too late to second-guess our mission analysis."

Even when the mission analysis might be flawed? Kolt thought.

"But sir, my instincts are that the stealth netting used on Kim Jung Un's armored trains is good enough to defeat the sensor," Hawk said, obviously a little frazzled. "If so, the SEALs won't know exactly which train car Seamstress is in."

"Why don't we just trust that the SEALs know what they are doing, Miss Tomlinson," Gangster said. He was clearly getting annoyed that his command influence was being questioned. "You better get some sleep. You have a big day tomorrow. Stick to the plan, call in your OPSKEDs, and we'll get this done."

Kolt could see Hawk's surprise at Gangster's conde-scending comments. Kolt certainly agreed with Hawk, but recognized the friction and knew how important it was that things go well, not just for Gangster, but for the good of the mission. Hell, for the future of the Unit.

"No worries, Carrie," Kolt said before Hawk could counter Gangster's last comments. "We're about to de-part for our staging area north of the Imjin River. We'll be up on comms. Ring us if you need us."

Kolt reached for the swipe pad, dragging the mouse up to the Skype dropdown menu and killing the call. He caught himself, wondering if he should have let Gang-ster have the last word with Hawk and let him hang up the call. He also realized that Hawk didn't have any tac-tical radios to call him if she wanted to.

Kolt stood up and turned to Gangster. "Are we sure about this thing?"

"Everything is synchronized and on schedule, Raynor," Gangster said. "Once you are in position, the force will be fully postured to move into the operation's next phase."

"I got that," Kolt said. "I'm talking about actions on the objective. I'm not feeling it on this one."

Myron Curtis stepped in. "Seamstress is the key to finally locating the mini-nuke storage sites. Without him, we all could be looking at the next World War on the heels of all the Pacific Fleet bases being decimated."

Kolt had said enough; he was on record. The wheels of war weren't going to stop tonight. No need to push it simply on Kolt Raynor's gut feeling. In fact, Kolt knew, the only thing that could cause a blowout was if Cindy Bird failed to tag Seamstress tomorrow morning.

Looking past Gangster's left shoulder, Kolt eyed Slapshot. "You good, Slap?"

"Yeah, boss, we're good," Slapshot said. "We've got a topped-off Kia Sedona. Ready to roll when you are."

Kolt turned toward JoJo. "You good with comms?"

"Way ahead of you, boss," JoJo said, having already been issued a cheap local Galaxy 4 from one of JCU communicators. He held it up with one hand and simply gave a thumbs-up with the other.

Reasserting some control, Gangster jumped in. "Raynor, you guys need to get moving. The SEALs are in their layup site, safe for now. The delegation meeting is on for tomorrow morning, zero two hundred Zulu. Stay on comms from here on out."

"No problem, Gangster," Kolt said, "this should be one to remember."

"Look, Raynor, the only thing that can make this mission an international incident is if your helos get anywhere near the DMZ. The SEALs will move the asset via ground, Seamstress is healthy and will be compliant. POTUS is ready to deny U.S. involvement."

"Got it," Kolt said.

Not one to be sidelined for the entire game, Curtis added two more cents. "Yeah, man, North Korean officials will be in the dark about who fucked up their railroad and will be too arrogant to admit to their millions that the incident was anything more than an accident or another assassination attempt by South Korean saboteurs."

"Your input is much appreciated, Curtis," Kolt said, smiling at the CIA operative and reaching to shake his hand again. "You guys have a good one, and if all goes well, who knows when we'll see each other again?"

"You're a little behind schedule, Raynor," Gangster said, breaking up their grab-assing.

"Yes, sir," Kolt said. "We're gone."

Kolt didn't much care for Gangster's condescending attitude, but he got it. If anyone had an ax to grind it was Gangster. Sure, he dicked the dog with letting the culture of killing get away from him while he was Noble

Zero-One. No denying he was entirely complicit. But Kolt wasn't there to take Gangster's belt, and letting him slip in a few unanswered jabs was no biggie. Given the importance of the ongoing mission, Kolt maintained a smart fight strategy, at least for the opening round.

Kolt also knew Gangster so bought into the entire toy soldier persona that he took the "courtesy to superior officers" thing, a phrase from the Ranger Creed, to the extreme. Which is why Kolt threw the "sir" salutation at him repeatedly.

Kolt turned to head for the door, pausing a moment to shake hands with both the JCU communicators and the SEAL LNO; these were guys he knew had been busting their asses behind the scenes to get the mission this far along.

"Major Raynor," Gangster said with a slight rise in his voice, "one last thing."

Kolt turned but didn't speak.

"Under no circumstances will you leave your staging area, or even pull the Little Birds out of the trucks, without a direct order from me," Gangster said, looking Kolt dead in the eyes.

"Yeah, I got it, man, no worries," Kolt said, taking another square shot to the chin.

"I'm not sure you do, Racer," Gangster said. "We don't need any of your so-called normal warrior shit on this one."

Holy shit! That was way below the belt.

"Roger, Gangster; your parade." Kolt looked at Slapshot, whose eyes screamed *Don't go there, boss.*

"We gotta roll, Racer," Slapshot whispered, grabbing Kolt's shoulder and turning him to the door.

"Let's not make it an issue," Kolt said, still looking at Gangster and deciding he was going to get the last word in.

"You've got a death wish, Racer." Gangster lowered

his voice a little to regain a little privacy from the others in the hangar.

Wrong motherfucking answer!

Now, for the first time, Kolt accepted that Rick Mahoney was the kind of guy you hate on first sight. The perfect square jaw and lady-killing dimples, the perfectly straight pearly whites, the thick dirty-blond hair without a hint of receding, the symmetrical triathlon body, and the rigid West Point style, suddenly harnessed enough power to buckle him like a knockout undercut to the floating rib. Gangster was pretty much machine made.

Kolt abruptly turned around, throwing Slapshot's hand off his right shoulder and closing the distance with Gangster. Kolt slammed both open-palm hands against Gangster's chest, shoving him backward like a rag doll, his Oakleys flying off his head and across the hangar floor. Digger caught the officer just before he hit the floor.

"Is it just me, man, or are you pushing my buttons?" Kolt barked, definitely catching the aroma of body wash.

Curtis stepped in front of Gangster as he regained his balance. From behind, Slapshot threw a bear hug around Kolt, slowing his momentum toward Gangster. If someone was about to throw their career in the Dumpster, looking to take the guard or slip in a leg sweep, Kolt figured the vast empty hangar space was as good a place as any.

"Adrenaline junkies are dangerous. You're so far removed from reality these days, have been for years now," Gangster yelled, not worried any longer if the entire Korean Peninsula heard him.

"You still sore over the Butcher hit?" Kolt said, collecting himself.

Gangster ignored the reference to the mission in Syria that was the tipping point of his downfall.

"If I had time, I'd relieve you right now," Gangster said.

"Make the time, big boy," Kolt said, "or back the fuck off!"

Digger and JoJo stepped in to help Slapshot show Kolt the door. Gangster didn't say another word, uncharacteristically letting Kolt get in the last one after all.

"Easy, boss, let's go!" Digger said. "Not the time or place."

Grand Hilton, Seoul, South Korea

Kolt and Slapshot didn't say a word as they rode the mirrored elevator to the fifth floor. They stepped off, paused to read the arrows on the wall directing them toward room 524, then turned right, heading down a plush hallway resembling an ugly Christmas sweater, passing the large mirrors and Korean paintings of Asian countryside and Buddhist and Confucian art.

They stopped in front of the door and noticed the small gold placard engraved in both Hangul and English, identifying the room as an executive suite. A green-and-white "No Disturb Thank You" sign hung around the lever-style door handle.

Kolt knocked three times. They waited.

"You're not going to deck her, are you?" Slapshot asked, ribbing Kolt a little after his riot with Gangster.

Kolt just looked at him, barely registering a smile, but appreciated that his teammate wasn't holding his earlier behavior against him.

Kolt knew they had the correct room; the polite gentleman at the front lobby desk was very accommodating, even with two Americans not necessarily meeting the five-star hotel's high expectations for dress. Three crisp U.S. one-hundred-dollar bills were more than enough to obtain his cooperation, but they knew it might take a little longer to gain room access, given the late hour and unannounced visit.

They checked their flanks before Kolt looked at Slapshot, who nodded.

Kolt knocked again, this time four times and with a little more authority.

A few seconds later, they heard the electric door lock disengage, and watched the lever quickly rotate toward the carpeted floor.

With the door cracked open a third of the way, Hawk leaned around to look at Kolt. No doubt she had checked who was outside the door through the peephole, surely seeing both Kolt and Slapshot in the fish-eye lens.

Hawk was all business, her bare feet—one set of toes covered with raspberry sherbet polish, the other yet to get the treatment—backing a few steps to open the door further. She held the door open, barely enough for them to squeeze through, immediately but delicately shutting it behind them.

"What's up? Nice pedicure," Kolt said, smiling wide and using his inside voice, picking up the aroma of woman freshly bathed with perfumed body wash.

"Crap, Kolt!" Hawk said, running both hands through her blond hair and clasping them behind her head for a few seconds. "What are you guys doing here?"

"I figured you'd be bummed to see me, but I did bring Slapshot here," Kolt said, trying to keep it light and keep Hawk calm. "It's all good, we'll only be here a few minutes."

Hawk looked at Slapshot, smiled as if to say hello, and dropped her hands to the sides of her spring green-and-pink pajama bottoms, looking every bit as if she just jumped out of a Victoria's Secret catalog. Hawk turned and shuffled toward the bed, plopping down on the edge of the thick white duvet cover.

"Sit down, you guys," Hawk said as she motioned to the suite's two red plush chairs behind the coffee table. "What's going on? Are we compromised already?"

"No, no, Hawk. All is good," Kolt said. Slapshot pulled his small backpack off his shoulder and set it on the table, sliding the nail polish and large flower arrangement out of the way. "We're about to catch up to the rest of the force to get across the Imjin River tonight."

"Okay, I'm freaking!" Hawk said as she turned and absentmindedly straightened the pillows. "I'm not feeling it, Kolt."

"Feeling what?" Kolt asked, surprised by her comment.

"Mission success," Hawk said. "I'm having second thoughts."

"What's your major malfunction?" Kolt asked, showing no mercy whatsoever. "Don't fucking worry about the SEALs."

Kolt understood Hawk's concern. Hell, he knew her part of the mission could very well be the most important part of the entire operation. Hawk doesn't tag Seamstress at the meeting tomorrow, the SEAL mission is a bust. *Too fucking late!*

"Look, Hawk," Kolt said, "everyone knows you have a tough job here. You are the key, no doubt."

"That's the problem, Kolt," Hawk said, "I'm all alone here. This isn't a simple Whistle-stop training event where I might receive a poor grade on some urban recce task. Holy hell, Kolt, what about your freaky phone call? If I screw this up it could start World War III."

Kolt turned to look at Slapshot, his expressionless face signaling this was all Kolt's problem to handle. Slapshot wasn't offering shit, good or bad. Kolt turned back to Hawk. She ran her fingers through her hair again, then knocked the bangs back off her face as if she was prepping for a fistfight.

Hawk's demeanor hit Kolt like a hurricane. His chest tightened and he struggled to fight the urge to swipe the coffee table clear with both hands and throw a chair through the window. This wasn't acceptable, not with the mission hanging in the balance. Kolt knew Hawk best, everyone knew that. He had seen her courage first-hand, seen her at her best when she'd saved his life in Cairo, at her worst after a month chained and caged, clinging to life, practically bathing in her own blood. But how could the female pilot program miss this stuff? Didn't the Unit psychs have this kind of thing identified years ago? No, this was much worse than a female problem forced on by nature. Sure, the singleton was cramping her style, but it had nothing to do with a menstrual cycle.

Kolt tightened his right fist, squeezing the plastic Kia key fob. He felt like calling Gangster right then, telling him the mission was an abort, telling him to exfil the SEALs tonight, while they still had a few more hours of darkness to safely cover their tracks.

Aborting the operation could be a no-brainer, but was it absolutely necessary? The SEALs would probably be okay, they'd make it out. But at what cost? An abort of a SEAL operation, well into phase two, even by their own frogmen, would be hugely problematic for JSOC, and given the mission's importance, any flowery expla-nation to the SECDEF would sound limp-wristed for sure. But, this was a hundred times worse—this wasn't SEALs aborting their own mission, this was Delta mak-ing the call. A call that couldn't be smoke-and-mirrored to cover the hard facts. Delta couldn't hold their own on this one, that was the only story here. Not only Delta, but the first potential female operator, already a highly decorated soldier, was having a meltdown.

"I don't even know what this guy looks like," Hawk said.

"We know," Kolt said. "You'll have to figure it out through introductions, or read the name tags, I guess."

"I'm fluent in Egyptian Arabic, not Hangul."

Kolt Raynor knew Cindy "Hawk" Bird. He knew her unquestionable quality, her unparalleled commitment, her potential. Hell, Kolt Raynor knew Hawk wasn't just a centerfold. She was more than a woman that had many an operator opting for an odd-colored protein shake over a super chili dog and fries at lunch. Indeed, she was a critical piece of Delta's value to the national objectives of the United States of America. She had performed before and she had to perform again. Even though nobody had a good idea of what Seamstress looked like these days, she just needed some hot hands.

"You done whining?" Kolt said, taking a chance this thing didn't get entirely out of control.

"Fuck you, Kolt!" Hawk said. "Sometimes you are a total asshole."

"Deserved," Kolt said. "I'll take that as you having your balance back. Look at his hands, analysts at Pine Gap swear they are the size of Ping-Pong paddles."

"Great," Hawk said. She took a long, slow breath and rolled back her shoulders before looking Kolt straight in the eyes. "Okay. Yeah, fucking okay. So, how close will you guys be to Panmunjom?"

"Straight line, eight klicks," Kolt said. "From Little Bird buildup to you, roughly fifteen minutes."

"Okay, that makes me feel much better," Hawk said with a forced smile as she traded looks with both of them.

"That's why we're here, Hawk," Kolt said. "This op is too important to the Unit to screw it up."

"You think I'm going to screw it up?" Hawk said, a little defensive. "Look, this whole thing has felt rushed to me. I don't exactly have a warm and fuzzy at this point, and frankly, feel a little in the dark about the planning, especially what the SEALs are doing."

"Just concentrate on your part," Kolt said, hoping the mood swing held. "The SEALs will be fine."

"What about you guys, if you have to help, or if the SEALs don't get on the train, how will you guys?"

"We've got a RRD sensor with us, too. We also have a few SIMON devices to breach the ballistic glass in the main engine car and the passenger car Seamstress is in. We'll pump some ferret rounds into both. The CS gas will get them to slow the train enough, at least to thirty miles an hour, for the MHs to put us on the roof of the right car. From there, it's tubular assault 101."

"Oh, is that all?" Hawk said without trying to hide her sarcasm. "I'll trade you."

"We know your piece of this is critical, but relax," Kolt said, trying to reassure her all was okay. "We're in your corner here, Hawk. We brought the Q dots."

"You are fucking kidding me," Hawk said, showing genuine relief.

"With the timeline pushed up, we figured the dip pouch wouldn't make it to Stockholm in time," Kolt said.

As Slapshot dug into the ruck to retrieve the Q dots, Kolt noticed the gray pinstriped suit and lavender blouse hanging on the full-length mirror. "Stockholm yard sale?"

"Krissy trousers with a work patch blazer and joy blouse," Hawk said, signaling she was returning to her old witty self. "Pure Swedish chic but worthless, courtesy of your favorite CIA buddy, Myron Curtis."

"Worthless?"

"The pants have no pockets," Hawk said, flipping her hands up like she was catching a beach ball.

Kolt laughed lightly. "We saw ole Curtis and his cane earlier. He looks healthy."

Slapshot pulled out a small white box and opened it, exposing three light green egg-shaped objects the size of golf balls sitting in padded cotton slots. He took one out, reached over the table, and handed it to Hawk.

"Check it out," Slapshot said. "It's a little delicate, it will bust if you sit on it, or squeeze it hard. You can puncture it with a paper clip, a ballpoint pen, whatever."

Hawk passed it between both hands, feeling the weight of the device, lightly pressing both sides to test the pliability and fullness.

"I'm not sure how I'll get the dots on Seamstress," Hawk said, holding it up, "but I'm going for it. I'm very worried the RRD tag the SEALs gave me won't work."

Kolt nodded his head and looked at Slapshot, then back at Hawk. "At least it matches the color of those shoes you have over there."

Hawk looked at the high heels Curtis had provided her and shook her head. "Curtis calls those nude-colored. They'll probably give me blisters as big as these Q dots."

"I figure you could gun that thing from deep center to home plate if needed," Kolt said, remembering Hawk's tomboy upbringing and how, as a young Cindy Bird on the Little League field with her five brothers, her dad had given her the nickname of Hawk because of the way she homed in on deep fly balls out to the warning track and then ignored the cutoff.

"I doubt that!" Hawk said, side-smiling and bouncing the Q dot lightly in her hand a few times. "Those days were a long time ago. After dislocating my right shoulder several times, I'd probably have trouble fielding a bunt."

"Seventh-inning adrenaline," Kolt said. "I bet you'd be surprised."

"You guys better get going," Hawk said.

"We've got some time; the trucks are waiting for us

near Munson," Kolt said. "What about your Bluetooth, any concerns about communicating from inside the meeting building on the DMZ?"

"Not sure really," Hawk said. "Why?"

"Wondering if the North Koreans wand people before they enter, if they forbid cells and stuff inside, or if the building might be set up with some type of stealth netting or umbrella jammer as well?"

"Is that legit?" Hawk asked. "Where did that come from?"

"From you, Hawk," Kolt said. "Hadn't thought about it till I heard your concerns about the train and then saw the Bluetooth on your ear in the Skype call."

"I don't know," Hawk said. "I guess if I need to call you, or the JOC at Inchon, I'll have to step outside. Curtis gave me a cell for the trip, can I assume it works at least outside at Panmunjom?"

"Curtis couldn't get that answer for you?" Kolt asked.

"No," Hawk said, "which is part of why I feel a little vulnerable here."

"What's up?" Kolt asked.

"The comms setup for one thing, but the lack of ISR coverage mainly." Hawk stood up to pace a few steps.

"Yeah, I'd be lying if we weren't a little concerned as well," Kolt said. "We did drag a SpyLite MicroB with us just in case."

"Can you put that up?" Hawk asked, showing a little more relief that she might have some eyes in the sky to monitor things. "While I'm at the meeting?"

"I can't promise you that," Kolt said, now regretting a little that he'd gotten her hopes up. Sure, if he was calling the shots, launching the uber-quiet mini UAV to pull in high-quality images and track Hawk's movements would be priority.

"They'd string us all up if that thing is spotted or burns in across the border," Kolt said. "POTUS's denial of U.S. involvement would be as shallow as Edward Snowden's whistleblower logic."

"I guess so," Hawk said as she sat back down, crossing her arms in front of her as if she was warding off the cold.

Stiff-arming the friction, Kolt pressed on. "Jot your number down and let's test it before I store it."

Hawk reached for a hotel pen and pad, her lean kettlebell shoulders and biceps twitching unconsciously, and scribbled the number on the paper before handing it to Slapshot.

Slapshot fat-fingered the number into the local Galaxy 4 and touched the green Call button to ring Hawk's phone. A few seconds later, Hawk's ringtone played, and after another second she killed the incoming call.

"Get some sleep, Hawk," Kolt said, "long day tomorrow, you've got my number. Anything changes, anything, take a piss break or something and call."

"Okay, you guys, too," Hawk said. "Hey, how did you get Colonel Mahoney to back off the Q dots? He sounded completely against it over Skype."

"Gangster doesn't know we are here, Hawk," Kolt said, "but we agree with you. This is too important of a concern to simply wish it away. Gangster has enough on his mind right now."

"Why am I not surprised?" Hawk said.

"Hey, don't stick your neck out too far, if you can only get the RRD tag secured and not the Q dots, that's the standard," Kolt said.

"Okay, Kolt."

"I'm serious, Hawk, don't be a hero," Kolt said, standing up and moving to the door.

"Not trying to be." Hawk followed them to the door. "Just looking to operate like everyone else."

NINETEEN

Deep in the heart of the night, the Smokey and the Bandit package, two KOREX tractor trailers with two MH6Ms each hidden inside, bumped along the road following Kolt and Slapshot's lead Kia Sedona. They crossed over the decades-old Freedom Bridge and continued north, taking the first east-bearing road. With far less noise and chaos than the original Smokey and the Bandit, they passed a sleepy South Korean military garrison before pulling off to the south side of the road.

Slapshot killed their headlights. Kolt exited the Kia and casually walked up to the locked double vehicle gates that led into an abandoned U.S. army garrison. Taking a beat to listen, Kolt hefted a pair of bolt cutters and cut the lock. When no alarm sounded, he pulled the gates open far enough for the larger trucks to pass through. Slapshot was now out of the Kia and at the black-and-white candy-striped barrier arm, cutting the lock that held it in the down position. A moment later the arm was up and the way forward was clear.

Camp Greaves had been home to several U.S. military units over the fifty years since the end of the Korean War, most notably the 1st Battalion, 506th Air

Assault Infantry. For almost twenty of those years, from 1987 through 2004, the Currahee battalion, its nickname Cherokee for "Stands Alone," enjoyed the prestige of being the closest American battalion to the North Korean menace, just three and a half klicks south of the DMZ. Even Adolf Hitler's alpine walking stick, one of the war trophies captured at the Eagle's Nest in Berchtesgaden in April 1945 and brought back by the Band of Brothers to the States, had found a home at Greaves.

Kolt got back in the Kia, this time behind the wheel, and followed the two trucks inside the fenced compound while Slapshot closed the gates and drop arm and replaced both locks with new ones before running to hop into the idling Kia.

"That went smooth," Slapshot said as he shut the door.

"Let's hope it all goes that smooth." Kolt put the Kia in gear and drove south up the hill, passing the trucks on the left. They passed where the dining facility used to stand and the ramshackle Bravo Company barracks on the right, then the forgotten Burger Bar and barbershop on the left.

The trucks followed Kolt's Kia as it made the left at the T intersection, still climbing another two hundred feet to the Y intersection. In sequence, the two trucks backed up the hill leading to the large one-story building, leaving them combat parked directly in front of the North of the River Inn, better known to former Currahee officers, men like Kolt Raynor, as simply the Notri.

With only the scuff of boots and a cough, men exited the trucks and walked into the Notri, their way forward facilitated by Slapshot and the bolt cutters. Kolt followed, looking around to see if anything was amiss, but everything seemed as it should. He was still thinking about Hawk, but he was able to compartmentalize that concern so he could focus on the here and now.

She'd had her soft moment, and he was pretty certain she'd overcome it. Time would tell soon enough.

Kolt stepped inside and found his way to the large, curtainless windows. The only light came from the moon and its reflection off the Imjin River and a few red-lens flashlights.

"We have one mission here, men." Kolt looked around at the assembled group of Noble Squadron and 160th Little Bird pilots. "We are to provide immediate QRF for Red Squadron," he said, reiterating what they all already knew from their extensive planning aboard the C17.

"We'll keep the Smokey package bundled up until the meeting at Panmunjom ends. We definitely don't need a curious local spotting us building up the MHs and compromising the entire mission."

"No change to the enemy situation. Minimal armed troops on the target train, but unknown numbers still. A hundred on the trail train. No known Red Guard garrisons near Six's ingress or egress route, just a few local rice farmers. Six will walk out with Seamstress."

"Contingencies if Six is compromised or runs into trouble, boss?" Digger asked.

"If shit goes bad, our priority is SEALs first, then Seamstress," Kolt said. "Obviously, if they need to evac a casualty or want to push the precious cargo out, we're available."

Digger's question continued to hang in the air. Kolt knew he hadn't answered it completely, and could feel the guys were not satisfied. He had already gotten the feeling that his men weren't too fired up about the mission. Most felt the rushed timeline and the lack of info from the CIA was very close to goat rope threshold, definitely high risk to the mission and high risk to the force.

Kolt knew he needed to address the worst-case

scenario, because one of them was about to ask it. Not simply to put his men at ease, but even more so to establish his creds with his new squadron. No doubt about it, some secretly blamed Kolt for Gangster's demise. He expected all eyes to be laser focused on his every move.

"I know the plan is a little weak. Six has little wiggle room out there; they are definitely at min force as it is," Kolt said, trying to make eye contact with all of them as he spoke. "We are definitely running the edge of minimal actionable intel here."

Slapshot spoke up. "We're good, boss, we know the risks."

"Roger," Kolt said, a little thankful Slapshot ran interference for him. "The last thing I'm looking to do is cross that border and execute an open-air takedown of a speeding armored train. Still, if it comes to that, there's no one else I'd rather do it with than you."

That was a little sunshine up their skirts, but Kolt meant it.

"Get your kit laid out for in extremis, two-man rule for radio watch, no white lights, and get some rack," Slapshot said, judging that Kolt was finished.

Kolt watched the assaulters move quietly toward the old hardwood dance floor to organize their kit. They would be delicately handling the thirty-inch-long SIMON devices, repackaging the 150-grain polymer-bonded explosive rifle grenades for flight and quick use from the air. Kolt knew the tactical shotguns would be loaded with the 12-gauge ferret rounds, shotshells containing powdered CS gas that upon impact spit out a nasty chemical payload.

Kolt noticed Slapshot and JoJo, off in the corner, breaking the seal on the SpyLite micro-UAV. Slapshot turned and Kolt caught his eye.

"We good with this, boss?" Slapshot asked. His

hesitation wasn't lost on Kolt; they both knew that the entire ten million troops from the Korean People's Army would have to crash the DMZ to even think about launching the platform.

"We humped it here," Kolt said. "Let's at least prep the wings and test the remote video terminal."

"Roger," Slapshot said before getting back at it.

Kolt took a quick nostalgic walk around the building. It had been a lifetime ago that he commanded an infantry rifle company during a yearlong hardship tour at this same camp. The television room, the long wooden bar still showing initials carved from decades of troops, the dining room, all missing the South Korean calligraphy and melted brass decorations that truly defined the place, brought back a wave of memories nonetheless.

Kolt walked toward the back glass door, slid it open, and stepped onto the back patio, the highest point in the forty-acre camp. It had seen better days—weeds and trees were threatening to engulf the place. He sucked in a chest full of fresh air coming off the Imjin, shaking slightly as he looked down at the water, then quickly lifted his eyes over the thousand-foot-wide river. From his vantage point, there were few visible lights in the distance; even the people of Munson-ri had turned in hours ago. This area hadn't changed much over the years and he knew the hardworking and active South Koreans would be up before sunrise, walking the ridgelines and tending the rice paddies.

"Shit!" Kolt whispered to himself. "Get it together, Kolt."

Looking at the Imjin brought other bodies of water to mind. His near-death dive in the spent fuel pool at Yellow Creek and recent dunking in the Atlantic Ocean swam into view and he did his best to push them away.

Kolt shook his head. Never before in his long career

had the stakes been higher. Not necessarily the potential loss of life for hundreds of thousands of innocent American citizens, but something much more personal.

We mess this op up and it's curtains for the Unit.

Sure, they needed to grab Seamstress. He was definitely the link to North Korea's miniature nuclear warhead plans. But did America need Delta? Couldn't this entire mission be handled just fine by SEAL Team Six? Riding the pods of a Little Bird certainly was not unique to Delta, a skill-level-one task for even any white special ops outfit. Hell, could we even handle this mission alone? What about the SEALs' course of action? Subsurface infil from the Yellow Sea up the Yesong River, dodging underwater mines most of the way? The Unit get that done?

Kolt bounced it around for a moment. What's the big equalizer? What exactly is it that we have on Six? How can we even argue POTUS's point in these massive across-the-military budget-cut times? Does America really need more than one killer force?

Then it hit Kolt. The female pilot program and Cindy "Hawk" Bird. Someone who should have died at Yellow Creek after a month of captivity and two gunshot wounds at close range was now in a major op. Hawk was the real G.I. Jane, an operator capable of infiltrating situations no men ever could.

"You need to go down for a few, boss," Slapshot said, walking up behind Kolt.

Kolt didn't respond. He remained locked on the haunting river water several hundred feet below the balcony, unable to break its straitjacket-like hold on him.

"Boss!" Slapshot said, circling in front of Kolt. "You good, man?"

"Yeah, I'm about to rack," Kolt said, blinking and coming back to himself.

"Place look the same to you?" Slapshot asked.

"Just about," Kolt said. "I thought we'd hear the North Korean propaganda being broadcasted from loudspeakers inside Propaganda Village. Always had us sleeping with one eye open."

"No shit?" Slapshot said.

"Urban legend is that nobody actually lived at Kijong-dong," Kolt said. "Supposedly the lights and loudspeakers were controlled by a single switch somewhere in Kaesong."

"Sounds legit to me."

"Sure never anticipated using the Camp Greaves Officers' Club as a safe house for the first covert U.S. military mission into North Korea in over sixty years."

"I'd prefer to be on the other side of the border though," Slapshot said. "However, my money says this entire Smokey and the Bandit effort will be just another rehearsal for a mission that will never happen."

"I hear ya, Slap," Kolt said. "Fingers crossed, though, we don't have to buzz the border tomorrow morning."

"You having second thoughts?" Slapshot asked. "Not letting Gangster bother you, are you?"

Kolt looked at Slapshot and raised his eyebrows in the dark.

"He's stressed, but I'm with Hawk on this one. This has the potential to go loud real quick on so many levels."

"The boys aren't too fired up about the less-than-lethal shit, Kolt."

"I'm not fired up about it either," Kolt said, "but that's the shit hand we've been dealt."

"Guys are thinking that Six is just doing this to stick another one in our face," Slap said, "another notch as POTUS's go-to guys."

"You?" Kolt asked, locking eyes with Slapshot.

"Boss, these guys know we've been together a long time, done a shit ton of crazy ops together." Slapshot's eyes bounced around Kolt's head as if he was afraid to maintain eye contact. "But I'm with them on this one. This whole op is jacked up. We're asking Hawk to hang it out without as much as a Boy Scout to lend her a hand. Six's course of action is fucked up on so many levels I don't know where to begin. Seems to me they are putting a lot of stock in stopping that train where they want it, and that the rubber bullets will work."

"That pretty much the way all the boys inside see it?"

"Not all, I'm sure," Slapshot said, "it just doesn't pass the common sense test."

"Brother, I won't leave Hawk hanging," Kolt said. "You know I won't."

"I know."

"That we can influence, at least pull Hawk out if shit goes bad," Kolt said, "but this QRF business is sketchy."

"Good to hear you say that, Kolt," Slapshot said, his shoulders dropping slightly in relief. "We're not much of a match for armed and fanatical North Korean troops in an armored train."

"Neither is Red Squadron if it goes bad."

TWENTY

Panmunjom, 38th parallel

"The meeting has been moved to across the MDL," Hawk said, just loud enough for her Bluetooth earpiece to pick up the tone, "I am in North Korea now."

"What?" Gangster said. "Why the move? That wasn't the plan."

Hawk had cringed at the thought of having to call Gangster with the change in plans, knowing he'd want more details than she had time to share. Now she could practically hear his heart pounding, in concert with his nervous footsteps as he was surely pacing the Inchon hangar, color-coded sync matrix in one hand as he wildly waved the other to get everyone's attention.

"It's field trip city out here," Hawk said in a hushed tone. "Every kindergartener in South Korea piled out of buses with a handful of helium balloons."

"Okay, stay calm and tell me, where exactly are you? Have you positively identified Seamstress?"

"Yes, I think so. But they are all over me," Hawk whispered as she tried to maintain a visual on the man she had pegged as Seamstress, walking up ahead. "Stand by."

Hawk reached up with her right hand, letting her raspberry-painted fingernails flip her neck-length hair just enough to make sure the earpiece was naturally concealed as she trailed the Korean delegation members along a manicured street to an unknown building, now fifty or sixty yards away. Not only was that smart, as being fingered for suspicious behavior by any of the shifty-eyed North Korean soldiers, who had been eye-fucking her since they arrived, could blow her mission to tag Seamstress, but her response to Gangster's irritating comment, from someone far removed from the X, would have been rated triple X for sure.

I am calm!

The eight males comprising the North Korean delegation, all dressed like off-the-rack penguins, perfect black-and-white everything, were confidently leading the way. The initial meeting spot inside the Military Armistice Commission building just wasn't getting it for the other team. Not more than a minute after Hawk believed she had PIDed Seamstress from across the long rectangular table, the North Koreans delivered a small but firm protest, specifically charging that the atmosphere inside the building was too historically militaristic given its exact position straddling the military demarcation line, the decades-old term for the manmade line hugging the 38th parallel, more or less. The South Korean delegation, now mingling with the northerners for what seemed like a casual walk for everyone but Hawk, had barely registered a concern.

The South Korean party members were pretty much a mirror image of their northern neighbors, if not for the two short elderly women in the party, most likely proudly symbolizing the human rights thing, and two of the six male members risking century-old protocol with their progressive Spanish gray suits and charcoal ties.

Hawk certainly wasn't as comfortable with the impromptu move, but of course, not her call. She knew the North Koreans were just flexing their muscles in front of her Swedish hosts, and as she followed from the rear of the pack she was surprised that the South Koreans seemed to be refreshingly comfortable around their enemies to the north. This looser atmosphere was one thing, not the most important thing. The impromptu relocation, a slight change to the tactical plan, prompted her to ring up Gangster at Inchon.

Hawk could hear the commotion going on back at Inchon, figuring Gangster and the staff were bracing for some bad news or anticipating changes to the sync matrix. Assuming she was not being observed directly, she spoke again, and winced a little from the new heels she was wearing. "Okay, I'm back."

"Give me your distance and direction from your last known point," Gangster demanded.

Crap! He wants my pace count? I knew we needed ISR to cover this meeting. "Not sure. Uh, moving northwest, gone about two hundred yards. I see a very tall tower with a huge North Korean flag flying."

"Where are you stopping?" Gangster said in an all-business tone.

"Looks like a light-orangish-colored building surrounded by trees, large steps out front center mass."

"You must be going to the Panmungak building or the Tongilgak conference hall," Gangster said.

"We just passed a three-story building with concrete steps on my right," Hawk said, hoping she wasn't interrupting the busy conversation she was hearing happening back at the hangar.

"Okay, confirmed. That is the Panmungak," Gangster said. "If you see the flagpole in Kijong-dong, then you must be headed to the Tongilgak."

Hawk really wasn't looking for an urban planning lesson from Gangster, she just wanted to let the command know about the change. She knew the first phone call they expected from her, according to the plan, was the OPSKED "Toyota," the code that the tag was on Seamstress, but a change is a change. Now she was wondering why she risked the call in the first place.

Hawk also knew Gangster wasn't sold on the female operator program. In fact, that was a definite understatement, as Gangster was well known around the building as a voice of contention from the very moment the pilot program had been briefed to the operators nearly two years ago. No, if Hawk was looking for any emotional support, Gangster was the last guy to expect it from. The former Delta man, now JSOC's man on the scene, only wanted to hear one thing from Hawk, or Cindy Bird, or even Carrie Tomlinson. The specific name didn't matter to him; the results did. Anything short of her accomplishing her mission to tag Seamstress would spread through the Unit Spine faster than an operator having an accidental discharge inside the house of horrors.

"What do you need from us?" Gangster asked.

"Gotta go," Hawk said. She reached into the jacket pocket just below her right breast, found the phone, felt for the power button, and mashed it to kill the call.

Hawk's stomach tightened. After the short cell call with Gangster, she wouldn't mind hearing his cartilage snapping, and other loud popping noises. Gangster had a mission to do and she appreciated his attention to detail and ability to synchronize complex operations, but a little personality goes a long way. He could save the mind fuck for sure. But, any energy wasted on policing Gangster, second-guessing herself, or worse, feeling sorry for herself, threatened her cover and risked compromise. She was the one dying to become a Delta operator and she knew damn well that if she pulled this off, the naysayers, those old-school graybeards back at Bragg, would have a hard time denying her.

Don't worry about Gangster, worry about the North Koreans.

The Six guys, patiently postured in the hills sixteen klicks west of her, hunkered down within striking distance of the electrified standard-gauge P'yŏngbu Line, certainly depended on her. As the operation's main effort, they had already set the remote-detonation explosive charges on the two bridges, Objectives Beaver and Bear, and were likely a little tense hoping to hear the signal that Seamstress had been successfully tagged. No Toyota call and no need to blow the bridges. No tag and the Six guys can call it an op and head back to the Yesong River. Hawk knew she was the key to success here. Fail to get close enough to place the RRD tag on Seamstress and they were mission abort for sure.

She looked around to see if anyone was watching her. Had she been seen talking to herself? She knew her actions may have drawn her additional scrutiny from watchful eyes, potentially creating obstacles to tagging Seamstress at best, and getting herself arrested for espionage at worst. The change in meeting location had bought her some time to think; it hadn't provided anything that might help her accomplish her mission. Which meant she had to think smart about every step, every move. She had to conceive, analyze, decipher, and decide her next move in warp speed, before she made a mistake she couldn't talk her way out of.

Hawk had never been exactly sure how she was going to successfully tag Seamstress anyway. Nobody else had any solid solutions either. Not the SEALs, not Myron Curtis, and not Kolt Raynor. Sure, all of them were type-A guys, had assholes and of course strong opinions, but none of them knew much more than Hawk about how things would go down at Panmunjom.

Hawk picked up her step to close with the Swedes, each step closer to the building creating more and more friction to blister her heels through her skin-tone-colored pantyhose. Trying to ignore the discomfort, she focused on reacquiring a bead on Seamstress. He was not an easy spot, dressed identically to the other North Koreans with the same jet-black hair and black suit over a white, collared shirt. Not a needle in a haystack, but if not for the slimmer build, it would have been easy to miss him.

Flanked by North Korean soldiers stair-stacked every other step (likely the tallest the military could produce, since they towered over the shorter delegation), and a half-dozen North Korean reporters with red armbands and Hangul markings on their left arms, the congregation climbed the smooth gray marble stairs to the front entrance. Hawk noticed their sloppy-fitting dress uniform jackets, in some odd shade that fell somewhere between olive drab green and worm dirt on the color chart, over pants of the same color, and black shoes. Polished dark leather gun belts were wrapped around their waists, appearing uncomfortably higher than their belly buttons, a holster on one side which, given the distinct hammer, Hawk figured to be holding a Czech model. Two leather magazine pouches on the off-hand side, set perfectly for rapid reloads should they run the pistol dry. Their heads were topped with bus driver–looking saucer hats with shiny black leather bills that made them appear to be ten feet tall. Postures perfect, at rigid attention, their eyes not shielded by dark sunglasses like their cousin guards to the south. No, the North Korean guards were not hiding the fact that they were there to make sure the South Koreans didn't pull anything funny that might embarrass the proud Democratic People's Republic of Korea. The menacing eyes were intimidating to guests of the hermit kingdom, the more the better.

Climbing the stairs, Hawk kept an eye on Seamstress as she tried not to turn an ankle in her heels. Besides causing her to lose major cool points, a tumble on the concrete would most likely strew the contents of her purse all over the place, sending the RRDs and quantum dots rolling down the stairs back toward South Korea. At least she wasn't carrying a handgun or a grenade, something that the North Korean troops would go ape shit about. The tall North Korean guards had been gawking at her since the Swedish delegation arrived, but in a different way than the SEALs had. What Hawk had smuggled across the MDL was not a deadly weapon, unless they were swallowed, maybe. However, given Hawk's mission, they were more important than a crate full of mortar rounds or a payload-heavy Stealth bomber.

As Seamstress entered the dark wooden door, Hawk lost sight of her target. She maneuvered toward the same door, rudely stepping around one of the South Korean dwarf-looking females, and entered the building. The delegation had been met by a welcoming party of a half dozen or so North Korean officials, likely caretakers of the buildings and grounds. With the others, Hawk shook hands with the hosts and gave the customary bow, smiling at each of them, struggling to not allow her eyes to bounce around the large foyer to search for Seamstress.

Then, out of the corner of her eye, she glimpsed a man separate himself from the crowd, make a turn around a corner, and vanish. Hawk couldn't be sure who had left, and quickly scanned the crowd like a counter sniper's spotter picking out a hostile in a crowded alley full of noncombatants. Hawk saw the two women and the two gray-suited South Koreans. Then she counted the penguins as nonchalantly as possible, conscious of moving her lips as she mouthed each number. Nine in all; one was missing.

Before she could make a decision, Hawk was interrupted by a female servant looking every bit the part of an expensive porcelain geisha doll, offering small hockey puck–shaped chocolate and lime green sweets and gold-crowned cups half full of hot tea. Simply following the lead of the others, Hawk helped herself to one of each.

Hawk drilled down, stepped through the crowd, trying to gain a position of advantage to see the faces of each Korean man dressed in a black suit. If not the face, at least enough to recognize Seamstress's distinct narrow build compared to the others.

No luck.

Was that Seamstress that moved away from the group? By now Hawk knew it must have been. She was certain she had covered the entire foyer, made a complete sweep, stolen a glimpse of every man there, and confirmed her target had left.

Shit!

Hawk ran the options quickly. She knew he wasn't trying to escape; maybe slip out a back door to make a mad dash for the MDL and the safety of South Korean soil. No, that would be suicide, even Seamstress knew that much. If that happened, the Czech CZ-82 pistols would be drawn and bullets would be flying, at least one of them having Seamstress's name on it. Besides, if he wanted to kill himself, he didn't need to take a long, impossibly slow ride on a bumpy train all the way from Pyongyang first.

The men's room! Gotta be it.

Hawk allowed herself to settle back down a bit, realizing she was over-amped. Seamstress hitting the head was natural; hell, the guy was pushing seventy. Trying to tag Seamstress in the men's room wasn't necessarily a bad idea, but definitely a high-risk idea.

As Hawk turned her attention back to the mingling crowd she noticed a female North Korean soldier enter the same door she had used. She was dressed similar to the men, but wore a fat olive beret with a gold emblem affixed to the front center. Like a Little League ball-player, she wore her headgear slipped back high on her head, affixing her straight black bangs perfectly flat to her forehead. Definitely not a looker, but she was just as armed and dangerous as the others. The soldier held up a brass bell and shook it rapidly, no different than a daycare teacher summoning the kids in from recess.

"Please, attention please," she said, "before have our discussions, we must secure hand-carried items and pocketbooks. Forbidden items are no allowed the Kim Il Sung Memorial Conference Room."

Hawk froze. The lady trooper's English was a little off, but Hawk knew exactly what she was saying.

Hawk tensed, shook violently inside, awakening a lot of haunted memories from the deepest recesses of her consciousness. Images of being inside the interrogation box at Black Ice, being beaten by Nadal the Romanian for days on end in that seedy hotel, and feeling her designer heel penetrate the terrorist's brain stem just before she ate two 9 mm slugs were now front and center. In those instances, like now, Hawk was unable to do a damn thing about it. If she had a pair of balls, they certainly had her by them now.

Forbidden items, yes, that's what she said.

Hawk knew she was facing mission failure, and she hadn't even so much as given a friendly greeting to Seamstress. Forget about tagging him now. No purse meant no RRD tags, no quantum dots. Sure, she might be able to hold on to her cell and Bluetooth, but for what benefit? Nobody wanted to hear from her again until she had done her job. Not until she had tagged that old man and sent him on his way back to the train at Panmun Station and the waiting SEALs.

Mission failure at Panmunjom was looking more and more possible. But what about her own status within the

Unit? What would failure here look like to the men back at Bragg? She could go back to the training cell if she called in a favor. Maybe Kolt could help, or even Colonel Webber might take pity on her. The NBC shop could use her too. Or, she could get those PCS orders to Fort Riley back. Yes, pack her shit, kiss her Special Forces boyfriend Troy good-bye, and top off the Volkswagen Beetle to begin the long drive.

Hawk had plenty of options if she wanted to fail, but only one option if she wanted to be knighted as a full-fledged Delta operator. An operator on par with the male operators in the Unit. Someone given equal pay and equal responsibility, someone held to the same standards and expectations. If Hawk wanted to make history within the special operations community, be the first female operator, she needed to make some Unit history in North Korea first.

"Miss Tomlinson, I'm sorry, can I have your purse, please?"

Hawk flinched as she looked dead in the eye of one of the dwarfs. She was kind enough all right, just doing her job, and as she reached for Hawk's pocketbook Hawk shuffled back in her heels, bumping into the snack table and knocking over one of the half-full teacups. Hawk quickly set her own cup and chocolate on the white tablecloth before clutching her lifeline tight to her chest. Lose control of the RRD tags and Q dots and she might as well Bluetooth the SEALs direct to tell them to bug out.

Hawk had to do something and she was out of time.

"Yes, ma'am, but in a minute," Hawk said, as she winked at the South Korean lady. "It's, uh, that time of the month and I really need to freshen up first, you understand."

Spinning ninety degrees on the balls of her feet, Hawk didn't wait for a response, and headed for the corner where she'd last seen Seamstress. She nodded politely to a second geisha, and without making a big deal about it, continued on for the hallway. Hawk hoped nobody noticed, at least not enough to question her, and if the bathrooms were just ahead, she had the perfect cover for action.

Hawk walked quickly down the solid white hallway, strangely sans any pictures or other decorations, save for the large and ubiquitous gaudy framed paintings of Kim Il Sung and Kim Jong Il. Her heels sounded off with each step on the polished tile floor as if they were sending a coded warning to Seamstress or a beacon to the North Korean soldiers.

Up ahead, she saw two hardwood doors, each with several Hangul letters that she couldn't understand. Hawk hurried to the doors, hoping they were the men's and women's rooms, and before she had to guess which one to enter, the left door swung open.

Seamstress!

Hawk held her purse close to her hip, lifted her heels, and jogged the last few steps toward the door. Seeing her approaching, Seamstress froze in the doorway, still holding the open door with his left hand. Hawk lifted her right hand, palm facing Seamstress, and laid a forward-moving Heisman on him that knocked him back into the restroom and onto his ass.

She quickly closed the door, turning the lock to secure it behind her. She knelt down next to Seamstress, who had already gone from shocked to pissed off. He was spouting off something unintelligible to Hawk but she knew it would make a hungover sailor proud.

"Mr. Pang," Hawk said, "do you speak English?" She wanted to dig into her purse and secure the tags, but knew she needed to confirm his identity and pass bona fides first.

"Yes, yes," Seamstress said. "Where is American CIA?"

So much for bona fides.

Hawk reached down, grabbed both of Kang Pang Su's hands, and held them palm up, waist high.

Large mitts, like an infielder's glove, but not really fat.

Not the correct protocol, or what Hawk was told by Myron Curtis to expect, but good enough for her, given the circumstances. He spoke English, obviously pretty good English, and at the moment Hawk knew that was a surprise party gift even Curtis couldn't predict.

"Great!" Hawk said. "Stay calm and give me a second."

Hawk pulled her designer purse sling over her head and placed it on the marble bathroom floor. She opened it and pulled out the two RRD tags and set them on the floor. She reached back into the purse, fished around in the small side pocket, and found the three light green egg-shaped Q dots. These she placed into the two pockets of her blazer. As soon as she placed the RRD tags she would be applying the Q dots next.

"Please take off your jacket," Hawk said. "We have to hurry."

"I defect, yes?" Seamstress said. "For political and ideological reasons me relinquish my status as a North Korean citizen."

Hawk heard every word, but it didn't register. "Your jacket, hurry!" Hawk said. "I need to mark you before you get back on the train."

"No, no, me no going back to Kaesong Station," Seamstress said. "You take across border now."

What? This guy's delusional.

Hanging her ass out on a singleton mission to place a tag on some old dude was one thing, humping his ass across a two-klick-wide demilitarized zone crammed full of land mines, razor wire, and interlocking machine-gun fire was another.

"Please, I beg you!"

"The jacket!"

"They will feed me to dogs," Seamstress said. "I know they on to me."

"That's not my mission, Mr. Pang," Hawk said. "I can't do that."

"I survive no another day."

"You have to get back on that train," Hawk said firmly. "It will be okay."

"No, I no can, no can," Seamstress said, showing obvious stress for the first time, "better shoot me here than let savages tear limbs off."

You can do this! she told herself, not really sure how.

Seamstress was scared shitless, but sneaking out of the building and running for the safety of South Korea was not part of the plan. As Hawk stared at the trembling Kang Pang Su, she allowed herself a moment to consider, what if? What if she audibled the mission and bolted with Seamstress? That course of action certainly had its advantages. For one, the SEALs would be off the hook. Beaver and Bear wouldn't need to be destroyed; they could melt back out of the country, nobody the wiser. Second, if Seamstress's angst was legit, if they really were onto him, then his personal scrutiny had likely changed. More North Korean soldiers surrounding the country's latest traitor inside the armored car would create definite trouble for SEAL Team Six, especially with the sketchy plan to use the less-than-lethal MAUL ammunition.

Conversely, Hawk knew the probability they would successfully make it out safely was ant-shit low, not even promising enough to register on the scale.

"Please, madam, you help me," Seamstress said as he cupped Hawk's right hand with both of his.

He shook so hard, Hawk began to worry he was going into shock.

"I can't help you," Hawk said. "You must get back on the train."

"I will not!" Seamstress said. "I defect today, I die trying."

Then it hit Hawk. This was fucking Delta Force, the premiere counterterrorist unit in the entire world. Paid, trained, and expected to solve the nation's most pressing national security problems. She remembered what Colonel Webber had said when she started her operator training course, almost two months ago now. *Operators are trained how to think, not what to think.* Yes, Gangster's comprehensive color-coded matrices, animated PowerPoint slides that Bill Gates would marvel at, and the SEALs' concept of operation were all good, while they lasted. But now, on the X, when the enemy gets a vote, all that plan A stuff had been overcome by events.

Fully knighted as the first female operator or not, on that morning, at that moment, as Carrie Tomlinson kneeled on the hard marble floor, she knew she was the most important member of Delta.

"Okay," Hawk said, nodding and smiling at Seamstress, "I'll help you defect."

Seamstress scrambled to his feet like anything but a man a few years shy of seventy. "Thank so much! Thank you! Thank you!"

He pulled out a folded piece of paper, about the size of a credit card, and handed it to Hawk. Surprised, she quickly unfolded enough of it to see a handwritten message in Hangul.

"What is this?" Hawk asked as she quickly refolded it.

"For my family."

Hawk yanked her left pant leg up to her knee, exposing the top of her knee-high hose. She peeled the edge back just enough to secure the note, pushing it an inch or so past the edge to be sure. She fixed her pants, grabbed the two RRD tags off the floor, and pushed to her feet, careful not to turn an ankle or bust a heel. Now standing face-to-face with Seamstress, she was stunned by how short he was, even accounting for her heels. She figured he was only about five foot three; five four, max.

Hawk reached into Seamstress's coat pockets, dropping a tag inside each as smoothly as a Times Square pickpocket when the ball drops. The SEALs wouldn't have to worry about him, but if they ran into trouble, somehow got separated, they might have a chance at recovering him.

"There back door," Seamstress said, squeezing Hawk's left arm, "I know way."

"Okay, but you have to stay calm," Hawk said. She pulled her cell from her pocket and powered it on.

Hawk cursed the slow startup sequence, watching it run its security protocols, tapping the Call Log button several times before it activated.

C'mon, c'mon.

"What doing?" Seamstress said, almost in panic mode. "We must now go!"

"Getting us some backup," Hawk said, "and maybe a safe lift over the land mines."

TWENTY-ONE

Objectives Beaver and Bear, North Korea

Ghillie-suited Master Chief Kleinsmith dropped both knees into the hardscrabble hillside that marked the SEALs' last covered and concealed position just as the sun was already shining high over the treeless hills to the east. The happy mounds, Korean graveyards crafted out of giant grass-covered dirt piles that resembled upside-down half grapefruits, where the dead were entombed in a seated position, provided their only cover for several hundred meters.

"That took longer than I wanted it to," he whispered to his mates only a few feet away.

Kleinsmith took a few deep breaths of the morning air. Strangely thick, it seemed to hang in his lungs, without a hint of wind moving across the hills. They'd had some trouble at OBJ Beaver, trying to get the C4 placed without making any noise that would certainly carry for miles, but happy to have finally placed the bulk explosives on the four vertical railroad track support beams with nobody the wiser.

But now, as the Six Team leader looked around the immediate desolate area, void of bushes or branches to build even a simple hide, not a rodent or bird or even an insect in sight, he wondered if they might have been safer back at the bridge. In fact, if not for the one water buffalo they'd bumped into last night moving to the shanty, North Korea was almost as lifeless as the moon, the result of a nationwide famine in the 1990s.

Kleinsmith didn't like it. He didn't like their current location, devoid of the basic requirements of any tactically sound operation—cover and concealment. He knew that, ghillie suits or not, anyone with a pair of binoculars would pick their torsos out from a klick away. This wasn't Afghanistan, where the sharp craggy rocks and rich foliage in the mountains offered protection to get the job done.

He cranked his head toward South Korea, running his eyes slightly downhill, searching for the ghillie-suited silhouettes of the other half of his Red Squadron troop.

Where the hell are the others?

"I don't see 'em," Kleinsmith said, not really expecting any comment from the others. "They should have beaten us back here."

"Me neither."

"We're an hour-plus behind schedule, I'm breaking radio silence," Kleinsmith said as he rotated onto his right side and reached for his push-to-talk near his left shoulder.

"Satan Seven-Two, Seven-One, check?"

Nothing. He waited a few long seconds, trying not to let worry enter his thoughts, or worse, let his fellow SEALs feel his angst. They had been through much tougher times, had come through much more complicated targets than this, and at the moment nobody was shooting at them. But, Kleinsmith also knew that the other team had half the distance to travel to reach OBJ Bear, and unless they had the same issues, dicking around with the explosive placement, his natural sixth sense couldn't help but peg hard right.

Sure, Satan Seven-Two could have engaged someone and he wouldn't have heard. Like him that morning, all his frogmen were running with cans. But, had they drilled someone, or been hard compromised, they certainly would have broken radio silence to fill him in.

"Satan Seven-Two, this is Satan Seven-One in the blind, over."

Kleinsmith heard one of his men whisper heavily, "Hold up, I see them."

Relieved, Kleinsmith released his hand mike and eased back to his belly to lower his silhouette. He looked around to his men, making sure they all were aware of the approaching patrol.

"Hey, heads up, friendlies," Kleinsmith said, "nine o'clock."

Eyeballing the SEALs slowly weaving through the shallow draw, the heads of the crouching SEALs just a foot or two below the far crest, his eyebrows popped.

"Who the hell are they carrying?" Kleinsmith asked.

Eight ghillie-suited SEALs in dark earth-tone patterns stopped about sixty feet short of Kleinsmith. He watched the leader, Machinist's Mate Danno, slowly move his left hand, palm facing toward the ground, up and down a few times, signaling the others to take a knee.

Kleinsmith's radio cracked. "Seven-One, Seven-Two, check?"

Kleinsmith reached for his mike again to answer Danno. "Seven-One, check."

He watched as two SEALs slowly lowered two bodies to the ground and rolled them on their backs.

"Whatya got?"

"Soft compromise," Danno whispered.

"Dead?"

"Negative," Danno replied coolly, "heavily sedated."

Kleinsmith slowly moved to his feet, tapped his prone partner on the back of the thigh, and whispered, "Back in a second."

He crossed the sixty feet of slightly sloped terrain at a crouch, careful with each step, carefully zigging and zagging between the five-foot-high happy mounds, before taking a knee next to his medic. Doc was already bent over one of the two supine men digging in his aid bag.

"Midz?" Kleinsmith asked, assuming the North Koreans had been drugged with midazolam.

"Yeah, time for another, too."

"What the fuck happened?" Kleinsmith asked as he watched Doc delicately hold a twenty-three-gauge medical needle and squirt a single drop of clear liquid from the business end.

"Sons of bitches spooked us near the bridge," Danno said, taking a knee next to Kleinsmith, "walked the fuck up on us like they owned the damn place until Roscoe hit on their scent."

"Damn, these guys are Red Guards," Kleinsmith said. "Roscoe get a bite?" Kleinsmith noticed the copper-colored Belgian Malinois sprawled on his belly, tongue threatening to snake out of the Hannibal Lecter–looking muzzle, breathing heavily a few yards away. His unblinking dark glassy eyes were steady state on the two Red Guards, waiting for a command, any command, to make his master happy and receive a treat.

"Nope, Streaker busted both of them with the less-than-lethal," Danno said, "both center mass to the chest."

"They armed?" Kleinsmith asked as he studied both bodies, looking for a rise in the chests, as if he didn't really know if they were dead or alive.

"Negative," Danno said.

Kleinsmith watched as Doc unbuckled the oversize and cheap brown utility belt that wrapped the Korean's narrow waist. Letting it flop to the dirt, Doc pulled the brown uniform shirt collar down on the middle-aged Korean to expose half of a large, swollen black-and-blue bruise, the definite point of impact of the rubber bullet. Doc released the collar and placed his gloved left hand gently but firmly on the man's forehead. He pushed down, naturally opening the mouth, to allow him to insert the needle between the inside of the cheek and the teeth and gums.

"Second dose to the buccal pouch?" Kleinsmith asked, pointing toward the inside of the Korean's cheek.

"Third," Danno answered.

"These guys are light sleepers," Doc said. "I'm about out though; maybe enough for one more dose."

Kleinsmith looked hard at the sedated paramilitary, then watched Doc slide on his knees, dragging his aid bag with him to the other numb Red Guard a few feet away. They could have been twins. Both wore identical brown, collared shirts made of Vinalon, the standard uniform of the Worker-Peasant Red Guards that make up the nation's civilian defense force. Top two buttons unsecured, possibly buttons missing. Sleeves rolled up to just under the elbows. Pants, the same swamp-brown color, at least a size or two too big, but blending in with the hillside better than their ghillies. Both in hand-me-down worn leather sandals over calloused feet that provided no hope to make a run for it should they wake up, as black flex ties secured their feet and ankles tight together. Kleinsmith knew their hands, hidden behind their backs, were flex-tied as well.

Hard, proud men full of midazolam, a powerful drug that peasants like these couldn't come by even if they were about to have a leg amputated inside Pyongyang's finest hospital. The drug works wonders, though, for presurgery jitters, and folks with money in North Korea or kin to the royal Kim clan could possibly confirm it inhibits unpleasant memories as well. In situations where killing the unwelcome busybody was against the combat rules of engagement, the drug was invaluable. But like any perfect drug, one had to respect the dose limits. Too much too often, and a man could end up checking out from a lethal injection. Of course, on any other field, they would be two dead men.

"Let's muzzle 'em too, Doc," Kleinsmith said. "Shouldn't be too long now before showtime, but who knows?"

"Will do, Dealer."

Kleinsmith stood to a crouch to move back to his side of the perimeter. He stopped, turned back around, still trying to process the yet unseen dangers this type of contingency presented.

"Ammo," Kleinsmith said. "How much?"

"Zilch on this guy." Doc kneeled next to one of them before turning to look at the other. "This cat only had seven rounds of AK ammo and one sharp-ass belly sticker."

"Damn, these guys must be in line to pick up their dead buddy's rifle."

"No way to win a war," Doc said.

"Rog," Kleinsmith said before turning away.

If nothing else, the intel on these guys was spot-on.

Kleinsmith slipped back in full crouch to his side of the perimeter. His shaded shadow looked like Sasquatch with a slung rifle given the super-stuffed shape of the ghillie. He looked at his Seiko dive watch, a few minutes before 0200 Zulu, and knew it wouldn't be long now before they heard the distinct clanking sound of the armored train making its return trip to Pyongyang. He'd never liked the idea of having to place the explosives during the daylight. That was just plain stupid from a tactical perspective, but his original plans to insert a day earlier, giving them two cycles of darkness to reach the barn, lay up for a day, then place the charges the following night, had been discarded the moment the radio teletypewriter at Pine Gap started buzzing with Seamstress's last punch tape message.

That was old news. This was the here and now. Their cover and concealment sucked and their night-vision goggles were now worthless, but all things considered, his men were postured for the hit. They had confirmed the armored train passing by at 140 yards' distance. As expected, a single rust-colored engine pulled the lead train, which Kleinsmith knew to be the advance party, with three Christmas-green through cars tricked out with a horizontal bright yellow racing stripe on both sides of each. Straight out of the target folder, almost two minutes behind, was the delegation's VIP train, sporting an additional through car but with an identical single engine doing the pulling. Finally, maybe five minutes behind the second train, a third set of cars identical to the lead. All three caboosed by a second rust-colored engine that would pull them back to Pyongyang after the meeting.

Kleinsmith was proud of their work so far. OPSKEDS transmitted on schedule, C4 planted, and the two wrongplace, wrong-time Red Guards sedated for the time being.

As Kleinsmith took a knee next to his communicator to make a SAT shot to Inchon and pass the next OPSKED to Gangster, he worried that any delay in the train could potentially screw their stay time. Kleinsmith worried as he turned back toward their two sleeping guests down the hill before lifting the hand mike.

Someone has to be missing these two jokers by now.

Camp Greaves, South Korea

Knowing Hawk was only a klick north of the Notri, Kolt had only managed a fitful sleep, even with an Ambien. As he and Noble Squadron roused, the checking and re-checking of gear commenced. Neatly arrayed on the floor against the walls of the dining room and dance floor, their combat kit was ready for efficient and rapid donning, no different than a New York City Jake's turn-out gear waiting on a five-alarm fire.

Kolt and Slapshot glassed two white passenger vans from the riverside balcony as the vehicles maneuvered slowly around the yellow-and-black road barriers that control vehicle speed on the bridge. With bellies full from some room-temperature army-issue Meals Ready-to-Eat vegetable lasagna and beef stew, they had confirmed everything was on schedule without a single cell call or radio transmission made.

Now they waited for a phone call from Gangster and the J-staff. Kolt needed one call, the phone call confirming that Hawk had passed OPSKED "Toyota" from Panmunjom, the one on the execution checklist that signified Seamstress had been tagged with the RRD.

"It's Gangster for you," Slapshot said as he passed the Galaxy 4 to Kolt. "By the way, SEALs have the explosives in place. Both bridges set to blow."

Kolt nodded, happy to take it, then paused a moment to watch Slapshot give a vulgar sign with his hand and mouth before he put it to his right ear.

"Go for Racer," Kolt said, forgetting he was on a cell and not a tactical radio.

"Your friend at Panmunjom called," Gangster said. "They changed the meeting location on her, she is inside North Korea now."

"What?" Kolt said, spinning around to move farther

away from his men, who were already kitted up and standing by. "Is her cover blown?"

"No," Gangster said, "she seems to be okay."

"Okay? She is inside North Korea by herself. That's not okay, that's life-threatening."

"She has PIDed Seamstress," Gangster said.

"Has she tagged him?" Kolt said. "We didn't get that OPSKED."

"No Toyota call yet, she is still working on it," Gangster said.

"Shit, Gangster, Hawk is hanging it out here," Kolt said. "I recommend we build the Little Birds up early just in case."

"Negative," Gangster said. "You could compromise the entire operation."

"Dude, just build them up, save ten minutes," Kolt said, "not fly them to Pyongyang."

"No, stay with the operational timeline on the sync matrix. There is nothing driving our contingencies yet."

"Then at least let me put our UAV up over Hawk."

"What fucking UAV?" Gangster demanded.

"We deployed with the SpyLite," Kolt said, now reminded that they hadn't shared that information yet, "standard loadout gear."

"Standard?" Gangster said. "Bullshit, Racer!"

"We'll keep it at max range for standoff, it's too small and quiet to see and no civilians live in the DMZ anyway," Kolt said, trying to put a happy face on Gangster's surprise.

"Damn it! I'm giving you an order, Major Raynor," Gangster said. "Do not put the SpyLite up."

"Roger," Kolt said, deciding his men didn't need to hear any more. "It's risky."

"You're damn right it is," Gangster said. "If that thing is spotted it could blow the entire mission. Or, if it burns in, especially over the border, we'll have an international incident on our hands that POTUS can't deny."

"Thanks for the update," Kolt said, trying to smooth out the catfight. "Ring us if anything changes."

Kolt waited for Gangster to kill the call from his end, surprised he didn't try to get in the last word, then slipped the cell into his right front thigh pocket on his Crye combat pants.

Kolt walked back toward his men lounging in the dining room of the Notri. They were fully kitted out, just waiting for the order to move to the KOREX trailers and build-up the helos.

"Slap!" Kolt said, looking around for his mate, "let's put the SkyLite up."

Slapshot approached Kolt, moving close enough to question the order without the others overhearing. "You sure about that, boss?"

"Yeah, I think we owe it to Hawk," Kolt said, looking past Slapshot and toward the other operators. "What do you think?"

"Did Gangster green-light us?"

"No, he didn't," Kolt said, almost afraid to look Slapshot in the eye, "in fact, he gave me a direct order not to launch it."

"In that case I think they'll be giving this squadron back to Gangster if you blow him off."

"I'm willing to take the chance," Kolt said.

"Fuck, Kolt, an order is a fucking order, man," Slapshot said, getting up in Kolt's face. "Don't jeopardize your career, this squadron, this mission by rocking the boat when it's not necessary."

"It is necessary."

"No, Kolt, it's not."

"Hawk needs it," Kolt said, amazed that Slap was pushing back this hard.

"Damn, boss, maybe you do have a death wish."

Where the hell did that come from?

Hearing that same accusation twice in less than forty-eight hours was a problem, and Kolt Raynor, like any other operator, knew it. Gangster's indictment last night was easy to ignore, but coming from Slapshot, a Unit noncom, it grabbed his attention. Hard punches like that, below the belt or not, if they weren't a kiss of death, were definitely a kiss with severe warning labels.

Kolt stood motionless, staring at Slapshot, who had turned away. He couldn't deny it. He heard Slapshot Lima Charlie, but did he really mean it? *A death wish? Bullshit! Not Slap, we're too tight, have been since day one.* Kolt knew he could not only trust his men with his life, but trust the lives of his kids, if he ever had any, with Slapshot. That kind of trust was uncommon; mates like that made things worth doing, even worth dying for if need be.

Damn it. Maybe Gangster is right. Maybe things would be much better around the Unit if Kolt Raynor just didn't get so damn lucky every time shit hit the fan. Eight fucking Purple Hearts and a dozen easy near-miss life-and-death episodes. Hell, it wasn't like Kolt hadn't given the other guy every chance in the world to take him out.

Kolt shook his head, dismissing that thought almost as fast as it came to him. He knew he was put on this earth to be a Delta Force operator. He knew he had a reputation as a damn fine operator, if also a rebel. A walking legend throughout the Unit Spine, someone to show off to visiting dignitaries and freshly starred general officers. Even so, Kolt wondered what the boys from Noble Squadron thought. How many of the guys sitting inside the Notri thought Kolt was off his rocker? For sure, he didn't know all of them as well as he did the men in Mike Squadron. That would take time. But, they certainly heard about all his bullshit, as Gangster couched it, over the years. And what about Hawk? Did she think he had lost all sense of normalcy too? Unable to respect the risk after so many bombs, so much blood, with death knocking over and over, during scores of deployments, turning targets night and day?

Few would argue that Kolt hadn't shouldered more than his share of the task over the years. Some say dumb luck got Kolt inside that hijacked American Airlines 767 from the cabin roof, took down American-born al Qaeda Daoud al-Amriki before he could assassinate the president, corralled Mohammad Ghafour in Pakistan, or drowned the slant-headed pointy-nosed Nadal the Romanian in a pool of nuclear spent fuel. Even dropping the Barrel Bomb Butcher wasn't enough to silence the critics. Actually, it multiplied them.

Kolt realized time was slipping away and made his choice. He'd made a career of operating intuitively, making instinct decisions, and sometimes wild-ass guesses that more often than not turned out okay. He'd been dropped from Delta's ranks twice, a first for an operator, but his resilience was just as unique. It would be more than just his ass if they lost the satellite feed that controlled the SpyLite from Greaves, or if the battery-powered laptop on the abandoned bar auto-rebooted. But, all things considered, he wasn't about to let Hawk go down alone. No, not to prevent World War III, not for Seamstress and his mini nuke warhead intel, and not for Gangster.

Not for shit.

"Slapshot," Kolt said, lightly grabbing him by the right arm just to get his undivided attention, "I hear you, but this one is on me."

"Rog," Slapshot said, "your call."

"Put the SpyLite up ASAP, push it over Panmunjom," Kolt said, "give it the max four-hour loiter time and program her GPS to recover back at Inchon near the hangar."

"Inchon?"

"Yeah, who knows where we might be by then? We need to sterilize this place."

Just as Slapshot turned to carry out Kolt's orders, the cell inside Kolt's thigh pocket vibrated. He let it buzz a few times, fully expecting it to be Gangster calling to either confirm he was playing well with others and hadn't ignored his last order about the SpyLite, or that Hawk had tagged Seamstress.

Kolt slipped the Galaxy 4 out of the pocket and looked at the screen.

Hawk?!

Kolt quickly answered, afraid she might hang up. "This is Racer, you good?"

"That depends," Hawk said. "Plan B in effect."

"What plan B?"

"I'm taking Seamstress across the MDL into South Korea," Hawk said. "Refuses to get on the train. He wants to defect."

"What the fuck?" Kolt said. "Slow down, give me some context, what's changed?"

"At the hotwash, Kolt, no time now."

Fuck! "Roger that," Kolt said. "We're putting a small UAV over you now. Where are you?"

"Orange two-story, but Kolt, I was hoping you could fly over here, just be close by in case. There are at least a dozen armed guards here."

Fuck me! First the SpyLite and now the Little Birds.

Kolt hesitated for a few seconds, realizing that what Hawk was asking him to do was much more dangerous than simply putting a small plastic plane in the air. Exposing the Little Birds before Seamstress was even back on the train was not smart, but flying even nap-of-the-earth to Panmunjom in broad daylight could be suicide. Kolt knew he didn't have too many options. In fact, only two came to mind: do as Hawk asks, or not.

"Kolt, are you there?" Hawk asked, sounding a little desperate. "Damn it! I could use some help here. I'm unarmed and not dressed for an E and E across the DMZ, especially dragging Seamstress with me."

"Shit, you're right, Hawk," Kolt said. Escaping with an old man would likely get them both killed. "We are en route. I'll keep the cell with me."

"Oh God!" Hawk said. "Someone is banging on the bathroom door. I might be busted. Gotta go."

"Trust your cover!" Kolt said. "Hawk? Hawk?"

Kolt looked at the Galaxy 4 to make sure she had hung up before he ran into the dining room, stopping at the edge of where the operators and helo pilots were catnapping or downing some army chow.

"Get it on!" Kolt barked. "Break out the MHs."

In an instant, everyone scrambled to their feet, reaching back down to grab their rifles, special equipment, and rucksacks before shuffling to the front door and outside to the KOREX trailers. The Delta team leaders and Night Stalker pilots moved toward Kolt, who dug a colored eight-by-ten aerial of the Joint Security Area out of his pocket.

"FRAGO," Kolt began, letting everyone know the fragmentary order he was about to issue trumped the original mission statement. "Hawk just called. She might be soft compromised at best. Seamstress wants to defect."

"Defect?" Slapshot asked. "When?"

"Right now," Kolt said. "Hawk is going to escort him across the MDL."

"We need ten minutes minimum to build the helos and perform safety-of-flight checks," one of the Night Stalker pilots said.

"Just pin the blades and crank 'em," Kolt said, "forget the safety checks."

"We should have SpyLite downlink in another five mikes or so," Slapshot said.

Kolt looked at Slapshot, happy he'd launched the UAV when he told him to and that he didn't dick around and waste time simply because he was against it.

"What about the less-than-lethal stuff?" Digger asked as he held up his MAUL-rigged rifle.

"We are already kitted out with it," Kolt said, "take it just in case."

"What about Gangster?" Slapshot asked.

"I'll call him myself," Kolt said, "let's get the Little Birds built."

As the key leaders and pilots filed out the front door carrying Kolt's orders to run the tails off the trailers, he dug the cell phone back out of his pocket. He knew they would be rolling the Little Birds off the back of the trailers one at a time, an exact reversal of how they were loaded at Osan Air Base. They would use the yak bar and ground-handling wheels to position them at the correct build-up before taking commands from the pilot to remove the wheels and raise each blade one at time using the blade pole. Reconfiguring them for flight required pinning the six main rotor blades in place and dropping the pods on both sides. Kolt wanted to help but they didn't expect him to. In fact, he knew they expected him to notify Gangster and the J-staff about the development.

Kolt would get to Gangster, but he knew he needed to check some things first. He moved to the bar, to where JoJo was busy punching buttons on the remote video terminal, the portable and rugged laptop-looking box that would allow control of the SpyLite as it searched for Hawk.

"Any video images yet?" Kolt asked as he looked over JoJo's back at the screen, hoping for some real-time intelligence.

"Just got it," JoJo said, "fuzzy in flight but once I stabilize it in orbit it should clear up."

Kolt opened his GTG of the JSA area. Graphed alphanumerically, it covered roughly a one-thousand-meter box that grabbed all the buildings along the MDL, including the two larger buildings in North Korea, which appeared to have an orange tint on the aerial.

He put his left forearm in front of JoJo. "Keep her on the South Korean side. Focus on these two buildings, in grid Charlie four and this one in Echo six."

"Got it."

"Pray this one doesn't blink on us," Kolt said.

"Or take a dive," JoJo said.

"Roger, grab me when you're over the buildings."

Kolt turned and walked away from JoJo, toward the front windows of the Notri. He pulled out the cell again and scrolled to Gangster's number, hitting the Call button as he paced the dance floor.

Three painfully long rings.

C'mon, answer the damn phone.

"What you got, Raynor?"

Kolt recognized the voice. "Hey, Curtis, Colonel Mahoney available?"

"Nope, tied up with Captain Yost and on a SAT call with the commanding general, I believe."

"Roger. Didn't know Yost was moving forward." Kolt wasn't necessarily surprised to hear the SEAL Team Six commander had joined the team at Inchon. He knew Webber, given the situation of the one killer force decision sitting in POTUS's inbox, would be commanding the operation from down range, too.

"Just got here, getting briefed up now," Curtis said.

"You guys aware of the change with Carrie?" Kolt asked.

"About changing buildings?" Curtis asked. "Yeah, she called us a while ago."

"Old news," Kolt said. "She is with Seamstress now."

"Exccllent. She tag him yet?"

"The train is a bust. He is defecting now," Kolt said as he looked out a window at the commotion. Two of the four birds were already slowly spinning their blades, and port-side passenger pods were in the down position, ready for customers.

"What?" Curtis asked, obviously confused by Kolt's comment. "When?"

"Now, as in right fucking now."

"Whose fucking idea was that?" Curtis asked. "The SEALs are set, in a perfect position to execute this thing."

"Seamstress's call, Carrie just doing her best to get it done."

"Shit, Raynor, I gotta tell Captain Yost and notify the embassy in Seoul."

"Look, if shit goes bad, we'll be ready to launch in about five minutes."

"What about the SEALs?" Curtis asked. "You leaving them hanging?"

"We have enough z-bags on the trucks to refuel once," Kolt said.

"Fuck, this is not good," Curtis said.

"Just pass the update to Gangster and Yost, will ya?" Kolt watched one of his operators reach high, grab the edge of one of the six rotor blades, and throw it forward, manually free-spinning the blades to a third Little Bird.

"I will," Curtis said. "Hey, wait. An intel update from Pine Gap was pushed to us a few minutes ago."

"Send it," Kolt said.

"Several of our analysts believe Seamstress knows more than just where the militarized nuke warheads are located."

"Like what?"

"Like that the Iranian scientists completed their work

over a month ago and that the missile test scheduled for a few days from now is just a diversion for something much worse."

"How much fucking worse?"

"Like the warheads are already loaded on their ICBMs and they are prepared to strike the Pacific Fleet and Washington state."

"What?" Kolt said, totally surprised by the news. "How good is the intel? Solid source?"

"Rock solid," Curtis said. "Seamstress just became a no-fail recovery."

Just then Kolt heard JoJo yelling from the bar.

"Boss, we got something. You better take a look."

"Stand by, Curtis," Kolt said as he speed-walked back to the bar.

Standing next to JoJo and looking at the screen, Kolt forced himself to blink several times. His mouth grew dry and he gaped. He forced it closed and swallowed heavily.

"Holy shit!" Kolt said. "What the hell is that?"

TWENTY-TWO

Joint Security Area, MDL

"Hawk?" JoJo asked.

Kolt stood right next to him, but he hesitated, not wanting to commit to confirming that the person they were zeroed in on, being dragged down the marble steps by three North Korean soldiers and onto the asphalt road, was in fact Cindy Bird. No, because Kolt knew saying that meant saying the mission was compromised. Saying that meant they had met the abort threshold and were at mission failure. No Seamstress, no intel dump about miniaturized nuclear warheads, and nothing to corroborate Myron Curtis's latest message traffic about a secret missile launch on U.S. PAC Fleet bases. Kolt didn't want to admit he was seeing Hawk, the Delta member Colonel Webber said was his responsibility. Hell no, he didn't. For starters, because doing so pretty much ensured POTUS would shutter Delta. But worse, it pretty much ensured they were on the cusp of World War III.

"Zoom in closer," Kolt said, stretching his neck toward the screen.

JoJo tapped the right arrow key several times, essentially closing the distance to the target area without switching the drone off autopilot and pushing its orbit closer.

Kolt focused on the body kicking and flailing in the middle of the street, a crowd of North Korean soldiers, a dozen or so gathering around, threatening to block the SpyLite's vision. As much as he wanted to believe he was imagining things, maybe hoping to wake up from an Ambien-induced nightmare, he couldn't argue with the definite contrast between the gray pantsuit and the hazel uniforms. And if not that, the daytime camera on the belly of the SpyLite was picking up the blond hair in living color.

"Fucking A right it's her," Kolt said, afraid to take his eyes from the video feed. "Get Slapshot in here; tell the boys to crank the birds."

JoJo slipped from his bar seat and bolted for the front door, leaving Kolt alone.

Kolt leaned forward, tapping the right arrow twice, zooming in close enough to definitely determine sex. Hawk, now partially hidden in the lower right-hand corner behind the auto-adjusting lat-long coordinates and the camera's center mass coordinates, was as non-compliant as a drug-crazed ex-con during a beat cop's wife-beating response, pulling and kicking, trying to escape.

"Take it easy, Hawk," Kolt whispered to himself as he felt Slapshot's presence. "Don't make it a big production."

Just then, Hawk raised her right knee at an odd Heisman-like angle as if she were in the middle of the P90X Cardio X and kung fu kicked out to her side, connecting with the ribcage of one of her accosters. He buckled over, and his bus driver cap fell to the street. Hawk brought her foot back in tight, raised her knee again straight up before slamming her nude-tone heels down on another soldier's left instep. Both released their grip, leaving only one soldier still holding her by the left arm.

Well, shit! Kolt flinched and tightened his abs as if he could feel the impact. Seeing Hawk fight back in heels didn't surprise Kolt. If she asked, Kolt would recommend passive resistance, maybe settle down and garner some pity, but who was he to judge?

The third soldier reached up with his right hand, grabbing a handful of blond hair from behind her head, and yanked it backward. Hawk didn't hesitate as she rotated her body counterclockwise to bump chests before delivering a textbook short stroke throat punch, forcing the soldier to release her hair and arm as he dropped to the street like a sack of rocks.

Kolt smiled for a few seconds, figuring the soldiers had expended all the female courtesies they would give today, expecting them to gang tackle her any second.

Then, Kolt realized there must be a sergeant in charge out there, because someone issued a command. He couldn't be positive, but the North Korean soldiers moved into a single rank, placing themselves shoulder to shoulder in a straight line, positioned between Hawk and the building they had exited behind them. It looked almost as if they were finished with Hawk, maybe satisfied with having removed her from the building, but now preparing to protect something.

Hawk backpedaled several steps, still clutching her purse but leaning to the right, half-barefoot, having left one heel behind. She put about thirty feet between herself and the problem, and put her right hand to her ear as if she was checking for blood.

Kolt looked back at the troops in line, half the group now offscreen. He tapped the back arrow key twice, zooming out to capture Hawk, the full line of soldiers, and the stairs of the building. The guards' legs were now spread shoulder-width apart, and Kolt watched them draw their sidearms in unison. They raised the pistols to the ready position, muzzles up near their right shoulders, as if someone was giving commands to an execution squad.

Shit!

Kolt's cell buzzed, startling him into taking his eyes off the downlink feed. He yanked it out just as Slapshot arrived.

Hawk?!

Kolt tapped the Answer button. "Hawk, get out of there!"

"Where are you guys?" Hawk said, her words coming in a rush.

"We're about to launch," Kolt said, looking back at the screen and now seeing she was making a phone call. "Get back to the MDL, to the South Korean guards."

"They have Seamstress, Kolt," Hawk said. "I tagged him but they might find the RRDs. They think I was confronting him about the regime's human rights record!"

"Fuck it!" Kolt said. "Get moving, we're coming."

Just as Kolt turned to walk away from the video image and head toward the Little Birds he heard Slapshot say something.

"Boss, is that Seamstress?"

Kolt turned back, stepped closer to the bar, and tapped the right arrow to zoom closer. Four or five other North Korean soldiers, one with a different style cap than the others, were dragging a shorter penguin down the same marble steps.

"Who the fuck knows?" Kolt said.

"Who else could it be?" Slapshot countered.

Hawk obviously could hear the two operators talking and jumped in. "Yes, that's him. We are so busted!"

"Stand by, Hawk," Kolt said, not necessarily because he had a solution, but more to give him time to think.

Kolt and Slapshot watched as the soldiers reached the bottom step and then gained the asphalt. They began dragging the man away from the line of troops, down the street and deeper into North Korea.

Think, Kolt, think!

Kolt ran the situation through his head quickly, searching for an answer he wasn't sure he would find. He knew Seamstress was now a dead man walking, soon to face a firing squad if he was lucky, or maybe the dogs if not. With no RRD tag, the chances of the SEALs finding him on the train were shot, if he was even put back on the train. Maybe they would just put a few rounds in the traitor's head and leave him on the side of the road.

"What about the Q dots?" Slapshot asked Kolt.

"The quantum dots," Kolt said, speaking to Hawk, "did you use them?"

"I didn't have time," Hawk said.

Just then, the front hood of a dark-colored vehicle entered the screen at the top. Kolt zoomed out several layers, revealing two four-doors parked up the road, maybe a football field or so away from Hawk and the execution party. By now, the soldiers manhandling Seamstress were halfway there.

"Exfil vehicles for sure, boss," Slapshot said.

Kolt didn't have any more time to think it through, not another second to run the options through some risk-assessment matrix, no fucking time to waste on building a PowerPoint CONOP to present to Gangster. He needed to do something, anything. Anything but continue to stand there offering no solutions to the problem.

"Hawk, where are the dots?"

"In my pockets still," Hawk said as she backpedaled a few more steps away from the line of upset North Korean troops.

"Use them now!" Kolt said, seeing Slapshot cut his eyes from the screen to him.

"What?" Hawk asked. "It's too late, Kolt, they have Seamstress. He's gone."

"No, Hawk, hear me out," Kolt said, taking inventory of his inflection, careful not to amp Hawk up even more.

"Use your gun, Hawk," Kolt said. "You can make that throw."

Kolt felt Slapshot cock his head, confused by the last comment. "Gun, dude?"

"She's got a rocket arm," Kolt said, "got her nickname from shagging bombs as a kid."

"Are you serious?" Hawk said as she threw her left arm in the air, obviously shocked at what she had just heard through her Bluetooth. "Stop oppressing your people!" Hawk shouted, doing her best to keep up her cover as a crazed delegate.

Kolt knew Hawk had three strikes at it. All she had to do was reach into her pockets and pull out the quantum dots, the three plastic eggs disguised as bottles of cologne, a gift from the Swedish delegation for their North Korean hosts.

"You have three tries, Hawk," Kolt said, "no different than gunning down a runner on third from the warning track in deep center."

"I can't make that throw, Kolt," Hawk said, her voice quivering, practically refusing to even try.

"I know you can," Kolt countered. "You did it dozens of times as a kid with your dad. Gun it once more."

"Christ, Kolt, they'll fucking shoot her if she pulls that shit," Slapshot said.

"Aw shit, you're right," Kolt said, resigned. "Forget that, Hawk, you probably don't have it anymore anyway."

"Damn you, Kolt Raynor," Hawk said.

Before Kolt could reply, letting her know he really didn't mean the cheap shot questioning her skills, a pack of suits burst from the front door of the orange building and hurried down the steps. At least a dozen, all in civilian dress, mostly black over black. The crowd moved around the intimidating firing party and toward Hawk.

Hawk reached into her jacket pockets.

"No she isn't," Slapshot said, pushing his face a little closer to the screen.

Kolt didn't respond, just watched the show almost in a paralyzed state, afraid to believe that Hawk might just attempt the throw.

"Hawk!" Kolt said into his cell. "Don't push it."

Hawk clutched one Q-dot in her left hand and two in her strong hand before stepping away from the rest of the gathering delegation. She figured that by tossing two on the first go she was bound to hit Seamstress.

Kolt heard Hawk speak in a normal, relaxed tone as if she had calmed down.

"Bottom of the seventh, tied score, winning run on third," Hawk said as she took two steps toward the thugs dragging Seamstress, now thirty feet or so from the safety of the vehicles.

Kolt updated Slapshot, both locked on the remote video screen. "She is going for it."

Hawk raised her hands chest level, cupped them as if the ball was hidden in the glove hand. She led with her left foot, the one still in the nude-tone heel, and crow-hopped with her bare right foot. In one smooth motion, she rotated at the waist, raised her throwing arm, and rifled the Q dots on a perfect horizontal.

Kolt and Slapshot watched them fly but couldn't tell where they hit.

Hawk turned quickly toward the crowd. Kolt could hear them screaming but couldn't understand what they were saying. Two men in dark suits ran toward Hawk just as the line of North Korean troops pointed their pistols at Hawk. The men stopped, apparently afraid to get too close to their wacked-out and obnoxious Swedish colleague.

"Shit!" Kolt said as he heard a gunshot through his cell. "Shots fired!"

"Leave it alone, Hawk!" Kolt yelled into his cell.

But Hawk was either not listening or ignoring Kolt now. She reached down with her left hand and ripped the remaining heel off, dropping it as if she was about to hit a hot shower.

"Free North Korea!" Hawk screamed at Seamstress, doing her best to explain her insane behavior.

"Hawk, acknowledge," Kolt demanded. "Abort the fucking op!"

By now, Kolt was certain the Swedish delegation was in full shock. Their American colleague's actions had not only broken up an important meeting, but threatened to get them all killed. And at the moment, Hawk no longer seemed to give two shits.

Hawk ran several steps closer to Seamstress, likely trying to improve her odds. Now barefooted, her movements looked pure and effortless. Hawk grabbed the remaining Q dot from her left hand, pulled her purse off her shoulder and dropped it to the street, then cupped her hands together again, going into another full windup. She turned her left shoulder toward home plate, crow-hopped, and uncorked a two-seam fastball directly at Seamstress. Just as she got the throw off, several North Korean soldiers grabbed her and forced her to the street. Now on her belly, her hands held behind her back, Hawk sent a final OPSKED over Bluetooth.

"I send Toyota."

Camp Greaves, South Korea

"We launching, boss?" Slapshot asked.

"Aww, shit," Kolt said as he watched Cindy Bird lifted to her feet, surrounded by North Korean guards and what he figured were both the South Korean and Swedish delegations. "I don't know, man, the train or Hawk?"

"Looks like Hawk might be going to jail, but hopefully on this side of the border," Slapshot said.

Kolt realized Hawk was being marched south, toward the original meeting building and the MDL.

"Get JoJo to pass Toyota to Inchon. Let the SEALs know he is tagged, but with the Q dots and not the RRDs. Their sensor won't help."

Kolt rubbed his short-haired beard nervously several times. He ran his fingers through his hair, flipping it out of his eyes, even though the first time did it. He turned away from the SpyLite's remote video terminal to see Slapshot leaving the building, out to get JoJo to pull up green SAT and update Gangster, and in turn, Kleinsmith and his men, that Hawk had done her part.

It had been a long time since he turned down an opportunity to launch with his men. But he knew he had a larger responsibility now, as a squadron commander, to respect the chain of command. Slapshot might not like it, but he sensed his longtime partner understood. If Gangster wanted Kolt and the QRF to launch, he'd order them to. And in the absence of orders, even though Hawk's performance was dicey, the situation was still under control. Launching helos across the DMZ in broad daylight required more than Hawk losing her cool. As long as she stayed true to her cover, Kolt figured she'd come out of it okay.

Kolt consciously felt for his cell phone, wondering if he should have just called instead of having JoJo pass the news over satellite. He turned back to the screen, and not seeing the crowd, reached for the arrow to zoom out.

Holy fuck!

Kolt leaped toward the bar and grabbed the video terminal with both hands. Careful not to inadvertently hit any buttons that might send the SpyLite barnstorming into North Korea, he turned toward his kit in the corner near the front door. Carrying the laptop over his left forearm like a newborn baby, he scooped up his assault vest, K-pot, and HK with his right hand and bolted for the front door.

TWENTY-THREE

Military Demarcation Line

Hawk looked back toward the mess she'd just broken free of. The North Korean guards were pushing the business-suited delegation members out of the way, helping each other to their feet, one guard even throwing Hawk's pin-stripe to the ground, another still supine, holding his left elbow.

Several pointed her way, their hands bobbing accusingly as if fingering a fan who might have interfered with a fly ball that was clearly playable by a hustling third baseman. She turned back, eyes on the path, consciously concerned about small unseen pebbles in the street gouging the bottom of her bare feet as she bolted for the safety of South Korean territory.

Not worried about having had her pantsuit jacket torn from her torso, she was just happy to have the elbow room to go full forty-yard sprint mode. She held on to her cell with her left hand as she held the Bluetooth to her ear with her right.

Her CrossFit legs pulled four more long but deli-cate strides before she turned again. Now their pistols were raised, probably slowing them a little, and they were screaming at her in undecipherable Korean, but no question: they were coming for her.

And fast.

No way, motherfuckers.

Hawk turned and eyed the center light blue buildings, the ones that straddled north and south territory evenly, and scanned for cover. Gunshots rang out. She instinctively ducked, fully expecting at least one of the North Korean guards' rounds to ventilate her torn mauve joy blouse. Nothing.

They all missed? The body is an acceptable bullet trap. *They couldn't all have missed.*

Hawk heard the shots, no doubt, but didn't hear the crack she knew always followed in a millisecond as the supersonic rounds screamed past a target's head. She knew the old pistols likely held shit ammo, with less stopping power than modern munitions, but she was still close enough to eat one. Hawk tried to increase her stride—even another inch could make a difference—but her shoeless feet weren't agreeing with the hard asphalt.

"Kolt! Kolt!" she screamed, hopeful the Bluetooth connection was somehow still active. "Answer me, damn it!"

Hawk stopped as she reached the first piece of ballistically suitable cover, a place that would provide enough mass to absorb the small-arms bullets.

Now standing in the sand bed, just around the corner of the center blue MAC building that straddled the MDL, Hawk bent over. She opened her mouth wide to grab air, panting desperately as her aortic valves pumped at time and a half, her sensory and motor neurons jousting like medieval knights preventing her from another step.

Hawk looked up and peered around the building corner, hoping the air-conditioning unit would help conceal her from her pursuers.

Still closing.

She turned her head toward South Korea, still thirty feet or so behind her, the exact line marked by a short concrete slab running from building to building, paralleling the MDL. Surprised, no, shocked to not see any shiny black helmets with thick white stripes, the helmets of South Korean guards that she might signal for help. Worse, no sign of U.S. Army troops behind her, armed soldiers that might help her to safety. The anticipated safety of South Korea didn't look so certain as she saw only the empty space of the five marble steps and three double glass doors of the massive Freedom House.

Shit!

Hawk knew she couldn't stop, no way, but she also knew that if she simply busted across the MDL without warning, she'd be stitched from cleavage to groin. She had already created an international incident, and even though word doesn't travel that fast, American JSA sharpshooters aim small and hit small.

But, debate too long now and she risked being grabbed again. And if the grudge-holding North Koreans got her in their clutches again, it would be curtains for sure. She had already proven too squirrely to hold on to and figured the North Koreans would simply line up their iron sights and execute her on the spot. Her act of love-crazed groupie had no doubt been viewed an act of espionage against the people of the DPRK. There was no stopping now, not on Gangster's sync matrix and not on hers.

She quickly looked around, left then right, then whipped her head to her six again, hoping like hell to finally catch a glimpse of a few rifle-bearing South Korean or U.S. Army soldiers holding the line. She knew they had to have heard the earlier gunshots.

Where the hell is everyone? Where the hell is Kolt?

Hawk pied the corner, staying low behind the air

conditioner, stealing one last look into North Korea before she knew she'd turn for the dark gravel bed that marked southern soil. If her pursuers planned to stop short of crossing the line, they sure weren't telegraphing their intentions. Without a weapon, she'd throw her hands into the sky surrender style and take her chances in South Korea.

Get moving, Hawk!

She heard the crack of two more rounds, but this time from behind her. She winced in pain, grabbed her right shoulder, and dropped prone to the sand next to the spray of blood drops that had beaten her there. She turned her head, her blond bangs barely obscuring the reflection from broken glass that had been blasted from the windowsill, now drawing her attention like a proctor is drawn to a performing class clown in the middle of a final exam. She looked up, toward the window, and directly into the business end of two smoking Czech CZ-82s double-gripped by two menacing and very serious-looking North Korean soldiers.

Party over!

Kolt Raynor quickly looked up from the remote video terminal, his thighs holding it tight by the edges as they sped toward the objective area at 152 knots, practically skidding across the treetops and happy mounds. He barely spotted the oddball rooftop of the Freedom House, the tallest building on the South Korean side of the Joint Security Area, and knew they were less than a minute out.

He gave one more glance at the screen, saw the video image of Hawk in a crowd between two of the three blue one-story buildings, and tapped in the four-number code to auto the SpyLite to its programmed recovery location.

He spun on his ass, reached behind him from the Little Bird's port-side external pod, and set the SpyLite laptop into the belly of Breaker Four-One. He pushed it as deep as he could, betting it wouldn't catch wind from under the auxiliary fuel tank, and called it good. He reached up to grab his Oakley goggles resting on his helmet, just above the plastic NVG mount, yanked on the elastic band, and dropped them in front of his eyes.

"Uhhhhh . . . say again last?" CW3 Stew Weeks, the Night Stalker air mission commander requested from the bubble cockpit only a few feet from Kolt. Weeks's tone revealed he wasn't all that fired up about Kolt's last directive, certainly because he had no idea what the flight conditions were at the JSA or how hot the landing zone might be. Without understanding a multitude of factors, like airspeed, temperature, and density altitude, the customer was asking for a high-fidelity maneuver with a dozen potential problems.

"I say again," Kolt said, pausing a moment after he keyed his hand mike, "put us on the X, directly east of the center blue building."

Kolt looked at the GRG on his left forearm showing a color satellite photo of Hawk's original meeting spot. He pulled a red pencil crayon from his vest, steadied his left forearm against the headwind, and drew an X exactly where he'd last seen Hawk on her back, with several North Korean soldiers only a few feet away. He slid the quarterback armband over his gloved left hand, leaned forward on the pod, and shoved it into the doorless cockpit, far enough to touch Weeks's left shoulder, just above the subdued American flag.

Weeks tilted his head down, his eyes hidden behind the smoke-colored face shield. Kolt figured he saw the GRG and probably the red X, by the shake of his head.

"Doubt I can clear the roof lines," Weeks transmitted over Helo common.

Kolt grabbed his push-to-talk. "Just get us close, Stew. Put two on the north side, buzz them as if on a

VI," he said, referencing a vertical interdiction. "Keep one in overwatch."

"Um, roger," Weeks said, pausing for a few seconds, letting Kolt know he wasn't entirely buying the hasty plan.

Kolt figured not only was Weeks hesitant about the X location, but asking him, the air mission commander, to put his other chalks, Breaker Four-Two, Four-Three, and Four-Four, into North Korea as if they were executing a vertical vehicle interdiction was off-the-charts suicidal. A moving vehicle was easy, they had standard procedures for those type of interdictions. What Kolt was asking for was anything but standard.

A few seconds later, Kolt and anyone else monitoring Helo Common heard the call.

"This is Breaker Four-One, I'm leading to the X. Four-Two bank wide right off me, then swing around from the east and buzz the blue buildings on the north side, break."

Kolt heard Weeks unkey his mike, hearing an audible click, then rekey to talk. "Four-Three follow Two, Four-Four aerial support. Standard offset VI formation for the customer."

As Kolt heard each pilot acknowledge the play he let out some air, and turned his MBITR radio back to his assault net.

"All elements, this is Noble Zero-One," Kolt said, knowing now was not the time for comms problems. "Eagle down between the blue buildings. I've got the SA so I've got the X, everyone else is buzzing the north side but staying airborne."

Kolt knew the order he'd just given his operators, arguably just as crazy of a command as he had issued in Ukraine about the Spetsnaz uniforms, at least one that meant anything, had to raise some eyebrows underneath the Ops-Core helmets and Oakleys on the other three birds. Kolt got it. He was a squadron commander now. His focus should be big-picture stuff, working external assets and friendly units, and coordinating contingencies. His days as Mike One-One, those glory years running as a troop commander, were long gone. Every member of Noble Squadron knew Kolt Raynor was the last guy that should be at the center of the X. Even Kolt knew it, which is why Kolt added the *SA* part to his last transmission, letting his men know that with the Spy-Lite feed, his helo had the only situational awareness of Hawk's exact location.

From the other side of the Breaker Four-One, Slapshot broke in. "We going in dirty, boss?"

TWENTY-FOUR

Hawk's fight-or-flight senses immediately drove her back to a knee, but the shock held her like a straitjacket, preventing her from running. She ran the options.

Run for it or give it up? Maybe I can hold true to my cover?

Hawk knew she wasn't hard compromised. She was absolutely sure her name tag, written in Hangul, said Carrie Tomlinson, Swedish delegation, not Cindy Bird, wannabe operator from the U.S. Army Delta Force. Sure, she had just been busted in the men's room, escorted out of the meeting. Had she left things alone then, she might have been directed back to the MDL without any more concern. The North Korean delegation, hell the South Korean delegation, would surely register a formal complaint about the actions of a female member of the Swedish delegation. Yes, a slap on the wrist, but manageable. But muscling the three North Korean guards before throwing things at their fellow thugs dragging a traitor to some vehicles only fed the shitstorm, definitely meeting the guards' threshold to draw their weapons and drop the hammers.

Hawk looked at her shoulder, her blouse now crimson red, blood oozing between her fingers as she held direct pressure. It wasn't a through and through, this she was certain of. She tried to slip her cell into her pants pocket several times before remembering her wardrobe disadvantage. She quickly slipped it into her skin-hugging black bra, down to the nipple, hoping her firm 34Cs would keep it secure.

Stand up slowly, Hawk, don't push it.

That was it, she had thought enough, and decided in an instant caution was the better part of valor. She did her job, Seamstress was tagged. She had seen the third Q dot find its mark, impacting directly between the shoulder blades of the back of Seamstress's ruffled black suit coat. She had saved another game from the warning track, gunning down that runner on third barreling toward home plate in the bottom of the ninth.

No, now was not the time to let perfect be the enemy of good enough. She'd end it now, raise her hands in surrender, and prepare to stay in the circle.

Hawk looked back toward the Freedom House. A flash of movement drew her.

About time!

Several South Korean soldiers had slipped into firing positions at the top of the marble stairs. Their black domes were barely peeking over the concrete benches and flowerpots, every bit the "Kilroy was here" impression. She didn't spot any long guns, but their drawn pistols were encouraging enough. Waving at others unseen by Hawk was all the better.

Hawk heard a faint buzzing sound, as if a swarm of killer bees had just joined the party. Though she was initially unable to place it, the sound registered as a remote-controlled drone. She looked up, but the overhanging corrugated rooflines of the two buildings blocked much of her vision of the sky.

She swiveled her head back toward North Korea,

running her eyes up the marble stairs of North Korea's version of the ROK Freedom House. At the top of the stairs, uniformed North Korean troops were busting out of Panmon Hall's two wooden front double doors, two at a time.

What about the RRDs?

In an instant, Hawk realized surrendering wouldn't work. They'd find the RRDs on Seamstress. They'd put two and two together. Practicing her peacetime detention techniques briefed well, until her unimpressed interrogators shoved the RRDs in front of her face. Playing her cover until she was blue in the face or not, she was guilty of espionage, pure and simple. And, once that was decided, she'd lose her head before POTUS pulled enough diplomatic rabbit tricks to secure her release.

Back at Fort Bragg, shitting herself in the Black Ice box had lasted only seventy-two hours. Nadal the Romanian's henchmen had their way with her for a month inside a forgotten bedbug-infested hooker's motel. No, isolation wasn't all the rage these days, and in an instant, she decided she wasn't going there again.

Okay, Cindy Bird, potential Delta operator, you're trained how to think, not what to think.

Hawk released her wounded deltoid and dug her bloody thirty-five-dollar fingernails into the sand. She raked out a handful, and pivoted on her knee.

Don't miss!

Hugging the building, Hawk threw the sand through the broken window, the bulk of it flying center mass between the light blue curtains. Enough of the sand grains found the eyes of the two North Korean soldiers and they flinched, one squeezing off another round that blew past Hawk's Bluetooth, missing her locks by a gnat's ass before ricocheting off the steel grating covering the concrete gutter on the opposite side of the open area.

Hawk broke for the concrete pad of the MDL. Immediately, broken glass sliced into her left heel, then into the ball of her right foot.

Just three, maybe two more steps from the gravel side, bullets stitched the sand around her feet. But one found its mark, striking her in the left calf, her forward momentum carrying her across the line and sending her barreling face-first, like Pete Rose in his peak years, into the gravel.

The hard impact bounced the Bluetooth from her ear and threatened to knock her unconscious. She slowly rolled to her back. Blood ran down her forehead from underneath her blond bangs, blurring both eyes. Blinking rapidly to clear her vision, she fought to stay conscious as she stared into the clear blue sky. Shaking her head, unable to focus on anything in particular, she barely made out a small white plane, very small, like the hobby toys she thought of earlier, buzz the two buildings only fifteen or so feet off the ground directly above her.

Hawk felt the hands of two North Korean soldiers clamp to her ankles. She tried to kick free but the grips were viselike. They began shuffling backward, dragging her back across the line, into the North Korean sand. Hawk dug her hands into the gravel, but unable to hold purchase, she was at the mercy of the two stronger men.

She struggled, determined not to go easy, and tried to roll left, then right, hoping to break their grip. Hawk felt them yank hard on both legs as if they timed it perfectly. Her head slammed into the concrete curb's corner edge on the gravel side. She felt for the wound. Broken skin. A deep gash.

That's it. I'm done!

Breaker Four-One dove from its approach altitude like a monster roller coaster cresting the scary apex, the part of the track where it feels as if someone just ripped your

heart from your chest. Leading the four-ship formation, Kolt's helo hugged the ground as it maneuvered
NASCAR fast just over the rotor wash–beaten trees.

The midday sun cast a menacing shadow on the
yielding poplars, pines, and happy mounds below,
clearly outlining the Killer Bee's bubbled cockpit and
tail boom as it sped to the target area. The distinct smell
of human waste and muddy water filling the foot-deep
rice paddies laid out in the fertile soil as far as the eye
could see reminded Kolt of a string of portable shitters
serviced by a battalion of marines in Kandahar.

By the angle, Kolt could make out the dangling lower
legs of the two operators on the opposite side pods,
Slapshot in the front with his ankles characteristically
crossed and straddling the pod like a mechanical bull.
Behind him, sitting sidesaddle, Kolt knew, was Master
Breacher Digger. He wasn't tough to spot, as the shadow
of his narrow titanium prosthesis contrasted with the
human form of his left calf.

Kolt turned back around and looked off in the distance past the thick poplar trees . Maybe a klick away
at his nine o'clock, Kolt spotted where he knew the 72-
Hour Bridge sat, the hallowed ground notorious for the
ax murders of 1976. That incident was the impetus for
the concrete pad between the blue buildings and the en-
forcement of the dividing line.

Now looking back in the direction of flight, Kolt spotted the large three-story Peace Hall, and farther, maybe
another two hundred feet distant, the unique oriental-
flavored roofline of the larger Freedom House. The
highly buffed and polished concrete walls and custom
glass windows in each were the pride and joy of South
Korea and were considered engineering marvels. Not
much had changed since he had visited the JSA many
years ago.

Kolt reached up for the coiled black radio cable,

traced his gloved fingers upward, feeling the connection between his MBITR and the electrical communications port embedded inside his SWAT black M50 protective mask. He pushed the male lead in again, expecting to take up the slack, but pleased the connection was solid. Communicating from under a gas mask, particularly if your audio amplifier was spotty, or cable connection loose, made for a cluster fuck on target.

Kolt thumb-pressed the mike, felt the marble-size voice meter with his lips, and spoke into the mini microphone. He knew it would be a miracle if all sixteen Noble Squadron members would clearly hear his call.

"We're here to grab Hawk, nothing else. MAULs only, stay on the pods, nobody get off."

Leading the formation of four MH-6M Little Birds, Kolt's chalk had a clear view of the manicured sunken garden, a sea of blue-and-white tourist buses, and the large odd-shaped monuments below, whipping past them as they approached the target like a strong side linebacker with the perfect angle. Weeks maneuvered the lead in behind the south side of the Freedom House, and Kolt knew he was banking the three-story building would mask their approach as long as possible. Kolt tapped his Salomon assault boots together several times, pushing blood flow and ensuring his feet hadn't fallen asleep.

Kolt turned around, looked to his six, past his hooked-in squadron communicator JoJo, and watched chalks two, three, and four pull hard right out of the staggered trail right formation, disappearing one at a time from his view, posturing for the aerial flanking maneuver.

Stop processing and start operating.

Kolt turned his HK over, two-fingered the charging handle, pulled it back a half inch or so, and eyeballed the ejection port.

Brass, check, weapon hot.

Kolt prayed he wouldn't need it. A gunfight with North Korean guards was to be avoided at all costs. Hawk throwing shit at North Korean officials to protest human rights abuses was one thing, but buzzing the MDL with weapons fire was a definite precursor to World War III.

Lock and loading was the norm, he knew his squadron's weapons were hot, but he also knew they would follow the rules of engagement and use the less-than-lethal munitions. Personally, though, Kolt wasn't interested in another mental mistake like the brain fart he'd had on the Barrel Bomb Butcher hit in Syria, and unless the North Koreans made it hard, he wouldn't be slinging brass.

Kolt made a conscious decision to breathe, feeling the chest area of his assault vest expand and contract. The headwind seeped between his ceramic chest plate and his combat shirt, cooling his sweat-covered pecs. He tried to relax as they approached the X, his exhales testing the de-mist properties of the smoke-colored lenses. Natural anxiety before any high-risk mission was the norm, but under a full protective mask where breathing is labored, the major worry was a fogged-up face mask. When that happened, it severely limited visibility, maybe forcing a guy to come out from under his mask, which, in a contaminated environment, was the sure-bet way to receive the ass clown award at the post-mission hotwash.

Through his Peltors Kolt heard Weeks over helo common, amazed that one man could juggle multiple inputs and process what he was seeing for the first time. The skill set, talent, and cool demeanor might not be common in all army aviators, but were required in the Night Stalker ranks.

"One minute! One minute!"

Kolt keyed his assault net to relay to the boys. "All elements, one minute!"

Fuck me!

Kolt pulled the beer-can-size canister from a nylon pouch on his assault vest. He had been carrying this same Triple Phaser in his kit for months now, knowing one day he might have a good reason to shed its weight. He looked at the aluminum-colored body, identified the red lettering confirming he was holding CS gas and not a high-concentrate screening smoke that could blind the pilot, and grabbed the flimsy OD green 100-mile-an-hour tape quick-release tab. He tore it free and flicked it from his gloved fingers. He slipped his trigger finger into the pull ring and yanked the safety pin out, his left-hand full grip maintaining pressure on the grenade's spoon.

"Smoke prepped, Slapshot!" Kolt said into his pro mask voice meter.

Breaker Four-One left the veiled protection provided by Freedom House's long shadow only seconds after entering, slipped crazy close over the last parked buses, around the east side of the building, and shot head on into the bright sunlight. Kolt noticed they were eye level with the second-floor balcony and left of the giant auburn gazebo covering the Panmunjom bell. And now, Kolt indeed knew, in direct line of sight of the North Korean checkpoint perched on a low hill only a few hundred feet away.

Kolt felt the helo break, the nose rising a foot or so, before overcorrecting to nose down as if he was on a playground teeter-totter with the neighborhood bully.

"Roger, I'm purple and you've got the gas," Slapshot confirmed, letting Kolt know he was holding a canister containing violet smoke.

Kolt braced as chalk one wobbled past the corner of

the building. The turbulence created by wind direction and terrain masking put the twenty-seven-foot-diameter main rotor blades perilously close to the building's massive corner pillar. Kolt leaned his back against the thin sheet-metal skin of the aircraft, holding tight to help the pilot manipulate the pedals and control the torque, staring straight into the large glass windows just above the Freedom House front doors. He looked toward his boots and saw several brown streetlight posts seemingly flying past, inches from the bird's tubular skids. Fleeting flashes of what Kolt knew to be South Korean, or even American troops, scattering for cover like a flash mob party busted by the law.

This is not good!

Kolt noticed he was holding his breath and exhaled slowly, trying to control his heart rate, concentrating on slow short breaths, desperately countering the anxiety inherent in assaulting under a full face mask.

Kolt heard Weeks again. "Ten seconds! Ten seconds!"

The lead helo crossed the spotless asphalt street, the white-and-yellow-painted lines a blur, before slowing to turn hard right, lifting Kolt and JoJo high in the air as the helo banked.

Feeling the Little Bird slow to line up with the correct buildings, Kolt turned around on the pod, testing every bit of his safety line's tensile strength. Stretching his neck to see, and ping-ponging his head to find a needle-head view, Kolt hoped to get a visual on Hawk.

Weeks shot his approach and flared, forcing the 4,300-hundred-pound bird's nose abruptly up and tail rotor toward the gravel side of the MDL. Kolt could tell the winds were adverse, quartering from the rear and driving up the power requirement and the resultant torque value needed to hold steady. They were on target, on time, but at a power setting that high an uncoordinated pedal movement, or a brief gust of wind, could drive the torque off the chart, busting the maximum continuous torque and putting them way outside the operational margin. If that happened, they might as well brace for impact. But this time, unlike the assault on the *Queen Mary 2* in the Atlantic Ocean, the crash and burn would definitely leave a bruise.

Kolt could feel Weeks struggling to hold the hover out of ground effect as the downwash of the six-bladed main rotor assembly pounded the corrugated steel covering the open gabled roof of the three light blue buildings. Spinning at close to 375 rpms, the composite blades generated a wind pressure that threatened to tear the metal screws from their settings. Sand on the North Korean side erupted into a massive dust ball, engulfing the front half of the MH-6M, but the gravel of the South Korean side was holding in place, not affected by the rotor wash.

"I've got eyes on," Slapshot sent over internal comms, "she's just below us."

Kolt grabbed the running end of his safety line, tug-checked it, and leaned out as far as he could to look past the skids and under the helo. He wasn't questioning Slapshot, but had to be sure, because winging it wasn't one of the approved contingencies.

There she was, lying on her back, arms out to her sides, her mauve top torn wide open exposing her black strapless bra. She seemed at peace, not fighting it, as if she'd frozen in time while making a snow angel at the beach. Several uniformed men were kneeling next to her, four, maybe five, all but one holding their saucer caps on their heads as the rotor wash pounded them. Kolt quickly sized them up.

North Koreans! Check!

One hatless soldier with a black pistol, aiming it right at Kolt maybe fifteen feet away, his black hair flapping violently in the down blast.

Shit!

Kolt tried to pull himself back toward the helo's skin, hoping the guy would choke, maybe jerk the trigger just before breaking the shot. Kolt heard at least three shots fired, and twice felt the blunt trauma impact of Thor's hammer against his level IV ceramic chest plate. The plate was heavy, a tad over six and a half pounds, but designed to stop multiple AK-47 hits. A plate sucks ass, until you fall in love with it.

Kolt buckled in pain, and his bladder released, involuntarily showering his legs with his own urine.

A nanosecond later, unable to control his voluntary skeletal muscles, he felt a sense of paralysis grab him underneath his Multicam. His grip on the Triple Phaser broke, the spoon disengaged and flew off, and the canister fell to the ground. Kolt was unable to hold on, and his ass slipped off the cornered edge of the pod. Gravity pulled him two feet below, just above the skid, his safety line the only thing still tethering him to the hovering Little Bird.

"Smoke out!"

Kolt thought he heard someone call his smoke, maybe JoJo, maybe the pilot, Weeks? Something grabbed him from behind the neck area of his assault vest, steadying him as the rotor wash turned the CS and sand violently over and over.

JoJo.

Kolt's torso rotated as JoJo tried to pull him up, causing his body to fall to the side and turn his chest toward the helo. Kolt hugged the skids with both arms, his rifle still slung but jabbing him uncomfortably in the groin.

Kolt noticed purple smoke lifting into the air, mixing with the sand and the CS gas's off-white shade.

Move Hawk, move!

Out of the corner of his eye, he spotted movement

behind the four-blade tail rotor, back in the road. Two ranks of helmeted South Korean troops, a dozen in each, maybe more, were short-stepping toward the X. Decked out in clear face shields and larger riot control body shields, they looked like they could have been handling an Occupy Wall Street callout.

Kolt's attention was drawn to the other pod, where he knew Slapshot and Digger were postured. A green nylon rope uncoiled past the starboard-side skid, only a few feet from him, as it fell heavily to the ground, landing only an arm's length from Hawk's right arm.

No! Don't do it!

Too late.

A fast rope had been deployed and in an instant, he watched Slapshot drop to the deck. On his tail, Digger followed.

Fuck! Get down there!

Knowing he couldn't reach his safety line snap link, Kolt reached for the straight blade cross-placed in a tan Kydex sheath on his chest, clipped on just over the American flag. He fumbled as he lifted it out and then reached behind him to catch the blade unseen on his nylon safety line.

On the ground, Hawk hadn't moved. Kolt worried about her inhaling the CS.

He saw the tops of Slapshot's and Digger's helmets, the tops of their shoulders, the call sign patches, and the upper receivers of their assault rifles as they aimed them at the North Koreans. Half obscured by the rotor wash, most were now holding their hats over their mouths, rubbing their eyes frantically, victims of the CS gas.

Slapshot held his fire, appearing to cover Digger. Just then, Kolt recognized the MAUL Digger was holding, a moment before he engaged three of the closest North Koreans. Each 12-gauge less-than-lethal blunt-impact round hit them in the upper torso, the kinetic energy behind the rubber balls knocking them over like pop-up carnival ducks.

Good play, Digger!

Kolt felt the helo slipping backward, away from the sandy North Korean side. Immediately, the rotor wash lost its flying sand and the dirty color cleared out. Kolt stopped trying to cut his safety line, knowing he didn't need to fall from the helo and add to the chaos. Pissing his pants was one thing, falling from a hovering helo was another story.

Kolt resheathed his custom Watson pocket fighter knife and turned to keep a visual on Slapshot and Digger. Kolt couldn't tell, his vision still obscured by the smoke. It had dissipated enough, though, to reveal that the North Korean guards had cleared the area, probably crawling to cover behind the building, not wanting to deal with the volatile mix of CS gas, rotor wash, purple smoke, and rubber bullets anymore.

Slapshot, or maybe Digger, looked to have already lifted Hawk to his shoulder in a fireman's carry. Yes, he saw Digger, heading toward the two South Korean ranks in riot control mode. Behind him, Slapshot was on a knee and bent over, appearing to pick something up. Whatever he grabbed, he shoved it in his right cargo pocket and turned to follow Digger.

Digger began to beat feet, his door-wide shoulders now square with the MDL, Hawk draped over his non-firing shoulder. He stepped onto the concrete slab with his left foot and took his first step back onto South Korean soil with his titanium prosthetic.

Kolt watched Digger face plant, crumbling into the gray gravel. Kolt thought he heard a gunshot, but couldn't be sure.

The leg!

Kolt saw it happen. He watched Digger's prosthetic

lower leg break away from his knee, watched him collapse, and watched Hawk heavily tumble from his shoulder.

Kolt keyed his mike to talk to Weeks. "Put us down! Down! Down!"

Kolt held his legs up above the skid as JoJo held his vest from above, allowing Breaker Four-One to set down in the center of the street, just behind the light blue MAC building and in front of the marble stairs leading up to the Freedom House. Kolt stood and reached for his snap link, unhooking as he watched JoJo do the same.

Kolt turned toward the cockpit and gave Weeks a clenched fist, the signal to hold what he had. Weeks would recognize the sign and stay in place, main rotor pumping in a ground hold, until the customer returned.

"Cover me!" Kolt yelled to JoJo while pointing to the easternmost building.

As Kolt cleared the outer edge of the spinning main rotor blades, he saw JoJo in his peripheral, moving to the closest corner of the building, the nearest spot of suitable cover and concealment.

Kolt took off, not at a dead sprint, but at a careful hurry as he approached the back side of the South Korean riot-control police.

"Make a hole!" Kolt yelled.

Kolt busted through the center of the two ranks, both hands on his HK at a low ready, and spotted Slapshot facing him on a knee. He hoped he wasn't going to be clubbed in the back of the head with one of the riot batons, and spotted Slapshot helping Digger to his feet, both with their eyes off the North Koreans. Behind the two operators, he saw Hawk curled up in a ball but on her right side, her upper body bouncing as if she was fighting a deep cough.

"Let's go! Let's go!" Kolt yelled as he approached the

MDL. He hadn't keyed his mike, was only yelling into his voice meter, and realized nobody could hear him from under the protective mask.

Through his mask's smoke-colored lens, Kolt spotted a North Korean soldier, hatless but proud. He appeared from the left side, clearing the corner and gaining the sandy soil. The soldier didn't seem to be in a big hurry as he raised his left arm and wiped his nose with his coat sleeve. He wasn't running, just walking with a purpose as if he knew exactly what he needed to do. Kolt couldn't be sure, but the North Korean looked like the same guy that had peppered his plate earlier.

Kolt took in a quick snapshot of the scene, studying the overall demeanor, assessing hostile intent, and searching for the hands. Yes, the hands—no matter what the North Korean thought, no matter who he might want to kill to protect the honor of the DPRK, if he wasn't carrying anything that clearly marked him as a threat to the force or threat to the mission, then Kolt had no choice.

Kolt ran it quickly. The guard looked like he might cause trouble, which in times past was enough to get ventilated. This, however, was North Korea, not Iraq or Afghanistan, or even those few peak months in Syria, and the days of Gangster turning a blind eye were behind them.

This was billed to the National Command Authority as a covert op. POTUS was on board to backstop the effort. But, smoking every fighting-age male that stood in the way of right and wrong wasn't authorized.

Indeed, people were watching, Kolt clearly knew. Not just his men—they were for sure—but also the entire black special operations community. The final game bracket had been set, the two Tier Ones would do battle—not for the hearts and minds of some third-world shithole tribal Shura who didn't want them there in the first place, though they were happy to accept the American taxpayer–funded water wells and two-room girls' schools; but for their very existence.

Kolt would have to leave him alone, maybe grab Digger's less-than-lethal MAUL, or dig out a nine-banger to clear him out. It had worked so well in Syria, most likely it would work again.

Kolt took two more steps toward Slapshot, knowing he wasn't stopping to help. Digger was good, Slapshot would see to it. Neither of them would want him to stop to help them. Kolt was going for Hawk. And now, Kolt knew the North Korean was going for Hawk, too.

Kolt took two steps, side-stepped around Slapshot, and reached for his Peltors. He slid them off the top of his head, stowing them around the back of his neck, the foam ear pads holding them firm and in place. He ripped his protective mask off his face, letting it drop to the gravel like a big league catcher tearing out of the box to field a high fly ball near the backstop.

Now, seeing things much clearer, his breathing easier, Kolt immediately wondered if he hadn't waited too long to discriminate.

Just then, out of the corner of his eye, Kolt spotted movement. Something small. Maybe a large dog, or even a few stray balloons. He tried to ignore it, tried to focus on the steely-eyed North Korean closing in on the knocked-out Hawk.

A gun! Son of a bitch!

The guard's intentions couldn't be mistaken now. A smooth draw, professionally clearing the black pistol from the brown leather holster. Closing the distance. Determined. He took three quick steps closer to Hawk as if he were teasing a rattlesnake and testing his common sense. In this case, Kolt knew, the soldier aimed to kill, but didn't want to step into South Korean soil to do it.

Kolt began to raise his rifle from the low ready, anticipating hand-to-hand combat if he could close the distance quick enough. He'd dot him with a muzzle tap if the guy's forehead was available, transition to a schoolhouse butt stroke if not. Kolt knew he didn't have time to borrow Digger's MAUL-equipped rifle, but knew his stand-up game could quickly trump less-than-lethal if it came to that.

What the hell? Where did she come from?

In an instant, Kolt realized the movement he had spotted in his peripheral vision, and ignored, was a little girl. Immediately, Kolt knew one of the kindergartners Hawk had complained about, whose teacher decided today was a good day to visit the DMZ, had bolted.

The jet black–haired little girl darted past Kolt, cute as a button decked out in what looked like a required school uniform of white shirt over a black skirt. Her hands up near her eyes, still clutching a large flimsy red-and-green souvenir bag, certainly obscuring her vision. She was obviously terrified by the gunfire, the helicopter that had hovered overhead, and most likely guys like Kolt, Slapshot, and Digger.

Heading directly into the path between the armed North Korean and the supine Hawk, the little girl was screaming bloody murder in her native tongue.

Kolt looked up, back to the North Korean who had already drawn his sidearm, then back to the back of the girl's flying hair.

Back to the shooter, back to the girl, and again to the shooter.

The North Korean lifted the pistol to a forty-five-degree angle, steadied his aim, holding the sights on the irksome female sprawled on the small gray pebbles.

Kolt knew he was too late. He just knew the North Korean wasn't going to take another half second of shame from the crazy female, even if he had to take an innocent South Korean to do it. Kolt knew Hawk was supposed to be a special guest of leader Kim Jong Un, a member of one of the few nations they enjoyed diplomatic relations with. The soldier wielding the gun most certainly had pegged the Swedish female as a spy. And in the hermit kingdom, both traitors and spies are met with the same discretion.

Shit!

Kolt dropped his rifle to the length of his sling, lunged forward, and grabbed the little girl by the back of her collared shirt, yanking her back into his arms. Now with her leather flats a foot off the ground, the girl kicked violently, her body trapping Kolt's rifle against his chest.

"Hawk!"

A nanosecond before the North Korean could fire, Hawk suddenly came to life. She rolled hard to her left, just before the guard broke the trigger.

Kolt saw the small-caliber bullet impact the gravel, picked up the forward spray of rock and dirt as it ricocheted along the bullet's path.

Holy crap! Possum?

Kolt didn't waste a second. He slid the girl in his arms around to his nonfiring side, using the same muscle memory used to transition from a dead rifle to his secondary weapon. Focused on the North Korean, he reached down, thumb-broke the holster hood, drew his earth-tone M1911A1, and indexed the gold bead front sight on the North Korean's yellow forehead just an inch or so below the man's freshly cut Halloween-black hair.

Kolt laid on the trigger once, let the trigger and sear reset, then quickly pulled pounds again, firing a controlled pair with his strong hand almost faster than the human ear could determine if one or two rounds were fired.

Kolt crossed the concrete slab, still clutching the girl, and leaned over the North Korean's limp body to administer a quick eye thump. No need in running until this guy was handled. Just as Kolt was about to two-finger-flick the right eye, he noticed both copper .45 caliber bullets had found the right side of the North Korean's forehead at an odd angle, appearing to impact the skull and rabbit upward, hugging his skull as they tore through his scalp, leaving him with what looked like two distinct parts in his military cut.

Kolt didn't bother finishing the eye thump and turned to Hawk. JoJo was already lifting her over his shoulder so he turned to check on Slapshot and Digger. He couldn't see them, and figured they had moved to the helo already.

Kolt moved to help clear the way for JoJo, forcefully moving a few of the riot control troops out of the way so they could get to the helo. Kolt set the girl down with the square-masked South Koreans, holstered his pistol, reacquired his long gun, and hoofed it to the waiting helo.

Slapshot had helped Digger onto the external pod, and turned around to help JoJo lay Hawk into the back of the MH-6M. Kolt watched, the wounds to her shoulder and calf obvious now. Hawk had come around, pretty much saved her own life, and was definitely alive. Kolt reached for the back of her head to keep it from banging on the metal floor as Slapshot moved back around the front of the helo and hooked back in on the starboard pod next to Digger.

Kolt and JoJo snap-linked back in at the port side and rotated to sit on the pod, legs now hanging free, boots just inches off the street. Kolt turned half around to check on Hawk. Snot was seeping from her nasal cavity, running down her cheeks and leaving a moisture path in her dirt-covered face. She was coughing sporadically, her lungs' answer to the amount of CS she had inhaled. Her shoeless feet were sticking out the opposite side, with Digger turned around and tearing away her skin-tone pantyhose, trying to assess the damage to her calf.

Hawk's gray pinstripe pants were noticeably soiled, a heavy mix of blood, sweat, and the churning sand. Her black bra was still intact, still modestly covering what it intended to cover. Her mauve blouse, torn, tattered, and stained, flapped freely with the rotor wind, unable to hide her defined abs, expanding in rhythm with her rapid breathing. There wasn't anything remotely military about her and no need for a cover story now.

Kolt reached in with his left hand and held pressure on Hawk's bleeder as he tried to manage the options available to him that certainly weren't covered in Gangster's sync matrix.

Now that was a total goat fuck!

Kolt keyed his mike. "This is Noble Zero-One, PC secure, all Eagles accounted for." He leaned over with his gloved right hand and signaled the pilot.

"Roger, customers aboard," Weeks acknowledged over helo common, cool as a cucumber.

Kolt saw Weeks acknowledge the thumbs-up, and felt Four-One increase power, softly lifting from the asphalt before rotating ninety degrees to the east. Just six feet or so off the ground, they were already moving back toward the red gazebo and looking to put distance between them and the problem. Just like a drunk who shows up, breaks a bunch of shit, pukes all over the sofa, and leaves the party without so much as an apology.

Kolt checked the status of his rifle as he heard Weeks transmit, "Four-One is out with five Eagles."

TWENTY-FIVE

"RELOADING!" Master Chief Kleinsmith yelled, trying to communicate over the thundering racket of belt-fed machine guns and small-arms fire.

With his dick in the dirt, he reached underneath his ghillie suit, trying to locate a fresh mag without taking his eyes off the enemy. Finding one, he caught a glimpse of a figure flying through the air, momentarily blocking the sun.

A fellow SEAL slid in on his right hip, just to Kleinsmith's immediate left, and rolled over prone to face back to the enemy as if he had been practicing break contact drills prior to puberty. Danno, Satan Seven-Two.

"We gotta go, man!" Danno said matter-of-factly as he stuck a tight cheek weld to his HK416's dark-earth-colored collapsible buttstock. Danno steadied his aim using both elbows and the bottom of the magazine.

"Half-baked plan, man, half fucking baked!" Kleinsmith said as he fully seated the fresh mag and rocked the safety off.

Kleinsmith knew Danno's firing position wasn't recommended, using the mag as a bipod, as it induced a lot of malfunctions, but he didn't really care at the moment. The Red Guards had proven to be sneaky little bastards, and smart, not silhouetting themselves and providing only small and fleeting targets to engage. Danno's heart had to be racing, his breathing maxed out, so if the prop helped Kleinsmith and the others safely peel off the bald ridgeline and get to the safety of the exfil corridor, so be it.

"We gotta go, Dealer!" Danno said just before he knocked off three well-aimed shots at teeny brown shades about two football fields away.

"Where's the two Red Guards?" Kleinsmith asked, not taking his eyes from his day optics.

"Fuck them, man, we left them!"

Kleinsmith shook his head, trying to clear his thoughts. He knew Danno was right. What the hell did they need with the two skinny and drugged-up detainees now?

Kleinsmith looked to his right, finding his communicator, Tanner, just as three or four enemy bullets impacted the dirt only a foot from the radioman.

"Tanner!" he said, "send war pa—"

"MOTHERFUCKER!" Tanner screamed. "I'm hit!"

Kleinsmith scooted on his belly, pushing himself backward five or six feet before combat rolling to his right several revolutions until he was abreast of Tanner.

"Where you hit?"

"Fucking forearm, man," Tanner said as he applied direct pressure to his wound while offering Kleinsmith the hand mike to the satellite radio. "I think comms are still good!"

Kleinsmith grabbed the mike, looked back at Danno, who was laying down consistent fire, enough to give the Red Guards pause about popping their melons up, and letting the others bound back.

"Heater One-Zero, Heater One-Zero, this is Satan Seven-One, over."

C'mon, c'mon.

Kleinsmith waited, knowing he didn't have a lot of time to wait on his commander, Captain Hank Yost, or anyone, for that matter, back at Inchon. He knew his gun was needed in the fight, but he also knew he needed the quick reaction force, especially with wounded SEALs that might not be able to make it to the border.

Negative contact.

"Heater One-Zero, Satan Seven-One in the blind," Kleinsmith transmitted, "I send War Path, I say again, War Path!"

Kleinsmith dropped the hand mike and looked past Danno, to the unseen Red Guards that had them pinned down. He ran the numbers quickly, pissed that one of his SEALs had been hit, hoping the Red Guards didn't have the ammunition to maintain a sustained rate of fire. If they stayed low, watched their silhouettes, and patiently sniped the little brown hats popping up and down like Whac-a-Mole, they'd melt back into the terrain under their ghillies and make their escape and evade corridor.

"Dealer!" Danno yelled from behind his rifle. "They're flanking us!"

"Blow the bridges?" Tanner asked.

The first forty or so klicks of the sixty-kilometer flight from the Joint Security Area at Panmunjom to Inchon were uneventful. Their handheld comms, line-of-sight radios with maximum operating ranges, allowed for a pleasant and uninterrupted ride, especially after shit-canning their protective masks as soon as they got south of Panmon Hall.

In essence, Kolt was in a commo blackout as the four Little Birds, now formed back into a staggered trail right formation, tooled along nap-of-the-earth into a head-wind at a crisp 146 knots.

Kolt turned to see Digger holding a fat polycarbonate syringe inside Hawk's calf wound. Digger depressed the plunger, which injected baby blue pill-sized sponges into Hawk's bleeder. Known as XStat, the sponges were designed to expand and soak up blood while putting much-needed pressure on the ruptured arteries. Digger stowed the syringe and began wrapping the wound with a pressure dressing. He motioned to Kolt from across the cabin, signaling with his blood-covered gloves that he was going to try to sit her up.

Kolt knew Hawk's head and shoulder bleeders needed to be above her heart, and gently released the pressure he had been holding on her shoulder wound. He watched Digger pull gently on her wrist to lift her torso, bending her at the waist, then rotating her around to put her back against the rear of the cabin, and lifting her feet into the bird.

Digger unclipped the chinstrap to his Kevlar brain bucket and slipped it off his head. Rushing wind grabbed his matted dirty-blond California-cool hair and threatened to pull out every strand. Digger lifted Hawk's calf and slid the helmet underneath the dressing, elevating the wound the best he could. Kolt saw it wasn't high enough, her wound still below the heart, and wasn't surprised to see Digger grab his titanium prosthetic from behind the pilot's seat and slide it under the helmet.

Digger reached underneath his vest and delicately pulled out the green parachute cord holding his meds around his neck. Holding up a red-capped syringe capsule, he placed it a few inches from Hawk's eyes, offering her an escape from reality.

Kolt knew if she was responsive, Digger wouldn't waste his morphine, but if not, he wouldn't hesitate to stick her.

Hawk shook her head side to side a couple of times,

saving her from the needle, prompting Digger to retract the offer and put the capsule away.

Kolt smiled and keyed his mike on helo common. "Breaker Four-One, casualty is responsive and stable, over." Hawk would need some more medical attention, no doubt, but she was coherent and alert, at least for the time being.

"Roger," Weeks answered before slowing the aircraft's speed to save fuel, now knowing he wasn't carrying an Eagle inside the golden hour.

Hawk reached up with her right hand to clear her bangs from her eyes and placed her trigger finger on her nose, closing one nostril at a time and blowing a snot monster from each onto her chest. She wiped her nose with the back of her forearm, looked at Kolt, and mouthed a quick *Thank you*.

Just as Kolt offered her a thumbs-up his Peltor came to life. It was Gangster, transmitting over the assault frequency.

"Noble Zero-One, acknowledge, over."

"Go for Zero-One."

"Red Squadron is in contact, I say again, hard compromised at Objective Beaver," Gangster said with an obvious tone of distress.

Holy fuck!

Kolt was shocked, uncertain as to how to respond. He knew he should be taking this call from the secluded Notri at Camp Greaves. His task was to serve as the quick reaction force for Kleinsmith and his SEAL mates, but now, having had to recover Hawk at Panmunjom, they weren't postured appropriately to perform their primary mission.

"Roger, orders?"

Kolt knew that response sounded lame. He braced for an ass wound over the net. He'd had no choice but to respond to Hawk's problem, and now needed to get her on the ground under a medic's care soon.

Kolt waited for what seemed like eternity for Gangster to respond. Nothing.

"This is Zero-One, send it."

"I need you to break out the Little Birds and launch the QRF to support the SEALs," Gangster said.

What the hell? In an instant, Kolt realized he hadn't notified Gangster that they had already serviced Hawk, had already deployed from Camp Greaves, had already created one international incident, and were not prepared to enter into a second one. Kolt had forgotten he was a squadron commander now, not a troop commander, and his focus should have been on notifying his higher command first, and acting second.

Aw shit!

"We are inbound your location, one wounded Eagle, litter but stable," Kolt transmitted, bracing for the response.

Again, a long silence from Gangster's end.

"Say again, Racer!" Gangster demanded. "You launched? For what?"

"We are about three mikes out, sitrep on the ground."

"Negative, negative, negative," Gangster said with deep disdain in his tone. "Turn around and head to Beaver immediately."

"Can't do it," Kolt said, careful with his inflection. A lot of people were listening on that net, especially his men—Gangster's old men—and even though they still had their fighting load of bullets and charges, their SI-MON devices, and most of their MAUL rubber rounds, he knew he needed some more situational awareness about Kleinsmith's shitstorm that he couldn't obtain from the pod of a Little Bird.

"Need fuel and a medic, then we'll turn."

Kolt looked at JoJo, who was nodding his head in approval.

"Noble Zero-One, this is Heater One-Zero, go ahead and put her down here. Tractor One and Two arrived, z-bags and medics waiting."

Startled by the response, Kolt didn't recognize the call sign, but he knew the voice. It was Captain Yost, the SEAL Team Six commander. He wasn't sure if he was in for an ass chewing or an attaboy for safely recovering Hawk, but he knew Yost to be a calm-headed commander and a seasoned SEAL leader.

"Roger," Kolt said.

"Quick FRAGO on the ground, hot refuel," Yost said. "Need to get you guys airborne ASAP!"

TWENTY-SIX

Inchon, South Korea

Kolt instinctively lifted his black Salomons a few inches as Breaker Four-One's tubular skids gently found the weed-covered and forgotten parking lot outside the hangar. Something about the idea of having his lower legs crushed always made him nervous.

Kolt unhooked, slipped off the pod, and turned toward the hangar area. He spotted the litter bearers and waved to get their attention. With the blades still spinning, Kolt reached high in the air, careful not to lop his gloved fingers off, and pumped his fist to get them to hurry the hell up. Seeing Kolt's signal, they started jogging toward the bird.

Greenpeace know about this place?

The place stunk like the black-market dock of a Panamanian trout farm. The aroma was worse than last night. He rubbed his nose with his sleeve and chalked it up to baking sun rays pulling every biohazard from the side-floating bloated bodies.

Kolt turned back toward Hawk, still sitting upright in the belly of the helo, holding her left deltoid with her right hand. Through the open cabin he noticed Digger had retrieved his leg. Now bent over the opposite pod, framed by the pearl white and aqua blue waters of the Yellow Sea, he was reattaching it to the male end of his right knee.

The idle engine still turning the blades drowned out the sound of the waves slapping against the riprap as if hiding the danger ahead. The rolling whitecaps, something Kolt knew the SEALs, and maybe Gangster, would frolic in, hadn't always given him pause, but that was another time.

Hawk looked comfortable, almost as if she thought they might be giving her a lift back to the Seoul Grand Hilton. She made eye contact with Kolt, smiled, and lifted her left hand in a thumbs-up.

"This is your final destination. Don't forget your belongings," Kolt yelled, trying to be heard over the engine noise as he passed Hawk her cell phone back. "We have one more leg though."

"Where are you guys going?" Hawk yelled.

"Troops in contact," Kolt said.

"I'm going!" Hawk said, letting go of her shoulder to try and close up her soiled blouse, and pulling her bandaged leg off of Digger's helmet to show she was ambulatory and not a liability.

"You're fucked up, you need attention," Kolt said. "We got this."

"You guys don't know the train like I do."

"I said we got this."

"You don't got shit, Kolt!" Hawk said, knocking her blond bangs out of her eyes and running her hair behind her right rear.

Kolt narrowed his eyes at Hawk, a little taken back by the smart-ass remark. Uncharacteristically informal for sure. In the past, ever since they'd first met inside Huske Hardware House years earlier, Hawk always made it a point to be respectful, if not of the rank, of the seasoned operator.

Kolt took a long pull on his CamelBak. He swirled the fresh water around his mouth for a few seconds before spitting out a long stream that splattered several unnamed weeds, essentially clearing the clam nets from his mouth.

"You're delirious," Kolt said, chalking it up to the shock she must be feeling, coupled with the blood loss. He motioned to the litter bearers to help her out and onto the litter.

"All yours, fellas."

"You guys don't know what Seamstress looks like," Hawk yelled, "only I do." She scooted a little farther away from the litter bearers like a kid avoiding Mommy, not ready to go to bed just yet.

"Look, Hawk, you aren't frickin' going, now get the hell out so we can refuel this thing."

She didn't budge. The litter bearers, in a high crouch under the spinning blades, stood dumbfounded. Kolt looked to his left, where two men in civilian clothes were approaching the nose of the helo, laboring to keep from dragging the heavy black z-bag they were holding between them.

Why didn't Digger just stick her?

Hawk leaned toward Kolt and handed him the folded-up note. Kolt opened it and cocked his head, a little confused.

"Field trip permission slip from your mother?" Kolt said before shoving it in his left shoulder pocket next to his chew.

"From Seamstress," Hawk said, "probably need to get it translated."

"You're still not going."

"Seamstress doesn't have an RRD on Kolt," Hawk said.

"We know," Kolt fired back, "you hit him with a Q dot."

"I missed!"

"You sent Toyota."

"I did," Hawk said, "but I hit his jacket, right between the shoulder blades."

"Good enough," Kolt said.

"Think about it, Kolt," Hawk fired back. "If I hit his head, they'd have to waterboard the shit out of him, cut his head off, or make him bob for apples for an hour to get rid of the Q dot crystals."

"Your point?"

"The point is that they probably stripped Seamstress naked by now, or best case, have taken off his jacket."

"No jacket, no crystals, no tag," Kolt said. "Is that it?"

Movement out of Kolt's peripheral grabbed him. The two refuelers had held up short of the bubble and lowered the z-bag to the deck by the side handles. As per standard procedure, they looked to the pilot for instructions. CW3 Stew Weeks extended his forefinger and turned it downward, issuing the signal to fill the main tank only.

Kolt then noticed Weeks manipulating some small knobs, frictioning down the cyclic and the collective. The pilot then took out a black nylon strap and placed it over the collective. Weeks unhooked his safety harness, bent forward in the seat, and wrapped a red-and-yellow bungee cord around the spring-loaded right pedal. These steps would maintain the Little Bird at flight idle, main rotors spinning, and allow him to unass without risking the aircraft yawing right.

Weeks leaned back, confirmed the rpms were holding steady, and began crawling out of the right side of the bubble cockpit.

Kolt turned back to the medics. "See about her left shoulder. Body wrap her if you have to, but get the bleeding stopped. Her head, too."

Kolt turned away from the cockpit, took a few steps

in a crouch to clear the blades, then went upright, following Weeks up the slight incline toward Slapshot and the rest of the boys. Some lounged in the rucksack flop and some were standing. Kolt slid his rifle around to his back, letting the sling hold it in place, muzzle down, as he approached the hangar. He was looking at the front door when it flew open; the first person out ruined his day.

Shit! Gangster.

On Gangster's heels, immediately following him out the door, was Captain Yost, the SEAL commander's barrel-chested body and hint of a beer gut filling up the fatal funnel completely. Next out was the SEAL LNO and a few others Kolt didn't recognize.

Guess we'll get plenty of opinions.

Yost was a legend, Kolt knew, on the battlefield and in every boardwalk bar and saloon in Virginia Beach. Even though he'd slowed down a little, the hard-man, dirty-fighter reputation he'd built as a young SEAL officer had stayed with him. Kolt knew Yost wasn't Dick Marcinko hard, but he was damn close. That was all good, for sure, but it needed to wait until they could hit oyster and beer night at CP Shuckers again. At the moment, Kolt only needed gas and a mad-minute intel dump.

Gangster went right for the jugular, not wasting any time. "Where the hell have you been?"

"Tied up, man," Kolt said as he unhooked his helmet from his assault vest. "Hawk's wounded but fine."

"What?" Gangster said, looking past Kolt and toward the helo. "How bad? Where is she?"

Kolt ignored Gangster's episode, pulled off his glove like a gentleman, and stepped toward Yost as he approached. Kolt extended his hand, taking the full seat of Yost's, and consciously doing grip battle, as he didn't want his old friend to best him.

"I still gotcha, Raynor," Yost said, smiling as he handed Kolt a bottle of water. Kolt could feel the ice-cold water through his tactical glove.

"Great to see you, sir," Kolt said. "Last time I believe I was dragging your ass across the Drina River east of Zvornick."

Yost smiled, laughed, and slapped Kolt on the back. Total bullshit of course, as the War on Terror had seen to it that they ran into each other every few months or so. Kolt also knew he owed Yost for saving his ass, keeping him from drowning in the river that night, some sixteen years ago. In fact, it hadn't been too long that Raynor and Yost were at the memorial chapel in Dam Neck, the services for the SEALs that had hit Nadal the Romanian's safe house in Sa'naa, Yemen, and run into a trap. Before that tragedy, Yost had requested Racer by name to deploy with his SEALs.

"Damn good to see you, too, Kolt," Yost said. "Look, Kleinsmith and the boys are in their E and E corridor but having a slow go of it with their casualties."

"Just waiting on gas, sir," Kolt said as he poured half the bottle of ice water on his head and took a deep swallow of the rest.

"Not sure they'll get through the DMZ and back inside South Korea in one piece," Yost said.

Gangster jumped in. "Kleinsmith blew Beaver and Bear."

"Old news now, right?" Kolt asked, knowing he and his men were only gassing up to QRF the SEALs and not try to recover Seamstress.

"No, it still matters. One of your missions is QRF, quick reaction force, but your little flight to Panmunjom took the quick right out of that," Gangster said.

"So the bridges are blown then, big deal," Kolt said, still not understanding exactly what they were looking at before they buzzed back across the MDL and into North Korea airspace.

"Not exactly sure, Raynor," Yost interrupted. "They think one or both might have gone low order, they couldn't confirm it."

"We are QRF, not a reserve assault force."

"You're both!" Gangster said.

"You're smoking crack—I've got twelve shooters and my headquarters element."

"Damn it, Rac—" Gangster said.

"Colonel Mahoney is right, though, we'll send Tractor One and Two to pick up Red Squadron at the DMZ; we need you to go after the train and Seamstress," Yost said.

"C'mon, sir, let's think this through a bit before we just go guns a-blazing into North Korea," Kolt said. "Have you guys put considerable thought into this?"

"Of course we have!" Gangster yelled.

Kolt saw Yost's eyes lock on Gangster, the unspoken message loud and clear, forcing the former Delta officer to check his mouth a little. It worked for the moment, but Kolt was sure it wasn't enough to plug his pie hole.

"What the hell do you think we have been doing here? What do you think the J-staff does?" Gangster said through clenched teeth. "We're way past mission analysis, and this exact situation is covered completely in our synchronization matrix."

"No problem with the J-staff, man, just saying you know how quick shit changes," Kolt said, trying to let Gangster off gently, knowing Yost was already an ally. "Color-coded Excel spreadsheets aren't always the answer."

"It's on the spreadsheet. Did you bother to read it?" Gangster said.

"What? It says somewhere to assault an armored train under way and protected by crack North Korean troops already spooked with four Little Birds and sixteen men?" Kolt said with no effort to hide the sarcasm. "What part of the surprise, speed, violence of action class in your operator training course did you miss?"

"Okay, chill out. Both of you," Yost said, trying to muffle his voice enough so the men of Noble Squadron huddled nearby didn't overhear. "Racer, tell us what you know. Why spooked?"

"Seamstress is tagged, with the Q dots, not the RRD," Kolt said, running the key points through his mental database. "Shit went sideways at the meeting, but Hawk got it done."

"How bad is she?" Yost asked with obvious concern.

Kolt looked away from Yost, making eye contact with Slapshot standing a few feet behind him. The Night Stalker pilot, dressed in a tan jumpsuit under his earth-tone survival vest, had edged closer to the discussion by now.

Kolt hesitated, searching for the right words, accurate words for sure, but not so dramatic as if to imply they might be combat ineffective.

"Hit twice. She's alert and getting patched up. We had to slot a guy though," Kolt said.

"You guys used lethal force?" Gangster asked Slapshot. "Killed a man? What the hell is wrong with you guys?"

"It was clutch. Linebacker depth, sir," Slapshot said as he wiped the sweat from his forehead.

Kolt lifted his hand as if to tell Slapshot he had this.

"My shots," Kolt said, still looking at Yost. "Wasn't looking to drop him, necessary though."

"That wasn't the plan, Raynor," Gangster scolded.

"The North Korean had other plans," Kolt said.

Kolt lifted the bottom of his assault vest with his left hand, reached near his belly button with the other, and yanked the Velcro flap open. He grabbed ahold of his hard armor ceramic plate, pulled toward his crotch, and slipped it from its hidden pouch.

Kolt held it up, showing Gangster and Yost the two spots where the North Korean's bullets spalled the outer covering. "These kind of plans."

"He saved a little girl's life," Weeks added, "had to be done."

"We have radios for this kind of thing, Racer," Yost said, signaling that he may not be entirely on the Kolt Raynor bandwagon.

Kolt dug the note out from his shoulder pocket, bringing the half-filled pouch of Red Man with it, and handed it to Yost. "Seamstress is compromised, taken away by thugs at gunpoint. Two shiny black four-door sedans, doubt we'd ever find them."

"Shit!" Myron Curtis said, jumping in from behind Yost and practically pickpocketing the note from the SEAL's hand. He had slipped up unseen by Kolt. "They won't stop until they get him to the train at Kaesong Station. They won't harm him, not yet anyway. That's the Workers' Party prerogative."

"We need to move then," Yost said.

Kolt had just finished two-fingering a golf-ball-size wad of leaf chew into the pocket between his cheek and gum, making his next response sound like he had a bag of marbles in his mouth.

"What the fuck, sir?" Kolt said. He wiped the tobacco residue from his fingers onto his Crye combat pants.

Curtis chimed in. "I agree. Seamstress is the mission. We have to get our hands on him or we condemn a lot of sailors and civilians to certain death."

"Now wait just one damn second here," Kolt said, trying to be the calming voice in the crowd. "Are we all comfortable with the intel that confirms that?"

"Roger," Yost said.

"I am totally," Curtis added, "as is Langley."

Kolt looked at Weeks. He was motionless, poised with a professional demeanor, ice in his veins, almost recruiting poster–like, giving no response one way or another.

"Damn it!" Kolt said, "I'm not taking the handful of men I have on a suicide mission into North Korea. No gunship support, no armed predator, no eyes in the sky, that's fucking suicide." Kolt knew enough not to push it, adding a quick, "Sir."

"I need you to reconsider, Kolt," Yost said.

Reconsider? What the hell does that mean?

"I'll do it, sir," Gangster said, turning toward Yost. "I'll take them back in."

Kolt looked at Yost, shocked by Gangster's balls. Surprisingly, Yost almost looked like he was actually considering it.

"Kolt?" Yost said, obviously giving him a chance to change his mind.

I'm being muscled here?

"Seamstress or not, even if we get lucky and grab the guy, we've probably started World War III anyway," Kolt said before quickly tilting his head to push a dark stream of tobacco juice away from the crowd.

"You don't have to go back out there, Kolt, but—"

Kolt turned quickly to CW3 Weeks. "You good with this, Stew?"

"No operational reason to say no," Weeks said.

"Fuck, all right, it's against my better judgment," Kolt said, now clearly on the spot. "Let's dirt-dive it real quick."

"No time for that, Raynor," Gangster said.

"You gotta get going, Kolt," Yost added.

"What the fuck is the rush?" Kolt said. He took a knee and yanked his straight blade from the sheath on his assault vest. "Let's at least give ourselves a fighting chance here. This ain't going to be a cake walk."

Kolt looked at Chief Weeks, nodded for him to kneel next to him, and began scraping a long fat line in the dirt. He scratched two arrows, one above the line, one below, then cut in small verticals to give the line an appearance of multiple train cars.

"All right, Stew," Kolt said as he pointed to each mark with the sharp end of the knife, "front of train here, direction of travel, and north-seeking arrow."

"Got it," Weeks said as he settled his knees into dirt.

"Dealer already blew the bridges. Let's assume they are nonpassable and that they won't test them," Kolt said, speaking with his hands as much as his blade. "Sync our approach with the train as it slows down."

"Optimal for the engine is ten miles per hour, fifteen is pushing it," Weeks said. He drew two ovals signifying Little Birds near the front left of the long line. "We'll snake in from their six, and drop Four-Three and Four-Four on the sleeper you think Seamstress is in."

"Shit, man, we don't even know if they put him on the train at Kaesong Station or not," Kolt said.

"Roger, which is why we need a simple plan, stick to our standard operating procedures," Weeks said as he drew two more circles above the center part of the train.

Yost jumped in. "I agree. Keep it simple." Yost quickly took a knee, leaving the others still bent over the makeshift terrain model. "You gotta get in the air, Kolt."

Why is Yost pushing us? What's with him? Is he worried about the fallout of failure here? Worried that if we don't grab Seamstress that POTUS might add a mark against SEAL Team Six?

Kolt looked at Weeks, ignoring the SEAL commander. The flight lead was still staring at the terrain model, rehearsing his actions in his head, maybe hoping things would change and someone with more sense than what was being displayed would abort this crazy, high-risk death ride. Weeks looked up, locked eyes with Kolt.

"We good, Stew?"

"I'm not gonna lie, Racer," Weeks said, "ain't feeling it on this one."

Weeks's last comment shook Kolt. He hadn't expected that, not from someone of Stew Weeks's character. Someone with his experience. The guy flew with ice in his veins, always had. Hell, Kolt just had to think back about twenty minutes ago at the JSA.

Stew Weeks was human, like everyone else, which is exactly what was boiling over in his gut.

Am I fucking jacked? Why am I not questioning this mission more? Do I have a death wish?

Kolt slapped Weeks on the shoulder, stood up, and resheathed his knife. "We'll go, but I need every operator available."

"I'm going, let me grab my kit." The SEAL LNO didn't hesitate, and turned for the hangar.

"Channel seven is the assault frequency," Kolt said. "Do a quick commex before you load."

Kolt looked Yost dead in the eye. "I've got room for you and Colonel Mahoney, sir."

"We both can't go," Yost said, "someone has to man the ship here."

"Gangster?" Kolt said, now locked in a visual game of chicken with the former Delta operator. Kolt knew Gangster was no slouch, certainly not a coward. But, he often ran his mouth first, like a moment ago, and Kolt didn't like it one damn bit.

"You in?" Kolt added.

Gangster hesitated, now seemingly trying to stir up the courage to match his earlier tough talk.

Kolt pressed it. "I've got room in my chalk. I could use your gun."

"I don't have a MAUL," Gangster said.

"You won't need it. Grab your shit!"

Gangster turned to Yost. "Sir, I'm going. I'll command and control from the target."

"Negative," Kolt quickly said, not letting Yost reply. "You're on the manifest as a shooter. Stay off my assault net, or stay here."

Kolt expected Gangster to detonate, but didn't care. Kolt needed assaulters, not micromanagement.

"Negative," Gangster said, "I outrank you."

"Rank don't mean shit out here."

"Who do you think you are, Raynor?" Gangster asked, inching closer to Kolt.

"I'm the fucking Noble Squadron commander, the ground force commander," Kolt said as he bowed up to match Gangster's move. "I'm the son of a bitch that is about to take my men across that damn border. You're welcome as a shooter, or give me your space."

"You have no authority to talk to—"

"Colonel Mahoney, grab your kit," Yost said, cutting off Gangster and trying to downplay the friction. "Raynor's got this. You work for him out there."

Without waiting for a response, Kolt turned to tell Slapshot to update the boys and get loaded, but he had already bolted. Kolt spotted him heading for the huddled men, replacing his helmet as he walked.

Kolt and Weeks moved back to the waiting Little Birds. Noticing the refuelers finishing up the last gravity-fed z-bags, Kolt knew the hot refuel was complete. Kolt reached the edge of the pilotless Breaker Four-One's main rotors, still rotating dangerously under the power of the Rolls-Royce engine, and paused at the obvious sight of blood on the floor of the cabin.

He turned back around, saw his men heading toward him and breaking for their respective chalks. He looked past them, hoping to see the SEAL LNO and Gangster exiting the hangar with their kit, but only seeing the two medics carrying Hawk on the stretcher through the door.

Just above the hangar, Kolt spotted something in the air, floating to the ground under a small white parachute. The SpyLite, having been autoset to recover to Inchon from Camp Greaves, drifted closer to the hangar's roof. The Christmas-green inflatable landing pad, now obvious underneath the spy plane's belly, cleared the edge of the roof by inches, seconds later impacting harmlessly with the spotted grass turf.

"That yours?" Weeks asked as he slipped his flight helmet back on his head.

"Depends who's asking," Kolt said.

TWENTY-SEVEN

Objectives Beaver and Bear

Burning it up at 155 knots for the last eight minutes, CW3 Stew Weeks flew a flat and true two-degree azimuth from Inchon to Objective Beaver and Bear. Kolt realized he was gorilla-gripping the edge of the pod, freaked by the water below him. Images of the training run on the *Queen Mary* and the blade strike that put them in the drink flashed in front of him.

Weeks hand-railed the baby blue waters of the Yellow Sea on the left while keeping South Korea to his right until he reached the marbled Ganghwa Peace Observatory that marked the northwesternmost point of South Korea. Maintaining a steady four hundred feet above ground level, the birds crossed the exact spot where the Imjin and Yesong Rivers joined, busting into restricted air space above the barbed-wire-heavy demilitarized zone and entering North Korea inside the same infil corridor that the SEALs used the night before.

Kolt released his death clutch on the outer pod and exhaled.

Processing what was happening in what felt like warp speed, Kolt forced himself to put the water issue behind him and think the more pressing problem through. They had standard operating procedures for these high-risk assaults, but usually they had better situational understanding. A compound was one thing, a moving train another.

Kolt keyed his mike. "Check nods, check nods."

Feeling Chief Weeks bank the helo right a few degrees, Kolt leaned out slightly to maintain vision at twelve o'clock. As they crossed the light brown and dry rice paddies and the greener hills southwest of Kaesong, Kolt reached up with his nonfiring hand to find the quick release holding his night-vision goggles up on his helmet. He thumbed the button, dropped them in front of his eye pro, and felt to make sure the lens caps were still on. Kolt looked through pin holes in the center of the caps, picking up various tints of cloudy lime green images passing by, and adjusted the focus ring for long-range recognition. Satisfied his optics were good, he lifted them away from his eyes and locked them into position.

"Target spotted, dead ahead," Chief Weeks said over helo common. "Uhh, half mile."

"I see smoke," Gangster said, "bridges must have blown."

Damn it! I knew I couldn't trust him.

"Confirm one," Weeks said, "not two."

"Definitely Bear has blown, can't be sure about Beaver," Gangster said.

Kolt had told Gangster back at Inchon, in no uncertain words, that he was strap-hanging as a shooter and not as a decision maker. Kolt snapped his head around to look into the cabin, picking up half of Gangster's body as the former Delta officer was on two knees and likely looking over the aux fuel tank and peering through the cockpit bubble, giving him the same perspective as Chief Weeks.

Kolt looked back to the front and extended his vision

deeper. He picked up on the train, and could tell it had stopped.

"Breaker Four-One Charlie Mike?" Weeks transmitted as he maintained altitude, speed, and azimuth toward the train and Objective Bear.

Kolt immediately picked up on Stew's tone. It was a question for sure, not a statement.

"Roger that," Gangster said. "Seamstress is on that train."

What?

Kolt forced himself to remain calm. This couldn't be another Syria, but damn it, hadn't Gangster paid attention in the briefings? Gangster had to know the North Korean order of battle, had to know that Kim Jung Un's train always traveled the railways bookended by twin trains. Regardless of destination or railway, the leader's armored train was always protected by time, distance, and armed soldiers in both directions. The route from Pyongyang to Kaesong was no different, something Kleinsmith had confirmed earlier that morning as the three trains passed their hide site. It wasn't just a standard and prudent protection measure, but a shell game to force any would-be saboteurs to guess which of the three trains the North Korean leader might be on.

"Do a go-around, Stew," Kolt transmitted.

"Say again," Weeks responded.

"I say again, abort the approach, burn holes for a minute," Kolt said. "That's not the train we want."

"Roger," Weeks said. "All elements, pulling out ninety degrees, follow my lead."

"Racer!" Gangster said, obviously heated by the call. "You can't be sure that's not the target train."

"I'm sure. That's the advance. The VIP train is second," Kolt said.

"We can't tell unless we get closer," Gangster said. "We need to push forward to better observe with the nods."

From the starboard pod at three hundred feet above ground level, Kolt Raynor's head was on swivel. Along with the rest of his element, he strained to keep eyes on the still-smoking Objective Bear as pilot Stew Weeks and Breaker Four-One took lead in a circular orbit.

Ain't that some shit? Weren't you against the Q dots last night? Something about the good idea fairy.

Kolt ignored Gangster's last transmission, knowing he didn't need an open-comms catfight right now. The four-ship Little Bird formation remained roughly a kilometer south of the SEALs' southern target, burning holes in the sky. From what Kolt could tell, the charge had detonated efficiently enough to get the job done.

"Looks like the train engineer couldn't get her stopped in time," Chief Weeks said from under his flight helmet.

Kolt agreed but didn't reply. He was seeing the same thing. Kleinsmith and his frogmen weren't postured to take advantage of their handiwork anymore, but they had done their job. The North Korean train's rust-colored engine had left the train tracks soon after reaching the lead edge of the bridge, and now teetered off the north side. Still hitched to the first passenger car, but hanging almost vertical above the gully below, it looked like a house of cards that could go at any moment.

Kolt counted three green passenger cars sporting horizontal yellow racing stripes, and a mirror-image engine serving as the caboose. The four cars provided enough counterbalance to prevent the entire five-car train from collapsing into the valley.

The SEALs' plan had been to trap the VIP train between the two blown bridges, but as often happens, Murphy had a vote. When the Red Guards compromised Kleinsmith's Red Squadron, they had no choice but to detonate early and bug out. It wasn't ideal, but it isolated

Seamstress's train on a three-mile stretch of track back to Kaesong Station.

Kolt knew he wasn't going to waste time trying to explain all that to Lieutenant Colonel Rick Mahoney.

Something vibrated in Kolt's right cargo pocket.

My cell?

Kolt keyed his mike as he reached to dig the phone out, careful not to drop it. "All elements, stand by. Cell call from the JOC."

"Raynor!" Kolt yelled into the phone, trying to overcome the engine noise as he slipped it under his right Peltor ear pad and pressed it close to his ear.

"Seamstress confirms the North Korean attack on the Pacific Fleet, Kolt. It's not a bluff!"

"Hawk?" Kolt yelled, unable to fully understand what she said. "Speak up!"

"Seamstress knows where the missile sites with the mini nuke warheads are, knows all about Marzban Tehrani. You have to bring him out alive."

"Working on it!" Kolt said, wondering why Yost hadn't seen to it that she had been shot full of morphine by now and drifted off to the candy slides in happy land. "Is that it? Kinda busy."

"We're struggling to translate the note, not done yet though," Hawk said.

"Shots fired!" CW3 Weeks announced over helo common.

"Roger," Slapshot said, "confirm muzzle blasts from here, too. Far for AKs though."

Kolt dropped the call with Hawk and shoved the cell back into his cargo pocket.

"Breaker Four-One, take us east toward Kaesong, hug the tracks," Kolt said.

"What the hell are you talking about, Raynor?" Gangster said.

Kolt bit his tongue and again ignored Gangster.

"Stew, we're looking for the next train. The one at Bear is the advance, not our target."

"Roger," Weeks said, "Breaker Four-One is out at nine o'clock. Staggered trail right."

North Korean VIP train

Kang Pang Su braced for the next blow, spitting blood from the left crook of his mouth that ran down the length of his wrinkled face. Every few seconds, enough warm blood pooled in one vertical crease to funnel a heavy drip of blood onto the collar of his white city shirt.

His right eye was already swollen shut, his eyelid grossly formed into a bubbled mess, forcing him to view the world through his bloodshot and black left eye.

"Who is the woman?" one of the uniformed guards demanded.

"I do not know," Kang said. Actually, it wasn't a lie. Kang had never met Cindy Bird before, but he wasn't ready to admit his collaboration against the people just yet.

"American CIA!" the guard shouted.

"No," Kang said, "I do not know. She was crazy!"

It had only been about a minute since several North Korean soldiers had thrown him to the carpeted floor before one lodged his boot on the side of Kang's face. They wasted no time in stripping Kang Pang Su of his dignity. Immediately after being loaded on the passenger car train at Kaesong Station, they yanked his black suit jacket off him, one arm at a time, and hung it on a tall coatrack near one of the ballistic windows before removing his shoes without bothering with the laces. Kang had tensed as they tugged violently at both pants legs, forcing the belt around his hips, and leaving his gray boxers a few inches lower than normal.

Kang heard the train bell and engine power up, and in a few seconds the engine began to slowly pull forward, heading west back to Pyongyang. He saw a soldier step behind him, felt a white blind slapped over his eyes and uncomfortably tied, pulling pieces of jet-black hair from their roots.

Kang felt someone's breath on his left ear, figured it was the soldier that tied the knot, and worried he might bite his earlobe next.

The guard whispered barely loud enough to drown out the sound of the propaganda footage looped on the interior wall television. "Traitor!"

Kang felt him test the ties securing his wrists behind his back.

Kang didn't reply, knowing there was not much he could do at the moment. Further resistance would likely only result in more backhands to the face, or toes of a boot to the ribs. He was going to die, of that he was sure. Deep in his heart he knew he deserved to. He had betrayed his country. All the anger and loss that had fueled his simmering rebellion had been washed away in a tidal wave of guilt and remorse.

"You are an embarrassment to the Democratic People's Republic of Korea."

Kang couldn't see the man speaking in front of him, but easily recognized the voice. It wasn't the guard, but someone of authority. Someone who Kang knew would be just as eager to kill Kang as he was to kill himself.

"Remove his blindfold."

Kang felt the blind pulled from his head, and winced at the hair that went with it. He blinked hard several times, trying to focus his left eye on the man in front of him.

"This, from the deputy secretary of science and education?" Pak Yong Chol said. "Just like your own son, you have dishonored your family."

Kang thought back to Kim Il Sung Square, where only a few weeks ago he and Pak had stood motionless, shoulder to shoulder, as they watched another traitor to the Motherland ravaged by starving dogs, torn apart limb from limb.

"I am innocent," Kang said. Despite his shame, he would not bow to this pig. "There has been a misunderstanding."

"A misunderstanding, you say?" Pak said, pulling both sides of his dress coat around his fat belly and fastening the lower button.

"Yes."

"Then you can explain these foreign items," Pak said as he held up two small white plastic devices.

Kang looked hard at the two odd objects in Pak's hands.

"Those are not mine," Kang said. "This I am sure of."

"They were in your coat pockets."

Kang recalled the American woman back in the men's room. She had put the two devices on the bathroom floor. Kang was certain he wasn't handed the devices, but vaguely recalled the women sticking both her hands into his coat pockets after they stood up. Yes, he now realized, she must be responsible.

Kang slumped forward, his shoulders dropped toward the floor. Denying the obvious was futile, he knew as much.

"May I have a sidearm?" Kang asked. "Allow me an honorable death."

Just then, the train slammed to a stop, knocking Kang off balance and tumbling him to the floor. Kang saw the heavier Pak stumble into one of the guards, both of them falling into the small side table. The screeching of the electric wheels was easily heard from inside the armored train.

One of the guards set the stool upright and helped Kang back to his seat.

"Blindfold the collaborator," Pak said.

The blindfold, still knotted in behind his head, was roughly slipped back over Kang's head and pushed down to cover his eyes.

Kang heard the forward door of the train car open. There was commotion for sure, several people moving quickly across the carpet.

"Saboteurs!"

TWENTY-EIGHT

Breaker Four-One led the four-ship formation northeast, hugging the railroad tracks at just over twenty-feet above ground level. The sky was clear and blue, ceiling and visibility unlimited, with the temperature comfortably in the low nineties. Kolt gave an approving nod as he felt the Little Bird slow, happy Chief Weeks had powered back to roughly fifty knots forward air speed. No need to rush headlong into an ambush before they had time to figure out the situation.

Kolt looked behind him, leaned out slightly to see around JoJo on the pod next to him, and spotted the other three black helos mirroring Weeks's altitude and speed. Focusing beyond Breaker Four-Four, the trail bird, Kolt noticed the small ridgeline they had passed less than a minute ago was now blocking their view of Objective Bear and the disabled train.

"Good spot on next train," Weeks transmitted, forcing Kolt to whip his helmeted head back to twelve o'clock. "Looks stopped."

Kolt squinted, held his hand above his eyes to shade them from the sun's bright light, and picked up the orange engine. The train was stopped, dead on the tracks, and Kolt noticed what looked like a few North Korean troops standing outside, mingling around. Several guards were posted up and down the track, spread out on both sides of the track every so often and roughly thirty feet from the train. Kolt studied them, surprised by their demeanor. The guards were facing away from the five train cars at a rigid position of attention as if they were pulling perimeter security at Hugh Hefner's Midsummer Night's Dream Party at the Playboy Mansion.

"We spooked them," Weeks said.

Kolt watched the guards turn around and jog back to the train. Something was happening, no doubt, but their actions looked rehearsed, almost routine. Kolt wasn't convinced they heard or saw the Little Birds approaching. In the distance, maybe a half mile beyond the train, Kolt saw what he was sure was the top of the Kaesong Station main building.

"Let's sit down for a minute," Gangster said. "We need to have some dialogue."

"Roger," Weeks said. "Trail formation, pit stop."

Damn it, Gangster!

Kolt felt Weeks lift the bird's nose, slowing his air speed to safely set her on the deck. Gangster's command decision irritated the hell out of Kolt, but at the moment, what he was seeing didn't give him much impetus to counter Gangster's call.

"She's moving," Slapshot said from the opposite outer pod, "heading away from us."

Kolt looked hard, immediately seeing Slapshot was right. "Stay airborne, Stew, stay airborne."

"Roger," Weeks said, as if he wasn't bothered in the least about being jerked around by two nagging mothers.

Kolt thought it through, trying to analyze what he was seeing and develop a quick course of action on the fly. Whatever he came up with wouldn't be easy, but he didn't have a lot of time to debate it.

"Options?" Kolt asked over the net, willing to accept any half-decent course of action his men or, at this point, even Gangster might have.

Kolt paused for a few moments, waiting for a response. Nothing.

Finally, Gangster broke in.

"Seamstress is in there. Best to wait until it stops and then isolate."

That's it? That's the input? You thought Seamstress was on the first train.

Kolt didn't entirely disagree with Gangster, as he assumed Seamstress was on the second train, too. Still, Gangster's wait-and-see course of action wasn't going to get it done. Kolt firmly believed allowing the train to return to the station evened the odds. If the North Koreans had time to consolidate and develop a defense plan, given their armored protection and scores of armed troops on board, possibly more armed North Koreans back at Kaesong Station, the risk to the force escalated off the charts. Doctrinally, special operations forces don't play even-Steven. Moreover, even though Kolt agreed the target was the middle train, the one currently headed east back to Kaesong, he knew nobody could be sure where Seamstress was.

Kolt keyed his mike to transmit his orders over the assault net. "All elements, this is Noble Zero-One, Black Snake, Black Snake."

Kolt didn't bother waiting for a reply before he sent his next command. He knew they would understand he wanted to approach the target in its blind spot, sneak up from the rear as if they were approaching a hijacked aircraft on a dark tarmac single file and dressed in black.

"I need Four-Four to take flight lead and put down

on the pulling engine. Four-One has the first green passenger car, Four-Two take the middle one, Four-Three the third. Everyone flows to middle car."

"This is Breaker Four-One, roger all," Stew Weeks said. "Four-Four take lead."

Kolt continued. "Controlled approach along the north side. All elements put a SIMON round through a window and follow it with ferret rounds. Then put down on the roofs and get inside."

Kolt picked up Breaker Four-Four maneuvering past his helo to take the lead as Weeks went nose down to increase forward air speed.

"Nods down," Slapshot said. "Call out the Q dot crystals if you spot them."

As the formation rapidly approached the rear of the slow-moving train, Kolt keyed on the three green passenger cars with yellow stripes and silver roofs. Each car had what looked like three gray roof hatches protruding skyward a foot or so, and he wondered if inserting through the roof was more viable than the personnel doors near the train couplers.

Twenty seconds later, three Little Birds pulled abreast of their respective target cars, just far enough away to prevent the Little Birds' main rotor span from striking the side of the green armored cars. Kolt knew his operators on the port-side pods were peering through the pinholes in their night vision goggles' plastic lens caps that protected them from the bright sunlight. With any luck, one of his men would spot the Q dot crystals inside a window.

Kolt looked down, figured they were moving ten, maybe fifteen miles an hour. He noticed they crossed a major two-lane highway that ran northwest, as the four birds hugged a single hard dirt road that ran along the north side of the train tracks.

"I see it!" Gangster said. "Positive ID of the Q dot."

"Roger that," Slapshot said, "eyes on. Middle car, second-to-last window."

Kolt strained to locate the Q dot crystals himself, trying to get a view through the cockpit, but Weeks's body in the right front seat blocked his view. Kolt leaned backward, hoping to have better luck looking through the cabin, but again, his vision was blocked, this time by Gangster, who was on both knees, practically leaning on the backs of Slapshot and Digger, like some kind of photo bomber.

Kolt saw Digger had removed his suppressor and was now sliding the thirty-inch-long SIMON grenade's tail fin assembly over the muzzle end of his HK416. Beyond Digger, Kolt now saw their proximity to the train. Even though they had the optimal angle on the windows for the standoff rifle grenade to work, he worried they might be closer than the minimum arming distance of the 150-grain munition.

"SIMONS!" Kolt said, "Fire the SIMONS!"

"Shit!" Slapshot said. "Compromise, compromise!"

Kolt tensed on the pod, bracing for what he had worried about. If Slapshot was calling compromise before any operators were able to put boots on the passenger car roofs, Kolt knew the assault was going sideways quick.

Just then, Kolt heard a massive and sustained amount of automatic fire. He knew it wasn't friendly. Dozens of 7.62 x 39 mm full-metal-jacketed bullets, the distinct cartridge of the Chinese knockoff Kalashnikov AK-47 rifle, ripped through the sky.

"I'm hit!"

Shit! Slapshot.

"Shots fired!" Weeks transmitted. "Breaker Four-One taking fire."

Kolt leaned forward on the pod, testing the tensile strength of his safety line, and noticed the bubble cockpit's glass now heavily spidered in several places, telling him bullets had torn through the windows. He couldn't tell if Weeks had been hit, but marveled at his nerve, knowing the seasoned 160th pilot would hold his position to allow his customers to continue the assault until his last breath, or until gravity took over.

Kolt heard more AK fire, easily discernable over the Little Bird's Rolls-Royce turboshaft.

"Four-One is out!"

Kolt felt Weeks go vertical in an instant, lifting the bird above the train and slipping it to the south, obviously trying to clear the kill zone and looking for safety. Now able to see all three green passenger cars, Kolt recognized the problem. North Korean soldiers, still in their brown saucer caps with red bands wrapped around the brim, had popped up outside the roof hatches. They still had their rifles in their hands, oddly with silver bayonets fixed, still aiming at the formation of Little Birds that had jumped to the south side of the track and were climbing away.

Out of his peripheral vision, Kolt picked up his communicator, JoJo, sitting immediately behind Kolt in the starboard pod. JoJo's rifle was horizontal, stock fully seated in his shoulder pocket, and placing well-aimed fire on the enemy troops. Kolt felt two of JoJo's spent brass cartridges hit his left shoulder as he lifted his own rifle to engage. Before he could get a round off, the North Koreans dropped out of sight, some leaving the gray hatches up, some closing them behind them.

"Slapshot," Kolt said, safing his weapon, "status?"

"Damn, I took one. Digger, too."

Kolt turned around on the pod, leaned back to look through the cabin, trying to assess the damage. Digger was buckled over at the waist, his green nylon safety line taut but still holding him to the pod. Slapshot had both hands on the back of Digger's tan assault vest, holding tight to his flash-bang pouch mounted just below the back of his neck.

Son of a bitch!

Kolt's attention was drawn closer, now toward Gangster, who was lying on his back and not moving.

Kolt yelled. "Gangster!"

Realizing he couldn't be heard, Kolt frantically reached for his push-to-talk. "Gangster, you good?"

No response.

Kolt strained to assess Gangster's wounds but couldn't see where he was hit or if his eyes were open. Slapshot had righted Digger and was able to lean his upper body back into the cabin. JoJo had unhooked and was now using hard points on the cabin floor to pull himself into the cabin near Gangster.

"Four-Four is Lame Duck!"

Damn!

The mission was going to shit in a hurry.

"This is Noble Zero-One, I need a status from all elements!"

"Breaker Four-Two is Lame Duck, losing pedals and collective slipping," the pilot said. "Several wounded Eagles on board."

"Breaker Four-Three is up."

As Kolt processed the data points, trying to assess what he was dealing with, he looked back toward the five-car train, still moving east and picking up speed.

Kolt began to hyperventilate, his chest rising rapidly, beating against the ceramic plate that had saved his life not more than an hour ago at Panmunjom. At that moment, assessing the situation, he knew they were razor close to abort threshold, and in turn, mission failure.

With several wounded operators and two of the four MH-6M Little Birds no longer airworthy, Kolt knew he was out of options. He hesitated to key his mike, resisting the urge to send a command he hadn't done in all his years in Delta. In fact, a command that he himself had ignored on more than one occasion, somehow coming out on top each time after the smoke cleared.

Kolt knew there had to be another way; there always was. He just needed time to solve the problem. Likely not even a minute. Seconds would likely do it.

Focus, Kolt, focus.

"Four-Four is Mayday, Mayday, Mayday."

That was it. Kolt knew a 160th pilot wouldn't make a Mayday call unless shit was bad, unless he had run through every last troubleshooting option, flicked every emergency toggle, pushed every recovery button, and applied every piece of insider knowledge they had gained over the years to trick their helicopter into doing things the manufacturer placed warning stickers about. Kolt knew now he had no choice but to make the call.

"This is Noble Zero-One," Kolt said, before pausing for a long second. "Abort, abort, abort!"

"Roger," Chief Stew Weeks repeated. "Abort, abort, abort!"

Kolt stole one more look back at the train. It had traveled another hundred meters or so farther away, and closer to the station. He focused on the roof hatches, making sure none of his operators or the Little Birds were going to get stuck again by a North Korean sharpshooter.

Just as he was satisfied they were safe to return to base, heading back to the DMZ and on to the JOC at Inchon, Kolt picked up on the shiny top of two black vehicles moving in the opposite direction of the train. He followed them until they cleared the rear train engine, now able to observe both sedans and their shadows against the light brown dirt road and partially green hills in the background. For some reason they looked familiar.

Kolt studied the vehicles, vaguely hearing Stew Weeks transmit his four helos' status back to the JOC. Kolt turned around, saw that his helo was now in trail, following the others southwest. Two of the Little Birds were definitely damaged, thick gray and black smoke billowing from the main rotor on one and the tail boom rotor on another. He wondered if they'd make it back across the border before they lost enough fuel or oil, locking the controls and forcing at best a controlled crash landing.

Kolt turned back to the two black sedans, still unable to place their familiarity.

Motherfucker!

In an instant, Kolt recognized the vehicles. Yes, he was certain they were the same two vehicles that he had seen on the SpyLite's video downlink from the Notri. The same two vehicles the North Korean guards at the DMZ had dragged Seamstress to after Hawk was muscled outside the meeting building.

"Stew, target spotted due north. Two black sedans."

"Uhhh," Weeks transmitted, "we're combat ineffective at this time. Two birds limping as it is."

"Hear me out," Kolt said. "Let Four-Three escort the two smoking birds back. We need to flex off and go for the vehicles."

Kolt looked back at JoJo, still inside the cockpit tending to Gangster. JoJo obviously heard Kolt's last transmission and was looking directly at his squadron commander.

Kolt gave JoJo a thumbs-up as he tried to yell over the engine noise, "Is he good?"

JoJo returned the thumbs-up and fumbled for his push-to-talk. "Strong pulse, just unconscious. Bullet struck his helmet."

"What are we doing, boss?" Slapshot asked, not hiding the fact that he wasn't entirely on board with Kolt's hasty idea to go after the two vehicles.

"Slap, those are the same vehicles that were at the meeting," Kolt said, "I'm positive."

"Racer, think it through," Slapshot said, "what are the odds Seamstress is in one?"

"Gut, Slap, that's all," Kolt said. "But it's logical."

"We saw the Q-dots, boss," Slapshot said, "inside the middle passenger car."

Kolt didn't have a lot of time to debate it with Slapshot. He remembered what Hawk had said back at Inchon when she refused to let the medics lift her out of the Little Bird. Maybe she was right, maybe they would have pulled Seamstress's jacket off, and if she was correct that her Q dot throw was only good enough to impact the shoulder blades of her target, then the possibility that the North Korean guards separated him from his jacket, thus removing the tag on Seamstress, wasn't too far-fetched.

Kolt looked at JoJo again, trying to gauge his opinion on what he was asking them to do. JoJo held up his fist, showed Kolt his gloved knuckles, and reached toward him. Kolt bumped knuckles with JoJo, happy to accept his communicator's vote of confidence.

"We're min force, Slap," Kolt said, hoping to get Slap's nod, too.

"One helo with three wounded?"

"Two sedans, Slap," Kolt said. "Odds in our favor."

Slapshot didn't respond. Kolt and Slapshot had been together a long time. So long that Kolt knew silence was consent from his squadron sergeant major. If not, Slapshot certainly would have resisted like a grizzly bear in a claw trap bed.

"How's Digger?" Kolt asked.

"Stable." Slapshot's reply was terse, but understandable.

Stew Weeks interrupted, transmitting over helo common, "Your call, Racer."

Kolt knew Captain Yost was monitoring everything transmitted over helo common. Yost had to know two of the aircraft had called out Lame Duck. He had to know several Eagles were wounded. So far, the SEAL Team Six commander had yet to jump in, which Kolt took as tacit support for what he wanted to do.

"Turn around," Kolt said.

"Roger. Four-Three, you are escort and return to base," Weeks said, "Four-One is out, inbound target."

Stew Weeks banked his MH-6M Little Bird hard right, forcing Kolt's torso practically horizontal, leaving him staring at the cloudless blue sky. The centrifugal force pressed Kolt's ass tight to the outer pod until Weeks went rotors level and nose down, looking for a direct line to the two black sedans heading away from them to the northwest.

Kolt keyed his mike. "Slapshot, hand me Digger's shotgun."

"We got it."

"You're both hit," Kolt said, "I'll take the windshield."

"I got it, boss!"

Kolt didn't reply, knowing Slapshot's wound must be superficial enough that he could still fight. Happy to at least have his squadron sergeant major's support, he didn't push it.

"Get us in front of the lead vehicle, Stew," Kolt said.

"Roger."

"Put your port side to the windshield," Kolt said, letting everyone know that he wasn't pushing the issue of who would fire the ferret rounds, putting CS gas through the windshield.

SEAL Captain Yost broke into the net from the JOC. "Breaker Four-One, this is Heater One-Zero, how's your ship?"

Stew Weeks didn't hesitate. He was still able to juggle his responsibilities single piloting an assault aircraft, loaded with wounded, and heading deeper into North Korea, looking for a fight.

"Systems solid," Weeks replied. "Fuel gauge a little jumpy is all."

"You need gas?" Yost asked.

"Negative," Weeks said, "should be good for now."

With an ear to Yost and Weeks, Kolt looked back into the cabin at JoJo, checking to see how Gangster was. JoJo was leaning over the former Delta officer, obscuring Kolt's view of exactly what he was doing.

Kolt leaned a few inches deeper, trying to assess Digger and Slapshot. Digger was moving, apparently on his own, as Kolt spotted him helping Slapshot lift the shotgun sling from around his neck. Kolt wanted to ask how bad both Digger's and Slapshot's wounds were, but reconsidered. They were alive, and obviously not critical, so Kolt decided to let things ride.

Kolt saw Slapshot raise the shotgun, shove a thumb up into the fixed magazine to raise the loading tray and check the chamber, confirming he had at least two ferret rounds loaded.

Slapshot broke squelch. "I've got the shotgun. Digger, take one of the front tires."

"Tunnel ahead," Weeks said.

Kolt looked up, noticed the tunnel up ahead, pissed he hadn't seen it first. Realizing Weeks didn't have enough room to position his helo in front of the lead vehicle before crashing into the mountainside, Kolt gave Weeks an out.

"Pull if you need to, take them on the far side."

"Hold on!" Weeks said.

Kolt felt the Little Bird accelerate and leaned slightly forward on the pod, keeping an eye on the two sedans as Weeks maneuvered in from the left. Now abreast with the lead vehicle, the tail rotor swung wide as Weeks banked hard right, holding a hard forty-degree angle to give Slapshot the correct angle of fire.

A moment later, Weeks pulled up and out, Kolt's boots barely missing the concrete roof of the tunnel embedded in the hillside.

"Good hits!" Slapshot said.

"Put us on the tunnel exit," Kolt said.

"Roger," Weeks said, as he continued to climb. Weeks hugged the lush green hillside, covered with scrub bushes and sporadic brown bald spots.

"There's gas all over the cabin floor," JoJo said. "We're leaking somewhere."

"I'm not seeing it," Weeks said, as he crested the hilltop and went nose down to the hardball road and the tunnel's exit. "Instruments solid."

Kolt kept his rifle aimed at the dark tunnel as the Little Bird touched down, just off the edge of the road. He unhooked and popped off the pod, immediately sprinting toward the U-shaped concrete tunnel entrance.

Surprised at not seeing the vehicles yet, Kolt turned to see JoJo on his heels.

"Nods down, let's go," Kolt said as he pulled the black plastic caps off his night vision goggles.

Kolt pushed down the right side of the tunnel, just a foot away from the wall, to not eat a rabbit round. He hoofed it opposite of the approach lane he knew the vehicles would likely be using, skittish of becoming roadkill. Up ahead, maybe another forty or fifty meters, he spotted the lead sedan cattycornered into the tunnel wall. The left front tire was flat and smoke billowed from under the hood. Through the smoke Kolt could barely make out the windshield, which bore the obvious marks of two shotgun rounds having penetrated into the cab.

Kolt and JoJo approached tactically, in depth with

max fire power forward, ready for any North Korean that might have survived the crash and had maintained the will to fight. The trail vehicle, now in sight, looked as if it might have rear-ended the lead vehicle.

It took Kolt only another ten seconds or so to reach the lead sedan. With the engine smoke affecting his nods, he lifted them off his eyes, locking them into place above his helmet. Kolt picked up the residual from the ferret rounds, practically tasting the gas as it slowly entered his nostrils. With his rifle aimed at the windshield he slowed his pace to a careful hurry, closing the distance until he could see into the cab through the driver's side window.

Two busted-up North Koreans were up front. The passenger was older and dressed in a dark suit. His face had smashed into the windshield, leaving a bloody imprint on the glass. He was buckled over and coughing from the effects of the CS, but alive. Kolt immediately assessed him as a possible match for Seamstress. The other occupant, a uniformed North Korean, was still behind the wheel and definitely unconscious. It looked like his nose had been caved in by the steering wheel.

Kolt quickly moved to the rear driver's side window, jamming his rifle's muzzle through the glass. Empty.

"Passenger is a possible jackpot," Kolt yelled to JoJo, letting him know to hold his fire.

Kolt resisted the urge to positively identify the coughing passenger, knowing they needed to secure the crisis site first.

Kolt heard tires squealing and turned to the trail vehicle. He saw someone behind the wheel, two hands gripped at ten and two o'clock. As it sped toward him, Kolt couldn't miss the determination in the driver's eyes, the specific look telling Kolt the guy wasn't driving scared. No, the driver was driving with intent to kill, headed straight for Kolt.

TWENTY-NINE

Kolt had only a second or two to react, with few options. He looked toward the tunnel wall, realizing the approaching vehicle would smash him like a bug on a windshield. He turned back to the smoking lead sedan and instinctively took a step and braced his nonfiring hand on the trunk. He launched his body up and onto the hood just as the front right bumper of the approaching car struck the left rear quarter panel, knocking the lead car a half length across the painted center line and throwing Kolt to the asphalt just as he picked up a strong whiff of burnt rubber.

Kolt tried to roll out of the fall, hoping to ball up as if he was executing a parachute landing fall, but the weight of his vest and gear killed his momentum and he flopped to the deck, landing hard on his strong side and Roscoe's bite wound. A shooting pain flew up through his shoulder blades as he ate the stock end of his HK416.

Kolt tried to roll into a prone position, struggling to right his rifle and get a bead on the tires. Searching for his red dot, Kolt caught an image just distant of the racing vehicle, partially framed by the bright light of day at the tunnel exit.

Slapshot!

Kolt heard several shots ring out, the noise easily suppressed by his Peltor hearing protection. Kolt fought to settle his red dot and control his breathing but the vehicle fishtailed violently, first bouncing off the right tunnel concrete wall, then crossing both lanes and careening into the left tunnel wall.

Kolt knew Slapshot must have taken both front tires for the driver to instantly lose control like that. Or, Slap decided to go directly for the driver.

Immediately, Kolt spotted a North Korean soldier step outside the driver's side and turn around, aiming a handgun at Kolt's face. Kolt dove back toward the smoking lead car, collapsing to both knees as three or four pistol shots rang out. Kolt heard the rounds whip by his head, one sounding as if it skipped off the pavement only a foot away. Kolt shuffled to the front quarter panel and hugged the tire for cover.

Kolt angled around the front bumper, saw the enemy soldier had mirrored his actions, now ducked behind the open driver's door. Kolt scooted backward a few more inches, out of the soldier's field of fire, and leaned forward, putting his helmet on the asphalt and trying to obtain a sight picture with his rifle turned sideways, ejection port down.

Shit!

Kolt knew he was too close to get a good angle and ripped his chin strap off and up, letting his Ops-Core helmet fall to the road. He leaned toward the road again, this time able to get his head close enough to the road to acquire a good cheek weld and observe the hidden North Korean's knees on the deck below the open door through his HOLO Sight optics.

Holding his red dot just below the door, Kolt sent two 5.56 rounds down range only a few inches off the road. The man fell from behind the door, now partially exposed and screaming in pain while holding his left knee and shin.

"Cover me!" Kolt yelled.

"Roger!" JoJo said.

Kolt popped to his feet, stepped wide around the front of the sedan, and rushed the trail car. Seeing the pistol on the deck, he kicked it down the road, then put his size-eleven Salomon into the wounded Korean's groin. Seeing the front seats were empty, Kolt quickly moved to the back seats, this time going for the door handle. He ripped it open with his nonfiring hand before reacquiring the upper receiver. Kolt spotted a fat old man, again, like the other one, wearing a black suit. His hands were already over his head, as if he had resigned himself to giving up and hoping he wouldn't be hurt.

Kolt heard a transmission through his Peltors. It was Weeks: "Getting low on fuel."

Already? Kolt thought Weeks's call was odd, knowing they had topped off the tank back at the JOC in Inchon.

Ignoring Weeks's call for the moment, Kolt froze as he noticed another man opposite the fat man in the backseat. It was another older man for sure, not as heavy as the other two, but either unconscious or dead. Strangely, this one was dressed in his birthday suit, if not for the baggy gray drawers, his hands hidden behind his back.

Kolt reached into the backseat, grabbed the suit collar of the fat man, and dragged him out to the hardball road. Kolt rolled him to his belly and dropped his right knee hard into the small of the North Korean's back.

"Grab the other guy," Kolt said.

"Rog," Slapshot said.

Kolt yanked a pair of flex cuffs from his assault vest, quickly flex-tying his man before moving around the vehicle to help Slapshot. The mostly naked man was lying on his belly, too, as Slapshot worked to set the teeth of his bolt cutters on a set of shiny handcuffs.

"He's alive," Slapshot said. "Our man?"

Kolt tapped his rifle's SureFire, white-lighting the man's hands. Kolt studied them as his squadron sergeant major worked to turn him over. Kolt lifted one of the hands, felt how oddly large it was, and gently set it back down. Kolt looked down to the man's feet. Fat and flat, flopped heavily to the street like two groupers scored on a deep-sea fishing outing.

"Jackpot!" Kolt transmitted. "I say again, Jackpot."

"Roger, Jackpot," Weeks said. "We need to go. Not sure we'll make the DMZ."

Kolt rotated his rifle to his back side, muzzle down, and leaned over to lift Seamstress over his right shoulder.

"I got him, boss," Slapshot said.

"You're wounded, man," Kolt said, looking at Slapshot's blood-soaked Multicam top. "No worries."

"What about the others?" Slapshot asked.

"Leave 'em," Kolt said as he turned back to the smoking vehicle where JoJo was still holding security. "JoJo, let's bolt."

Slapshot led the way back to the tunnel exit, toward the waiting Little Bird. JoJo brought up the rear, maintaining security at six o'clock, allowing Kolt to concentrate on carrying the precious cargo.

"Eagles coming out!" Slapshot transmitted, signaling Gangster and Digger that friendlies were exiting the dark tunnel.

Still twenty or so meters from the spinning Little Bird, Kolt noticed someone standing near his pod. It was Gangster, his thick latte brown hair blowing heavily in the rotor wash, his helmet under his arm like he was carrying a football. Kolt looked closer as he closed the distance, and realized Gangster also had his assault vest off, holding it in his other hand, his rifle slung.

What the hell?

Kolt laid Seamstress down on his external pod as Slapshot helped to position him into the cabin. Smelling a heavy odor of fuel, Kolt eyeballed Gangster as he stepped in, handing his helmet to Slapshot, then awkwardly trying to affix his assault vest around the topless Seamstress. Kolt watched as Gangster connected the Velcro straps around Seamstress's waist. It definitely wasn't one-size-fits-all, but it would work.

Slapshot secured Gangster's helmet over Seamstress's head before climbing into the cabin and then turning to help Gangster slide the North Korean into the cabin. Gangster's efforts were a funny sight, but Kolt knew it was smart. No need to have hung it out on a high-risk mission and have the precious cargo get smoked by a lucky round from a hidden North Korean sniper or a Red Guard paramilitary in the hills.

"Good call," Kolt yelled, looking at Gangster. "You okay?"

Gangster turned to Kolt and locked eyes. "Where's your helmet and nods?"

Kolt had practically forgotten about dumping his headgear to get a shot but ignored the comment, wiping the two snot snakes hanging from his nostrils with his sleeve before keying his hand mike and moving to straddle the front of the personnel pod. Kolt took a long pull on his CamelBak, swirled the water around his mouth several times, and spit it out onto the hot asphalt.

"Breaker Four-One, this is Noble Zero-One," Kolt said, "we're up with one PC."

"Roger, Four-One is out with five Eagles plus one," Weeks said. "I'm not sure I can lift us all."

Kolt felt Weeks give the bird max power as the helo

vibrated like an unbalanced overstuffed washing machine.

C'mon, c'mon, Stew, get us airborne.

Kolt felt the bird lift off the deck a few inches but quickly drop the skids back to the two-lane road.

"We're heavy," Weeks transmitted.

"Nothing to shed, brother," Kolt said. "Gotta make it work."

Then, just as Kolt finished his transmission, he felt the Little Bird climb. Slow but steady. Several seconds later, Weeks turned a quarter port side, climbed to roughly thirty feet, and slowly lowered the cockpit nose as he accelerated southwest toward the border.

"Looking for the Yesong River corridor," Weeks transmitted. "We're a chip shot at this speed."

Kolt knew Weeks was right. Overweight, practically limping home, they were sitting ducks for even the most unskilled North Korean marksmen, but Kolt wasn't keen on the over-water route.

Kolt thought back to the *Queen Mary 2* again, wishing now his men had the horse collars that inflate automatically in four inches of water. Or, truth be told, that there was at least one for the squadron commander.

He knew they had too much kit on to swim, and nobody had a wet suit with built-in buoyancy hidden under their Crye Precision fatigues. No, the safety precautions they enjoyed flying over the Atlantic weren't available in North Korea and, at the moment, Kolt was willing to take his chances on a land-based crash landing rather than another dip in the drink.

Facing sideways on the pod, Kolt turned around to check on Seamstress and Gangster. Both were sitting shoulder to shoulder, backs against the rear of the cabin. Closest to Kolt was an odd sight, a mostly naked man with a dark-earth helmet and a heavy, oversize black assault vest like a man on a street corner wearing a two-sided advertisement. Next to Seamstress, on the opposite side and still under his Peltors, Gangster appeared calm, his head leaning back on the flat-black aluminum, padded by his thick hair. Gangster held his HK416 on his lap with both hands. Kolt looked back at Seamstress, quickly inventorying the radio, three pouched thirty-round magazines, a frag grenade, and Gangster's Glock holstered on the chest area just below a small embroidered subdued American flag.

Up ahead, Kolt could easily make out the western edge of North Korea terrain, and in spots, revealed between the scorched-earth-looking rolling hills, could see the reflection off the glass-smooth Yesong River. Subconsciously, Kolt allowed himself to relax a little, blowing off his water demons and focusing on reaching the JOC and dropping off the precious cargo to competent authority. He wiped his nose again, happy to have cleaned his system of the last trace of CS and, for the first time in the last two hours, consciously released the straitjacket-like tension that had gripped him. He wondered about his wounded men on the other Little Birds and if they had returned to base yet. He thought of Slapshot and Digger, both wounded but alive, and how proud he was of their unvarnished courage. Kolt knew he'd get an earful from them at the hotwash. It definitely wouldn't be the first time, but his skin was as thick as an elephant's.

The vibration in Kolt's right cargo pocket yanked him back to the present.

Hawk?

He pulled out his cell phone, careful not to drop it to the turf below, and held his off hand over the screen to locate the green Answer button.

"We're en route," Kolt said, correctly assuming it was Cindy Bird on the other end again. "How are you feeling?"

"Listen, Kolt, Seamstress is suicidal," Hawk said. "Where is he?"

"Chill, he's in our helo, right behind me, packaged and napping."

"No, Kolt, we finished translating the letter. He is genuinely ashamed of betraying his country and family. He knows he is going to be fed to the dogs," Hawk said.

"We're good, Hawk," Kolt said. "About twenty mikes out." Before Hawk could answer, Kolt remembered the Glock and the frag grenade still on the vest now draped over Seamstress. Kolt turned quickly in panic, drilled down immediately to the vest to locate both tools of death that, if Hawk was right, Seamstress could use if he truly wanted to off himself.

Seamstress appeared calm, his head turned toward Slapshot and Digger, staring blankly out the starboard side of the helo.

"Just be careful, Kolt," Hawk said.

"Yes, Mother."

"Bingo, Bingo, Bingo!" Weeks reported.

Shit!

Kolt tensed and shoved the cell back in his cargo pocket, knowing their Little Bird was now flying on fumes, and wondered where pilot Chief Weeks's head was at.

"We need to put her down?" Kolt asked over helo common. For Kolt, he'd rather set her down and wait on gas or hump it across the DMZ to the safety of South Korea. Ten times out of ten, it beat another water landing.

"Not yet," Weeks answered after a short pause. "I'll know when it's time. Still RTB."

Kolt didn't like the answer, not one bit, but he understood the pecking order. On target, on the ground, it was the Kolt Raynor show. In the air, inside a heavier-than-specs Night Stalker Little Bird struggling to reach a safe area, it was the pilot in command's show.

Kolt resisted the urge to look down at the water as Weeks maneuvered into the current like he was easing a hot rod off an on-ramp into rush-hour traffic. The air was different above the brackish river, moist and laced with the sulky odor of fish and salt.

Single-ship formation Breaker Four-One tooled along at roughly one hundred feet above the water level and holding to a tight 120 knots max air speed. Kolt looked at his communicator, JoJo. He was relaxed and focused on the coast buzzing by below them, certainly looking to spot trouble before a Red Guard paramilitary dished it out.

Be careful, Kolt.

Kolt thought again about Hawk's last words, half grinning like the Cheshire Cat. Besides the fuel problem, he was confident their shit was tight.

Suddenly, Kolt felt pressure on his left shoulder. For a moment, he assumed it was JoJo trying to get his attention and turned around. As soon as he did, a blur of color flew past him, with something semi-soft slapping him in his face.

Momentarily stunned, Kolt shook off the surprise impact, and leaned over to catch a glimpse of what had just fallen from the helo.

Holy shit!

The weight of Gangster's helmet and vest driving his naked and frail body to the dark blue waters below, Seamstress had jumped! As the North Korean impacted the surface like a man who no longer cared, Kolt realized Hawk was right. Seamstress had lost his marbles and was suicidal indeed.

Kolt watched Seamstress go subsurface, the impact jarring Gangster's helmet off, and reached for his push-to-talk.

"Stew, turn around," Kolt transmitted. "The PC jumped ship!"

"Roger," Weeks said, "we're pushing it, though."

Kolt knew Weeks had to be staring at the fuel gauge needle, likely pegged all the way to the left.

Damn it!

Kolt felt Gangster's presence behind him and to his left as Weeks banked a hard 180. Along with JoJo, the three were straining to get a look at the spot where Seamstress had gone in.

Kolt wanted to get on the radio and give Gangster shit for letting the precious cargo bail out. As the ground force commander, Kolt was responsible for Seamstress, but he'd figured he could count on Gangster to at least keep the guy from shooting himself with the Glock or swan diving from the Little Bird.

"Here's good," Kolt transmitted. "He went in directly below."

Kolt felt Weeks slow to a steady hover, then wobble more than usual, likely due to the weight of the load and the last drops of fuel running through the Rolls-Royce.

"I don't see him," JoJo said.

Kolt didn't respond, just kept looking at the river below, trying to determine the current and if the floating helmet was a good indication of exactly where Seamstress might be.

What Kolt saw next freaked him out.

Launching off the pod as if he was on a cliff-jumping vacation in Curaçao while Weeks fought the aircraft's wobble, Gangster's kitless body, light and athletic, arced upward toward the deadly spinning main rotor blades. Instantly, a red mist of blood and brains impacted Kolt's face, covering the clear lenses of his safety goggles and speckling his face.

Gangster!

Kolt frantically wiped the crimson-colored blood spatter from his lenses, smearing them enough to just watch the ball of Multicam fall free to the river below, impacting only a few feet from the still-floating helmet. Fighting the shock of what just happened, Kolt clung to the Little Bird pod as if he was afraid of being pulled into the river next. That, he knew, wasn't going to happen. Subconsciously, Kolt reached over to grab JoJo, the way a father reaches over to the passenger seat to protect a child when he has to suddenly slam on the brakes.

Kolt struggled to process the data points of the problem before him. In less than a minute, both Seamstress and Gangster had left the cabin of the helo, and neither appeared to be okay. Gangster was floating facedown but Kolt couldn't be sure if he was dead, just unconscious, or what. And the reason they had come to North Korea—the first American troops, armed to the teeth, to set foot inside the isolated nation in sixty years—was nowhere to be seen.

A hard-won mission, one that cost Delta numerous wounded and the sacrifice of several high-tech helicopters, and potentially threatened a third world war, had vanished.

Kolt felt the helo steady out, certainly due to jettisoning two bodies from the cabin, as he studied the water below. Kolt ran the options as Weeks descended a little toward the water. Slapshot and Digger were both wounded; neither of them would survive a jump to help Gangster. Kolt turned to JoJo, the youngest of the Delta guys on Breaker Four-One. JoJo had a family, two kids not yet in grade school. Seamstress was just another mission, not someone to sacrifice your life for. It wasn't personal like September 11th was. That had worn off the day we stepped on Iraqi soil back in 2003. And now, just like with chasing Saddam, it was just business.

Kolt realized Slapshot might have been right, back on the porch of the Notri. Maybe Kolt did have a death wish. Maybe he had always wanted to go down in a blaze of glory, assaulting an enemy bunker and trench-line singlehandedly, all Audie Murphy–like. He realized the only thing holding him back now was that debilitating fear of the water he had psychologically battled since he had drowned in the spent-fuel pool back at Yellow Creek Nuclear Power Plant.

C'mon, Kolt, deal with it!

Kolt looked back down to the water, saw Gangster still floating, then back to JoJo. They both locked eyes, sending unspoken signals that neither could understand. Kolt knew JoJo wasn't expected to follow the circus act into the river, and he also figured JoJo wouldn't expect his new squadron commander to take a dip either.

Fuck it!

Kolt yanked his HK416 rifle over his head and shoved it into the cabin. He pulled his Peltors off and unhooked the coiled cable to clear them from his vest before laying the headset near his rifle. Pulling the quick-release tabs to his assault vest, he controlled both the chest and back pieces as they separated, pushing them both into the cabin.

JoJo grabbed Kolt's fatigue sleeve. The grip was hard, telling Kolt his partner on the pod thought what he was doing was stupid.

"Boss, don't, man!" JoJo yelled, barely heard over the buzzing blades above them.

Kolt looked at JoJo, grabbed his communicator's gloved hand, and lifted it from his arm.

"I'm good!"

Kolt pushed off the black aluminum pod and, from about sixty feet, dropped feet-first with his arms spread out to the sides to limit the distance he would sink on impact. He hit like a sack of wet shit on concrete. A vicious jolt ran up the length of his body as half a gallon of water shot up his nose. He surfaced a few seconds later, gasping for air. He immediately looked for Gangster, figuring Seamstress was gone. He needed to get

Gangster the life-saving attention he needed or, barring that, recover his body so that he wasn't left behind in enemy territory.

As he swam toward his Delta mate, something bumped Kolt from below.

Shark!

Kolt flailed at the air, trying to climb out of the river on an invisible staircase before he realized he was panicking. As he calmed down he realized it must be Seamstress.

Kolt dove to investigate, feeling left, then right, and then spreading his hands out to increase his chances. Kolt felt skin and rolled his hand over a bony forearm, dragging his grip up to a hand that seemed larger than life. With both hands, Kolt pulled on the arm, trying to prevent the current from pulling Seamstress deeper.

Kolt made some headway, and after a few seconds, was able to pop Seamstress's head out of the water. The man looked like a train wreck, almost certainly dead by now.

Holding Seamstress from behind, arm over the right shoulder and grasping the left side of his chest, Kolt reached around with his left hand and felt for the quick releases to Gangster's vest. They weren't easy to find by feel, and Kolt could only find one. He yanked it, pulling the flexible cotter pin from its housing, separating the left side of the vest. Kolt fumbled with the vest, eventually pushing it off Seamstress's body and letting it float away.

Kolt looked downstream, surprised to see he was still close to Gangster. He had a better view of his mate's head now, the top of which was missing several inches at least, sliced clean off, and swathes of his long brown hair matted to the edge of the scalped wound and floating in the water.

Kolt dragged Seamstress toward Gangster, pulling

long strokes with his left arm while scissor-kicking below the surface. Kolt struggled to stay above water, knowing his natural buoyancy wouldn't be enough to keep all three of them above the surface. Kolt reached his right ankle first, and a few seconds later reached his head. Kolt worked to turn Gangster over, checked for a pulse. Nothing.

Something hit the water a few feet away. It was a black life vest, obviously thrown from the helo hovering above him, the rotor wash sending giant concentric ripples of water. Kolt reached long for the vest, retrieving it with two fingers, just as a second vest hit the water inches from him.

With one hand, Kolt shoved one of the vests underneath Gangster's chest, then simply held the second one under his left armpit. For the moment, they were able to stay afloat, giving Kolt a spell of relief.

With Gangster's fate decided, Kolt rolled Seamstress's head back a few inches. He placed two fingers on his neck, feeling for a pulse. With the downward beating of the rotors, Kolt couldn't be sure if he felt a pulse or not. If there was one, it was faint and weak.

Kolt turned Seamstress's face toward him, pinched the North Korean's nose and locked lips, giving the old man two long rescue breaths. Kolt reached under the man's ribcage, balled his right fist below his chest, and gave a hard upward thrust. Seamstress didn't respond.

Kolt scissor-kicked to keep his body upright, spitting river water out as fast as it entered his mouth. Kolt gave another thrust, then another, and another.

Suddenly, Seamstress coughed. Water spurted from deep in his lungs, exiting his mouth like an ice-bucket challenge.

Kolt looked at Seamstress, then up at the hovering Little Bird, and gave a raised thumbs-up, signaling he was alive.

Kolt turned back toward his mate Gangster, and in an instant, Kolt felt the weight of the world come crumbling down on him.

He wept and he wept as only a man who has lost a brother in arms can.

CONCLUSION

"Chill out, Hawk," Kolt said as he wedged his backside against the heavy steel door before pulling Hawk's wheelchair into the spine of the Unit hallway, "you crushed it."

"Bullshit, Racer!" Hawk said. "The board members ripped me a new one in there."

Happy Hawk couldn't see his face, Kolt didn't answer right away. He knew Cindy Bird was right. The Commander's Board had been especially hard on her for the past three-plus hours, even taking a piss break halfway through the soft interrogation.

Kolt knew nothing was off-limits at a Commander's Board when selecting operators for the Unit. Sure, outside the compound, they were total gentlemen, opening car doors for their wives, handling honey-do lists with patience after returning from long deployments, and never forgetting anniversary dates or Valentine's Day. But the graybeards weren't going to let Hawk become the first female Delta operator without taking some skin first.

Kolt had sat poker-faced as they had opened old

wounds about the circumstances of her father's death in Fallujah, swarmed her with technical questions about this and that piece of operator kit, and had the skeletons in her closet either tap-dancing or looking to run for the hills. Yes, Kolt knew Cindy "Hawk" Bird had proven beyond a shadow of a doubt that she was fully capable of entering the ranks as a Delta operator. After turning numerous holy-shit targets with Hawk, she had his vote. But Kolt was easy; it was the other board members she had to convince. The graybeards of the Unit were charged with ensuring the right guy, not necessarily the best guy, was knighted, and they had pushed more of her buttons than a cosmonaut attempting reentry. Their votes were still being debated.

"You'll know before close of business today," Kolt said, pushing her down the large hallway toward the Unit memorial garden. "Let's go pay our respects to your father."

"Do you think POTUS will do it?" Hawk asked, changing the subject. "Stealth bomb the mini nuke sites?"

"I don't know. The North Koreans know we have Seamstress, which means they know everything he knew, we know, too. It's mutually assured destruction all over again."

Kolt pushed Hawk through the threshold of the double glass doors, held open by Slapshot, who gave Kolt the stink eye for being late. Kolt smiled. It was beyond joy to see Slap there to scold him, and know that the rest of Noble Squadron and the crews of the Little Birds had made it back alive.

Kolt maneuvered Hawk toward the front of the crowd, careful not to bump her bandaged and elevated left leg on any of the guests' chair legs. A small army of attendees—current and former operators, family members, and specially invited friends of the Unit—were on hand for the unveiling of the latest Eagles to be immortalized into the growing list.

"And the Unit and Six?"

"After enduring a million questions, now you're full of them," Kolt said. He wondered about that, too. Everyone did. Delta had performed miracles with Six not far behind. Unless POTUS had an aneurism he had to see that America needed both.

Kolt looked toward the far right of the wall, at the black cloth tarp still hiding the true names of former Delta squadron commander Gangster, and the two snipers killed in action in the Ukraine, Philly and Max. He knew their names, like so many before them, had been patiently and professionally hammer-and-chiseled into the giant triangle-shaped black marble wall by a world-renowned craftsman.

Kolt swallowed hard, self-consciously hoping nobody would notice his unmanageable discomfort with the entire situation. He scanned the other names on the wall, and realized that the names had more than doubled since he had joined Delta.

Great Americans and warriors. Kolt saw each of their grizzled faces crystal clear, and would swear he could hear TJ's last words again, see his last breath after saving POTUS on Marine One, even seeing in the deep recesses of his consciousness the marble headstones in Arlington's Section 60 for Musket, Rocky, and Jet. Kolt could see the reflection off the wall of the gathered crowd, who seemed to be staring him down with accusing eyes as if he were responsible for all of them. If they weren't launching blame darts, the graybeards certainly would.

Farther to the left, Kolt noticed "Michael Leland Bird" inscribed, Hawk's dad, and figured she was looking at the same. Some on the wall had died in training, most in hard-fought battle, even some who sacrificed it all pulling a gig with the CIA abroad.

Kolt eased Hawk into a slot of chairs, most taken by family members of the deceased, but next to Colonel Webber's wife. The board had caused them to be fashionably late, and Kolt instantly realized the spot next to the commander's eccentric and meddlesome wife probably wasn't the best, given Hawk's situation.

Kolt looked toward the podium for Colonel Webber but didn't see him. He did notice the Unit chaplain standing tall and confident in his military dress blue uniform over perfectly glossed jump boots. Kolt knew the chaplain hated this part of his job, had struggled personally at times with the finality of it all, but his demeanor and personality were perfect for these dark occasions.

Kolt noticed the three triangle-folded American flags held by three Unit members. All close friends and mates of the fallen, who had the unenviable task of soon presenting the colors to the dead's next of kin. They had drawn the short straws.

Kolt moved his eyes back across the wall, stopping on the chiseled quote credited to former army secretary John O. Marsh Jr. during a visit to the compound twenty-five years earlier. Kolt read silently.

IN DELTA'S RANKS IS A SPECIAL BREED. THEY HEAR AND MARCH TO A DISTANT DRUMMER. SECRECY PROTECTS THEIR MISSION AND CONCEALS THEIR PERSONAL DEEDS. UNSUNG, THEY ARE DARING CONSUMMATE PROFESSIONALS. COMMITTED, DEDICATED, ANONYMOUS—THEY BELONG TO A TINY FRATERNITY WHOSE COMMON BOND IS UNCOMMON VALOR.

Kolt finished reading just when he heard Mrs. Webber address Hawk.

"Oh my God, Sergeant Bird, every time I see you it's as if you just survived a train wreck."

"Uhh, yes ma'am," Hawk said. "I've always been a little accident prone."

Mrs. Webber leaned closer to Hawk and cupped her hand near her mouth. "Honey, you must have given your mother fits."

"I inherited it."

"What was it this time?" Webber's wife asked. "Another car accident?"

"Vacation booboo, actually," Hawk said.

Kolt caught some movement behind him and he turned. Webber and several of the graybeards had entered the garden and were moving to their designated places for the ceremony to commence. They hadn't changed clothes, still wearing the same Multicam fatigues they wore at Hawk's board. That told Kolt—and in a few seconds, as soon as they came around the crowd and into Hawk's view, she'd assume the same—that they must have debated her acceptance until they were forced to break for the ceremony. The jury was likely still out.

Kolt noticed Mrs. Webber lean over toward Hawk again and strained to hear her next comment. "You really should be more careful," she said. "You spend more time in the aid station than the operators do, it seems."

"Yes, ma'am," Hawk said before turning her head and leaning back to look up at Kolt. Kolt hid the amusement, barely showed concern, and simply rolled his eyes slowly as if he was worried someone might be watching.

Webber stepped to the podium, adjusted the microphone with both hands, raising it a few inches to mouth level, and became Henry V for the umpteenth time in his three years-plus as Delta Force's commander.

"We few, we happy few, we band of brothers. For he today that sheds his blood with me shall be my brother. Be he ne'er so vile, this day shall gentle his condition."

Kolt thought about it. Felt his stomach turn and pulse race under his fatigue top. He reached up with his left hand, flipped the hair out of his eye, discreetly wiped the tear that had run down his left cheek, and focused on the black cloth that was ceremoniously being removed from the black marble wall by the chaplain and Unit sergeant major.

Kolt read his three mates' names relief carved in perfect Baskerville Old Face font, felt a deep sense of responsibility mixed with vulnerability, felt his sweaty palms roll around Hawk's wheelchair handles, and asked himself if it all had been worth it.

In a second, he came to one hard conclusion.

It had to be.